Hunted

I held my breath and heard his footsteps stop. I still didn't look at him. I was afraid if I did that, I would turn around, run back to him, and hurl myself into his arms.

I was almost to the old metal grate when I heard the first croaking caw. The sound stopped me like I'd run into a brick wall. I whirled around. Heath was standing in the freezing rain under the tree just a few feet from his truck. I spared hardly a glance for him. My eyes darted up into the dark branches of the ice-bowed tree.

Within the shadows of the naked boughs a darkness stirred. It reminded me of something, and I blinked, staring at it and trying to remember where I'd seen something like it before. Then the image shifted . . . changed . . . I gasped as it became more visible. Neferet! She was clinging to a thick, ice-slick branch that leaned against the roof of the depot. Her eyes blazed crimson and her hair whipped around her crazily, like she had been caught in a sudden wind.

Neferet smiled at me. Her expression was so purely evil that I felt frozen in place.

Then, as I stared up in horror, her image shifted again, wavered, and where the image of the tainted High Priestess had been, there was now a huge Raven Mocker. The thing perched on the side of the depot roof wasn't human and it wasn't animal. It was a terrible mutated mixture of both.

BY P. C. AND KRISTIN CAST

The House of Night Series
Marked
Betrayed
Chosen
Untamed
Hunted
Tempted

Hunted

A House of Night Novel

P. C. and KRISTIN CAST

Book Five of the
HOUSE OF NIGHT
series

www.atombooks.co.uk

ATOM

First published in the United States in 2009 by
St Martin's Press
First published in Great Britain in 2009 by Atom
Reprinted 2009 (four times)

Copyright © 2009 by P. C. and Kristin Cast

The moral right of the authors has been asserted.

A CIP catalogue record for this book
is available from the British Library.

ISBN 978-1-90565-457-4

Typeset in Granjon by Palimpsest Book Production Limited,
Grangemouth, Stirlingshire

Printed in the UK by CPI Mackays, Chatham, ME5 8TD

Papers used by Atom are natural, renewable and recyclable
products sourced from well-managed forests and certified
in accordance with the rules of the Forest Stewardship Council.

Mixed Sources
Product group from well-managed
forests and other controlled sources
www.fsc.org Cert no. SGS-COC-004081
© 1996 Forest Stewardship Council

Atom
An imprint of
Little, Brown Book Group
100 Victoria Embankment
London EC4Y 0DY

An Hachette UK Company
www.hachette.co.uk

www.atombooks.co.uk

This one is for John Maslin — ex-student,
research aide, and brainstormer extraordinaire.
An all-around great guy who bears a striking
resemblance to our Damien . . . hmmm . . .

Acknowledgments

We'd like to send big XXXOOOs to our lovely UK team at Little, Brown Atom, with a special THANK YOU to Samantha Smith for saving me when I was food poisoned in London. Gack!

As always, we are indebted to our agent and friend, Meredith Bernstein.

We would like to thank the many fans who are so supportive of this series and who make appearances such fun for Kristin and me. A special thanks to the freshman classes at Will Rogers High School in Tulsa, Oklahoma, who adopted *Marked* in their English classes and who made our visit to their very cool school a great time!

And while we are mentioning cool schools, we have to thank a group of long-time fans – the teachers from the Jenks, Oklahoma, school system. We heart us some Jenks teachers! (See y'all at the next signing!)

CHAPTER ONE

THE DREAM BEGAN WITH THE SOUND OF WINGS. IN retrospect I realize I should have known that was a bad sign, what with the Raven Mockers being set loose and all, but in my dream it was just background noise, kinda like a fan whirring or the TV turned on to QVC.

In my dream I was standing in the middle of a beautiful meadow. It was night, but there was an enormous full moon hovering just above the trees that framed the meadow. It cast a silver-blue light strong enough to throw shadows and made everything look like it was underwater, an impression that was strengthened by the gentle breeze blowing the soft grasses against my bare legs in sweeps and whirls like waves lapping sweetly against a shore. That same wind was lifting my thick dark hair from my naked shoulders and it felt like silk floating against my skin.

Bare legs? Naked shoulders?

I looked down and let out a little yip of surprise. I was wearing a seriously short buckskin minidress. The top of it was cut in a wide V, front and back, so that it hung off my shoulders, leaving lots of skin visible. The dress itself was amazing. It was white and decorated with fringe, feathers, and shells and seemed to glow in the moonlight. All over it was beaded with intricate designs that were impossibly beautiful.

My imagination is so darn cool!

The dress tickled a memory, but I ignored it. I didn't want to think too hard – I was dreaming! Instead of pondering déjà vu moments I danced gracefully through the meadow, wondering if Zac Efron or even Johnny Depp was going to suddenly appear and flirt outrageously with me.

I peeked around as I twirled and swayed with the wind and thought I saw the shadows flicker and move oddly within the massive trees. I stopped and was trying to squint so I could get a closer look at what was going on in the darkness. Knowing me and my weird dreams, I'd created bottles of brown pop hanging from the limbs like bizarre fruit, just waiting for me to pick them.

That's when he appeared.

At the edge of the meadow, just inside the shadows of the trees, a shape materialized. I could see his body because the moonlight caught the smooth, naked lines of his skin.

Naked?

I stopped. Had my imagination lost its mind? I wasn't really up to frolicking around a meadow with a naked guy, even if he was the amazingly mysterious Mr Johnny Depp.

'You hesitate, my love?'

At the sound of his voice a shiver passed through my body, and terrible, mocking laughter whispered through the leaves of the trees.

'Who are you?' I was glad that my dream voice didn't betray the fear I was feeling.

His laughter was as deep and beautiful as his voice, and as frightening. It echoed in the limbs of the watching trees until it drifted almost visible in the air around me.

'Do you pretend you do not know me?'

His voice brushed against my body, making the little hairs on my arms stand up.

'Yeah, I know you. I made you up. This is *my* dream. You're a mixture of Zac and Johnny.' I hesitated, peering at him. I spoke non-chalantly even though my heart was beating like crazy because it was already obvious this guy was not a mixture of those two actors. 'Well, maybe you're Superman or Prince Charming,' I said, reaching for anything but the truth.

'I am no figment of your imagination. You know me. Your soul knows me.'

I hadn't moved my feet, but my body was slowly being drawn toward him, like his voice was pulling me. I reached him and looked up and up . . .

It was Kalona. I'd known him from the first words he'd spoken. I just hadn't wanted to admit it to myself. How could I have dreamed him?

Nightmare – this had to be a nightmare and not a dream.

His body was naked, but it wasn't completely substantial. His form wavered and shifted in time with the caressing breeze. Behind him, in the dark green shadows of the trees, I could see the ghostly shapes of his children, the Raven Mockers, as they clung to the limbs with the hands and feet of men and stared at me with men's eyes from the mutated faces of birds.

'Do you still claim not to know me?'

His eyes were dark – a starless sky. They seemed the most substantial thing about him. That and his liquid voice. *Even though this is a nightmare, it's still mine. I can just wake up! I want to wake up! I want to wake up!*

But I didn't. I couldn't. I wasn't in control. Kalona was. He'd built this dream, this dark, nightmare meadow, and somehow brought me there, closing the door to reality behind us.

'What do you want?' I said the words quickly so he couldn't hear my voice shaking.

'You know what I want, my love. I want you.'

'I am *not* your love.'

'Of course you are.' He moved this time, stepping so close

4

to me that I could feel the chill that came from his insubstantial body. '*My A-ya.*'

A-ya had been the name of the maiden the Cherokee Wise Women had created to trap him centuries ago. Panic spiked through me. 'I'm not A-ya!'

'*You command the elements,*' his voice was a caress, awful and wonderful, compelling and terrifying.

'Gifts from my Goddess,' I said.

'*Once before you commanded the elements. You were made from them. Fashioned to love me.*' His massive dark wings stirred and lifted. Beating forward softly, they enfolded me in a spectral embrace that was cold as frost.

'No! You must have me mixed up with someone else. I'm not A-ya.'

'*You're wrong, my love. I feel her within you.*'

His wings pressed against my body, drawing me closer to him. Even though his physical form was only semi-substantial, I could feel him. His wings were soft. Winter cold against the warmth of my dreaming self. The outline of his body was frigid mist. It burned my skin, sending electric currents through me, heating me with a desire I didn't want to feel but was powerless to resist.

His laugh was seductive. I wanted to drown in it. I leaned forward, closing my eyes and gasping aloud as the chill of his spirit brushed against my breasts, sending shooting sensations that were painful but deliciously erotic to places in my body that made me feel out of control.

'*You like the pain. It brings you pleasure.*' His wings got more insistent, his body harder and colder and more passionately painful as it pressed against mine. '*Surrender to me.*' His voice, already beautiful, was unimaginably seductive as he became aroused. '*I spent centuries in your arms. This time our joining will be controlled by me, and you will revel in the pleasure I can bring you. Throw off the shackles of your distant goddess and come to me. Be my love, truly, in body as well as soul and I will give you the world!*'

The meaning of his words penetrated through the haze of pain and pleasure like sunlight burning away dew. I found my will again, and stumbled out of the embrace of his wings. Tendrils of icy black smoke snaked around my body, clinging . . . touching . . . caressing . . .

I shook myself like a pissed cat shaking off rain and the dark wisps slid from my body. 'No! I'm not your love. I'm not A-ya. And I'll never turn my back on Nyx!'

When I spoke Nyx's name, the nightmare shattered.

I sat straight up in bed, shaking and gasping. Stevie Rae was sleeping soundly beside me, but Nala was wide awake. She was growling softly. Her back was arched, her body was totally puffed up, and she was staring slit-eyed at the air above me.

'Ah, hell!' I shrieked and bounded off the bed, spinning around and looking up, expecting to see Kalona hovering like a giant batbird over us.

Nothing. There was nothing there.

I grabbed Nala and sat on the bed. With trembling hands I petted her over and over. 'It was just a bad dream . . . it was just a bad dream . . . it was just a bad dream,' I told her, but I knew it was a lie.

Kalona was real, and somehow he was able to reach me through my dreams.

CHAPTER TWO

OKAY, SO KALONA CAN GET INTO YOUR DREAMS, BUT YOU'RE awake now, so pull yourself together! I told myself sternly as I petted Nala and let my cat's familiar purr soothe me. Stevie Rae stirred in her sleep and murmured something I couldn't hear. Then, still sleeping, she smiled and sighed. I looked down at her, glad that she was having better luck with her dreams.

Gently I pulled back the blanket she'd curled up under and breathed a sigh of relief when I saw no blood seeping through the bandage that covered the terrible arrow wound that had pierced her.

She stirred again. This time Stevie Rae's eyes fluttered and opened. She looked confused for a second, then she smiled sleepily up at me.

'How are you feeling?' I asked.

'I'm okay,' she said groggily. 'Don't worry so much.'

'It's a little hard not to worry when my best friend keeps dying,' I said, smiling back at her.

'I didn't die this time. I just almost died.'

'My nerves are telling me to tell you there's not a big difference in that "almost" to them.'

'Tell your nerves to be quiet and go to sleep,' Stevie Rae said, closing her eyes and pulling the blanket back up over her. 'I'm okay,' she repeated. 'We're all going to be okay.' Then her breathing deepened and I swear in less time than it took for me to blink, she was asleep.

I stifled my big sigh and scooted back on the bed, trying to get comfortable. Nala curled up between Stevie Rae and me, and gave me a disgruntled *mee-uf-ow!* that I knew meant she wanted me to relax and go to sleep.

Sleep? And possibly dream again? Uh, no. Not likely.

Instead I kept an eye on Stevie Rae's breathing and petted Nala absently. It was so darn weird how normal everything seemed here in the little bubble of peace we'd made. Looking at sleeping Stevie Rae I found it almost impossible to believe that just a few hours ago she'd had an arrow sticking through her chest and we had had to escape from the House of Night as chaos tore our world apart. Unwilling to allow myself to sleep, my exhausted thoughts circled back, replaying the events of the night. And as I sifted through them, I was amazed anew that any of us had survived . . .

I remembered that Stevie Rae had, unbelievably, asked me to get a pencil and some paper 'cause she thought it would be a good time to make a list of stuff that we needed to get down in the tunnels so that we'd have the right supplies and whatnot if we had to stay hidden for a while.

She'd asked me that, in a totally calm voice, while she was sitting in front of me with an arrow stuck through her chest. I remember looking at her, getting really sick to my stomach, and then looking away and saying, 'Stevie Rae, I'm not so sure this is a good time to be making lists.'

'Ouch! Dang, that hurts worse than gettin' one of those goat-head thistles stuck in your foot.' Stevie Rae had sucked air and flinched, but still managed to smile over her shoulder at Darius, who had ripped open the back of her shirt to expose the arrow that was sticking out of the middle of her back. 'Sorry, I didn't mean it's your fault that it hurts. What'd you say your name was again?'

'I am Darius, Priestess.'

'He's a Son of Erebus warrior,' Aphrodite had added, giving him a surprisingly sweet smile. I describe it as surprisingly sweet because Aphrodite is usually selfish, spoiled, hateful, and kinda hard to tolerate in general, even though I'm starting to like her. In other words, she's definitely not sweet, but it was becoming clearer and clearer that she *really* had a thing for Darius, hence the unusual sweetness.

'Please. His warrior-ness is obvious. He's built like a mountain,' Shaunee had said, giving Darius an appreciative leer.

'A totally hot mountain,' Erin echoed and made kiss noises at Darius.

'He's taken, Twin freaks, so go play with each other,' Aphrodite automatically snapped at them, but it had seemed to me that she didn't have her heart in the insult. Actually, now that I was thinking about it again, she'd sounded almost nice.

Oh, by the way, Erin and Shaunee are soul twins, not biological twins, being as Erin is a blonde-haired blue-eyed Oklahoma girl and Shaunee is a caramel-colored easterner of Jamaican descent. But genetics didn't matter with them – they might as well have been separated at birth and then rejoined by twin radar.

'Oh, yeah. Thanks for reminding us that our boyfriends aren't here,' Shaunee said.

''Cause they're probably being eaten by man-bird freaks,' Erin said.

'Hey, cheer up. Zoey's grandma didn't say the Raven Mockers actually *ate* people. She said they just picked them up with their humongous beaks and threw them against a wall or whatever over and over again until every bone in their body was broken,' Aphrodite told the Twins with a light-hearted grin.

'Uh, Aphrodite, I don't think you're helping,' I said. Though she was right. Actually, as scary as it sounded, she and the Twins both might have been right. I hadn't wanted to think about that too long, so I'd turned my attention back to my injured best friend. She'd looked absolutely horrible – pale, sweaty, and covered with blood. 'Stevie Rae, don't you think we should get you to a—'

'I got it! I got it!' Just then Jack had burst into the little side-tunnel area that had been made into Stevie Rae's room, followed closely by the yellow Lab that rarely let the kid out of her sight. He was flushed and brandishing a white briefcase-looking thing that had a big red cross on it. 'It was right where you said it'd be, Stevie Rae. In that kinda kitchen-tunnel place.'

'And as soon as I get my breath I'll tell you how pleasantly surprised I was when I discovered the working refrigerators and microwaves,' Damien said, following Jack into the room, breathing heavily and dramatically holding on to his side. 'You'll have to explain to me how you managed to get all of that down here, including the electricity to run it.' Damien paused, caught sight of Stevie Rae's bloody, ripped shirt and the arrow that still protruded from her back, and his pink cheeks blanched white. 'You'll have to explain *after* you're fixed up and not en brochette anymore.'

'En— Huh?' Shaunee said.

'Bro— What?' Erin said.

'It's French for something being skewered, usually food, cretins. "The world going insane and evil letting slip the birds of war"' – he raised his brows at the Twins as he deliberately misquoted Shakespeare, obviously expecting them to recognize it, which they just as obviously didn't – 'does not excuse sloppy vocabulary.' Then he turned back to Darius. 'Oh, I did find these in a not-so-sanitary pile of tools.' And lifted what looked like giant scissors.

'Bring the wire cutters and the first aid kit here,' Darius said in an all-business voice.

'What are you going to do with the wire cutters?' Jack asked.

'I'm going to cut the quill end of the arrow off so that I can pull it the rest of the way through the priestess's body. Then she can begin to heal,' Darius said simply.

Jack gasped and fell back against Damien, who put an arm around him. Duchess, the yellow Lab who had become completely attached to Jack since her original owner, a fledgling kid named James Stark, had died and then un-died and shot an arrow through Stevie Rae as part of an evil plot to let loose Kalona, a nasty fallen angel (yes, looking back on it I see that it's complex and even kinda confusing, but that seems to be typical for evil plots), whined and leaned against his leg.

Oh, Jack and Damien are a couple. Which means they're gay teenagers. Hello. It happens. More often than you'd expect. Wait, scratch that. It happens more often than *parents* expect.

'Damien, maybe you and Jack could, uh, go back to that kitchen you found and see if you can whip up something for us to eat,' I said, trying to think up things for them to do that didn't include staring at Stevie Rae. 'I'll bet we'd all feel better if we ate something.'

'I'd probably puke,' Stevie Rae said. 'That is, unless it's blood.'

She tried to shrug apologetically, but broke off the movement with a gasp and turned even whiter than her already totally pale complexion.

'Yeah, not really hungry over here, either,' Shaunee said, gawking at the arrow that was poking out of Stevie Rae's back with the same kind of fascination that made people rubberneck at car wrecks.

'Ditto, Twin,' Erin said. She was looking everywhere but at Stevie Rae.

I was just opening my mouth to tell them I really didn't care if they were hungry or not, I just wanted to keep them busy *and* away from Stevie Rae for a while, when Erik Night hurried into the room.

'Got it!' he said. He was holding a *really* old combo CD-cassette-radio that was humongous. It was one of those things they used to call boom boxes way back in the day. Like the 1980s. Without looking at Stevie Rae, he set it on the table that was close to her and Darius and started fiddling with the ginormic, glaringly silver knobs, muttering that he hoped it could pick up something down here.

'Where's Venus?' Stevie Rae asked Erik. It obviously hurt for her to talk, and her voice had gone all shaky.

Erik had glanced back toward the round, blanket-draped entrance to the room that served as a door, which was empty. 'She was right behind me. I thought she'd come in here and—' Then he did look at Stevie Rae, and his words fell away. 'Ah, man, that must really hurt,' he said softly. 'You look bad, Stevie Rae.'

She tried, and failed, to smile at him. 'Well, I've felt better. I'm glad Venus helped you out with the boom box. Sometimes we can actually get some of the radio stations down here.'

'Yeah, that's what Venus said,' Erik said vaguely. He was staring at the arrow sticking out of Stevie Rae's bare back.

Even through my worry about Stevie Rae I'd started to wonder about the absent Venus and tried like hell to remember what she looked like. Last time I'd gotten a really good look at the red fledglings, they hadn't been 'red' yet, which means the outline of a crescent moon in the middle of their foreheads had still been sapphire-colored like all fledglings' tattoos are when they're first Marked. But these fledglings died. Then un-died. And they had all been blood-sucking, crazed monsters until Stevie Rae went through a type of Change. Somehow Aphrodite's humanity (who knew she had any?) mixed with the power of the five elements – all of which I can control – and voilà! Stevie Rae got her humanity back, along with some gorgeous adult vampyre tattoos that look like vines and flowers framing her face. But instead of the tattoo being dark blue, it had turned red. As in the color of fresh blood. When that happened to Stevie Rae, all the undead-dead kids' fledgling tattoos had turned red, too. And they got their humanity back. In theory. I really hadn't been around them or Stevie Rae enough since her Change to know for sure that everything was one hundred percent with all of them. Oh, and Aphrodite lost her Mark – totally. So she's supposedly human again, even though she still has visions.

All of this explains why the last time I'd spent any time with Venus she was more than kinda disgusting-looking since she was very nastily undead. But now she'd been fixed – or at least sort of – and I knew that she'd hung with Aphrodite before she died (and un-died), which means she had to have been totally gorgeous because Aphrodite didn't believe in ugly friends.

Okay, before I sound like an über-jealous freak let me explain: Erik Night is to-die-for hot in a Superman-Clark Kent kind of way and, to carry through with the superhero analogy, he's also talented and honestly a good guy. Er, vampyre. Recently Changed vampyre at that. He is also my boyfriend. Er, ex-boyfriend. Recently ex-boyfriend at that. Sadly, that means I'm going to be ridiculously jealous of anyone, even one of the kinda freaky red fledglings, who might be catching too much of his interest (too much = any).

Darius's businesslike voice had, thankfully, interrupted my inner babbling.

'The radio can wait. Right now, Stevie Rae must be attended to. She will need a clean shirt and blood as soon as I get through with this.' Darius spoke as he put the first aid kit on Stevie Rae's bedside table, opened it, and busily pulled out gauze and alcohol and some scary stuff.

That had definitely shut everybody up.

'You know I love y'all like white bread, don't you?' Stevie Rae said, giving us a brave smile. My friends and I had nodded woodenly. 'Okay, so you won't take it the wrong way if I say that all of y'all but Zoey need to go find somethin' to keep

16

yourselves busy while Darius yanks this arrow outta my chest.'

'All of them except me? No no no no no. Why do you want me to stay?'

I saw humor in Stevie Rae's pain-filled eyes. ''Cause you're our High Priestess, Z. You gotta stay and help Darius. Plus, you've already seen me die once; how much worse could this be than that?' Then she paused and her eyes widened as she stared at the palms of my still dorkishly raised hands and blurted, 'Holy crap, Z, look at your hands!'

I turned my hands over so I could see what the hell she was staring at, and felt my own eyes widen. Tattoos spread across my palms, the same beautiful intricate pattern of lattice-work swirls that decorated my face and neck and stretched down either side of my spine and around my waist. *How could I have forgotten?* I'd felt the familiar burning flash across my palms as we all escaped into the safety of the tunnels. I'd realized then what that burning meant. My goddess, Nyx, the personification of Night, had Marked me again as exclusively hers. Had set me apart, again, from all the other fledglings and vampyres in the world. No other fledgling had a filled-in, expanded Mark. That only happened after a kid went through the Change, and then the outline of the crescent moon on the forehead was filled in and expanded to a unique, one-of-a-kind tattoo that framed the face, proclaiming to the world that he or she was a vampyre.

So my face proclaimed that I was a vampyre, but my body said I was still a fledgling. And the rest of my tattoos? Well, that was something that had never happened before – not to a fledgling and not to a vamp, and even now I wasn't one hundred percent sure what it meant.

'Wow, Z, they're amazing,' Damien's voice came from beside me. Hesitantly, he touched my palm.

I looked up from my hands to his friendly brown eyes, searching them for any trace of a change in the way he saw me. I looked for signs of hero worship or nervousness or, even worse, fear. And what I had seen was just Damien – my friend – and the warmth of his smile.

'I felt it happening before, when we first got down here. I— I guess I just forgot,' I said.

'That's our Z,' Jack said. 'Only she could forget something that's practically a miracle.'

'More than practically,' Shaunee said.

'But it's a Zoey miracle. They happen pretty much all the time,' Erin said matter-of-factly.

'I can't keep a tattoo and she's covered in them,' Aphrodite said. 'Figures.' But her smile took the bite from her words.

'They are the Mark of our Goddess's favor, showing that you are, indeed, traveling the path she would choose for you. You are our High Priestess,' Darius spoke solemnly. 'The one Nyx has Chosen. And, Priestess, I need your aid with Stevie Rae.'

'Ah, hell,' I muttered, chewing my lip nervously and balling my hands into fists, hiding my exotic new tattoos.

'Oh, for crap's sake! I'll stay and help,' Aphrodite marched over to where Stevie Rae was sitting on the edge of her bed.

'Blood and pain don't bother me at all as long as they're not mine.'

'I should take this closer to the entrance to the tunnels. I'd probably have more luck getting reception there,' Erik said, and without so much as a glance at me, or a word about my new tattoos, he disappeared through the blanket door.

'You know, I think food really was a good idea,' Damien said, taking Jack's hand and starting to follow Erik out of the room.

'Yeah, Damien and I are gay. That means that we are guaranteed to be good cooks,' Jack said.

'We're with them,' Shaunee said.

'Yeah, we're not as convinced about the genetics of gay good cooking. We'd better supervise,' Erin said.

'The blood. Don't forget the blood. Laced with wine, if you have it. She'll need it to recover,' Darius said.

'One of the refrigerators is full of blood. Then find Venus,' Stevie Rae said, grimacing again as Darius took an alcohol wipe and began to clean the dried blood on her back from the skin around the protruding arrow. 'She likes wine. Tell her what you need and she'll get it for you.'

The Twins hesitated, passing a look between each other. Erin spoke for both of them. 'Stevie Rae, are the red kids really okay? I mean, these *are* the kids who killed the Union football players and grabbed Z's human boyfriend, aren't they?'

'Ex-boyfriend,' I said, but they ignored me.

'Venus just helped Erik,' Stevie Rae said. 'And Aphrodite stayed here for two days. She's still in one piece.'

'Yeah, but Erik is a big, healthy male vamp. He'd be hard to bite,' Shaunee said.

'Even though he is definitely yummy,' Erin said.

'True, Twin.' Both of them had given me apologetic shrugs before Shaunee continued. 'And Aphrodite is so damn nasty that no one would want to bite her.'

'But we're little bits of vanilla and chocolate. We'd tempt even the nicest bloodsucking monster,' Erin said.

'Your mom's a bloodsucking monster,' Aphrodite said, smiling sweetly.

'If y'all don't stop bickering, I'm gonna bite *you*!' Stevie Rae yelled, then winced again and made little panting sounds as she tried to breathe through the pain.

'Guys, you're making her hurt herself, and you're giving me a headache.' I said it quickly, getting more and more worried about how bad Stevie Rae looked by the second. 'Stevie Rae says the red fledglings are okay. We just escaped from all hell breaking loose at the House of Night with them and they didn't try to eat any of us on the way here. So make nice, and go find Venus, like Stevie Rae said.'

'Z, that's not a big mark in their favor,' Damien said. 'We were running for our lives. No one had time to eat anyone.'

'Stevie Rae, once and for all – are the red fledglings safe?' I asked.

'I really wish y'all would concentrate on being nicer and accepting them. You know it's not their fault they died and then un-died.'

'See, they're fine,' I said. It was only later that I would remember that Stevie Rae never really answered my question about whether the red fledglings were really safe.

'All right, but we're holding Stevie Rae responsible,' Shaunee said.

'Yeah, if one of them tries to chomp on us, we're going to have words with her about it after she's better,' Erin said.

'Blood and wine. Now. Less talking. More doing,' Darius said bluntly.

They all scurried out of the room, leaving me with Darius, Aphrodite, and my best friend, currently en brochette.

Hell.

CHAPTER THREE

'SERIOUSLY, DARIUS. CAN'T WE DO THIS ANOTHER WAY? SOME other more hospital-like way. In a hospital. With doctors and waiting rooms for friends to wait in while the . . . the . . .' I'd made a semi-panicky gesture at the arrow sticking through Stevie Rae's body. 'While the *stuff* is fixed.'

'There may be a better way, but not under these conditions. I have limited supplies down here, and if you took a moment to think about it, Priestess, I do not believe you would want any of us to go aboveground to one of the city hospitals tonight,' Darius said.

I chewed my lip silently, thinking that he was right but still trying to come up with a less horrifying alternative.

'No. I'm not going back up there. Not only is Kalona free, along with his totally gross bird babies, but I can't get caught aboveground when the sun rises, and I can feel that sunrise isn't that far away. I don't think I could survive it already hurting like this. Z, you're just gonna have to do it,' said Stevie Rae.

'You want me to push on the arrow while you hold her still?' Aphrodite asked.

'No, watching it will probably be worse than helping with it,' I said.

'I'll do my best not to scream too loud,' Stevie Rae said.

She'd been serious, which made my heart squeeze then, just like it did now as I thought back. 'Oh, honey! Scream all you want. Hell, I'll scream along with you.' I looked at Darius. 'I'm ready whenever you are.'

'I will cut off the feathered end of the arrow that is still protruding from the front of her chest. When I do that, you take this,' he handed me a wad of gauze that was wet with alcohol, 'and press it over the cut-off end. When I have a good grip on the front of the arrow I'll tell you to push. Push hard while I pull. It should come out fairly easily.'

'But it might hurt just a little?' Stevie Rae said, sounding faint.

'Priestess,' Darius rested his big hand on her shoulder. 'This will hurt quite a bit more than a little.'

23

'That's why I'm here,' Aphrodite said. 'I'll be holding on to you so you don't flail about as you writhe in pain and mess up Darius's plan.' She hesitated, and then added, 'But you need to know if you go all crazy from agony and bite me *again*, I'm going to knock the shit right out of you.'

'Aphrodite. I'm not gonna bite you. Again,' Stevie Rae said.

'Let's just get this over with,' I said.

Before Darius ripped off what remained of Stevie Rae's shirt he said, 'Priestess, I must bare your breasts.'

'Well, I've been thinkin' about that while you've been workin' on my back. You're kinda like a doctor, aren't you?'

'All of the Sons of Erebus are trained in the medicine field so that we can care for our wounded brothers.' He relaxed his stern expression for a moment and smiled at Stevie Rae. 'So, yes, you may think of me as a physician.'

'Then I'm fine with you seeing my boobies. Doctors are trained not to care about that kind of stuff.'

'Let's hope his training hasn't been *that* thorough,' Aphrodite muttered.

Darius gave her a quick wink. I made a gagging sound, which made Stevie Rae giggle and then gasp when the movement caused her pain. She tried to smile reassuringly at me, but she was way too pale and shaky to pull it off.

It was about then that I really started to worry. Back at the House of Night the undead-dead Stark followed Neferet's pain-in-the-butt orders and shot Stevie Rae. Blood had spilled out of her body at an alarming rate, so much so that it had made the ground around her look like it was bleeding, which fulfilled the stupid prophecy to free the stupid fallen angel, Kalona, from his gazillion-year imprisonment in the earth. Stevie Rae looked like all of the blood in her body had been left on the ground and even though she'd done pretty well up until then, and been walking and talking and mostly conscious, she was quickly fading into a ghostly white nothing before our eyes.

'Ready, Zoey?' Darius asked, making me jump.

Fear had made my teeth chatter so hard that I barely managed to stutter, 'Y-yeah.'

'Stevie Rae?' he said gently. 'Are you prepared?'

'As I'll ever be, I guess. But I can tell you I really wish stuff like this would quit happenin' to me.'

'Aphrodite?' He'd looked to her next.

Aphrodite moved so that she was kneeling on the floor in front of the bed and took both of Stevie Rae's forearms in a strong handhold. 'Try not to flail too much,' she told Stevie Rae.

'I'll do my best.'

'On three,' Darius said, with the shears poised to close on the feather end of the arrow. 'One . . . two . . . three!'

Then everything happened fast. He'd clipped off the end of the arrow like he'd just cut through a tiny twig.

'Cover it!' He barked the command at me, and I'd pressed the gauze against the inch or so of arrow that still stuck out of the front of Stevie Rae's chest squarely between her boobies while he moved around behind her. Stevie Rae's eyes had been squeezed closed. She was breathing in short little panting gasps again, and sweat was beading on her face. 'Again on three, only this time you push against the end of the arrow,' Darius said.

I'd wanted to stop everything and scream *No, let's just wrap her up and take our chances getting her to a hospital*, but Darius had already begun counting. 'One . . . two . . . three!'

I shoved against the hard, newly sliced end of the arrow as Darius, bracing himself with one hand against Stevie Rae's shoulder, pulled the arrow from her body with one swift, awful-sounding jerk.

Stevie Rae did scream. So did I. So did Aphrodite. And then Stevie Rae slumped forward into my arms.

'Keep the gauze pressed against the wound.' Darius quickly and efficiently cleaned the newly exposed hole in Stevie Rae's back.

I remembered repeating over and over, 'It's okay. It's okay. It's out now. It's all over now . . .'

Looking back, I remember that Aphrodite and I had both been sobbing. Stevie Rae's head had been pressed against my shoulder, so I couldn't see her face, but I could feel wetness leaking down my shirt. When Darius lifted her gently and laid her back on the bed so that he could dress the entry wound I felt a jolt of pure fear stab through me.

I'd never seen anyone look as pale as Stevie Rae – anyone who was still alive, that is. Her eyes were squeezed tight shut, but red-tinged tears made horrible tracks down her cheeks, the slight pink in stark contrast to her almost transparent colorless skin.

'Stevie Rae? Are you okay?' I could see her chest rising and falling, but she hadn't opened her eyes and she wasn't making any noise.

'I'm . . . still . . . here.' She whispered the words with long pauses between them. 'But . . . kinda . . . floating . . . above . . . y'all.'

'She's not bleeding,' Aphrodite said in a low voice.

'She has nothing left to bleed,' Darius said as he taped the gauze to her chest.

'The arrow missed her heart,' I said. 'Its purpose wasn't to kill her. It was to bleed her.'

'We are lucky, indeed, that the fledgling missed his mark,' Darius said.

His words still went round and round inside my head because I knew what none of the rest of them did, that it was impossible for Stark to miss his mark. His gift from Nyx had been that his aim was always true, that he always hit whatever it was he aimed at, even if that sometimes had horrible consequences. Our Goddess had told me herself that once she gave a gift, she never took it back, so even though Stark had died and then come back as a twisted version of himself, he still would have hit her heart and killed Stevie Rae if that had been his intention. So did that mean there was more of Stark's humanity left than there had seemed to be? He'd called my name; he'd recognized me. I'd shivered, reliving the chemistry that had sparked between us right before he died.

'Priestess? Did you not hear me?' Darius and Aphrodite had been staring at me.

'Oh, sorry. Sorry. I was distracted by . . .' I hadn't wanted to explain that I was thinking about the guy who had almost killed my best friend. I still didn't want to explain that.

'Priestess, I was saying, if Stevie Rae doesn't get blood, this wound, though it missed her heart, could very well be the death of her.' The warrior shook his head while he examined Stevie Rae. 'Though I cannot tell you for sure that she will heal. She is a new kind of vampyre and I do not know how her body will react, but were she one of my brother warriors, I would be very concerned.'

I had drawn a deep breath and readied myself before saying to Stevie Rae, 'Okay. Well. Forget waiting for the Twins and their bloodmobile. Bite me.'

Her eyes fluttered open and she somehow managed the hint of a smile. 'Human blood, Z,' she said before closing her eyes again.

'She's probably right. Human blood always has a more powerful effect on us than fledgling or even vampyre blood,' Darius said.

'Well, then, I'll run and get the Twins,' I said, even though I hadn't had any real idea where I would be running to.

'Fresh blood would work better than that bland, refrigerated stuff,' Darius said.

He hadn't so much as glanced at Aphrodite, but she definitely got the message. 'Oh, for crap's sake! I'm supposed to let her bite me? Again!'

I blinked, not sure what to say. Thankfully, Darius came to the rescue.

'Ask yourself what your Goddess would have you do,' he said.

'Well, shit! This being one of the good guys really, *really*

28

sucks. Literally.' She sighed, stood up, and pushed back a sleeve of her black velvet dress. Holding her wrist in front of Stevie Rae's face, she said, 'Fine. Go ahead. Bite me. But you owe me big-time. Again. And I do not know why I'm the one who keeps saving your life. I mean, I don't even—' Her words were choked off with a little yip of *yikes!*

It's still kinda disconcerting to think about what happened next. When Stevie Rae grabbed Aphrodite's arm I saw her entire expression change. She instantly went from my sweet BFF to a feral stranger. Her eyes glowed a nasty dark red, and with a scary hiss she bit the crap out of Aphrodite's wrist.

Then Aphrodite's *yikes* turned into a disturbingly sensual moan and her eyes closed as Stevie Rae's mouth latched on to her, breaking the skin easily and causing the hot, pulsing blood to flow as my best friend greedily sucked and swallowed like a predator.

Okay, yes. It was disturbing and nasty, but it was also weirdly erotic. I know it felt good – it had to. That's how vampyres are made. Even being bit by a fledgling will cause the bitee (a human) and the biter (a fledgling) both to experience a very real jolt of intense sexual pleasure. It's how we survive. The old myths about vamps ripping open throats and taking victims by force is pretty much bullpoop – well, unless someone pisses off a vamp pretty badly. And then, even though his or her throat is being ripped out, the bitee would probably like it.

Anyway, we are what we are. And from observing what was going on with Stevie Rae and Aphrodite, it was clear that red vampyres definitely had the whole bring-your-human-pleasure phenomenon going. I mean, Aphrodite had even leaned suggest-ively into Darius, who wrapped an arm around her and bent to kiss her as Stevie Rae continued sucking on her wrist.

The kiss between the warrior and Aphrodite had so much sizzle to it I swear I could almost see sparks flying. Darius held her carefully so that he didn't cause Stevie Rae to wrench her wrist. Aphrodite wrapped her free arm around him and gave herself to him with an openness that showed exactly how much she trusted him. I felt guilty watching, even though there was an undeniably sexy beauty to what was happening between them.

'Okay. Awkward.'

'Seriously. Could have gone my whole life without seeing that.'

I'd looked away from Stevie Rae and company to see the Twins standing just inside the blanketed door. Erin was holding several packets of what were obviously bags of blood. Shaunee was holding a bottle of some kind of red wine and a glass, as in the typical kitchen variety that Mom pours the iced tea into.

Duchess pushed past them and came wagging doggily into the room with Jack close behind her.

'Ohmigod, girl-on-girl action while the guy gets the bene-fits,' Jack said.

'Interesting . . . to think some guys would really find that a turn-on.' Damien had come into the room behind Jack and was holding a paper bag and peering at Stevie Rae, Aphrodite, and Darius like he was watching a science experiment.

Darius managed to break the kiss, pulling Aphrodite close to him and holding her tight against his chest. 'Priestess, this will humiliate her,' he told me in a low, urgent voice. I didn't bother to take time to wonder which *her* he was referring to, Aphrodite or Stevie Rae. Before he finished the sentence, I was already moving toward the Twins.

'I'll take that,' I said, grabbing a bag o' blood from Erin. Totally diverting their attention from the scene on the bed, I used my teeth to tear open the packet like it was a bag of skittles, being sure I got a nice amount of blood on my mouth. 'Hold the glass for me,' I told Shaunee. She did as I commanded, even though she was giving me an *eew* look. Paying her no attention, I poured most of the blood into the glass, making a point of licking my lips and catching the spattering of red that hung on them. Deliberately I upended the baggie and slurped out the remaining blood before I tossed the flattened pouch aside. Then I took the glass of blood from her. 'Now the wine,' I said. The bottle had already been opened, so all Shaunee had to do was pull out the cork. I held up the glass. I'd filled it about three-fourths full with blood, so it took no time to add the wine and fill the cup. 'Thanks,' I said briskly and turned, marching back to the bed.

With a business-like movement I'd taken Aphrodite's upper arm and pulled, disengaging her from Stevie Rae's surprisingly gentle hold. I discreetly stepped in front of her, blocking the view of my best friend's mostly naked body from the gawking masses, a.k.a., the Twins, Damien, and Jack.

Stevie Rae glared up at me, her eyes glowing and her lips

curled back to expose sharp, blood-reddened teeth. Even though I was shocked by how monsterlike she looked, I kept my voice calm and even added a touch of annoyance to it. 'Okay, that's enough. Try this now.'

Stevie Rae snarled at me.

Weirdly enough, Aphrodite had made a sound that echoed Stevie Rae's snarl. WTF? I'd wanted to turn to Aphrodite to see what was going on with her, but I'd known it was best to stay focused on my best friend – who was growling at me.

'I said enough!' I'd snapped in a voice low enough that I hoped my words couldn't be overheard by everyone else. 'Get it together, Stevie Rae. You've had enough from Aphrodite. Drink. This. Now.' I distinctly separated the words, and then I shoved the blood and wine mixture into her hands.

A change came over her face and she blinked and looked unfocused. I guided the glass to her lips, and as soon as the scent of it hit her, she started gulping it down. She was drinking greedily, so I'd allowed myself a second to glance over at Aphrodite. Still in Darius's arms, she looked okay, though more than a little dazed, and she was staring wide-eyed at Stevie Rae.

I'd felt a prickle of unease skitter down my spine at the shocked expression on Aphrodite's face, which turned out to be an accurate premonition of weirdness to come. But then I turned my attention to my gawking friends. 'Damien,' I made my voice sharp. 'Stevie Rae needs a shirt. Can you find her one?'

'The laundry basket. There're clean shirts in it,' Stevie Rae said between gulps. She sounded and looked more like herself again. With a shaky hand she gestured to a pile of stuff. Damien nodded and hurried across the room.

'Let me see your wrist,' Darius said to Aphrodite.

Without speaking she'd turned her back to the staring Twins and Jack and gave her arm to Darius, so I had been the only one who really saw what he did. The warrior lifted her wrist to his mouth. Without taking his eyes from hers, his tongue snaked out and ran over the ridge of bite marks that were still dripping scarlet. Her breath caught, and I saw that she was trembling, but the moment his tongue touched the wound the bleeding began to clot. I had been watching closely, so I didn't miss the way Darius's eyes had widened suddenly in surprise.

'Well, shit,' I heard Aphrodite say softly to him. 'It's true, isn't it?'

'It is true,' he answered her in a low voice meant for her alone.

'Shit!' Aphrodite repeated, looking upset.

Darius smiled, and I saw a definite glint of amusement in his eyes. Then he kissed her wrist gently and said, 'No matter; it will not affect us.'

'Promise?' she whispered.

'I give you my word. You did well, my beauty. Your blood saved her life.'

For a moment I saw Aphrodite's unguarded expression. She shook her head slightly and her smile was tinged with honest wonder and more than a little sarcasm. 'And why the hell I have to keep saving Stevie Rae's country-bumpkin ass I do not know. All I can say is that I used to be really, *really*

33

bad, so I have an unbelievable amount of shit I have to make up for.' She cleared her throat and ran the back of her hand shakily across her forehead.

'Do you need something to drink?' I asked, wondering what the hell the two of them were talking about, but not wanting to ask just then because they obviously didn't want the whole room to know.

'Yes.' Stevie Rae surprised me by answering for her.

'Here's a shirt,' Damien said. He'd approached the bed, saw that Stevie Rae, who had gone from gulping to sipping from the glass, was partially naked, and averted his eyes.

'Thanks.' I gave him a quick smile, took the shirt from him, and tossed it to Stevie Rae. Then I looked back at the Twins. The swallows of blood had begun to work in my body, and the exhaustion that had pressed down on me since I'd had to call all five of the elements and control them while we escaped from the House of Night finally had lessened enough for me to think again. 'Okay, guys, bring the blood and wine over here. Do you have another glass for Aphrodite?'

Before they could answer Aphrodite spoke up. 'Uh, no blood for me. I have one word for that: disgusting. But I will take the booze.'

'We didn't bring another glass,' Erin said. 'She'll have to drink out of the bottle like a peasant.'

'Sorry, kinda,' Shaunee said insincerely, handing Aphrodite the bottle. 'So, as a human, can you explain to us what it's like to get your blood sucked by a vamp?'

'Yeah, inquiring minds want to know 'cause you looked

like you were liking it, and we didn't know you swung that way,' Erin said.

'Did you brain-sharers not pay any attention in Vamp Soc class?' Aphrodite said before she tipped up the bottle and drank from it.

'Well, I've read the physiology section of *The Fledgling Handbook*,' Damien said. 'Vampyre saliva has coagulants, anti-coagulants, and endorphins that act on the pleasure zones of the brain, human and vamp. You know, Aphrodite is right. You two really should pay better attention in class. School's supposed to be more than a social event.' He finished primly while Jack nodded enthusiastically.

'You know, Twin, what with all the drama going on above – the release of an evil fallen angel and his goons – and the House of Night pretty much in panic mode, there might not be school for a while,' Shaunee said.

'Excellent point, Twin,' Erin said. 'Which means we won't need Queen Damien and his tutorness for a while.'

'So we could, I dunno, hold him down and pull out his hair? What do you think?' Shaunee said.

'Sounds fun,' Erin said.

'Great. I'm drinking cheap red wine out of a bottle. Miss Teen Country Vamp just bit me – again. And now I'm going to be witness to a nerd herd rumble.' Sounding much more like her bitchy self, Aphrodite sighed dramatically and plopped down on the end of the bed next to Darius. 'Well, at least being human means I can probably get drunk. Maybe I can stay that way for the next ten years or so.'

'I don't have enough wine for that.' We all looked up as a red fledgling entered the room, followed by several others who clustered behind her in the shadows. 'And that isn't *cheap* red wine. I don't do cheap anything.'

Everyone else turned their attention to the red fledgling as she spoke, but I'd been watching Aphrodite gripe at the Twins (and was getting ready to step in and tell everyone to shut up), so I saw the brief flash of what looked like a mixture of embarrassment and discomfort cross Aphrodite's face before she got a handle on her expression and said coolly, 'Nerd herd, this is Venus. Dorkamese Twins and Damien, you should remember my ex-roommate who died about six months or so ago.'

'Actually, it seems reports of my death were premature,' the pretty blonde said smoothly. Then something totally bizarre happened. Venus paused and sniffed the air. I mean she literally lifted her chin and took several short, sharp sniffs in Aphrodite's general direction. The red fledglings that still clustered together behind her followed her lead, and I watched them sniff, too. Then Venus's blue eyes widened and in a very amused voice she said, 'Well . . . well . . . well . . . how interesting.'

'Venus, do not—' Stevie Rae began, but Aphrodite cut her off.

'No. It doesn't matter. Everyone might as well know.'

With a mean smile the blonde continued. 'I was just going to say how interesting it is that Stevie Rae and Aphrodite have Imprinted.'

CHAPTER FOUR

I HAD TO CLAMP MY JAWS SHUT TO KEEP FROM GASPING along with the Twins.

'Ohmigod! Imprinted! Really?' Jack blurted.

Aphrodite shrugged. 'Apparently.' I thought she looked way too nonchalant, and she was totally avoiding even glancing in Stevie Rae's direction, but I think almost everyone else in the room was fooled by her 'whatever' attitude.

'Well, spank me and call me your baby!' Shaunee said.

'Make that a double spanking, Twin,' Erin chimed in. And then the two of them burst into semi-hysterical giggles.

'I think it's interesting.' Damien spoke up so he could be heard over the cackling Twins.

'Me, too,' Jack said. 'In a freaky, ohmigod way.'

'Sounds like Karma has finally caught up with Aphrodite,' Venus said with a sneer that made her beauty turn reptilian.

'Venus, Aphrodite just saved my life. Again. And it's really not right that you're being ugly to her,' Stevie Rae said.

Aphrodite finally looked at Stevie Rae. 'Do *not* start doing that.'

'Doin' what?' Stevie Rae asked.

'Standing up for me! We may have somefucking how Imprinted, and that's bad enough. But Do. Not. Go. All. BFF. On. Me!' she said slowly and distinctly.

'Your bein' hateful will not change this,' Stevie Rae said.

'Look, I'm just going to play like *this* never happened.' A wave of giggles from the Twins had Aphrodite glaring their way. 'Dorkamese Twins, I will figure out a way to smother both of you while you sleep if you do not stop laughing at me.'

Naturally, the Twins erupted into louder guffaws.

Turning her back on them, Aphrodite faced me. 'So, like I was saying before I was rudely interrupted times ten: pain-in-the-ass Venus, this is Zoey, the super-fledgling I'm sure you've heard so much about, and Darius, the Son of Erebus warrior who you will *not* be sneaking around with, and Jack. He won't be sneaking around with you, either, but mostly because he's gay as a French pastry. His other half is Damien, the guy who is staring at me like a fucking science project.

You already know that the Twins are the laughing heads over there.'

I could feel Venus's eyes on me, so I managed to tear my gaze from Aphrodite (Imprinted! To Stevie Rae!) to look at her. Sure enough, she was staring at me with an intense expression that made me instantly defensive. I was still trying to decide whether my negative reaction to Venus was because she was (obviously) a bitch, because she had been skulking around the tunnels with Erik, or because I had a bad feeling about the red fledglings in general, when she spoke up.

'Zoey and I have already met, but it was unofficial. Seems last time I saw her she was trying to kill us.'

I put a hand on my hip and met her cold, blue-eyed stare. 'While we're taking this trip down Memory Lane, you might want to get a clue. *I* wasn't trying to kill anyone. *I* was trying to save a human kid you guys were trying to eat. Unlike you, *I* would have much rather been at IHOP munching on chocolate-chip pancakes than football players.'

'That doesn't make the girl you killed any less dead,' Venus said as the red fledglings behind her stirred restlessly.

'Z? You killed someone?' Jack asked.

I opened my mouth to answer, but Venus beat me to it. 'She did. Elizabeth No Last Name.'

'I had to,' I said simply, speaking to Jack and ignoring Venus and the red fledglings, even though something about them had the little hairs on the back of my neck standing on end. 'They weren't letting Heath and me out of here alive.' Then I turned my attention back to Venus. She had an icy beauty.

Venus was sleek and sexy in a pair of tight designer jeans and a simple cropped black tank that had a rhinestone skull's head on it. Her hair was long and thick and the kind of blonde that looked golden. In other words, she was definitely attractive enough to hang with Aphrodite, which was saying something, because Aphrodite is totally gorgeous. And, like Aphrodite used to be, Venus was obviously a hateful bitch, and probably had been one before she died and un-died. I narrowed my eyes at her. 'Look, I told you guys to back off and let us out of here. You didn't. I did what I had to then to protect someone I cared about – and you all should know I'd do it again.' My eyes shifted from Venus to the fledglings behind her while I stifled the urge to reach for a couple of the elements and have wind and fire put a little added punch to my threat.

Venus glared back at me.

'Okay, y'all have got to learn to get along. Are you remembering that the entire outside world might be against us, or at least filled with scary booger monsters?' Stevie Rae sounded tired but herself. She sat up, gingerly straightening her Dixie Chicks T-shirt and slowly leaning back against the pillows Darius had propped behind her. 'So, like Tim Gunn on *Project Runway* would say, let's make it work.'

'Ooooh, I love that show,' Jack gushed.

I heard a couple of the red fledglings mumble agreement and decided Stevie Rae might have had a point during one of our many trash TV arguments: Reality shows could make the world a better place and bring peace to all mankind.

'Making it work sounds good to me.' Even though my internal alarm was still warning me that all was not sweetness and light with the red fledglings, I smiled at Stevie Rae, who dimpled back at me. Okay, she obviously believed we could figure out a way to get along. So maybe my alarm system was misfiring simply because Venus was a hateful bitch, and not because she and the rest of them were evil incarnate.

'Good. So, first, could I please have a refill of that blood and wine? Heavy on the blood part.' She held her empty glass out toward the Twins, who gratefully moved closer to Stevie Rae's bed and farther away from the group of red fledglings. I noticed Damien and Jack, with Duchess by his side, had also managed to make their way over to where I was standing. 'Thanks,' she said when Erin took her glass. 'And there're some scissors in the drawer over there so you don't have to rip it open with your teeth.' She gave me a little eye roll. While Erin and Shaunee were busy getting Stevie Rae more bloody wine, she studied the little group of red fledglings. 'Look, we already talked about this. You know y'all are gonna have to make nice with Zoey and the rest of the kids.' She glanced up at Darius and smiled, 'Well, kids and vamps, that is.'

'Hey, excuse me, guys. I need to get through.'

I'd bristled automatically as Erik pushed through the crowd at the door. If someone (Venus) tried to bite him, someone (me) was gonna kick her ass. Period.

Ignoring the tension in the room, Darius said, 'What does the radio report is happening in the world above?'

Erik shook his head. 'I can't get anything in. I even went up into the basement. Nothing but static. Couldn't get my cell phone to work, either. I did hear a bunch of thunder and could see flashings of massive lightning. It's still raining, even though it's getting colder, which means it'll probably turn to ice. Plus, the wind's kicked up like crazy. I couldn't tell if the weather was natural, or if Kalona and those bird things were causing it. Either way, that's probably what's knocking the radio stations and cell towers off-line. I thought you'd want to know, so I came back down.' I saw his eyes move from Darius to arrowless Stevie Rae and he smiled. 'You look better.'

'Aphrodite saved her by letting Stevie Rae drink her blood,' Shaunee said, and then giggled.

'Yeah, and now the two of them have Imprinted,' Erin finished in a rush, and then joined Shaunee's laughter.

'Wow, you're kidding. Right?' he said, sounding totally shocked.

'No, they are not kidding,' Venus said smoothly.

'Huh. Well. That's interesting.' I watched Erik's lips twitch as he stared at Aphrodite. She totally ignored him and kept drinking straight from the wine bottle she clutched in her hand. He stifled a big laugh with a cough, and then his eyes lit on Venus. He nodded, his normal easygoing, popular self. 'Hi again, Venus.'

'Erik,' she said, with a feral smile that made me want to squash her like a bug.

'Aphrodite was right to start introductions,' Stevie Rae said, and before Aphrodite could interrupt, she hurried on, 'And, no, I'm not saying that because we're Imprinted.'

'I really wish you would all quit talking about it,' Aphrodite muttered.

Stevie Rae continued as if she hadn't heard her. 'I think being polite is a real good idea, and introductions are always polite. Y'all already know Venus,' she said, and then moved on quickly. 'So I'll start with Elliott.'

A redheaded kid stepped forward. Okay, dying and un-dying hadn't improved this kid any. He was still pudgy and pale with a frizzy ball of carrot-colored, uncombed hair sticking up in odd places on his head. 'I'm Elliott,' he said.

Everyone nodded at him. 'Next is Montoya,' Stevie Rae said.

A short, Hispanic guy who looked seriously thuggish with his sagging pants and his multiple piercings nodded his head, sending his thick dark hair waving around his face. 'Hi,' he said with just a touch of an accent and a surprisingly cute, warm smile. 'And that's Shannon Compton.' Stevie Rae ran her first and last name together, so that it sounded like Shannoncompton.

'Shannoncompton? Hey, didn't you read the spotlight piece in *The Vagina Monologues* last year at the school perform-ance?' Damien asked.

Her pretty face brightened. 'Yeah, that was me.'

'I remember because I just love *The Vagina Monologues*. They're so empowering,' Damien said. 'And then right after the show you . . . um . . .' His voice trailed off and he fidgeted.

'I died?' Shannoncompton added helpfully.

'Yeah, exactly,' Damien said.

'Oh, gosh, that's too bad,' Jack said.

Aphrodite sighed. 'She's not dead anymore, morons.'

'And this is Sophie.' Stevie Rae said quickly, frowning at Aphrodite, who was already sounding tipsy. A tall brunette stepped a little forward and gave us a tentative friendly smile. 'Hi,' she said.

We waved and muttered hellos. I was actually feeling better about the red fledglings now that they were becoming individuals – and not individuals who were trying to chomp on us. Or at least at that moment they weren't.

'Dallas is next.' Stevie Rae pointed to a kid standing behind Venus. At the sound of his name he kinda slouched around her and mumbled what sounded like a version of hi. He would have been totally unremarkable looking if it hadn't been for the quick intelligence in his eyes and the kinda flirty smile he threw Stevie Rae. *Hm*, I thought, *wonder if something's going on there?* 'Dallas was born in Houston, which we all think is odd and confusing,' Stevie Rae was saying.

The kid shrugged. 'It's a gross story my dad tells about him and my mom making me in Dallas. I never wanted the details.'

'Ugh, parent sex,' Shaunee said.

'Completely disgusting,' Erin agreed.

I could see a little laugh ripple through the group of red fledglings at the Twins' comments, making the tension that had been hanging between our two groups begin to really loosen up.

'Next is Anthony, who everyone calls Ant.'

Ant waved awkwardly at us and said hi. Well, it was obvious why everyone called him Ant. He was one of those little kids. You know, the ones that look, like, ten when they're really fourteen and supposed to have gone through puberty already. Then, as if to provide the biggest contrast possible, Stevie Rae moved on to the next kid. 'This is Johnny B.'

Johnny B was tall and built. He reminded me of Heath with his athletic body and the easy confidence with which he held himself. 'Hey,' he said, flashing white teeth and obviously checking out the Twins, who raised their brows at him and checked him out right back.

'Next is Gerarty. She's the best artist I've ever known. She's started to decorate parts of the tunnels. It's gonna look majorly cool when she gets done.' Stevie Rae beamed at yet another blonde, only Gerarty wasn't all tall and Barbie-like. She was pretty, but her blonde hair was more dishwater than platinum, and cut in a seventies shag. She nodded at us and looked uncomfortable.

'And last but not least is Kramisha.'

A black girl twitched out of the group. It was a testament to how distracted I'd been with Venus and Aphrodite and Stevie Rae that I hadn't noticed her before then. She had on a form-fitting bright yellow shirt cut low to show the top of her black lace bra and a pair of high-waisted, skintight cropped jeans that were cinched up with a wide leather belt that matched her chunky gold shoes. Her hair was cut geometrically into a short poof on her head, and half of it was dyed bright orange.

'Let's get it straight right now that I'm not sharin' my bed with no one,' Kramisha said, weaving her head around and looking bored and pissed off at the same time.

'Kramisha, I told you about a zillion times, don't make an issue outta somethin' that isn't one,' Stevie Rae said.

'I just want to be clear about myself,' Kramisha said.

'Fine. You're clear.' Stevie Rae paused and looked up at me expectantly. 'Okay, that's my group.'

'And these are the extent of the red fledglings?' Darius asked before I could launch into my introductions.

Stevie Rae chewed the inside of her cheek and didn't meet Darius's eyes. 'Yeah, these are all of my red fledglings.'

Ah oh, that's her I'm-not-telling-the-whole-truth look. I knew it, but when she met my eyes, hers so clearly begged me not to say anything that I decided to keep my mouth shut and get the whole story when we weren't the focus of everybody's attention.

But me putting off questioning Stevie Rae didn't put off the *feeling* that had come back, alarm bells ringing inside my head, loud and clear, at her evasion. There was definitely something going on with the red fledglings, and I didn't think that something was going to be good.

I cleared my throat. 'Well, I'm Zoey Redbird.' I tried to sound polite and normal in a situation that didn't feel either.

'I've told y'all about Zoey. She has an affinity for all five elements, and it's through her powers that I was able to Change and we were all given our humanity back,' Stevie Rae said. I noticed she was looking directly at Venus.

'Well, it wasn't just through me that happened. My friends had a lot to do with it, too.' I nodded at Aphrodite, who was still drinking directly from the bottle of wine. 'You guys obviously know Aphrodite. She's a human now, but let's just say she's not normal,' I said, completely avoiding the subject of her fresh Imprint with Stevie Rae.

Aphrodite snorted, but didn't say anything.

'This is Erin and Shaunee, the Twins. Erin has an affinity for water, Shaunee's affinity is fire.' The Twins nodded and said hi.

'Damien and Jack are a couple,' I said. 'Damien's affinity is air. Jack is our audiovisual guy.'

'Hi,' Damien said.

'Hey there,' Jack said. He lifted the bag he was still carrying. 'I made sandwiches. Anyone hungry?'

'Can someone explain why that dog's in here?' Venus said, totally ignoring Jack's friendly overture.

'She's here 'cause she's mine,' Jack said. 'She stays with me.' He reached down and petted Duchess's soft ears.

'Duchess stays with Jack,' I said firmly, giving Venus a hard look and thinking that I could happily strangle her with Duchess's leash before I continued with the intros. 'And this is Erik Night.'

'I remember you from drama class,' Shannoncompton said, her cheeks turning pink. 'You're really famous.'

47

'Hi, Shannon.' Erik smiled easily at her. 'Nice to see you again.'

'I remember you, too. You were with Aphrodite,' Venus said.

'Not anymore,' Aphrodite said quickly, giving Darius *a look*.

'Obviously. You're not a fledgling anymore,' Venus said in a silky voice that sounded way too interested. 'When did you Change?'

'Just a few days ago,' he said. 'I was on my way to the European acting academy when Shekinah asked that I take Professor Nolan's place temporarily at the House of Night.'

'Wow, I knew that High Priestess looked familiar. That was actually Shekinah!' Shannoncompton said. 'I saw her just before she started toward that winged guy and—' She stopped talking and picked at her lip worriedly.

'And she was killed by Neferet,' I bluntly finished for her.

'Was she? Do you know that for certain?' Darius asked.

'She's dead and I saw Neferet do it. I think she killed her with her mind,' I said.

'Queen Tsi Sgili,' Damien murmured. 'It's true then.'

'I need all of this explained to me,' Darius said curtly.

'And this is our Son of Erebus warrior, Darius,' I said.

'He's right,' Stevie Rae said. 'We need what happened tonight explained to us.'

'Not just tonight's happenings,' Darius said. His gaze rested on the group of unusual fledglings. 'I need information if I am to protect you. I must know everything that has been going on.'

'Agreed,' I said, glad beyond words that we had an experienced Son of Erebus in our group.

'We could eat and talk,' Jack said. When I looked at him, he gave me a big smile. 'It always helps to eat with each other. A meal makes things better.'

'Unless *you're* the meal,' I heard Aphrodite mutter.

'Jack's right,' Stevie Rae said. 'Why don't y'all go grab some of the egg crates we have in the kitchen and some bags of chips and whatnot. Let's eat while we talk.'

'Would the whatnot be more blood?' Venus said.

'Yes, it would,' Stevie Rae said matter-of-factly, clearly not wanting to make a big deal out of the blood issue.

'Fine. I'll go get some more,' Venus said.

'Hey, while you're getting blood, grab me another bottle of wine,' Aphrodite said.

'You know I'm not into charity, so you'll be paying me back,' Venus said.

'I remember,' Aphrodite said. 'And you should remember that I pay my debts.'

'Yeah, that's how you used to be, but seems you've made a change,' she said.

'No shit? You mean you just now noticed I turned human?'

'Not what I was talking about. So just replace the wine,' she added before leaving the room.

'Hey, weren't y'all roomies?' Stevie Rae asked Aphrodite.

Aphrodite ignored Stevie Rae and I had the urge to shake her and yell, *Not talking to her or looking at her is not going to break your Imprint*.

'Yes, they were,' Erik said into the dead air, reminding me that because he and Aphrodite used to be together, he would know her roommate, maybe too well.

'Yeah, well, things change.' Aphrodite found her voice.

'People change,' I said, pulling my gaze from Erik.

Aphrodite met my eyes. Her lips curled up in a sad, sarcastic smile. 'And that is too damn true,' she said.

CHAPTER FIVE

'SO WE HAVE P.B. AND J., BOLOGNA, AND PROCESSED AMERICAN cheese slices.' Jack said the 'processed American cheese slices' part like he was reluctantly offering us worms and mud. 'And my personal gourmet *Top Chef* concoction: mayonnaise, peanut butter, and lettuce on wheat bread.'

'Okay, Jack. Nasty,' Shaunee said.

'Have you lost your damn mind?' Erin said.

'Gay white boy is weird,' Kramisha said, snagging one of the bologna and cheese sandwiches.

The Twins nodded and made 'yep' noises as Kramisha joined them on a nearby egg crate.

Jack looked mortally offended. 'I think they're good, and you guys should try things before you disrespect them.'

'I'll try one of them,' said Shannoncompton sweetly.

'Thanks.' Jack grinned and handed her a sandwich wrapped in a paper towel.

There was the rustling of a lot of paper as all of us crowded into Stevie Rae's room, grabbed sandwiches, and passed bags of chips around. I was surprised to see the amount of food and chips and brown pop (yea for brown pop!). It made a weird, surreal mixture with the bottles of red wine and bags of blood that were being shared. I sat on the bed with Aphrodite and Darius and Stevie Rae, who was looking better and better. For a second, with the normal sounds of kids eating and talking, it was easy to imagine that we were just in a kind of ratty building at the House of Night and forget that we were in a tunnel under the city and that all of our lives were in the process of never being the same. For a second, we were nothing but a group of kids, some friends, some not, and we were just hanging out together.

'Tell me what you know of the creature that rose from the earth and the bird beings that followed him.' Darius's words made the whole just-hanging-out façade crumple like a house of cards.

'Sadly, we don't know as much about him as I wish we did, and what we do know comes from my grandma.' I swallowed down the tightness in my throat that mentioning her caused. 'Grandma's in a coma, so she can't help us right now.'

'Oh, Z! I'm so sorry! What happened?' Stevie Rae cried, touching my arm.

'The official version is she was in a car accident. The truth is that the accident was caused by the Raven Mockers because she knew too much about them,' I said.

'Raven Mockers – those are the beings that came out of the earth after the winged man appeared?' Darius said.

I nodded. 'They're his children – what happened after he raped the women of my grandma's people more than a thousand years ago. When Kalona broke out of the ground their bodies were returned to them.'

'And you know these things because they are creatures from Cherokee legend?' Darius said.

'Actually, we know these things because in the vision Aphrodite had a couple days ago she was shown what we figured out was a prophecy about Kalona returning. It was written in Grandma's handwriting, so we called her – told her about it. She recognized the references and came to the House of Night to help us.' I paused, steadying my voice. 'That's why the Raven Mockers attacked her.'

'I really wish we had that prophecy,' Damien said. 'I'd like to take a look at it again now that Kalona has actually been set free.'

'That's easy enough,' Aphrodite said. She took a long drink from her bottle of wine, hiccupped a little, and then recited:

'Ancient one sleeping, waiting to arise
When earth's power bleeds sacred red
The mark strikes true; Queen Tsi Sgili will devise
He shall be washed from his entombing bed

Through the hand of the dead he is free
Terrible beauty, monstrous sight
Ruled again they shall be
Women shall kneel to his dark might

Kalona's song sounds sweet
As we slaughter with cold heat.'

'Wow! Well done, you!' Jack said, clapping his hands.

Aphrodite inclined her head regally and said, 'Thank you . . . Thank you . . . It was nothing. Really.' And then went back to her wine.

I made a mental note to keep an eye on her drinking. Okay, yeah, she'd been through a bunch of stress lately, and being bitten – twice – by Stevie Rae and, bizarrely enough, Imprinting with her couldn't be particularly good for her nerves, but the last thing we needed was Vision Girl to turn into Drunk Vision Girl.

Darius nodded thoughtfully. 'Kalona is the ancient one, but that doesn't explain what type of being he is.'

'Grandma said that the easiest way to describe him is to think of him as a fallen angel, an immortal being that walked the earth in ancient times. Seems there were a bunch of them that showed up in the mythology of many cultures, like ancient Greece and the Old Testament.'

'Yeah, on vacation from heaven or whatever, they decided women were hot, and so they *mated* with them,' Aphrodite said, slurring her words a little. 'Mated – that's an uptight way to say that they fu—'

'Thanks, Aphrodite. I'll take it from there,' I said. I was glad she had stopped her silent pouting, but wasn't so sure that her drunken sarcasm was much better. Wordlessly Damien handed me a sandwich and nodded at Aphrodite. I passed the sandwich to Aphrodite telling her, 'Eat something.' Then I took up the thread of the story. 'So Kalona started getting with Cherokee women and became bizarrely addicted to sex. The women rejected him and he started raping them and enslaving the men of the tribe. A group of Wise Women called Ghigua made a maiden out of the earth to trap him.'

'Huh?' Stevie Rae said. 'You mean like a dirt doll?'

'Yeah, only an attractive one. Each of the women gave the doll a particular gift, then they breathed life into her and named her A-ya. Kalona wanted A-ya, and she ran from him, leading him to a cave deep in the ground. He followed her into the cave, even though he usually avoided anything that was under-ground, and that's where they managed to trap him.'

'That is why you brought us here, into these tunnels,' Darius said.

I nodded.

'So we are to think of Kalona as a dangerous immortal and the Raven Mockers as his servants. Who is the other creature mentioned in the prophecy and also by Damien, a Queen Tsi Sgili?' Darius said.

'According to Grandma, the Tsi Sgili are really awful Cherokee witches. Don't think cool Wiccans or Priestesses. They're not good at all, but more like demons, really, except that they are mortal and known for their psychic abilities, especially the ability to kill with their minds,' I said. 'Neferet is the queen the prophecy was talking about.'

'But Neferet announced to the House of Night that Kalona is Erebus on earth, and her consort, as if she had become the literal incarnation of Nyx,' Darius said slowly, as if he was reasoning through it aloud.

'She's lying. Really, she's turned from Nyx,' I said. 'I've known it for a while, but acting openly against her has been pretty close to impossible. I mean, look what happened tonight. Everyone saw Stevie Rae and the red fledglings and they didn't turn on her. Except for Shekinah, they barely even blinked even after she ordered Stark to shoot.'

'Which is why she got Stark transferred from the Chicago House of Night to Tulsa,' Damien said. When just about everyone gave him confused looks, he explained. 'Stark is James Stark, the fledgling who won the gold medal at the Summer Games for archery. Neferet wanted him here so she could use him to shoot Stevie Rae.'

'Makes sense,' Aphrodite said. 'We already know Neferet has something to do with fledglings un-dying. Obviously she wanted to use him, and her plan worked because he's definitely undead and under her control.' She looked pleased at her powers of deduction and upended the bottle of wine for another long drink.

'Guess I'm just lucky his aim wasn't so good now that he died and then came back,' Stevie Rae said.

'That's not it.' My mouth spoke before I could shut myself up. 'He missed your heart on purpose.'

'What do ya mean?' Stevie Rae asked.

'Before Stark died, he told me about his gift from Nyx. He never misses. He can't. He always hits the mark he aims at.'

'Then if he missed killing Stevie Rae on purpose, that must mean he's not totally under Neferet's influence,' Damien said.

'He did say your name,' Erik said. His piercing blue eyes seemed to see deep inside me. 'I remember that distinctly. Before he shot Stevie Rae he definitely recognized you. He even said he'd come back to you.'

'I was with him when he died,' I said, returning Erik's questioning gaze and trying not to look as guilty as I felt for being attracted to yet another guy besides him. 'Right before he died I told Stark that fledglings at our House of Night were coming back from the dead. That's what he was talking about.'

'Well, there was obviously a connection between the two of you,' Darius said. 'And it probably saved Stevie Rae's life.'

'But Stark definitely wasn't himself,' I said, looking away from Erik. It had just been a few days ago that I'd kissed Stark and he'd died in my arms, but it seemed like forever had passed. 'He was obviously under Neferet's influence, even if he was trying to resist her.'

'Yeah, it's like she put a spell on him or something,' Jack said.

'Hang on, that reminds me,' Damien said. 'I definitely noticed how almost everyone acted awestruck and even a little disoriented when Kalona appeared.'

Venus snorted, sounding very much like Aphrodite at her most sarcastic (and least attractive). 'Everyone except us.' She made a gesture that took in all of the red fledglings. 'We knew he was evil and totally full of bullshit from the second we saw him.'

'How?' I asked abruptly. 'How did you guys know? All the other fledglings, well, except us, actually fell to their knees at the sight of him. Even the Sons of Erebus warriors didn't move against him.' I'd felt drawn to him, too, but I didn't want to admit that in front of Venus.

Venus shrugged. 'It was just obvious. Yeah, he was hot and all, but come on! He exploded from the ground after Stevie Rae bled all over it.'

I watched her closely, thinking that maybe the reason she recognized Kalona's evil was that she was too darn familiar with evil.

'Look, he had wings. That ain't right,' Kramisha added, fragmenting my attention. 'My mama told me don't trust no white boy, even a pretty one. I'm thinkin' a pretty white boy with wings explodin' up from the ground in a mess of blood and ugly-ass bird things is double trouble.'

'She has a point,' said Jack, obviously forgetting he was a pretty white boy.

'I have to share something,' Damien said. We managed to pull our attention from Kramisha to him. 'If I hadn't been in the middle of a fully cast circle, surrounded by you guys with Aphrodite yelling at us to stay together and get out of there, I might have fallen to my knees, too.'

I felt a prickle of unease. 'What about you guys?' I asked the Twins.

'He was hot,' Shaunee said.

'Majorly,' Erin said. She looked at Shaunee. Her Twin nodded, so she continued, 'He would've gotten to us, too. If Aphrodite hadn't been shrieking unattractively at us to keep the circle together, we'd still be back there in the middle of that mess.'

'Which would not be good,' Shaunee said.

'That's all I'm sayin',' Kramisha added.

'Again I save members of the nerd herd,' Aphrodite slurred.

'Just eat your sandwich,' I told her. Then I turned to Erik. 'How about you? Did he make you want to . . . ?' I trailed off, not sure how to put it.

'Stay and worship him?' Erik inserted, and I nodded. 'Well, I did feel his power. But, remember, I already knew something was up with Neferet. If she was into him, I figured I didn't want anything to do with him. So I just kept myself focused on other things.'

Our eyes met and held. Of course Erik had known it wasn't all good with Neferet, because he'd witnessed me confronting her. Plus, by then he'd realized I'd only cheated on him and been with the Vamp Poet Laureate, Loren Blake, because

Neferet had set him up to seduce me and isolate me from my friends.

'So the red fledglings aren't affected by Kalona like regular fledglings are,' Darius was saying. 'Although it seems regular fledglings can control the effect he has on them if they have to. And what Erik is describing, coupled with my reaction to him, tells me that perhaps vampyres are less susceptible to him than fledglings.' He paused and looked at Jack. 'Did you want to stay and worship Kalona?'

Jack shook his head. 'Nope. But I didn't really look at him that much. I mean, I was real worried about Stevie Rae, and then I was just thinking about staying with Damien. Plus, Duchess was upset about S-T-A-R-K.' He spelled the name while he petted Duchess. 'And I had to take care of her.'

'Why weren't you affected by him?' I asked Darius.

I saw his eyes flit to Aphrodite, who was tipsily nibbling on a sandwich.

'I had other things on my mind.' He paused. 'Although I did feel his draw. And remember I'm in a slightly different position than my brother warriors. None of them have been as intimate with your group. When a Son of Erebus takes on an assignment of protection, as I did when I began escorting you and Aphrodite, it becomes a strong bond.' He gave me a warm smile. 'Often a High Priestess is protected by the same group of warriors for her entire life. It is no accident that we are named after our Goddess's faithful consort, Erebus.'

I smiled back at him and hoped that Aphrodite wouldn't be a butt and break his honorable heart.

'What do you think is happening up there right now?' Jack asked suddenly.

Everyone looked at the curved ceiling of the little tunnel room, and I knew I wasn't the only one glad of the thickness of the earth between us and 'up there.'

'I don't know,' I said, using the truthful answer instead of something meaningless like *I'm sure everything's going to be okay*. I thought hard, choosing my words carefully. 'We know that an ancient immortal has broken free of the earth's imprisonment. We know that he brings with him creatures that are like demons, and that the last time he walked the earth he raped women and made men his slaves. We know that our High Priestess and maybe even what's left of the House of Night have, well, for lack of a better description, gone over to the Dark Side.'

Into the silent pause that followed my words Erik said, 'A *Star Wars* analogy always works.'

I grinned at him, then sobered as I continued. 'What we don't know is how much damage Kalona and the Raven Mockers have done in the community. Erik said there was some kind of electrical storm going on along with the rain and ice, but that might not have been caused by supernatural means. This is Oklahoma, and the weather can be totally bizarre.'

'*Ooooooo-klahoma!* Home of dustnadoes and ice storms that kick ass,' Aphrodite said.

I stifled a sigh and ignored Imprinted Drunk Vision Girl. 'But then again, on the "what we do know" side is the fact that we're pretty safe down here. We have food and shelter and whatnot.' *At least I hoped we were okay down here.* I patted the bed I was sitting on, which really did have some cute light green linens on it. 'Hey, speaking of the "and whatnot," how did you guys get this stuff down here?' I asked Stevie Rae. 'Not that I'm trying to be mean, but this bed and your table and fridges and other things are a serious improvement over the dirty rags and other grossness I saw down here a month or so ago.'

She gave me her cute Stevie Rae smile and said, 'That's mostly thanks to Aphrodite.'

'Aphrodite?' I asked, lifting my brows and staring at her along with everyone else.

'What can I say? I've become the poster child for do-gooders. Thank god I'm attractive,' Aphrodite said and then belched like a guy. 'Oops, *scusa*,' she slurred.

'*Scusa?*' Jack said.

'Italian, dork,' Aphrodite said. 'Broaden your gay horizons.'

'So what does Aphrodite have to do with the stuff you have down here?' I interrupted what was sure to become some serious bickering.

'She bought this stuff. Actually, it was her idea,' Stevie Rae said.

'*Scusa?*' I said, not even trying to stifle my grin.

'I stayed down here for two days. Did you expect me to live in a hovel? Not hardly. Have credit cards, will decorate. I think that's on my family crest along with a very dry martini,' she said. 'There's a Pottery Barn in Utica Square right down the street. They deliver. So does Home Depot, which is also not far from here, although I wasn't aware of that until one of the red freaks enlightened me because I do not shop at appliance stores.'

'They're not freaks,' Stevie Rae said.

'Oh, bite me,' Aphrodite said.

'She already has,' Venus said.

Aphrodite glared woozily in her direction, but before she could get out a drunken retort, the kid called Dallas said, 'I knew the Home Depot was there.' My friends and I looked at him. He shrugged. 'I'm good at building things.'

'Home Depot and Pottery Barn delivered down here?' Erik said.

'Well, not technically,' Stevie Rae said. 'But they do deliver to the Tribune Lofts which are practically next door. And with a little, uh, friendly persuasion they brought the stuff here and then totally forgot once they left. So, ta-da! New stuff.'

'I still don't understand. How could the humans have been persuaded to come down here?' Darius said.

I sighed. 'Something you should know about red vampyres—'

'And red fledglings, too, only it's not quite as strong with them,' Stevie Rae interrupted me.

'And red fledglings,' I corrected. 'They have a mind-control thing they can do with humans.'

'That sounds a lot meaner than it is,' Stevie Rae assured Darius quickly. 'I just tweaked the delivery guys' memories.

I didn't mind-control them. We don't go in for using our powers to be all hateful and stuff.' She gave the group of red fledglings a look. 'Right?'

The group muttered 'Right,' but I noticed Venus didn't say anything, and Kramisha glanced around the room guiltily.

'They can control the minds of humans. They cannot bear direct sunlight. Their powers of recovery are excellent. They need to commune with the earth to feel truly comfortable,' Darius said. 'Am I leaving anything else out?'

'Yeah,' Aphrodite said. 'They bite.'

CHAPTER SIX

'THAT'S IT. I'M CUTTING YOU OFF,' I TOLD APHRODITE AS the red fledglings erupted into laughter.

'Aphrodite – she crazy even when she not drunk and Imprinted,' Kramisha said. 'We all used to her, though.'

'But, yes,' I continued, answering Darius through the laughter of the masses. 'All of those things are true about the red fledglings.'

'And the one red vampyre.' Stevie Rae sounded tired but proud. 'Oh, and I can also tell you that sunrise was exactly' – she paused, cocking her head like she was listening to crickets – 'sixty-three minutes ago.'

'All adult vampyres know when the sun rises,' Darius said.

'I'll bet it doesn't make all vamps as sleepy as it makes me.' Stevie Rae punctuated her words with a big yawn.

'No, it usually doesn't,' Darius said.

'Well, it makes me real sleepy,' she said. 'Especially today, which I bet has somethin' to do with that stupid arrow that used to be stickin' through me.'

Since Stevie Rae had mentioned it, I was feeling majorly exhausted again now that my jolt o' blood had worn off. I looked around at our mixed group of red and blue and saw dark circles under eyes and lots of stifled yawns. Kalona and the problems at the House of Night nagged at my mind, as well as my increasingly strong feeling that everything was not as it seemed with the red fledglings, but I was too tired to deal with all of it.

Wishing I could burst into tears, I cleared my throat, refocused, and said, 'How about we all get some sleep? We're fairly safe here, and there's really nothing any of us can do about what's going on upstairs when we're so tired we're all practically asleep on our feet.'

'Agreed,' Darius said. 'But I think we should set watches at the entrances to the tunnels – with your approval, Priestess, just in case.'

'Yeah, that's probably smart,' I said. 'Stevie Rae, are there any other entrances to the tunnels besides the one through the depot?'

'Z, I thought you knew that there're tunnels that connect to a bunch of the old downtown buildings,' Stevie Rae said. 'This section is part of that system.'

'But no one comes down here and uses these particular tunnels except you guys, do they?'

'Well, no, not this part of them, 'cause everyone thinks they're old and nasty and abandoned.'

'Could be because they are old and nasty and abandoned,' Aphrodite slurred sarcastically. I noticed she'd ignored the fact that I'd cut her off and started on her second bottle of wine.

'That's not right. They ain't nasty and abandoned,' Kramisha spoke up, frowning at Aphrodite. 'We're here and we been decorating. You should know 'cause we used your got-no-limit gold card to buy the stuff.'

'Did you use incorrect grammar at the same time? Like you are now?' Aphrodite said as she peered blurrily at Kramisha from around Darius.

'Look, I know you human and just been awkwardly Imprinted with Stevie Rae, not to mentioned you gettin' totally trashed, so I'd hate to use my superior red fledgling skills to kick your bony ass, but if you talk about me again I'm gonna forget to be nice,' Kramisha said.

'Can we not focus on the bad guys who might be trying to eat us instead of bickering with each other?' I said wearily. 'Stevie Rae, do the other tunnels connect to these?'

'Yeah, but they're sealed off, or at least that's what it would look like to everyone else.'

'Is there only one entrance from this section of tunnels to the public ones?' Darius asked.

'Only one that I know of. And it was blocked by some

seriously thick metal doors. How 'bout y'all? Have you found any more?' Stevie Rae said.

'Well, maybe,' Ant said.

'Maybe?' Stevie Rae said.

'I was exploring and I found something, but the opening to it was little even for me, so I didn't go into it. I meant to go back and poke around with a shovel or, better yet, with Johnny B's muscles, but I just haven't yet.'

Johnny B grinned and flexed for us. I ignored him, but the Twins tittered appreciatively.

'So, basically, what you guys are saying is that besides the depot entrance, there's one we know of for sure that links these tunnels to the other ones?' I said.

'Sounds about right,' Stevie Rae said.

'Then I advise you to post two guards, Priestess,' Darius said. 'One at the depot entrance and one at the known entrance to the other tunnel system.'

'Okay, that sounds like a good idea,' I said.

'I'll take first shift on the depot entrance,' Darius said. 'Erik, you should take over for me there. It's our most vulnerable place, so full vampyres should guard it.'

Erik nodded. 'Agreed.'

'Jack and I will take the first shift guarding the sealed-off entrance to the downtown tunnels,' Damien said. 'That is, if it's okay with you guys.'

'Yeah, we could even plan some menus and write down some things we need for the kitchen,' Jack said.

'Sounds good,' I said, smiling at Jack and Damien.

'I agree. Shaunee and Erin, could you relieve them for the next shift?' Darius said.

The Twins shrugged. 'Okay with us,' Erin said.

'Good. I think it wise that we don't use the red fledglings to guard the entrances during daylight hours,' Darius said.

'Hey, we can kick some ass,' Johnny B spoke up, looking all jockish and testosterone filled.

'It's not that,' I said, guessing what Darius meant. 'We need to let you guys sleep during the day so that you can stand guard at night when you're strongest. Which means, hopefully, you'll be stronger than the creatures who will be coming against us.' What I didn't say was that, even had Darius not spoken up because of the daylight issue with the red fledglings, I would have said something. I didn't want to be 'protected' by Stevie Rae's kids until I felt surer about them.

'Oh, well. Yeah. We can do that. I'm cool with protecting a priestess and her group,' Johnny B said, giving me a cocky wink.

I stifled an eye roll. Even without the red fledgling issue, the last thing I needed was another football player-like guy in my life. My eyes slid over to Erik and I had to force myself not to jump guiltily. Yes, he'd been watching me. Great. He'd mostly ignored me since we'd gotten to the tunnels and chose the instant when some other guy was acting flirty to stare at me.

Jack held up his hand like a good little student. 'Um, question . . .'

'Yes, Jack,' I said.

'Where do *we* sleep?'

'Good question.' I turned to Stevie Rae. 'Where *do* we sleep?'

Johnny B spoke up before Stevie Rae could answer. 'For the record, I'm willing to share my bed. My heart is more giving than Kramisha's.'

'It ain't your *heart* you wanna share,' Kramisha said.

'Don't go hatin' on me, baby!' Johnny B said, trying (unsuccessfully) to sound black.

Kramisha rolled her eyes at him. 'You so crazy.'

'Well, we have some sleeping bags,' Stevie Rae broke in, sounding like she was on the verge of falling asleep. 'Venus, could you show Zoey and the rest of the kids where they are? I guess y'all can sleep in whosever room you want to.' She paused and smiled wearily at Kramisha. 'Except Kramisha doesn't share her bed.'

'But you can stay in my room. That's cool with me,' Kramisha said. 'Just not on the bed.'

'Do all of you guys have rooms now?' I couldn't keep the surprise from my voice. This was all so different from the first time I'd been down here. Then the kids could barely have been called humanoid, and the tunnels were dark and dirty and creepy. Now the room we were crammed into was cozy, lit by flickering oil lanterns and candles, and the furniture was comfortable, obviously new, and even had cute matching pillows on the bed. It all seemed so normal. Was I just imagining that there was weird stuff going on with them because I was so darn tired I could hardly think?

'Any of us who wanted his or her own room has one,' Venus answered me. 'They're really not hard to fix up. In this part of the tunnels there're lots of little dead ends. We've been turning them into real rooms. I definitely have my own room.' She smiled at Erik. I had to remind myself it probably wasn't ethical to evoke fire and have it burn all the hair off her bobble-head.

'This is probably where most of the bootleg liquor was stored during Prohibition,' Damien said. 'It's logical because this is right here at the train tracks, and it would have been easy to sneak stuff in and out at night.'

'That's so cool and romantic!' Jack sighed. 'I mean, the whole 1920s flapper thing and juke joints and gangsters.'

Damien smiled indulgently at Jack. 'Actually, Prohibition lasted in Tulsa until 1957.'

'Well, never mind. That's not so romantic. That's more like gay Bible Belt stuff.' He giggled. 'Gay! Hee hee.'

'You're funny and cute. That's why I love you,' Damien said, kissing Jack smack on the mouth and causing Duchess to bark happily.

'Okay, barf,' Aphrodite said.

'Oh, and I have one more question,' Jack said, frowning at Aphrodite.

As he started to put his hand up, I said, 'Yes, Jack. What is it?'

'Where do we potty?'

'Potty? Did he really just say potty?' Aphrodite giggled until she snorted. We ignored her.

71

'That's easy,' Stevie Rae said around a giant yawn. 'Venus, would you show them?'

'You have a bathroom?' What? There was working plumbing in the tunnels?

Venus sneered a guess-you-don't-know-everything look at me. 'Bathrooms, actually. With showers.'

'Hot water showers?' Jack said enthusiastically.

'Of course. We're not barbarians,' Venus said.

'How?' I said.

'They're in the depot building above us,' Stevie Rae said. 'We've done a lot of exploring in the building. It's totally boarded up, so no one can get in, except from the basement entrance, so we control who comes and goes.'

'And we don't let just anyone in,' Venus added, looking a little dangerous.

Okay, honestly, I was liking her less and less with every second. And this time it had nothing to do with her drooling over Erik.

'Exclussssssive. My kind of place,' Aphrodite said, then she burped.

'Anyway' – Stevie Rae rolled her eyes at Aphrodite – 'we were checking out the depot and we found two locker rooms – a guy's and a girl's. We figured they were for the depot employees. There's even a gym up there, too. Dallas did the rest.' She plopped tiredly back on her pillows, giving Dallas a go-ahead-and-tell-the-rest-of-it gesture.

Dallas shrugged nonchalantly, but his grin said he knew he'd done something cool. 'I just found the water-main connection to the depot and opened it up. The pipes were all still good.'

'That's not all you did,' Stevie Rae said.

He grinned at her and again I caught a *thing* between them. Hm . . . I was definitely going to get the scoop from Stevie Rae later.

'Well, I also figured out how to turn on the electricity. That started the water heaters again, and then Aphrodite's credit card got us the extra-long extension cords and such that I spliced into the old tunnel lighting system. A little work here and there, and we have hot water up there and electricity down here.'

'Wow,' Jack said. 'That's really cool.'

'Impressive,' Damien agreed.

Dallas just kept grinning.

'So do you want to use the facilities or not?' Venus said. I thought she sounded grumpy, or maybe 'bitchy' was a better descriptive word.

'Yeah!' Jack said happily. 'I could definitely use a hot shower before we go on duty.'

'Uh, what's the status on your hair-care products down here?' Shaunee asked.

'Oh, girl. I took care of that first thing after I got my sense back. Do not worry. I got you covered,' Kramisha said, standing up and brushing crumbs from her butt-hugging jeans.

'Excellent,' Erin said. 'Let's go.'

I hung back as everyone started to file out of Stevie Rae's room.

73

'Hey, Z, you wanna be my roomie again?' Stevie Rae looked exhausted, but she was smiling her old smile at me.

'Absolutely,' I said. Our gazes slid over to Aphrodite, who was still perched on the end of her bed, half-leaning against Darius.

'Aphrodite, go get yourself a sleepin' bag. You can crash in here, too,' Stevie Rae said.

'Okay, look. No damn way am I sleeping with you,' she said, trying hard not to slur her words. 'Our Imprint is not *that* kind of Imprint. And even if I was gay, which I'm not, you are not my type.'

'Aphrodite, I was not makin' a move on you. That's just stupid,' Stevie Rae said.

'I'm just letting you know. I'm also letting you know that I'm breaking this damn Imprint the first second I can figure out how.'

Stevie Rae sighed. 'Don't do somethin' that's gonna hurt either one of us. I've had enough with stuff hurtin' for a while.'

I'd been listening to the exchange between them with frank interest. I mean, I'd been Imprinted with my human boyfriend, Heath, so I knew something about being linked to a human through the magic of blood. I also knew something about breaking an Imprint – and it could be very painful.

'Zoey, is it too much to ask that you stop gawking at me!' Aphrodite burst out, making me jump guiltily.

'I'm not gawking,' I lied.

'Whatever. Just stop.'

74

'An Imprint is nothing to be ashamed of, my beauty,' Darius said, putting his arm around Aphrodite gently.

'It is weird, though,' Stevie Rae said.

Darius smiled kindly at her. 'There are many types of Imprints.'

'Well, ours is not the drink-your-blood-and-have-sex-with-you type,' Aphrodite said.

'Of course it is not,' Darius kissed her on her forehead.

'Which means you can sleep in here without being freaked out,' Stevie Rae said.

'And again I say hell no. Plus, I'm going with Darius. I'll be on duty with him,' Aphrodite said decisively, raising her half-empty second bottle of wine in a weird, drunken salute.

'Darius has to guard the entrance to the tunnels. He doesn't need to be takin' care of your drunk behind,' Stevie Rae told her.

'I. Am. Going. With. Darius,' Aphrodite repeated slowly and stubbornly.

'She may come with me,' Darius, said, unsuccessfully trying to hide a smile. 'I'll get a sleeping bag for her. I do not believe she will be much trouble, and I like to keep her close to me.'

'Not much trouble?' I said. Stevie Rae and I raised our brows at him. I swear his high, chiseled cheeks blushed just a smidgen of pink.

'He must be thinkin' of another Aphrodite. One we don't know,' Stevie Rae said.

'Come on,' Aphrodite said, getting unsteadily to her feet. 'I know where they keep the stupid sleeping bags. Just ignore them.'

She gave us a hilarious attempt at a scowl, which turned into another manly belch, grabbed Darius's hand, and staggered from the room while Stevie Rae and I laughed.

Before he ducked under the blanket, Darius spoke over his shoulder to Erik, who I'd almost forgotten was still lingering in the room. Almost.

'Erik, get some sleep. I will wake you for the second shift.'

'Sounds good. I'll be . . .' Erik hesitated.

'Dallas's room is just down the tunnel from here. I'll bet he wouldn't mind if you roomed with him,' Stevie Rae said.

'Okay, that's where I'll be,' Erik said.

Darius nodded. 'Priestess, would you check the bandages on Stevie Rae's wounds? If they need to be changed—'

'If they need to be changed, I can do it,' I interrupted. Hell, I'd already helped shove an arrow through her chest. I could certainly change a Band-Aid without freaking.

'Well, if you need me, simply have a fledgling—'

The warrior's sentence was cut off as Aphrodite jerked hard enough on his hand to pull him from the room. Then she stuck her head back through the doorway. 'Good f-ing night. Don't bother us.' And she disappeared.

'Better him than me,' I heard Erik mutter as he watched the blanket swing back into place. I made no attempt to hide my smile. I was glad Erik wasn't still interested in Aphrodite. Erik met my eyes. And slowly he smiled, too.

CHAPTER SEVEN

'NO, YOU TWO GO ON. CATCH UP WITH THE OTHERS. I'M JUST gonna sleep,' Stevie Rae said as she curled onto her side, moving gingerly.

There was a grumpy *mee-uf-ow* and a chubby little orange ball of fur padded into the room and jumped up on Stevie Rae's bed.

'Nala!' Stevie Rae scratched the top of my cat's head. 'Hey, I've missed you.'

Nala sneezed in Stevie Rae's face and then made three rotations on the pillow beside her head, lay down, and started up her purr engine. Stevie Rae and I grinned at each other.

Okay – SPECIAL NOTE: Duchess, Jack's yellow Lab, is an anomaly. Stark brought her with him when he transferred to our school from the Chicago House of Night. Then he died. Jack adopted her. Then Stark un-died, but was obviously not himself, 'cause the first thing he did was shoot an arrow through Stevie Rae. Hence the fact Duchess is still with Jack. Plus I think the kid's really getting attached to her.

Anyway, when the group of us escaped from the House of Night, our cats, plus Duchess, followed us. So seeing Nala making herself comfortable added a comfy, homelike touch to Stevie Rae's room for Stevie Rae and me.

'You and Erik go on. Get a shower or whatever,' Stevie Rae repeated sleepily as she cuddled with Nala. 'Nal and I'll take a little nap. Oh, you can catch the rest of them if you go out, turn left, and then keep circling to your right. The entrance to the depot is by the room where we keep the fridges.'

'Hey, Darius said I should check your bandages,' I reminded her.

'Later,' she yawned massively. 'They're fine.'

'Okay, if you say so.' I tried not to show the relief I felt. No way was I ever going to be anything resembling a nurse. 'Get some sleep. I'll be back in a little while,' I said. I swear she was out before Erik and I ducked through the checkered blanket.

We turned to our left and walked without saying anything for a little way. The tunnels were less creepy than when I'd been down here before, but that didn't make them unclaustrophobic and bright and cheery. Every few yards there were lanterns staked with what looked like railroad spikes into the cement walls at about eye level, but the dampness permeated everything. We hadn't gone far when something caught at the corner of my eyes and I slowed down, peering into the heavy shadows between the lanterns.

'What is it?' Erik asked softly.

My stomach tightened with fear. 'I don't know, I—' My words broke off as something exploded out of the darkness at me. I'd opened my mouth to shriek, imagining feral red fledglings or, worse, the horror of the Raven Mockers. But Erik's arm went around me and he pulled me out of the way of half a dozen bats, who fluttered past.

'They're as scared of you as you are of them,' he said, taking his arm from around me as soon as the creatures were past us.

I shuddered, trying to force my heart to beat regularly again. 'Okay, no possible way could they be as scared of me as I am of them. Eesh, bats are rats with wings.'

He chuckled as we started walking again. 'I thought pigeons were rats with wings.'

'Bat, pigeons, ravens – I don't care about distinctions right now. Any fluttery, flappy thing is not cool with me.'

'I see your point,' he said, smiling at me. His smile didn't do much to help my heartbeat slow down, and as we kept walking, I swear I could still feel the warmth of his arm around my shoulders. In a few more feet we came to a section of the tunnel that was as amazing as it was surprising. Erik and I stopped and stared.

'Wow, that is majorly cool,' I said.

'Yeah, wow,' Erik agreed with me. 'This must be the work of that Gerarty girl. Didn't Stevie Rae introduce her as being an artist who's been decorating the tunnels?'

'Yeah, but I didn't expect anything like this.' Forgetting about the bats, I traced my hand over the beautifully complex pattern of flowers and hearts and birds and all sorts of swirls, all entwined to make a brightly painted mosaic that seemed to breathe life and magic into this little section of the dreary, claustrophobic walls.

'People, humans and vamps, would pay a fortune for art like this.' Erik didn't add, *if the world could ever know about the red fledglings and vamps*, but the thought hung unspoken in the air between us.

'Hopefully, people will,' I said. 'It would be nice if the red fledglings could become known to the rest of the world.' Plus, I added to myself, if they were out in the open, maybe my lingering questions about their powers and their tendencies could be more easily resolved. 'Anyway, I think vampyres and humans should have better relationships,' I added.

'Like you and your human boyfriend?' He asked the question quietly, with no hint of sarcasm.

I met his gaze steadily. 'I'm not with Heath anymore.'

'Are you sure?'

'I'm sure,' I said.

'Okay. Good.' That was all he said, and we started walking again, silent and lost in our own thoughts.

Not long after that the tunnel curved slightly to the right, which was the direction we were supposed to follow, but on our left there was an arched exit covered with another blanket. This one was black fake velvet decorated with a tacky picture of Elvis in a white jumpsuit.

'Must be Dallas's room,' I guessed.

Erik hesitated only a moment, then he brushed aside the blanket and we peeked in. It wasn't very big, and Dallas didn't have a bed, just a couple of mattresses piled on top of each other on the floor, but he did have a bright red comforter and matching red pillowcases (there was a big lump under the comforter, which I assumed was the sleeping Dallas), a table that held a bunch of stuff that the light wasn't good enough for me to see, and a couple of black beanbag chairs. On the curved wall over the bed was a poster of . . . I squinted at it, trying to see . . .

'Jessica Alba in *Sin City*. The kid has excellent taste. She's one hot vamp actress,' Erik said quietly so as not to wake Dallas.

I frowned at him and pulled the Elvis blanket door closed.

'What? It's not in *my* bedroom,' he said.

'Let's just catch up with everyone else,' I said, and started walking again.

'Hey,' he said after a few minutes of dead air. 'I owe you a big thanks.'

'Me? For what?' I looked over at him.

He met my eyes. 'For saving me from being left up there in the middle of that mess.'

'I didn't save you from that. You came along with us of your own free will.'

He shook his head. 'No, I'm pretty sure you saved me because without you I don't think I would have had any free will.'

He stopped and touched my arm, gently turning me so that I faced him. I looked up into his brilliant blue eyes, which were framed by his adult vampyre Mark, an intricate pattern that gave the impression of a mask, making his totally gorgeous Clark Kent-Superman-look go all Zorro-like and insanely hot. But Erik was more than just supergorgeous. Erik was talented and an honestly nice guy. I hated that we had broken up. I hated that I'd caused us to break up. In spite of everything that had happened, I wanted to be his girlfriend again. I wanted him to trust me again. I missed him so darn much . . .

'I really miss you!' I realized I'd blurted the words I'd been thinking when his eyes widened and his sexy lips curved up.

'I'm right here.'

I could feel my face flush hot all the way from my neck up and I knew I'd turned a bright, unattractive red. 'Well, you just being *here* isn't what I mean,' I said lamely.

His smile widened. 'Don't you want to know how you saved me?'

'Yeah, of course.' I wished I could fan my face so that some of the beet color might go away.

'You saved me because, instead of being hypnotized by the power of Kalona, I was thinking about you.'

'You were?'

82

'Do you know how amazing you were when you cast that circle?'

I shook my head, caught by the brightness in his blue eyes. I didn't want to breathe. I didn't want to do anything that might spoil what was happening between us.

'You were incredible – beautiful and powerful and confident. You were all I could think of.'

'I cut your hand,' was all I could make my mouth say.

'You had to. It was part of the ritual.' He lifted his hand and turned it palm up so that I could see the thin ribbon that sliced down the meaty pad under his thumb.

I trailed a finger lightly along the pink line. 'I hated to hurt you.'

He took my hand in his and turned it over so that the sapphire-colored tattoos that covered my palms were visible. Then, much as I had just done, he lightly traced his finger across my skin. I shivered, but didn't pull away.

'I didn't feel any pain when you cut me. All I felt was you. The heat of your body. The way you smell. The way you feel in my arms. That's why that creature didn't affect me. That's why I didn't believe Neferet. You saved me, Zoey.'

'Even after all that's happened between us, you can say that?' My eyes were filling with tears, and I had to blink fast to keep them from spilling over.

I watched as Erik took a deep breath. He looked like he was a diver getting ready to jump off a high, dangerous cliff. Then, in one rush, he said, 'I love you, Z. All that's happened between us hasn't changed that, even when I wanted it to.'

He cupped my face in his hands. 'I couldn't be fooled by Neferet or hypnotized by Kalona because I'm already a fool for you, hypnotized by what I feel for you. I still want to be with you, Zoey, if you'll just say yes.'

'Yes,' I whispered without one instant of hesitation.

He bent and his lips met mine. I opened my mouth and accepted his familiar kiss. His taste was the same; his touch was the same. I slid my arms up and around his broad shoulders and pressed myself against him, hardly able to believe that he'd forgiven me – that he still wanted me – still loved me.

'Zoey,' he murmured against my lips. 'I've missed you, too.'

Then he kissed me again, and I swear he made me dizzy. It was different than kissing him before – before he'd become a full vampyre – before I'd lost my virginity to another man. Now it was like he knew a secret, but I was in on it. I felt his moan more than I heard it, and then I also felt the hard coolness of the wall of the tunnel against my back as he turned me in his arms and trapped me there. One of his hands, low on my back, was firmly pressing me into him. The other I felt sliding down the side of my body, skimming my ceremonial dress and traveling down the back of my thigh until he found the hem, then his fingers were finding their way up and under it, warm against the coolness of my naked flesh.

Naked flesh?

Backed against the wall of a tunnel?

Being groped in the dark?

And the worst thought of all hit me: *Did Erik think because*

I'd had sex (once!) that now it was open season on nailing Zoey? Ah, crap!

I wasn't going to do this. Not here. Not like this. Hell, I didn't even know if I was ready to *do it* again at all. The one and only time I'd had sex had ended disastrously and had been the biggest mistake of my life. It had definitely not turned me into some kind of nympho ho!

I pushed against Erik's chest and pulled my mouth from his. He didn't seem to mind. Actually, he hardly seemed to notice. He just kept grinding against me and moved his lips to my neck.

'Erik, please stop,' I said breathlessly.

'Umm, you taste so good.'

He sounded so sexy and turned-on that for a moment I was confused about what I really wanted. I mean, I did want to be with him again, and he was totally hot and familiar and . . .

I had just begun to relax into him when I glimpsed something over his shoulder. Fear stabbed me as I realized the something had eyes glowing red from a deep, wavering sea of blackness that seemed to pool and writhe in the air like a ghost made of nothing but darkness.

'Erik! Stop. Now.' I shoved hard against his chest and he stumbled back half a step. My heart beating wildly, I moved quickly so that I could face whatever was there behind him. There were no red eyes glowing at me, but I swear I saw an inky darkness within the black of shadow. As I blinked and focused my eyes, the weirdness disappeared, leaving nothing but Erik and me and a dark, silent tunnel.

Suddenly, from the opposite direction, I heard the click of shoes against concrete and I drew in a deep breath, readying myself to call whatever element I'd need to combat this new faceless threat, when Kramisha stepped calmly out of the shadows. She gave Erik a long, considering look and said, 'Boyyyy, you is workin' it here in the tunnel? Damn! You got some game.'

Erik turned to her as he tucked me under his arm. I didn't need to look up at him to know that he had an easy smile on his face. Erik was a seriously good actor. The face he was showing Kramisha was under control, with just the right amount of sexy, got-caught-in-the-act to it.

'Hey there, Kramisha,' he said smoothly.

On the other hand you have me. I could barely stand, let alone speak. I knew my face was beet red and my lips looked bruised and damp. Hell, *I* probably looked bruised and damp. 'Kramisha, did you see anything over there in the tunnel?' I jerked my chin in the direction of the shadows behind us and managed to sound only semi-porn star and breathless.

'No, girl, I only seen you and your boy here sucking face,' Kramisha said quickly.

I wondered if maybe she hadn't answered a little too quickly.

'Aww! Are Erik and Z making out? That's so sweet!' Seemingly from nowhere, Jack suddenly materialized behind Kramisha, Duchess woofing and wagging by his side.

'Z, don't freak. You probably just saw more of those bats,' Erik said, squeezing my shoulder reassuringly before he nodded at Jack. 'Hey there, Jack. I thought you'd be basking in a hot shower by now.'

'He's gonna, but he came to help me get some towels and stuff,' Kramisha said. 'And, yeah, there is definitely bats down here. They don't mess with us if we don't mess with them.' Then she yawned and did a seriously impressive stretch that made her look like a long, lean black cat. 'Since you here, how 'bout you two helping Jack carry the stuff back to the showers and I'll just take me a little beauty sleep?'

'No problem. We'd be glad to help,' I said, regaining my voice and feeling like a moron for letting bats in a dark tunnel almost scare the poopie out of me. Jeesh, I must really need some sleep. 'Erik and I were just heading to the bathrooms.'

Kramisha gave us a long, slow look that wasn't any less knowing because she was sleepy. 'Uh-huh. You looked like you was headin' to the bathrooms.'

I felt myself blush again.

She turned, and I thought she was going to (bizarrely) walk right into the tunnel wall behind her, but instead she disappeared into it. Then I heard a match strike and a flickering lantern illuminated a hollowed-out section of the tunnel, just a little bit smaller than Dallas's room. Kramisha hung the lantern on a spike and then looked over her shoulder at us.

'Well? What you waitin' for?'

'Oh, yeah, okay,' I said.

Jack, Duchess, Erik, and I moved up beside Kramisha to look into the new room. It actually had shelves built into the squared cement walls and looked just like a tidy closet. I gazed at neat piles of folded towels and, weirdly enough, big puffy bathrobes that Duchess was nosing around.

'Is that dog sanitary?' Kramisha asked.

'Damien says that a dog's mouth is cleaner than a human's,' Jack said, patting the big yellow Lab on her head.

'We ain't humans,' Kramisha said. 'So could you please keep her big wet nose off the merchandise?'

'Fine. But try to remember that she's been through a trauma and her feelings are easily hurt.'

While Jack pulled Duchess over to him and had a very serious conversation with her about keeping her nose off things, I stared at the piles of stuff. 'Huh. Who knew all this was here?'

'Aphrodite,' Kramisha said as she filled our arms with terry cloth. 'She paid for it. Or her mama's gold-card money did. You wouldn't believe all the stuff you can order from Pottery Barn if you got unlimited credit. It's made me decide once and for all on my future career.'

'Really? What do you want to do?' Jack asked. Duchess sitting politely beside him, he held his arms out to be filled with towels and robes.

'I'm gonna be an author. One of those rich ones. With an unlimited gold card. Do you know people act different to you when you got you some serious credit?'

'Yeah, I guess. I have seen store people kiss the Twins' butts,' Jack said. 'Their families have money, too.' He whispered the last part like it was a big secret, which it wasn't. Everyone knew the Twins' parents were rich. Okay, not Aphrodite rich, but still. They'd bought me boots for my birthday that cost almost $400. That's definitely rich to me.

'Well. I decided I like me some butt-kissing. So I'm gonna get me some. Okay, that's enough stuff. Come on. I'll walk partway back with you, but when we get to my room, I'm crashing. Jack, you can find the way back to the showers, can't you?'

'Yep,' he said.

We walked down the tunnel, following it as it curved to the right. The next blanketed doorway we came to was covered with a shimmering strip of purple silk.

'This here's my room.' Kramisha saw me staring at the amazing material masquerading as a door, and she smiled. 'It's a curtain from Pier One. They don't deliver, but they do take unlimited gold cards.'

'It's a great color,' I said, thinking how moronic it was for me to be imagining booger monsters in every shadow when the place had been Pier One-decorated.

'Thanks. I like me some color. It's an important part of decoration. Wanna see my room?'

'Yeah,' I said.

'Definitely,' Jack said.

Kramisha looked from Jack to Duchess. 'She potty trained?'

Jack bristled. 'Of course. She's a perfect lady.'

'She better be,' Kramisha grumbled, then she pulled the curtain to the side and made a graceful flourish with her free hand. 'You may enter my space.'

Kramisha's room was about twice the size of Stevie Rae's.

She had two lanterns and a dozen scented candles lit, which gave the fresh-paint smell a hint of citrus. She'd obviously recently painted the round cement walls a bright lime color. Her furniture was dark wood – bed, dresser, nightstand, and bookcase. She didn't have any chairs, but piled around the room were huge satin pillows in bold purples and pinks, which matched the linens on her bed. On said bed were half a dozen books, with bookmarks in them or lying open, like she was in the middle of reading all of them at the same time. I noticed that they, along with the books in the bookcase, had Dewey Decimal stickers on their spines. Kramisha noticed me noticing.

'Central Library downtown. They stay open real late on weekends.'

'I didn't know the library let you check out this many books at the same time,' Jack said.

Kramisha fidgeted. 'They don't. Not technically. Not 'less you do a little this and a little that with they minds. I'll give 'em back soon as I can get to Borders and buy my own,' she added.

I sighed and added 'committing library theft' to the list in my head of things the red fledglings needed to be encouraged to stop doing, and as I made the mental addition I also chastised myself. Kramisha definitely looked guilty about ripping off library books. Would a kid who still had monstrous tendencies be worried about petty theft? *No, no, hell no*, I told myself, automatically wandering over to the bed to read some of the titles. There was a huge copy of the complete works of Shakespeare, as well as an illustrated hardback of *Jane Eyre*, which was piled on top of a book called *The Silver Metal Lover* by Tanith Lee. There was also a hardback edition of *Dragon-flight* by Anne McCaffrey lying beside *Thug-A-Licious, Candy Licker*, and *G-Spot* by an author whose name was blazed as Noire. Those three books were open with their extremely nasty-looking covers spread wide. Totally curious, I put my pile of towels down on the bright pink bedspreaded bed, picked up *Thug-A-Licious*, and began reading at the open page.

I swear my retinas started to burn with the heat of the scene.

'Book porn. I like it,' Erik said from over my shoulder.

'Um, they some of my research.' Kramisha quickly plucked the book from my fingers, shooting Erik a smooth look. 'And from what I seen out there, you don't need no help.'

I felt my face get hot again and sighed.

'Hey, cool poetry,' I heard Jack say. Glad for the distraction, I looked up to see Jack pointing at several posters neatly hot-glued to Kramisha's green walls. They were filled with poetry, all written in the same curling script in different colors of fluorescent Magic Markers.

'You like it?' Kramisha said.

'Yeah, it's great. I really like poetry,' Jack said.

'They mine. I wrote 'em,' Kramisha said.

'Are you kidding? Man, I thought they were from a book or something. You're really good,' Jack said.

'Thanks, I told you I'm gonna be an author. A famous, rich one with major gold-card power.'

I vaguely heard Erik join the discussion. All of my attention had become focused on one short poem that was written in black on a blood-red poster. 'You wrote that one, too?' I asked, not caring that I was interrupting their discussion of whether they liked Robert Frost better than Emily Dickinson.

'I wrote all o' them,' she said. 'I always did like writin', but since I was Marked I been doing it more and more. They just come to me. I been hopin' I can write more than poems. I like 'em and all, but poets, they don't make no money. See, I researched careers at Central Library, too, 'cause, you know, it stay open late. Anyhow, them poets don't make—'

'Kramisha' – I cut her off – 'when did you write that one?' My stomach felt funny and my mouth had gone dry.

'I wrote all them in the past few days. You know, since Stevie Rae got us our sense back. Before that I didn't think much 'bout anything 'cept eatin' humans.' She smiled apologetically and lifted one shoulder.

'So you wrote that one – the one in black – in the past couple of days?' I pointed at the poem.

Shadows in shadows
He watches through
dreams
Wings black as Africa
Body strong as stone
Done waiting
The ravens call.

Jack gasped as he read it for the first time.

'Oh, Goddess!' I heard Erik say under his breath as he, too, read the poem.

'That's easy. It's the last one I wrote — just yesterday. I was . . .' Her words ran out as she understood our reactions. 'Shit! It's 'bout him!'

CHAPTER EIGHT

'WHAT MADE YOU WRITE IT?' I ASKED, STILL STARING AT THE black words.

Kramisha had sat down heavily on her bed, all of a sudden looking almost as exhausted as Stevie Rae. She was shaking her head back and forth, back and forth, making her orange and black hair dance against her smooth cheeks. 'It just come to me, like all the stuff I write do. Things just come into my head, and then I write it down.'

'What did you think it meant?' Jack asked, patting her arm gently, a lot like he patted Duchess (she was curled up by his feet).

'I didn't really think 'bout it. It come to me. I write it. That's all.' She paused, glanced up at the poster board, and then looked quickly away, as if what she saw scared her.

'Are these all poems you've written in the days since Stevie Rae Changed?' I shifted my attention to the other poems. There were several haiku.

Eyes watching always
Shadows in shadows they wait
A black feather falls

First accepted, loved
Then betrayed – spit in the face
Vengeance sweet like dots

'Sweet, blessed Nyx.' Erik's shocked voice came from behind me, kept low for my ears alone to hear. 'They're all about him.'

'What does "sweet like dots" mean?' Jack was asking Kramisha.

'You know – dippin' dots. I love me some dippin' dots,' she said.

Erik and I moved around Kramisha's room. The more I read, the tighter the knot my stomach curled into.

They done
*   Wrong*
Like ink from a busted pen
*   Thrown away 'cause of someone else*

Used up
But he come back
 Dressed in night
Fine as a king
With his queen
 The wrong
Made right
 So right

'Kramisha, what were you thinking about when you wrote this one?' I asked her, pointing at the last one I'd read.

She shrugged that one shoulder again. 'I guess I thought 'bout how we out of the House of Night, but we shouldn't be. I mean, I know it's best for us underground, but it just don't feel right that only Neferet know about us. She a wrong kind of High Priestess.'

'Kramisha, would you do me a favor and copy down all of these poems?'

'You think I messed up, don't you?'

'No. I do *not* think you messed up,' I assured her, hoping I was being guided correctly by my instincts and wasn't just chasing bats in the darkness again. 'I think you've been given a gift from Nyx. I just want to be sure we use your gift in the right way.'

'I think she's Vamp Poet Laureate material, and a major improvement over our last one,' Erik said.

I looked up at him sharply, and he shrugged and grinned. 'It was just a thought, that's all.'

Okay, even though it made me uncomfortable to think about Loren, especially when Erik had been the one to bring him up, I felt the rightness of what he was saying down deep in my gut, which said more about Kramisha's true nature than what my exhausted guessing and my apparently over-active imagination were telling me. Nyx obviously had her hand on this kid. *What the hell. I'm the only High Priestess we have. I can make a proclamation.* 'Kramisha, I'm going to make you our first Poet Laureate.'

'Whaaaaat?! Are you kiddin'? You kiddin', ain't ya?'

'I'm not kidding. We're a new kind of vamp group. We're a *civilized* new kind of vamp group, and that means we need a Poet Laureate. You're it.'

'Um, I agree and everything with you, Z, but doesn't the council have to vote on a new Poet Laureate?' Jack said.

'Yep, and I have my Council down here with me.' I realized Jack had been talking about *the* Council of Nyx, the one Shekinah had been head of that ruled all vampyres. But I had a Council also, a Prefect Council, acknowledged by the school, made up of me, Erik, the Twins, Damien, Aphrodite, and Stevie Rae.

'Kramisha has my vote,' Erik said.

'See, it's practically official,' I said.

'Yea!' Jack cheered.

'It's a crazy idea, but I like it.' Kramisha beamed.

'So, write those poems down for me before you go to sleep, 'kay?'

'Yeah, I can do that.'

'Come on, Jack. Our Poet Laureate needs to get her sleep,' Erik said. 'Hey, congratulations, Kramisha.'

'Yeah, big congrats!' Jack said, giving Kramisha a hug.

'Y'all go on now. I got work to do. Then I gotta get my rest. A Poet Laureate do have to look her best,' Kramisha said primly, finishing up with a couplet.

Erik and I followed Jack and Duchess out of Kramisha's room and down the tunnel.

'Was that poem really about Kalona?' Jack said.

'I think they all were,' I said. 'Do you?' I asked Erik.

He nodded grimly.

'Ohmigod! What's that mean?' Jack said.

'I don't have a clue. Nyx is at work, though. I can feel it. The prophecy came to us in poem form. Now this? It can't be a coincidence.'

'If it's the work of the Goddess, then there must be some way we can use it to help us,' Erik said.

'Yeah, that's what I think, too.'

'We just have to figure out how,' Erik said.

'That's gonna take someone with more brains than me,' I said. There was a short pause, and then the three of us spoke together, 'Damien.'

Spooky shadows, bats, and my worries about the red fledglings temporarily forgotten, I hurried down the tunnel with Erik and Jack.

'The door to the depot's over here.' Jack led us through the surprisingly homelike kitchen to a side room that was obviously a pantry, though I'd bet what used to be stored there was more liquid than the bags of chips and boxes of cereal it now held. All along one wall, rolled neatly, piled side by side and on top of each other, were a bunch of puffy sleeping bags and pillows.

'So is that the way into the depot?' I pointed to a wooden pull-down staircase in the corner of the storage closet that led up to an open door.

'Yeah, that's it.' Jack said.

Jack went first and I followed him, poking my head up into the supposedly abandoned building. My first impression was of darkness and dust, fragmented every few minutes by what looked like a strobe-light effect of flashes of sudden brightness leaking through the boarded-up windows and door. When I heard the rumble of thunder, I understood and remembered what Erik had said about a major thunderstorm going on, which wouldn't be unusual for Tulsa, even in early January.

But this wasn't a normal day, and I couldn't help but believe this also wasn't a normal thunderstorm.

Before I did any looking around I pulled my cell phone out of my purse. I opened it. No service.

'Mine hasn't worked, either. Not since we got here,' Erik said.

'Mine's charging down in the kitchen, but I know Damien checked his when we got up here, and he didn't have any service, either.'

'You know bad weather can knock the towers out,' Erik

said in response to what I'm sure was my sickeningly worried expression. 'Remember that big storm a month or so ago? My cell didn't work for three entire days.'

'Thanks for trying to make me feel better, but I just . . . just don't believe this is a natural phenomenon.'

'Yeah,' he said quietly. 'I know.'

I drew a deep breath. Well, natural or not, we were going to have to deal with it, and right now there wasn't a darn thing we could do about our isolation here. There was a storm raging outside, and we weren't ready to face it yet.

So first things first. I squared my shoulders and looked around. We'd come up in a little room that had a half wall, and then bank teller-like windows cut in the real wall, complete with tarnished brass bars on the front. I decided quickly it must have been the depot ticket office. From there we entered a huge room. The floor was marble and it still looked slick and butterlike in the dimness. The walls were weird, though. All kinda rough and bare from the floor up to about a foot or so above my head, and then the decorations started. They were blurred by dust and time and inattention, and there were cobwebs hanging all over (eesh, first bats and now spiders!), but the vibrant old Art Deco colors were still visible, telling stories of Native American mosaic patterns, feather headdresses, horses, leather, and fringe.

I gazed around at the corroded beauty, and thought *this could make a great school*. It was big and it had the same kind of grace as many of Tulsa's downtown buildings had, thanks to the oil boom and 1920s Art Deco styling. Lost in thought of what might someday be, I walked across the empty lobby, peeking around, noticing hallways that stretched off from this one big room, leading to others, wondering if there were enough of them for several classrooms. We took one of those hallways and it dead-ended at wide double glass doors. Jack bobbed his head at them. 'That's the gym.' We all gazed through the time-dirtied glass. In the nonlight I could just make out blobs of shapes that looked like great sleeping beasts from a dead world. 'And over there's the door to the boys' locker room.' Jack pointed to a closed door to the right of the gym. "And there's the girls".'

'Okay, well, I'm going to hit the showers,' I said lamely. 'Erik, would you and Jack let Damien know about Kramisha's poems? Tell him if he has to talk to me about it I'll be in Stevie Rae's room, hopefully sound asleep for at least a few hours. If it can wait, we'll all meet and try to figure out what it could mean after we've rested.' I shifted the towels and bathrobes I'd been clutching so I could wipe sleepily at my face.

'You need to rest, Z. Not even you can go through all of this and keep functioning without sleep,' Erik said.

'Yeah, if Damien wasn't staying awake with me, I'd be scared of falling asleep on watch duty,' Jack said, and yawned for punctuation.

'The Twins will take over from you soon.' I smiled at Jack. 'Just hold on till then.' My smile widened to include Erik. 'I'll see you soon. Both of you.'

I started to turn away and Erik's touch on my arm stopped me. 'Hey, we're together again. Aren't we?'

I met Erik's eyes and saw his vulnerability through the pretend confidence of his smile. He wouldn't understand if I said I needed to talk to him about, well, sex before I agreed to get back together with him. That would hurt his ego as well as his heart and then I'd be back where I was before, with me kicking myself for being the cause of us being apart.

So I simply said, 'Yeah, we're together again.'

The sweet vulnerability was reflected in the kiss he bent to place on my lips. It wasn't a groping, demanding, we're-gonna-have-sex-now kiss. It was a warm, gentle, I'm-so-glad-we're-back-together kiss, and it utterly melted me.

'Get some sleep. I'll see you soon,' he whispered. He kissed my forehead quickly, then he and Jack disappeared through the boys' locker room door.

I stood there for a while, just looking at the closed door and thinking. Had I been wrong about the change in Erik? Had I misunderstood what was behind his passion in the tunnel? After all, he wasn't a fledgling anymore. He was a fully Changed, adult vampyre. That made him a man, even though he was still nineteen, just like he'd been less than a week ago, before he'd Changed.

Maybe the increase in the sexual tension between us was natural, and not just because he thought I was a skank now that I'd given up my virginity. *Erik was a man*, I repeated the thought to myself. I already knew from the disaster with Loren Blake that being with a man was different than being with a boy or a fledgling. *Erik was a fully Changed vampyre, like Loren had been*. The thought sent nervous skitters through

102

my body. 'Like Loren' wasn't a particularly good analogy. But Erik definitely was not Loren! Erik had never used me or lied to me. Erik was Changed, but he was still the Erik I knew and might even love. I really shouldn't be stressing myself out with worrying about this. The sex thing would work itself out. I mean, compared to an ancient immortal coming after us, Neferet having the school in her evil clutches, me freaking about whether there is or isn't something bizarre going on with the red fledglings, Grandma being in a coma, and the nasty Raven Mockers wreaking havoc in Tulsa, whether or not Erik would try to pressure me into having sex with him should be a stress break, or at least a stress vacation. Shouldn't it?

'Z! There you are. Would you come on?' Erin stuck her head out of the girls' locker room door. There was a huge cloud of steam wafting around behind her and I could see that she was wearing only her bra and panties (matching, of course, from Victoria's Secret).

With an effort I put Erik out of my mind. 'Sorry . . . sorry, I'm coming,' I said and hurried into the locker room.

CHAPTER NINE

OKAY, TAKING A GROUP SHOWER WITH GIRLS WHO HAD affinities for water and fire was an experience that went from awkward to interesting to pretty darn funny.

At first it was awkward because, well, even though we're all girls, we're not exactly used to communal showers. These weren't horribly barbaric. There were about half a dozen shower heads (which were all bright and shiny and new-looking – I'm sure thanks to either Kramisha or Dallas or both, with help from Aphrodite's popular gold card). Each of them had a separate shower stall one right after another. No, there weren't any doors or shower curtains or anything.

Actually, there was a rail at the top of each one, so my guess was that there used to be shower curtains back in the day, but they were long gone. Oh, the stalls for the toilets did have doors, even if they didn't want to stay latched. So it was awkward to be naked with my friends at first. But we *are* all girls, hetero girls at that, so we really weren't interested in each other's boobies and such, no matter how hard that is for guys to comprehend, so the awkward part didn't last long. Plus, the entire locker room was filled with dense steam, which gave the illusion of privacy.

Then, after I picked my shower stall, chose from the lovely assortment of bath and hair products, and started to soap up, it hit me that it was *really* steamy. As in unnaturally so. And that the 'unnaturally so' was happening because *all* of the shower heads, even in the unoccupied stalls, were shooting jets of hot water from them, causing warm mist to rise and swirl, almost as thick as smoke.

Hmm . . .

'Hey!' I stuck my head over my stall trying to see the Twins in their showers. 'Are you guys doing something to the water?'

'Huh?' Shaunee said, wiping shampoo bubbles out of her eyes. 'What?'

'This,' I flailed my arms causing the thick mist to billow around me dreamily. 'All of *this* doesn't seem like it's happening without some help from certain someones who know how to manipulate fire and water.'

'Us? Miss Fire and Miss Water?' Erin said. I could barely

see the top of her bright blonde head through the steam. 'Whatever could she mean, Twin?'

'I do believe our Z is implying we'd use our goddess-given affinities for something as selfish as making thick, warm, sweet-smelling mist to help relax all of us after we've just had a day that was ever so horrible,' Shaunee said with mock Southern Belle innocence.

'Would we do that, Twin?' Erin asked.

'We absolutely would, Twin,' Shaunee said.

'For shame, Twin. For shame,' Erin said with mock severity. And then they dissolved into twin giggles.

I rolled my eyes at them, but realized Shaunee had been right. The mist was sweet-smelling. It reminded me of spring rain, filled with the fresh scents of flowers and grass, and it was warm – no, the water was hot, like a lazy summer day at the beach. The truth was even though the room was occasionally semi-illuminated by flashes of lightning from the storm that was raging outside, and even though the booming thunder was uncomfortably loud, the atmosphere the Twins had created was utterly soothing.

So here's where the interesting part came in. I decided that there was not one darn thing wrong with the Twins using their gifts to make us feel warm and clean and comfy. We'd just gone through a horrible experience – been chased from our home by weird bird-man-demon things – and now we were basically trapped in this old building and the tunnels beneath us in the middle of an unnaturally violent winter storm without any way of communicating with the outside world short of walking outside. Uh, and none of us wanted to do that, storm or no storm. So why not indulge ourselves a little?

'Hey, are you sending any of this over to the guys' locker room?' I asked as I scrubbed my hair.

'Nope,' Shaunee said happily.

'Nada.' Erin grinned.

I smiled back at them. 'It's good to be a girl.'

'Yeah, even if we do have to get butt-ass naked together and shower in what looks like a line of horse stalls,' Erin said.

I giggled. 'Horse stalls. I think that makes you guys nags.'

'Nags! Us?' Erin said.

'Oh no, she did not just call us nags,' Shaunee said.

'Get her!' Erin yelled, and she flung her hands at me, causing water to pelt me from all sides.

Of course it didn't really hurt, so it made me giggle even more.

'I'm heating her up, Twin!' Shaunee said, flicking her fingers at me, and my skin was suddenly very, *very* warm. So much so that the steam in my stall doubled.

In between giggles I whispered, 'Wind, come to me,' and instantly felt the brush of power surround me. Swirling my fingers in the steamy mist that engulfed me, I said, 'Wind, send all this back to the Twins!' Then I pursed my lips and blew gently in their direction. With a mighty *whoosh* the mist and heat and water whirled around me once, twice, and then blew directly at the Twins, who screeched and laughed and tried to fight back. Of course they couldn't win. I mean, come on!

I can call on all five elements, but it was a hilarious version of a pillow fight/water fight that left all of us drenched and breathless with laughter.

We finally called a truce. Okay, more accurately, I made the Twins yell, 'We give! We give!' several times, and then I graciously accepted their surrender. It was wonderful to slip into soft terry-cloth robes and feel all squeaky clean and sleepy. We draped our clothes around the shower stalls and called water and mist once more to steam them, and then I commanded fire and air to blow them dry. Then the three of us drifted back down to the tunnels, ignoring the crack-and-boom show that was playing outside, secure in the fact that we were surrounded by the earth and protected by male vampyres who would no way let anyone sneak up on us.

I'd say Stevie Rae had been dead to the world when I got back to her room, but the phrasing scared me. She'd been dead, or almost dead, too many times for my nerves. I will admit I tiptoed over to her and stood there staring to make sure she was breathing before going to my side of the bed and easing myself in under the covers. Nala put her head up and sneezed at me, clearly unhappy at being disturbed, but she padded sleepily over to me and curled up on my pillow, resting one little white paw on my cheek. I smiled at her and, clean and warm and very, very tired, fell instantly to sleep.

Then I'd had that horrible dream, which brought me back to current time. I'd hoped replaying everything that had happened in the past several hours would be like counting sheep and maybe help me drift back into a dreamless sleep. But it was no use. I was too freaked about Kalona and too worried about what I was supposed to do next.

My cell phone was on the bedside table and I picked it up, checking the time: 2:05 P.M. So, great, I'd gotten a whopping three hours of sleep. No wonder I felt like my eyes had sand in them. Brown pop. I needed some brown pop in the worst way.

I checked Stevie Rae again before I left the room, this time being careful not to wake her up. She was curled up on her side, snoring softly and looking about twelve years old. It was hard to imagine her ever having blood-red eyes, snarling dangerously, and chomping on Aphrodite with such intensity that the two of them had Imprinted. I sighed, feeling like the entire world was pressing down on me. How was I supposed to deal with all of this, especially when the good guys sometimes seemed bad, and the bad guys were so... so... Images of Stark and Kalona passed through my mind, making me feel terribly confused and stressed out.

No, I told myself firmly, *you shared a kiss with Stark as he was dying. He was a different kid before Neferet messed with him, but now she has messed with him and you have to remember that. You shared a nightmare with Kalona. Period. That's all there was to it.*

The fact that in my nightmare Kalona had insisted I was A-ya was just crazy. It wasn't true. Sure, I'd felt drawn to him, but so had practically everyone else. Plus, I was me, and A-ya had been, well, *dirt* until the Ghigua women had

109

breathed life and special gifts into her. *I must look like her, weird as that is*, I told myself. *Or maybe he'd called me A-ya just to mess with my head.* That seemed more than possible, especially if Neferet had told him stuff about me.

Nala had settled back down on the pillow beside Stevie Rae and was purring again with her eyes shut. Obviously there were no nightmare monsters lurking about because Nala would have been freaked. Glad at least of that, I gave her head and Stevie Rae's a little pat – neither opened her eyes – and then ducked through the blanket door and into the hallway.

The tunnels were absolutely silent. I was glad that the oil lanterns were still lit; darkness and I weren't exactly on good terms right then. I'll also admit that, even though I kept a wary eye on the shadows between lights for bats and whatnot, it did feel reassuring to be snuggly underground and not anywhere near open, moonlit meadows or trees with ghostly shadows perched in them. I shivered. *No. Don't think about it.*

On the way to the kitchen I paused by Kramisha's doorway and peeked quietly in. I could just make out her head in the middle of her bed under mounds of purple comforter and pink pillows. The Twins were zonked out on sleeping bags with their hateful cat, Beelzebub, curled up on the floor between them.

I closed the blanket flap quietly, not wanting to wake up the Twins before it was their turn to be on watch. Actually, I should grab my brown pop and relieve Damien and Jack and tell them to let the Twins sleep. I definitely wouldn't be doing any more sleeping for a while – like years. Okay, just kidding. Sort of.

No one was in the kitchen. The only sound was the small, homelike hum of the refrigerators. The first one I opened caused me to take a little step back in shock. The entire fridge was filled with sealed baggies full of blood. Seriously. And, of course, my mouth started to water.

I slammed the door shut.

And then reconsidered and opened it again. Resolutely, I grabbed a baggie. I'd had next to no sleep. I was under major stress. A stupid immortal fallen angel bad guy was after me and calling me some dead dirt-girl's name. Let's face it, I needed a lot more than brown pop to get through the day.

I found the scissors in the top drawer of the butcher block island and, before I could guilt or gross myself out of it, snipped open the bag and upended it.

I know, I know. My slurping down blood like it was from a collapsible juice box sounds completely nasty, but it was delicious. It didn't taste like blood, or at least not that coppery, salty way blood used to taste to me before I was Marked. It was delicious and electrifying, like drinking rare gourmet honey mixed with wine (if you like wine) mixed with Red Bull (but better tasting). I could feel it spreading through my body, giving me a jolt of energy that chased away the lingering terror of my nightmare.

I crumpled up the empty baggie and tossed it in the big garbage can in the corner of the room. *Then* I grabbed a bottle of brown pop and a bag of nacho-cheese Doritos. I mean, my breath already smelled gross from the blood. Might as well have Doritos for breakfast.

Then I realized: one, I didn't know where Damien and Jack were, and two, I really needed to call Sister Mary Angela and find out how Grandma was doing.

Yeah, I know it sounds weird that I was calling a nun. It sounds even weirder that I trusted said nun with my grandma's life. Literally. But all the weirdness stopped the moment I met Sister Mary Angela, prioress of the Benedictine nuns of Tulsa. Besides doing nun stuff (praying and whatnot), Sister Mary Angela and the nuns from the abbey run Tulsa Street Cats, which is how I met her. I'd decided that House of Night fledglings needed to get more active in the community. I mean, the House of Night had been in Tulsa for upward of five years, but it was like we were a little island of our own. Everyone with any sense knows isolation and ignorance equal prejudice – hello, I read Martin Luther King Jr's 'Letter From Birmingham Jail' at the beginning of my sophomore year. Anyway, what with two vampyre professors being nastily murdered, Shekinah had agreed with my idea of helping a community charity, as long as I was well protected. Which was how Darius had gotten so involved with me and my group. So, I'd chosen Street Cats, well, 'cause what with all the cats at the House of Night, it just made sense.

Sister Mary Angela and I had hit it off from the moment we met. She's cool and spiritual, and wise and nonjudgmental. She even thinks that Nyx is just another version of the Virgin

Mary (and Mary is majorly important to the Benedictine Sisters). So I guess you could say Sister Mary Angela and I became friends, and when Grandma was attacked by the Raven Mockers and ended up in St John's Hospital in a coma, it was Sister Mary Angela I called to sit with her and protect her from the Raven Mockers hurting her again. When all hell broke loose at the House of Night and Neferet killed Shekinah and had Stark shoot Stevie Rae, Kalona rose, and the Raven Mockers became substantial, it was Sister Mary Angela who got Grandma safely belowground.

Or at least in theory she was supposed to have gotten Grandma, and the rest of the sisters, underground. I hadn't talked to her since last night, just before our cell service was cut off.

So, in order of importance, I needed to call Sister Mary Angela – assuming my phone was working again – and then get directions to Damien and Jack so I could relieve them. Figuring I could kill two birds at once, I retraced my path back down the tunnel, heading for the basement entrance and Darius. He'd know how to get to the boys, and I could probably get cell service in the basement – unless the aboveground world had gone all postapocalypse and cell service was out forever. Thankfully, being filled with blood made me feel slightly optimistic, and even the possibility of a disgusting (and unattractive) *I Am Legend*-type world didn't seem utterly hopeless.

One thing at a time. I'd just take it one thing at a time. First, I'd find out how Grandma was. Then I'd relieve Damien and Jack. Then I'd try to think my way through that awful nightmare.

I remembered the dark angel's voice and the way pain and pleasure had somehow melded into one when he touched me and called me his love. I jerked my mind from those kinds of thoughts. Pain couldn't equal pleasure. What I had felt in the dream was just that, *a dream*, and by the definition of 'dream' (or nightmare) that meant it wasn't real. And I was definitely not Kalona's love.

It was about then that I also realized some of the nerves skittering through my body *were* fearful, and that had nothing to do with Kalona. While I'd been preoccupied with thinking about him I'd been pretty much ignoring the subconscious tightening in my body. My heartbeat had sped up again. My stomach rolled. I had the distinct and terrifying feeling that I was being watched.

I spun around, expecting to see – at the very least – bats flapping nastily around. But there was nothing except the dead silence of the deserted, lantern-lit tunnel stretching behind me.

'You are utterly freaking out,' I said aloud to myself.

As if my words had caused it, the lantern closest to me went out.

Dread filled me, and I started backing down the tunnel, keeping my eyes open for anything that might be more than my imagination. And I backed into the metal ladder that had been welded to the wall and led up into the basement of the depot. Giddy with relief at finding the end of the tunnels, I balanced my can of brown pop in one hand and smooshed the big bag of my breakfast Doritos noisily in the other. I had just started to climb when a strong male arm appeared from above, scaring the bejeezus out of me.

'Here, give me the pop and chips. You're going to fall right on your butt trying to hold on to them and the ladder.'

My gaze flew up to see Erik smiling down at me. I swallowed quickly and gave him a perky 'Thanks!' Handing him the pop and chips, I made my way more easily up the rest of the ladder.

The basement was several degrees colder than it was in the tunnels, which felt good on my fear-flushed face.

'I like that I can still make you blush,' Erik told me, stroking my hot cheek.

I almost blurted that I was freaked by shadows and unseen crap down in the tunnels, but I could imagine him laughing and accusing me of jumping at bats again. And what if I was just ultrasensitive because of the dream? Did I really want to talk to Erik, or anybody, about Kalona right then?

No.

Instead I said, 'It's cold up here, and you know I hate it when I blush.'

'Yeah, the temperature's dropped like crazy in the past few hours. It's going to be an icy mess out there. You know, I think you're adorable with those pink cheeks.'

'You and my grandma are the only two people in the world who think that,' I said, smiling begrudgingly at him.

'Well, that puts me in good company.' Erik chuckled,

reaching for a chip while I glanced around the basement. Everything was quiet up here, too, but not scarily quiet like the stupid tunnels. Erik had a chair pulled over near the entrance to below and beside it were a couple of oil lanterns (brightly burning), a half-empty liter bottle of Mountain Dew (eesh!), and, surprise, surprise, Bram Stoker's *Dracula* with a bookmark stuck in it at about the halfway point. I waggled my brows at him.

'What? I borrowed it from Kramisha.' He was smiling kinda guiltily, which made him look like an adorable little boy. 'So, I admit it. I've been curious about the book ever since you told me a while ago that it's one of your favorites. I'm only about halfway through, so do not tell me what happens.'

I grinned at him, flattered that he was reading *Dracula* just because of me. 'Oh, please,' I teased. 'You know how the book ends. Everybody knows how the book ends.' I really loved that Erik was this big, tall, hot, studly guy who reads all sorts of books and watches old *Star Wars* movies. My grin got wider. 'Sooooo, you're liking it?'

'Yeah, I am. Even though I didn't really expect to.' His grin mirrored mine. 'I mean, come on. It is a little old school, what with the vamps being monsters and all.'

My mind instantly went to Neferet, whom I considered a monster in a beautiful disguise, and to my unanswered questions about the red fledglings, but I pulled my thoughts away from all that, not wanting darkness to intrude on this moment with Erik. Refocusing on *Dracula*, I said, 'Well, yeah, Dracula is supposed to be a monster and all, but I always feel sorry for him.'

'You feel sorry for him?' Erik was obviously surprised. 'Z, he's pure evil.'

'I know, but he loves Mina. How can something that's pure evil know love?'

'Hey, I'm not that far in it yet! Don't give it away.'

I rolled my eyes at him. 'Erik, you have to know Dracula goes after Mina. He bites her and she starts to change. It's through Mina that the Count is tracked and eventually—'

'Stop!' Erik said, laughing as he grabbed me and covered my mouth. 'I wasn't kidding. I don't want you to tell me how it ends.'

My mouth was covered by his hand, but I knew my eyes were smiling at him.

'If I take my hand away, do you promise to be good?'

I nodded.

Slowly, he uncovered my mouth, but he made no move to step away from me. It felt nice to be close to him. He was gazing down at me, with a small smile still tugging at the corners of his mouth. I thought about how hot he was and how glad I was that we were together again, and I said, 'Want me to tell you how I *wish* the book ended?'

His brows lifted. 'How you *wish*? Which means you won't really be telling me the ending?'

'Cross my heart.' Automatically, I crossed my heart. We were standing so close that the back of my hand brushed his chest.

'Tell me.' His voice had gone deep and intimate.

'I wish Dracula hadn't let everyone come between him and Mina. He should have bitten Mina, made her like him, and then taken her away so they could be together forever – and lived happily ever after.'

'Because they're the same and they belong together,' he said.

I looked up into Erik's amazing blue eyes and saw that all the kidding had gone out of them.

'Yeah, even if bad things happened in their past. They'd have to forgive each other for the bad stuff, but I think they could have.'

'I know they could have. I think when two people care about each other enough, anything can be forgiven.'

Obviously Erik and I weren't talking about fictional characters from an old book. We were talking about ourselves, testing each other to see if we could actually make it work between us.

I had to forgive Erik for being so awful to me after he'd caught me with Loren. And he had been horrible, but the truth was I'd hurt Erik a lot more than he'd hurt me – and not just with Loren. When I'd first started dating Erik, I'd still had a relationship with Heath, my human boyfriend. It had pissed Erik off that I had been seeing him and Heath at the same time, but he'd believed that I would come to my senses eventually and understand that Heath was a part of my old world, my old life, and that he wouldn't fit into my future like Erik would.

And Erik had a point. Now that the Imprint with Heath had been broken, which I knew for sure because he and I had had a very ugly scene when I ran into him just a couple of days ago at Charlie's Chicken (of all places). My ridiculous mistake in having sex with Loren had had a domino effect of messing up lots of things in my life. One very big mess-up was the painful way it had broken my Imprint with Heath, and he'd made it clear he didn't ever want to see me again. Sure, I'd warned Heath about the Raven Mockers and Kalona being loose, told him to get himself and his family to safety, but it was over between Heath and me, just like it had been over between Loren and me (even before he'd been killed), which is really how it should be.

I continued to meet Erik's gaze. 'So you like my version of *Dracula*?'

'I like your ending – the one where the two of them are vampyres and they have a happily-ever-after, especially because they care enough to get over their past mistakes.'

Still smiling, Erik bent to kiss me. His lips were soft and warm, and he tasted like Doritos and Mountain Dew, which wasn't as nasty as you might think. His arms went around me, and he pulled me close, deepening the kiss. It felt good to be in his arms. So good that at first I managed to tune out the little alarm bells that were ringing in the rational part of my mind as Erik's hands slid down my back to cup my butt. But when he pressed me hard against him, grinding intimately into me, the lovely warm fog he'd started inside me began to clear. I liked him touching me. But what I didn't like was the feeling that his touch had suddenly become too aggressive, too insistent, too *she is mine, I want her, and I'm going to have her now*.

He must have felt me stiffen because he pulled back, gave me an easy smile, and then said, 'So, what are you doing up here?'

I blinked, disoriented at the instant change in him. I took a little step away from him and grabbed my pop from where he'd put it on his chair, taking a big gulp and pulling myself together. Finally I managed to say, 'Oh, I, uh, came to talk to Darius and see if my cell would work.' I fished into my pocket for it and then held it up like a dork. Glancing at it, I could see three bars lit up. 'Yea! It looks like it might!'

'Well, the rain changing to ice stopped not too long ago, and I haven't heard any thunder for a while, either. If we don't get another wave of this crappy weather, service might actually stay up. Hope that's a good sign.'

'Yeah, me, too, I'll try to call Sister Mary Angela in a sec and check on Grandma.' My words were coming easier now. I studied Erik as we talked. He seemed so nice and normal, just his usual good-guy self. Had I been overreacting about his kiss? Had what happened with Loren made me too sensitive? Realizing there was a bunch of dead air between us and Erik was starting to give me a questioning look, I said quickly, 'So, where is Darius?'

'I relieved him early. I woke up and couldn't get back to sleep, and I figured he's going to need the extra rest since he's basically our entire army.'

'Was Aphrodite still trashed?'

'She was passed out. Darius carried her out of here. She's going to have a killer hangover when she wakes up.' He sounded pleased at the prospect. 'He was going to Dallas's room to sleep. He hasn't been gone long, so maybe you won't even have to wake him up.'

'Well, I really just wanted directions to Damien and Jack. I couldn't sleep, either, so I thought I'd relieve them and let the Twins rest.'

'Oh, that's easy. I can tell you how to find them. They're not far from the entrance up into the depot we took before.'

'Good, I don't really want to bother Darius if he's actually resting. You're right. Our army needs to get some sleep.' I paused and then added, in a way-too-nonchalant tone, 'Hey, you didn't notice anything, uh, weird in the tunnels on the way up here, did you?'

'Weird? Like what?'

I didn't want to say blackness, because, well, they were tunnels and for them to be dark wasn't weird. Plus, as I'd already imagined, I could hear Erik reminding me of how much the bats had freaked me out. So I blurted, 'Like the lanterns suddenly going out.'

He shrugged and shook his head. 'Nope, but that's really not all that weird. I'm sure the red fledglings have to refill their oil pretty often, and I would bet that recent events have messed up their schedule for that.'

'Yeah, that makes sense.' And it did. So, just for that little moment I let myself feel a sense of relief that even then I knew deep down wasn't real, and grinned at Erik. He smiled back at me and there we were, grinning at each other. I reminded myself that Erik really was a great boyfriend. I'd been glad that he and I were back together. I was still glad we were back together, wasn't I? Couldn't I just stay glad and not let the good things we had between us be messed up because I was freaked that he was going to want more from me than I could give him right now?

Farther to the back of my mind I shoved the memory of the kiss Stark and I had shared and Kalona's nightmare visit and how he'd made me feel things no guy had ever come close to making me feel.

I stood up so abruptly I almost knocked the chair over. 'I gotta call Sister Mary Angela!'

Erik gave me an odd look, but only said, 'Okay, walk a little way over there, but don't get too close to the door. If anyone's hanging around outside I don't want them to hear you.'

I nodded and gave him what I hoped didn't look like a guilty smile. Then I walked a little ways through the basement, which, I noticed, also wasn't as disgusting now as it had been last time I'd been down here. Stevie Rae and her group had obviously done a lot of cleaning and throwing away of the street people's stuff that had been littering the place before. And, happily, it didn't smell like urine anymore, which was a definite improvement.

I pressed Sister Mary Angela's number and mentally crossed my fingers while it said it was calling . . . calling . . . and then it actually rang, once, twice, three times . . . My stomach was just starting to hurt when she answered. The connection was really crappy, but at least I could understand her.

'Oh, Zoey! I'm so glad you called,' said Sister Mary Angela.

'Sister, are you okay? Is Grandma?'

'She's fine . . . all fine. We're . . .' She was definitely breaking up now.

'Sister, I can't hear you very well. Where are you? Is Grandma conscious?'

'Grand . . . is conscious. We're under the abbey, but . . .' There was static and then suddenly I could hear her clearly. 'Are you influencing the weather, Zoey?'

'Me? No! What about Grandma? Are you guys safe in the abbey basement?'

'. . . fine. Not to worry, we . . .'

And the line went dead.

'Hell! This connection sucks so much!' I paced a short path of frustration while I tried to call her back. Nothing. I had service, but the screen kept saying that it was a lost call. I tried several more times before I saw that, not only was I not getting her back, but my phone was getting ready to die. 'Hell!' I repeated.

'What did she say?' Erik had come up behind me.

'Not much, 'cause I lost the connection and can't get it back. But I did manage to hear her say that she's okay and Grandma's okay. I even think she's finally conscious.'

'That's really good news! Don't worry; everything's going to be fine. The nuns have your grandma safe underground, right?'

I nodded, feeling stupidly close to tears that were really more because of frustration than fear for Grandma. I completely trusted Sister Mary Angela, so if she said Grandma was okay, then I believed her. 'It's hard not knowing what's going on. Not just with Grandma, but with everything out there.' I jerked my thumb up at the outside world.

Erik stepped up beside me and his warm hand closed over mine. He turned me so that I was facing him, and then with his thumb he gently traced the new tattoos that covered my palm. 'Hey, we'll get through this. Nyx is at work here, remember? Just look at your hands to see proof of her favor. Yeah, our group is small, but we're strong and we know we're on the right side.'

Just then my phone made the little chime that said I had a text message. 'Oh, good. Maybe this is Sister Mary Angela.' I flipped open the phone and stared at the message, not really getting it.

All fledglings and vampyres are to return
to the House of Night immediately.

'What the hell?' I said, still staring at my phone's screen.

'Let me see,' Erik said. I flipped the phone so he could read it. He nodded slowly, as if the text confirmed something he'd already thought about. 'It's Neferet. And even though it's sounding like one of those schoolwide text broadcasts, I'd bet she's talking directly to us.'

'Are you sure it's her?'

'Yeah, I recognize her number.'

'She gave you her phone number?' I tried not to sound as annoyed as that made me feel, but I doubt I was very successful.

Erik shrugged. 'Yeah, she gave it to me before I left for Europe. Said if I ever needed anything I could call her.'

I snorted.

Erik smiled. 'Are you jealous?'

'No!' I lied. 'She's just such a manipulative bitch that it makes me mad.'

'Well, she's definitely into some bad shit with Kalona.'

'Yeah, that's for sure, and we're not going back to the House of Night. At least not right now.'

'I think you're right about that. We need to find out more about what's happened above before we make our next move. Plus, if your instincts are telling you we need to stay clear of the school, then that's what we should do.'

I looked up at him. He smiled reassuringly down at me and brushed a strand of my hair back from my face. His eyes were warm and kind, not sex crazed and possessive. Jeesh, I had to get a grip on myself. Erik made me feel safe. He believed what he was saying. He believed in me.

'Thank you,' I said. 'Thanks for still believing in me.'

'I'll always believe in you, Zoey,' he said. 'Always.' Erik wrapped me in his arms and kissed me.

The door to the outside was wrenched open, letting in the murky light of a stormy afternoon and a blast of frigid air. Erik whirled, pushing me behind him. I felt a heart-thundering rush of pure fear.

'Get below! Get Darius!' Erik shouted as he moved forward to face the figure silhouetted against the gray upper world.

I had started to run back to the basement ladder when Heath's voice stopped me.

'Hey, is that you, Zo?'

CHAPTER TEN

'HEATH!' I HURRIED TOWARD HIM, PRACTICALLY SHOUTING my relief that it was him and not a terrifying Raven Mocker or worse, an ancient immortal with eyes like the night sky and a voice like a forbidden secret.

'Heath?' Erik didn't sound nearly as pleased. He grabbed my arm so I couldn't run past him. He frowned, still managing to stay protectively in front of me. 'You mean your human boyfriend?'

'*Ex*-boyfriend,' Heath and I said at the same time.

'Hey, aren't you that Erik guy? Zo's fledgling ex-boyfriend?' Heath said. He ignored the three stairs that emptied into the basement and jumped lightly down, looking every inch (and I do mean at least six feet tall with kinda curly, sandy, blond-brown hair and the cutest eyes and guy dimples you have ever seen) the star quarterback he was. Yes, I'll admit it freely, my high-school boyfriend was a cliché, but at least he was an adorable one.

'Boyfriend.' Erik's voice was flint. 'Not ex. Just like vampyre, not fledgling.'

'Oh. I'd say congrats on the makeup with Zo and on not drowning in your own blood, but that would pretty much be bullshit 'cause I wouldn't mean it. Know what I mean, dude?' He talked as he walked around Erik to snag my wrist, but before he could pull me into a big hug he glanced down and saw the new tattoos covering my palms. 'Whoa! Now that is majorly cool! So, your goddess is still takin' care of you?'

'Yeah, she is,' I said.

'I'm glad,' he said and pulled me into the hug I'd been expecting. 'Damn, I've been worried about you!' Then he held me at arm's length and checked me out. 'You all in once piece?'

'I'm fine,' I said, a little breathlessly. I mean, last time I'd seen Heath he'd been breaking up with me. Plus, I could smell him when he hugged me and he smelled amazing. Like home mixed with my childhood mixed with something that was delicious and exciting and was calling to me from everywhere his skin touched mine. I knew what was calling me – his blood. And that messed with more than my head.

'Excellent.' Heath let go of my wrist and I took a quick little half step away from him and toward Erik. I saw a flash of pain go through Heath's eyes, but it was only there for a second before he grinned nonchalantly and shrugged like the hug hadn't been a big deal because he and I were just friends now. 'Yeah, well, I figured you were okay. I mean, I thought even though that *blood thing* between us broke, I'd still know if something bad happened to you.' He'd said the words 'blood thing' with a sexy emphasis that had Erik stirring beside me. 'But I needed to see for myself. Plus, I wanted to ask what-the-fuck about the weird call last night?'

'Call?' Erik said. His eyes were guarded when he looked at me.

'Yes, call.' I lifted my chin. Erik might be my boyfriend again, but no way was I going to put up with his being all possessive and insanely jealous. The thought flitted through my mind that maybe Erik wouldn't ever be able to really trust me after what had happened between us, and I'd have to put up with some obsessive jealousy. I'd kinda earned it. But I said in a cool voice, 'I called Heath to warn him about the Raven Mockers and tell him to get his family to safety. He and I aren't together, but that doesn't mean I want anything bad to happen to him.'

'Raven Mockers?' Heath asked.

'What's going on out there?' Erik asked, his voice all business.

'Goin' on? What do ya mean? Like the major storm that's been goin' on since about midnight, and has turned into a mess of ice, or the gang bullshit that happened? And what're Raven Mockers?'

'Gang bullshit? What do you mean by that?' Erik snapped.

'No. I'm not sayin' shit till you answer my question.'

'Raven Mockers are demonlike creatures from Cherokee legend,' I answered. 'Up until about midnight last night, they were only evil spirits, but all that changed when their daddy, an immortal named Kalona, broke free from his prison inside the earth, and is now making his new address the Tulsa House of Night.'

'You really think it's a good idea to tell him all that?' Erik said.

'Hey, why don't you let Zoey decide what she wants to tell me and what she doesn't want to tell me?' Heath puffed up like he was dying to take a swing at Erik.

Erik puffed right back at him. 'You're a *human*,' he said the word like it was an STD. 'You can't handle the same things we can handle. Try remembering that I had to help save your stupid human ass from a bunch of vamp ghosts just a couple months ago.'

'Zoey saved me, not you! And I've been *handling* Zoey for about a zillion years longer than you've even known her.'

'Yeah? How often has your stupid human ass put her in danger since she's been Marked?'

That unpuffed Heath. 'Look, I'm not putting her in danger by coming here. I just wanted to be sure she was okay. I tried to call a couple of times, but cell service is messed up.'

'Heath, it's not me being in danger by you being here that I'm worried about. It's you being in danger,' I said, giving Erik a hard you-should-shut-up-now look.

'Yeah, I already know about those nasty fledgling kids who tried to chomp on me last time we were here. I don't remember real well everything that happened, but I remembered enough to bring this.' He reached into the pocket of his camo Carhartt and came out with a dangerous-looking black, snubbed-nose gun. 'It's my dad's,' he said proudly. 'I even have extra clips of ammo with me. I figured if they tried to eat me again, I could shoot whatever you couldn't zap.'

'Heath, do not tell me you're carrying a loaded gun in your pocket,' I said.

'Zo, I have the safety on and the first bullet in the clip is empty. I'm not a total moron.'

Erik snorted sarcastically. Heath narrowed his eyes at him.

I spoke quickly into the testosterone-filled air before they started banging on their chests. 'The fledglings don't eat people anymore, Heath, so you're not going to have to shoot anyone. When I said I was worried about you being safe, I meant because of the Raven Mockers.'

'And she answered your question. Now what's this about gang stuff going on?'

Heath shrugged. 'It's all over the news. 'Course, the electricity keeps going out and the stupid cable has been knocked out all day, along with the cell service being sucky. But they say that some gang went nuts last night about midnight, some kind of New Year's initiation thing. Chera Kimiko on Fox News called it a bloodbath. Cops were late in responding 'cause of the storm. Some people were killed in midtown, which is freaking everyone 'cause midtown isn't exactly gang

131

central, so a bunch of rich white folks have lost their minds. Last time I watched the news they were yelling about calling in the National Guard, even though the cops are saying everything is under control.' He paused and I could practically see the wheels in his head turning. 'Hey, midtown! That's where the House of Night is.' Heath looked from me to Erik and then back to me. 'So it wasn't gang bullshit. It was those raven thingies.'

'Brilliant,' Erik muttered.

'Yes, it was really the Raven Mockers. They started the attack when we were escaping from the House of Night,' I said before he and Erik could snipe at each other again. 'The news didn't say anything at all about weird creatures attacking people?'

'Nope. They said a gang attacked people. Killed some of them by slitting their throats. Is that what those Raven Mockers do?'

I remembered how one had attacked me at the House of Night, almost making one of Aphrodite's two death visions for me come true by trying to cut my throat – and that was before they got their physical bodies all the way back. I shivered. 'Yeah, that seems to be what they do, but I really don't know much about them. Grandma knows more, but they made her get in a car accident.'

'Ah, Zo, Grandma was in an accident? Damn! I'm so sorry. Is she gonna be okay?' Heath was genuinely upset. He was a big favorite of Grandma's and had gone out to her lavender farm with me more times than I could count.

'She's going to be okay. She has to be,' I said firmly. 'The Benedictine nuns are taking care of her in the basement under their abbey over there at Lewis and Twenty-first.'

'Basement? Nuns? Huh? Shouldn't she be in the hospital?'

'She was before Kalona rose and the Raven Mockers got their nasty part-human, part-bird bodies back.'

His face squidged up. 'Part human, part bird? That sounds creepy.'

'It's worse than you can imagine, and they're big, too. And mean. Okay, Heath, you have to listen to me. Kalona is an immortal, a fallen angel.'

'By "fallen" you mean that he's not a good guy anymore and doesn't float around with wings playing a harp?'

'He has wings. Big black ones,' Erik said. 'But he's not a good guy, and everything we know about him says he's always been evil.'

'No, he hasn't.' Okay, my mouth said that, but I really hadn't meant it to.

Both guys gawked at me. I smiled nervously.

'Well, uh, according to my grandma, Kalona used to be an angel, so I guess I just figured that he used to be a good guy. I mean, a long time ago.'

'I think we should just assume he's evil. Totally evil,' Erik said.

'A bunch of people were hurt last night. I don't know how many killed, but it was bad. If this Kalona guy is behind it, I'd say he's evil,' Heath said.

'Okay, yeah, well, you guys are probably right,' I said.

What the hell was the matter with me? I knew better than just about anyone how evil Kalona was! I'd felt his dark power. I knew Neferet was all mixed up with him, so mixed up with him that she'd decided to turn her back on Nyx. Okay, all of that definitely spelled E-V-I-L.

'Hang on. I almost forgot about this.' Erik hurried back to his chair and Heath and I followed him. From the shadow beside it, he pulled out the ginormic boom box radio-cassette-CD monstrosity.

'Let me see if I can get anything in.' He messed with the enormous silver knobs, and pretty soon a very staticky Channel 8 came on. The announcer was being all serious and talking quickly.

'To repeat our special report on the gang violence in midtown Tulsa last night, Tulsa P.D. reiterates that the city is safe and the problem under control. To quote the chief of police, "It was an initiation ritual by a new gang that calls itself Mockers. Leaders of the gang have been arrested and the streets of midtown Tulsa are, once again, safe for our citizens."' The newsman continued, 'Of course Tulsa and the surrounding area is under a severe winter storm watch until tomorrow evening, so we caution you not to travel unless it is an emergency situation. We're expecting at least six more inches of rain mixed with ice, which will hamper PSO's attempts to restore power to the many neighborhoods that lost electricity last night. Stay tuned for updates and a complete weather report on the five o'clock news in half an hour.

'We have one more community announcement: All House of

Night staff and students have been recalled to the school due to the impending weather. Again, all House of Night staff and students have been asked to return to school. Stay tuned for updates. We return you to our scheduled programming.'

'There was no gang in midtown last night,' I said. 'That's the most ridiculous thing I've ever heard!'

'She fixed it. She manipulated the press and probably the public, too,' Erik said, looking grim.

'Is the "she" that High Priestess who messed with my mind?' Heath asked me.

'No,' Erik said.

'Yes,' I said at the same time. I frowned at Erik. 'He needs to know the truth to protect himself.'

'The less he knows, the better it is for him,' Erik insisted.

'No, see, that's what I thought before, and that's why everyone was so mad at me. That's also why I made some major mistakes.' I looked from Erik to Heath. 'If I hadn't kept so many secrets and had trusted my friends to handle themselves, I might have talked more and messed up less.'

Erik sighed. 'Okay, I see your point.' He looked at Heath. 'Her name is Neferet. She's the High Priestess at the House of Night. She's powerful. Very powerful. And she's psychic.'

'Yeah, I already know she can do stuff with her mind. That's how she messed with me. She made me forget chunks of things that happened. I've just started to remember them.'

'Does it make your head hurt?' I asked him, remembering the pain I'd had to work through when I'd broken the memory blocks Neferet had put in my mind.

'Yeah. It hurts, but it's getting a lot better.' He smiled his familiar, forgiving smile and my heart squeezed.

'Neferet is also some kind of queen for Kalona,' Erik continued.

'So she's bad news all the way around,' Heath said.

'Bad news and dangerous. Don't forget that,' I said. 'Also, Kalona can't stand to be underground. He couldn't before he was imprisoned in the earth by Cherokee women, and now that he's escaped, my guess is he's going to be even leerier of the earth. So remember, you're safe underground.'

'What about the Raven Mockers?'

I shook my head. 'We just don't know. None have come down here, but that doesn't mean much.' I thought about the darkness in the tunnels below and the bad feeling it was giving me, but I didn't know what the hell it actually was: Red fledglings? Raven Mockers? Some *other* faceless thing that Kalona was sending against us? Or was it as simple as my imagination? The only thing I knew for sure was that I'd sound like an idiot crying wolf if I babbled a bunch of maybes, which meant, for the time being, I kept my mouth shut.

'Well, it's Saturday, but we don't have school because it's still winter break until Wednesday, and if this ice storm hits as hard as they say it's going to, we might be out for the whole week,' Heath was saying. 'It should be easy to keep safe, even if the Raven Mockers attack again and their attack moves from midtown Tulsa to Broken Arrow.'

My stomach felt hollow. 'And they might. Neferet knows

I'm from Broken Arrow, and she knows there are still people I care about there.'

'So she might send the Raven Mockers to Broken Arrow just to mess you up?' Heath said.

I nodded. 'Especially when my group and I ignore the call to return to school.'

'But wait, Zo. You *have* to be at school around a bunch of vamps or you and all the rest of the fledglings will get sick, right?'

'I'm here,' Erik spoke up. 'And so is another full vampyre. Not to mention Stevie Rae.'

'Isn't she all gross and undead?' Heath said.

'Not anymore,' I said. 'She's Changed into a different kind of vamp, one with red tattoos. And all of the gross fledglings that tried to eat you – well, they're red fledglings now, and aren't so gross.'

'Huh,' Heath said. 'Well, I'm glad your BFF's okay.'

'Me, too.' I smiled.

'So are three adult vamps enough to keep you guys from getting sick?' Heath asked.

'We'll have to be. Heath, you need to go,' Erik said abruptly.

Heath and I looked at him. I realized I'd been grinning a lot at Heath and really liking that he and I were talking again.

'The ice storm,' Erik continued. 'It's not smart for him to get stuck here, and that's what's going to happen if he's still here when the sun sets.' Erik paused and then said, 'Which is going to happen in about half an hour. How long did it take you to get from Broken Arrow to here?'

Heath frowned. 'Almost two hours. The roads are bad.'

It should have only taken him about thirty minutes to get from his place to the depot. Erik was right. Heath had to go home. Not only were we clueless about how much danger we might be in from Kalona, but I wasn't one hundred percent sure Heath would be safe around the red fledglings. Besides my questions about them, the truth was no matter what they were or weren't now, Heath was one hundred percent human, with lots of yummy, fresh, warm, sexy, pumping blood (I ignored the fact that my mouth was watering just thinking about it), and I had no idea about their willpower limits.

'Erik's right, Heath. You can't get stuck outside tonight, especially this close to midtown. Besides the ice, we don't know what's up with the Raven Mockers.'

Heath looked at me like he and I were completely alone. 'You're worried about me.'

My throat felt dry. This was so not a conversation I wanted to have in front of Erik. 'Of course I worry about you. We've been friends a long time.' I could feel Erik's eyes on me. I forced myself not to fidget guiltily and added, 'Friends worry about friends.'

Heath's smile was slow and intimate. 'Friends. Right.'

'Time for you to go.' Erik sounded pissed.

Without looking at Erik, Heath said, 'I'll go when Zo tells me to.'

'It's time for you to go, Heath,' I said quickly.

Heath's eyes stayed locked with mine for several heartbeats.

'Fine. Whatever,' he said. Then he turned to Erik. 'So you're a real vamp now, huh?'

'Yes.'

Heath looked him up and down. The two guys were close to the same height. Erik was taller, but Heath was the more muscular of the two. Still, both guys looked like they could handle themselves in a fight. I felt myself tense. Was Heath going to throw a punch at Erik?

'People say male vamps are big into protecting their priest-esses. Is that right?'

'That's right,' Erik said.

'Good. Then I expect you to be sure Zoey stays safe.'

'Nothing's going to happen to her as long as I'm alive,' Erik said.

'Make sure it doesn't.' Heath's voice had lost the charming, easy-going tone with which he usually spoke. It had gone hard and dangerous. 'Because if you let anything happen to her, I'm going to find you, and vampyre or no vampyre, I am going to kick your ass.'

CHAPTER ELEVEN

I MOVED QUICKLY, PUTTING MYSELF BETWEEN THE TWO OF them. 'Stop it!' I shouted. 'I have way too much to worry about right now to also have to pull you two off each other. Jeesh, talk about immature.' Both guys kept glaring at each other over my head. 'I said, stop it!' And I smacked their chests. That made them blink and shift their attention to me. Now it was my turn to do the glaring. 'You know, you two are ridiculous with your puffing up and your testosterone and crap. I mean, I could summon the elements and kick *both* of your butts.'

Heath shuffled his feet and looked embarrassed. Then he grinned at me, like a cute little boy whose mommy had just yelled at him. 'Sorry, Zo. I forget you have some major mojo going on.'

'Yeah, sorry,' Erik said. 'I know I don't have anything to worry about with you and him.' And he finished with a smirk at Heath.

Heath looked at me like he expected me to say something like *well, actually you need to worry, Erik, because I still like Heath*, but I didn't. I couldn't. No matter what was going on between Erik and me, Heath was part of my old world, and he fit better in my past than in my present or future. Heath being one hundred percent human meant he was one hundred percent more vulnerable to being seriously hurt if something attacked us.

'Okay, I'm out of here,' Heath said into the awkward silence. He spun around and started to walk toward the door to the outside and was almost there when he paused and looked back at me. 'But first I really do need to talk to you, Zo. Alone.'

'I'm not going anywhere,' Erik said.

'No one asked you to,' Heath said. 'Zo, would you come outside with me for a minute?'

'Hell no,' Erik said, moving toward me possessively. 'She's not going anywhere with you.'

I was frowning up at Erik, about to tell him that he really wasn't the boss of me, when he did something that totally, utterly, and completely pissed me off. He actually grabbed my wrist and jerked me toward him, even though I hadn't taken one step to follow Heath.

An automatic reflex had me yanking my wrist from his grasp.

His blue eyes narrowed at me. At that instant he looked mad and mean, and seemed more a stranger than a boyfriend.

'You're not going anywhere with him,' he repeated to me.

My temper spiked. I cannot stand being bullied. It was one of the reasons my mom's new husband and I never got along. At his core, the Step-loser was nothing more than a big bully. Suddenly I was seeing that same attitude reflected in Erik. I knew it would break my heart later, but just then my anger was burning too hot for any other emotion to cool my reaction.

I didn't yell. I didn't scream and smack him like I really wanted to. Instead, all I did was shake my head and say in my coldest voice, 'Erik, enough. Just because we're back together doesn't mean you can tell me what to do.'

'How about does it mean you don't cheat on me again with your human boyfriend?' Erik snapped.

I gasped and took a step back from him like he'd slapped me. 'Why the hell do you think you can talk to me like that?' My stomach clenched up so hard I thought I was going to be sick, but I ignored it, meeting Erik's angry glare with a steely stare of my own. 'As your girlfriend, you've just pissed me off. As your High Priestess, you've just insulted me. And as someone with a working brain, you've made me wonder if you've lost every bit of your sense. What do you think I'm going to do in the minute or so I'd be alone with Heath standing outside in the parking lot during an ice storm?

Lie down and let him do me right there on the cement? Is that really the kind of girl you think I am?'

Erik didn't say anything; he just kept glaring at me.

In the electric silence Heath's chuckle was supermocking. 'Hey, Erik, let me give you a little advice about our Zo. She really, really, *really* doesn't like it when you try to tell her what to do. And that's how she's been since, uh, I dunno, third grade or so. I mean, even before she got the vamp mojo from her goddess, she hated to be bossed around.' Heath held out his hand to me. 'So would ya walk outside with me for just a sec so we can talk without an audience?'

'Yes, yes I would. I think I need some fresh air,' I said. Ignoring Erik's pissed-off stare and Heath's offered hand, I stomped over to the metal grating that looked way more closed and secure than it was and with an annoyed shove pushed it aside and walked out into a very nasty winter evening. The blast of cold wet air felt good on my heated face, and I breathed deep, trying to calm down and not shriek my frustration with Erik up into the bruised gray of the sky.

At first I thought it was raining, but pretty quickly I realized it was more like the sky was spitting little pieces of ice. It wasn't coming down thick, but it was constant, and the parking lot, railroad tracks, and the side of the old depot building were already starting to take on the weird magical look of being gilded with ice.

'My truck's just over there.' Heath pointed to where his truck was parked at the edge of the deserted parking lot, under a tree that had obviously at one time been planted as

143

an ornament near the sidewalk that wrapped around the depot. Years of being ignored and not pruned had really messed with it, though, and instead of fitting neatly into its circular opening in the cement, the tree had grown way bigger than it should have and its roots had broken the sidewalk around it. Its ice-slick limbs swayed precariously close to the old granite building; some of them were actually leaning on the roof. Just looking up at the tree made me cringe. If we got much more ice, the poor old thing was probably going to shatter into zillions of pieces.

'Here,' Heath held one side of his coat up over my head. 'Come on over to my truck so we can talk out of this mess.'

I glanced around at the gray, soggy landscape. Nothing seemed frightening or freaky – as in half-man, half-bird grossness. It was just wet and cold and empty.

'Okay, yeah,' I said, and let Heath lead me over to his truck. I probably shouldn't have let him hold his coat over me and tuck me close to his side while I clutched on to him to keep from falling on the ice-slick pavement, but it felt so familiar and easy to be with him that I didn't even hesitate. Let's face it, Heath's been in my life since I was in grade school. I was literally more comfortable with him than with anyone else in the world, except for my Grandma. No matter what was going on, or not going on, between us, Heath was like family to me. Actually, he's better than the vast majority of my family. It was hard to imagine trying to treat him all formally like he was a stranger. After all, Heath had been my friend before he'd become my boyfriend. *But he can never just be my friend*

144

again; there'll always be more between us than that, whispered my conscience, but I ignored it.

We got to his truck and Heath opened the door for me, the interior smelling of an odd, familiar mixture of Heath and Armor All. (Heath is a neat freak about his truck; I swear you could eat off the seats.) Instead of sliding in, I hesitated. Sitting next to him in the cab of his truck was just too intimate, too reminiscent of the years I had been his girlfriend. So instead, I pulled a little away from him and half sat, half leaned on the end of the passenger's seat, enough out of the icy rain to stay semi-dry. Heath gave me a sad smile, like he understood that I was doing my best to resist being with him again, and leaned against the inside of the open door.

'Okay, what did you want to talk to me about?'

'I don't like you being here. I don't remember everything, but I do remember enough to know that the tunnels down there are bad news. I know you said those undead kids have changed, but I still don't like you being down there with them. It doesn't seem safe,' he said, looking serious and worried.

'Well, I don't blame you for thinking it's disgusting down there, but it really has changed. The kids are different, too. They have their humanity back. Plus, it's the safest place for us right now.'

Heath studied my face for a long time, then he let out a heavy sigh. 'You're the one who's the priestess and stuff like that, so you know what you're doing. It just feels weird to me. Are you sure you shouldn't go back to the House of

Night? Maybe this fallen angel guy isn't as bad as you think he is.'

'No, Heath, he's bad. Just trust me on this one. And the Raven Mockers are seriously dangerous. It's not safe to go back to school. You didn't see him when he rose out of the ground. It's like he can put a spell on fledglings and vampyres. It's really creepy. You already know how powerful Neferet is. Well, I think Kalona is even more powerful than her.'

'That is bad,' Heath agreed.

'Yeah.'

Heath nodded and didn't say anything. He just looked at me. I looked back at him, and somehow got caught by his sweet, brown-eyed gaze. I'd been sitting there in silence for a while, just looking into his eyes, when I started to be intensely aware of him. I could smell Heath. It was the nice, soapy, Heath smell that I'd grown up with. He was standing close enough to me that I could feel the heat from his body.

Slowly, without saying a word, Heath took my hand and turned it over so that he could look at the intricate tattoos that decorated it. He traced the pattern with one of his fingers.

'It's really amazing that this has happened to you,' he said softly, still studying my hand. 'Sometimes when I'm waking up in the morning I forget that you've been Marked and you're at the House of Night, and the first thing I think is how much I'm looking forward to knowing you're going to be at the game Friday night watching me play. Or that I can't wait to see you before school getting sausage rolls and your brown pop at Daylight Donuts.' He looked up from my hand

and into my eyes. 'And then I wake all the way up and remember that you won't be there for any of those things. That wasn't so bad when we were Imprinted, 'cause I still felt like I had a chance, that I still had a part of you. But now even that's gone.'

Heath made my insides tremble. 'I'm sorry, Heath. I— I just don't know what else to say. I can't change any of this.'

'Yes, you can.' Heath lifted my hand and pressed my palm against his black Broken Arrow Tigers football shirt just over his heart. 'Can you feel it beating?' he whispered.

I nodded. I could feel his heartbeat, steady and strong, if a little fast. It reminded me of the incredibly delicious blood that was pounding through his veins and how good it would feel to take just a tiny little bite of him . . . And now the pounding of my heart was beating in double time along with his.

'Last time I saw you, I said that it hurt too much to love you. But I was wrong about that. The truth is it hurts too much *not* to love you,' Heath said.

'Heath, no. We can't.' My voice was rough as I tried to talk through the desire I was feeling for him.

'Of course we can, babe. We're good at being together. We've had lots of practice at it.' Heath stepped closer to me. He took the pointing finger of my hand from his chest and ran his thumb lightly over my nicely manicured nail. 'Is it true that your fingernails are hard enough that they can cut through skin?'

I nodded. I knew I should walk away and back down to

the tunnels and the life that waited for me there, but I couldn't. Heath was also a life that waited for me and right or wrong it was almost impossible for me to walk away from him.

Heath took my finger and lifted it so that my nail was pressed lightly against the soft place where his neck curved into his shoulder.

'Cut me, Zo. Drink my blood again.' His voice was deep and harsh with desire. 'We're already connected. We'll always be connected. So put the Imprint back between us where it belongs.'

He pressed my fingernail harder against his neck. We were both breathing heavily now. When my nail broke through his skin, making a small scratch on his neck, I watched, mesmerized, as an exquisitely thin ribbon of scarlet sprang up against the paleness of his skin.

The smell hit me then, the utterly familiar scent of Heath's blood. The blood I'd once Imprinted as my own. Nothing can compare to the scent of fresh human blood, not another fledgling's and not even an adult vampyre's blood is as compelling, as hypnotically desirable. I felt myself leaning toward him.

'Yes, babe, yes. Drink from me, Zo. Remember how good it feels?' Heath whispered while his hand on my waist pulled me into him.

Couldn't I just take one little taste? So what if I Imprinted with Heath, again? Hell, of course, we'd Imprint. And that's not so bad. I loved being Imprinted with him. He'd liked it, too, until—

Until I'd broken the Imprint along with his heart and quite possibly irreparably damaged his soul.

I shoved him away and lurched out of the cab of the truck, stepping quickly around Heath. The icy rain actually felt good as it fell on my face, cooling the heat of my bloodlust.

'I have to go back, Heath,' I said, trying hard to get my breathing and my racing heart under control. 'You have to go back, too, where you belong. And that's not here.'

'Zoey, what's wrong?' He took a step toward me, and I moved one more step away from him. 'What did I do?'

'Nothing. It's— It's not you, Heath.' I pushed my wet hair back from my face. 'You're great. You've always been great, and I do love you. That's why this can't happen between us again. Imprinting with me isn't good for you, especially not right now.'

'Why don't you let me worry about what's good for me and what's not?'

'Because you don't think straight when it comes to me and you!' I shouted. 'Remember how painful it was when our Imprint broke? Remember how you said it made you feel like you wanted to die?'

'Then don't break it again.'

'It's not that simple. My life isn't that simple anymore.'

'Maybe you're just making it too complicated. There's you. There's me. We love each other, and we have since we were kids, so we should be together. The end,' he said.

'Life isn't a book, Heath! There's no guarantee of a happy ending,' I said.

149

'I don't need a guarantee if I have you.'

'That's just it. You don't have me, Heath. You can't. Not anymore.' I shook my head and held up my hand to stop him when he started to say something else. 'No! I can't do this right now. I just want you to get in your truck and go back to B.A. I'm going to go back down there. To my people and my vampyre boyfriend.'

'Oh, please! You and that vamp asshole? No way are you going to put up with his crap, Zo.'

'This isn't just about Erik and me. The truth is you and I can't happen, Heath. You need to forget about me and go on with your life. Your *human* life.' I turned my back on him and made myself walk away. When I heard him following me, I didn't look back. I just yelled, 'No! I want you to leave, Heath, and I don't want you to come back. Ever.'

I held my breath and heard his footsteps stop. I still didn't look at him. I was afraid if I did that, I would turn around, run back to him, and hurl myself into his arms.

I was almost to the old metal grate when I heard the first croaking caw. The sound stopped me like I'd run into a brick wall. I whirled around. Heath was standing in the freezing rain under the tree just a few feet from his truck. I spared hardly a glance for him. My eyes darted up into the dark branches of the ice-bowed tree.

Within the shadows of the naked boughs a darkness stirred. It reminded me of something, and I blinked, staring at it and trying to remember where I'd seen something like it before.

Then the image shifted . . . changed . . . I gasped as it became more visible. Neferet! She was clinging to a thick, ice-slick branch that leaned against the roof of the depot. Her eyes blazed crimson and her hair whipped around her crazily, like she had been caught in a sudden wind.

Neferet smiled at me. Her expression was so purely evil that I felt frozen in place.

Then, as I stared up in horror, her image shifted again, wavered, and where the image of the tainted High Priestess had been, there was now a huge Raven Mocker. The thing perched on the side of the depot roof wasn't human and it wasn't animal. It was a terrible mutated mixture of both. It was staring at me with eyes the color of blood and the shape of a man. Its human arms and legs were naked, looking vile and perverted emerging from the body of a gigantic raven. I could see its forked tongue and the glistening saliva that dripped hungrily from that horrible maw.

'Zoey, what's going on?' Heath said. And before I could tell him not to, he followed my gaze, looking up at the icy limbs that rested against the roof of the depot. 'What the fuck?' But as I saw the realization of what the creature must be cross his face, the bird thing turned its glowing red eyes from Heath to me.

'Zzzzzoey?' It breathed my name, its voice sounding wrong and flat and utterly inhuman. 'We havvvve been loooooking for you.'

My body felt frozen. My mind was screaming inside my head, *they've been looking for me!* But nothing came out of my mouth – no warning to Heath. Not even the shrill girl-scream that filled my throat.

'My father will be very pleasssssed when I presssssent you to him,' the Mocker hissed, spreading his wings as if he was preparing to fly down and snatch me up.

'I'll have to say "hell no" to that little messed-up plan of yours,' Heath yelled.

CHAPTER TWELVE

I TORE MY HORRIFIED GAZE FROM THE RAVEN MOCKER TO see Heath standing just a couple of feet in front of me. He had his gun out and was holding it before him, pointing it directly at the creature in the tree.

'Puny human!' the thing screeched. 'You think to ssssstop an Old One?'

Everything went into fast-forward then. The creature exploded from the tree at the same time my body thawed and I sprinted forward. I saw Heath squeeze the trigger and heard the deafening blast of the gun, but the Raven Mocker was moving with inhuman speed. It dodged, and the place Heath had been aiming at was empty the instant before the bullet sliced through the air, embedding itself in the ice-coated tree. As the thing flew toward Heath, I saw its jagged talons curling into claws and I remembered how, even in spirit form, a creature like this had almost sliced through my neck. Now the Raven Mockers had their bodies returned to them and I knew unless I did something fast, this one was going to kill Heath.

With a scream I gave voice to my fear and rage as I launched myself at Heath, knocking him aside a moment before the Raven Mocker reached him so that the creature struck me instead. I didn't feel any pain then, just an odd pressure against my skin, starting at the top of my left shoulder and slicing across the upper part of my chest, above my breasts, all the way to my right shoulder. The force of the blow spun me around in a half circle so that I was still facing the Raven Mocker as it flew past us and then dropped to the ground on its terrible human legs.

Its blood-colored eyes widened as it looked at me. 'No!' it cried in a voice that could belong to no sane being. 'He wantssss you alive!'

'Zoey! Oh, God, Zoey! Get behind me!' Heath was yelling at me as he tried to scramble to his feet, but he slipped on the icy pavement that had somehow turned a wet red. He fell hard.

I glanced at him and thought how weird it was that even though he was right next to me it sounded like he was yelling from way down a long tunnel.

I didn't understand why, but my knees gave way and I

dropped to the pavement. The awful rustle of the Raven Mocker's huge wings drew my gaze back to the creature. Sure enough, the thing had spread its wings. Obviously it was going to come for me. I lifted my hand, which felt heavy and warm. When I glanced at it, I was shocked to see that it was drenched in blood. *Blood? Is that what's all over the pavement? That's odd*. With a mental shrug I disregarded the pooling blood and shouted, 'Wind, come to me!'

At least I thought I shouted. What really came out of my mouth was barely a whisper. Thankfully, wind is a good listener because the air instantly began to swirl around me.

'Keep that thing on the ground,' I said. Wind instantly obeyed, and a lovely mini-tornado engulfed the grotesque birdman, causing its wings to be useless. With a terrible screeching sound the thing tucked its useless wings against its back and began to trudge toward me, ducking its mutated head against the battering of wind.

'Zoey! Shit, Zoey!' Heath was suddenly beside me. His strong arm was around me, which felt really good because I was thinking that I might want to fall over.

I smiled at him, wondering why he was crying. 'Just a sec. Gotta finish off that thing.' Wearily, I turned my attention back to the birdman. 'Fire, I need you.' Heat was there, warming the swirling air around me. Then I used the finger of the bloody hand I was still holding upright and I pointed it at the thing that was getting closer and closer to Heath and me. 'Burn it up,' I commanded.

The warmth that had been surrounding me changed tempo,

going from gentle heat to a column of consuming flame. It followed the direction of my pointing finger and of my will, and it plowed into the Raven Mocker, engulfing it in an angry yellow flame. The air was filled with the awful scent of roasting meat and burnt feathers. I thought I might puke.

'Oh, ugh. Fire, thank you. Wind, before you leave, could you please blow that nasty smell away?' It was so strange that I thought I was saying all this stuff really loud, but my voice was actually coming out as a weak little whisper. The elements obeyed me anyway, which was good, because a wave of sickening dizziness washed over me and I was suddenly slumping against Heath, unable to hold myself upright anymore.

I tried to understand what was wrong with me, but my thoughts were all muddied, and for some reason knowing exactly what was going on didn't seem very important.

Way off in the distance I heard running feet, and then I was looking up at Heath's tear-streaked face as he yelled, 'Help! We're over here! Zoey needs help!'

Next thing I knew, Erik's face had joined Heath's. All I could think was *oh, great, they're going to start growling at each other again*. But they didn't. Actually, Erik's reaction when he looked down at me started to make me feel kinda concerned, in a detached, only vaguely interested way.

'Shit!' he said, and his face turned really pale. Without saying another word Erik ripped off his shirt (which was the cool black long-sleeved Polo he'd been wearing at our last ritual), making buttons pop all over. I blinked in surprise, thinking that he looked really good in just his little wifebeater

T-shirt. I mean, seriously, he has a hot body. He dropped down on the other side of me.

'Sorry, this is probably going to hurt.' Erik balled up his shirt and pressed it against my chest.

Pain did slice through me then, and I gasped.

'Oh, Goddess! Sorry, Z, sorry!' Erik kept saying over and over.

I looked down to see what was making me hurt like that and was utterly shocked to see that my whole body was drenched in blood.

'Wh-what—' I tried to frame a question, but the pain mixed with the increasingly strong feeling of numbness made it difficult for me to speak.

'We have to get her to Darius. He'll know what to do,' Erik said.

'I'll carry her. Just lead me to this Darius guy,' Heath said.

Erik nodded. 'Let's go!'

Heath looked down at me. 'I have to move you, Z. Just hang in there, okay?'

I tried to nod, but the movement ended in another gasp when Heath picked me up and, clutching me to his chest like I was an overgrown infant, he ran, slipping and sliding, after Erik.

The trip back down into the tunnels was a nightmare I'll never forget. Heath rushed after Erik through the basement. When they got to the metal ladder that led down to the tunnel system, they paused only for a second.

'I'll hand her down to you,' Heath said.

Erik nodded and disappeared down the hole. Heath walked to the edge of it. 'Sorry, babe,' he said. 'I know this must be awful for you.' Then he kissed me lightly on my forehead before he squatted and somehow passed me to Erik, who was standing below us.

I say 'somehow' because I was busy screaming in pain and I wasn't really paying close attention to the logistics of what was actually going on.

Next thing I knew Heath had dropped lightly to the tunnel floor and Erik handed me back to him.

'I'm going to run ahead and find Darius. You keep following the main tunnel. Don't take any of the turnoffs. Stay where it's best lit and I'll come back to you with Darius.'

'Who is Darius?' Heath said, but he was speaking to empty air. Erik had already sprinted away.

'He's lots faster than I thought he was,' I tried to say, but a weak jumble of words was all that whispered from my mouth. And I noticed the lantern that I was sure had gone out right before I'd climbed up into the basement was lit again. 'That's weird' was what I meant to say. Instead, I barely heard myself mumble something that sounded like 'Thhhhat's weeeer' over the pounding of my heart in my ears.

'Shhh,' Heath soothed as he started out as quickly as he could without jiggling me so badly that he made me scream again. 'You stay with me, Zo. Don't close your eyes. Keep watching me. Keep with me.' Heath kept talking and talking, which was really annoying because my chest hurt really bad and all I wanted to do was close my eyes and go to sleep.

'Gotta rest,' I murmured.

'No! There's no resting! Hey, let's pretend like we're in that *Titanic* movie you used to watch over and over again. You know, the one with Leonardo DiStupio.'

'DiCaprio,' I whispered, irritated at the fact that after all these years Heath was still jealous that when I was a kid I'd had a crush on Leonardo. Or as I liked to think of him, 'my boyfriend Leo.'

'Whatever,' he said. 'Remember how you said if you'd been Rose you would really never have let him go? Okay, well, let's do a little reenactment. I'm the gay-looking DiCaprio and you're Rose. You have to keep your eyes open and on my face, or you'll have let me go and I'll turn into a huge gay Popsicle.'

'Dork,' I managed.

Heath grinned. 'Just never let me go, Rose. Okay?'

Okay, it was a stupid reenactment, but I'll admit that he hooked me. It had driven me crazy since the first time I'd seen the movie (and bawled my eyes out – and I do mean one of those shoulder-heaving, ugly snot cries). Stupid Rose says she'll never let him go, but then she does. And why couldn't she have scooted over and let Leo/Jack get on that floating board thing with her? There was plenty of room. So while my foggy mind circled round and round that heart-wrenching scene from one of my favorite movies, Heath held me tight in his arms and ran.

He'd just followed a gentle curve in the tunnel when Erik found us. Darius was at his shoulder. Heath came to a stop and it was then that I realized how hard he was breathing. Huh. I wondered abstractly if I should be embarrassed that I was heavy.

Darius took one look at me and started barking commands at Erik.

'I'm taking her to Stevie Rae's room. I'll get there well ahead of you, but I'll need this human to join me there, so show him where to go. Then you get the Twins and Damien. Wake up Aphrodite. We may need her, too.' Darius turned to Heath. 'I will take Zoey.'

Heath hesitated. I could tell he didn't want to let me go. Darius's stony look softened. 'Do not fear. I am a Son of Erebus and I give you my oath that I will always protect her.'

Reluctantly Heath transferred me to Darius's strong arms. The warrior looked grimly down at me. 'I'm going to move fast. Remember to trust me.'

I nodded weakly, and even though I knew what was coming next, I was still amazed as Darius took off, moving with a speed that blurred the walls of the tunnel and made my head spin. Once before I'd experienced Darius's amazing ability to practically teleport from one place to another, and it wasn't any less breathtaking the second time.

It seemed only seconds had passed when Darius came to an abrupt halt in front of the blanketed entrance to Stevie Rae's room. He shoved inside. Stevie Rae was sitting up, rubbing her eyes and peering blurrily at us. Then her mouth opened in utter shock and she bounded off the bed.

'Zoey! What happened?'

'Raven Mocker,' Darius said. 'Clear those things off that table.'

Stevie Rae knocked the stuff off the table that sat by the end of her bed. I wanted to protest that she really shouldn't make such a mess. I mean, I was sure she'd broken a glass or two and sent a whole bunch of DVDs flying across the room, but not only was my voice not working right, but I was really busy trying not to pass out from the terrible pain that was slicing through the top part of my body as Darius placed me on the table.

'What can we do? What can we do?' Stevie Rae repeated the question. I thought she looked like a little lost girl and I noticed that she was crying, too.

'Take her hand. Talk to her. Keep her conscious,' Darius said. And then he turned away and started throwing stuff out of the first aid kit.

'Zoey, can you hear me?' I could feel that Stevie Rae had hold of my hand, but just barely.

It took what felt like a superhuman effort, but I whispered, 'Yeah.'

Stevie Rae clutched my hand harder. 'You're gonna be okay. 'Kay? Nothin' can happen to you, 'cause I don't know what I'd do—' Her voice caught on a sob, and then she said, 'You can't die 'cause you've always believed the best of me, so I've tried to be what you believe I am. Without you, well, I'm afraid the good in me will die, too, and I'll give in to the darkness. Plus, there are so many things I still need to tell you. Important things.'

I wanted to tell her not to be silly, that she wasn't making sense and I wasn't going anywhere, but through the pain and the numbness I was starting to get a strange feeling. The only way I could describe it was as a sense of not-rightness. Whatever had happened, whatever was going on with me, that was the source of the not-rightness. And this new feeling, more than the blood – more than the fear in my friends' faces – was telling me that something was so wrong with me that I might, indeed, be going somewhere.

It was then that the pain began to recede, and I decided that if this was what it felt like to die, then it was better than living and hurting like hell.

Heath burst into the room, came straight to me, and took my other hand. He barely looked at Stevie Rae. Instead, he smoothed the hair out of my face.

'How are ya, babe? Still holding on?'

I tried to smile at him, but he seemed so far away that I couldn't make the change in expression reach him.

The Twins ran into the room with Kramisha close behind them.

'Oh no!' Erin stopped several feet from where I was and pressed her hand against her mouth.

'Zoey?' I thought Shaunee looked confused. Then she blinked several times, her gaze traveled down my body, and she burst into tears.

'That don't look good,' Kramisha said. 'Not good at all.' She paused and then her eyes went from me to Heath, whose attention was so focused on me I swear he didn't look like he'd notice if a giant white elephant in a tutu danced into the room. 'Ain't that the human kid who was down here before?'

I don't know why, but except for my own body, which didn't seem to belong to me anymore, I had become majorly aware of everything that was going on around me. The Twins were holding hands and bawling so hard snot was running from their noses. Darius was still digging through the first aid kit. Stevie Rae was patting my hand and trying (unsuccessfully) not to cry. Heath was whispering silly butchered lines from *Titanic* to me. In other words, everyone was focused on me – except Kramisha. She was staring hungrily at Heath. Little warning bells started ringing in my mind and I tried to struggle to regain awareness of my body. I needed to warn Heath to be on his guard. I needed to tell him he should leave this place before something bad happened to him.

'Heath,' I managed to whisper.

'I'm here, babe. I'm not going anywhere.'

I did a mental eye roll. Heath and his heroics were cute and all, but I was afraid they were going to get him eaten by Stevie Rae's red fledglings.

'Hey, ain't you the human kid who was down here before? The one Zoey came after?' Kramisha had moved closer to Heath. Her eyes had taken on a red tint that was a gigantic warning sign. Was I the only one who could see danger in the intense way she was staring at him?

'Darius!' I finally gasped.

Thankfully, the warrior looked up from rummaging through the first aid kit. I flicked my eyes from his to where

Kramisha was practically drooling on Heath and saw understanding cross Darius's face.

'Kramisha. Leave the room. Now,' Darius snapped.

She hesitated, then dragged her red gaze from Heath to look directly at me. *Go!* I mouthed the word. Her eyes didn't change, but Kramisha nodded once and walked quickly from the room.

It was then that Aphrodite slapped the doorway blanket aside and made her grand entrance. Looking seriously like poopie, she scowled at the room.

'Damn it, this Imprint is a pain in the ass! Stevie Rae, could you not get a handle on yourself and keep your emotional bullshit under control and show just a smidge of respect for those of us who can still have hangovers that would kill the average—' She finally managed to focus her blurry vision enough to actually see me. Her face, already pale and hollow-eyed, blanched so that it looked a sickly shade of fish-belly white. 'Oh, Goddess! Zoey!' She started shaking her head back and forth, back and forth as she rushed over to me. 'No, Zoey. No. I didn't see this.' She was talking earnestly to me. 'I never saw this. You beat the first death vision I had. The next one wasn't supposed to be you being cut again. The next was supposed to be you drowning. No! This isn't right!'

I tried to say something, but she'd already rounded on Heath.

'You! What the fuck are you doing here?'

'I— I came to see if she was okay,' Heath stammered, obviously freaked by her intensity.

Aphrodite shook her head again. 'No. You aren't supposed to be here. This isn't right.' She paused and her eyes narrowed at Heath. 'You caused this, didn't you?'

I watched Heath's eyes fill with tears. 'Yeah, I think I did,' he said.

CHAPTER THIRTEEN

DAMIEN, JACK, AND ERIK RAN INTO THE ROOM, FOLLOWED closely by Duchess. Jack took one look at me, screamed like a girl, and fainted. Damien caught him in time to keep him from falling and bashing his head on the floor. He laid him down on Stevie Rae's bed while the poor confused Lab whined and stared with big, worried brown eyes from Jack to Damien and me, and then back to Jack again. Damien joined everyone else, including Erik, who was crowding around me. Darius waded into the group, parting kids like he was a vampyre Moses and they were the fledgling Red Sea.

'They need to cast a circle and focus the healing powers of the elements on Zoey,' Darius told Aphrodite.

She nodded, touched my forehead gently, and then started snapping commands at my friends.

'Nerd herd! Take your places. Let's get this circle cast.'

Shaunee and Erin stared blankly at her. Damien, his voice thick with tears, said, 'I— I don't know which direction is east.'

Stevie Rae squeezed my hand again before letting it go. 'I do. I always know where north is, so I can show you where east is, too,' she told Damien.

'Make the circle around the table,' Darius said. 'And give me the sheet from that bed.'

Damien grabbed the top sheet from Stevie Rae's bed, murmuring to an awake and crying Jack that it was going to be okay. He handed the sheet to Darius.

'Stay with me, Priestess,' he told me. He glanced at Heath and Erik. 'Keep talking to her, both of you.'

Erik took the hand Stevie Rae had let loose. 'I'm here, Z.' He threaded his fingers with mine. 'You have to make it through this. We need you.' He paused and his beautiful blue eyes met mine. 'I need you, and I'm sorry about all that stuff before.'

Then Heath raised my other hand to his lips, kissing it softly. 'Hey, Zo, did I tell you I haven't had one drink for more than two months?'

It was seriously weird to have both of my guys there. I was glad they weren't banging their chests at each other, but I understood that might not be a particularly good thing because it meant that I was hurt even worse than I'd realized.

'That's good, huh? I've totally stopped drinking,' Heath said.

I tried to smile at him. It *was* good. The reason I'd broken up with Heath right before I was Marked was his drinking. It had totally gotten out of control, and—

Darius pulled Erik's wadded-up shirt from my chest and quickly ripped the top of my dress in half so that I felt the cool air of the tunnel against my blood-drenched skin.

'Sweet Goddess, no!' Erik blurted.

'Ah, shit!' Heath was shaking his head back and forth. 'This is bad. Really bad. No one can live with—'

'No *human* can live with this kind of wound, but she's not a human and I'm not going to let her die.' Darius interrupted Heath as he (thankfully) covered my naked boobs with the sheet.

I made the mistake of glancing down. Maybe it was a good thing that I didn't have the energy to scream. There was a long laceration that went all the way from the top of my left shoulder, across my chest a couple of inches above my breasts, and didn't end until it sliced through the skin on my right shoulder. The cut was deep and jagged. The edges of my skin flapped sickeningly apart, showing way more muscle and fat and layers of skin than I was ever meant to see. Blood seeped from all along the terrible wound, but not as much blood as I would expect. Was that because I was running out of it? Hell! It was probably because I was running out! My breath started to come in hysterical little pants.

'Zoey, look at me,' Erik said. When I kept staring down at the wound Darius was pressing thick pads of gauze against, Erik took my chin gently in his hand and turned my face up, forcing me to look at him. 'You're going to be fine. You have to be fine.'

'Yeah, Zo. Just don't look at it,' Heath said. 'You know, like you told me whenever I messed myself up playing football. You used to say, "Just don't look at it and it won't hurt so bad."'

Erik let loose of my chin and I managed to nod. Had I been able to talk I would have told both of them, *Hell no, I'm not looking at it again!* I'd already scared the crap out of myself. No need to revisit it.

'Get that circle cast,' Darius said.

'We're ready,' Damien said.

I looked around (definitely avoiding glancing down at myself again) to see that Damien, Stevie Rae, and the Twins had taken their positions in a circle around us.

'Then get it cast!' Darius snapped.

There was a pause into which Erin finally spoke. 'But Zoey always casts the circles. We never have.'

'I'll do it.' Aphrodite stepped within the circle and marched over to Damien. Damien gave her a look that even I could see was filled with doubt. 'You don't have to be a fledgling or a vampyre to cast a circle. All you have to be is attached to Nyx. And I'm attached to Nyx,' she said firmly. 'But I need you guys to be behind me on this. Are you?'

Damien paused long enough to look at me. With an effort that seemed to sap the last of my strength, I nodded at him. He smiled at me and nodded back.

'I'm behind you,' Damien told Aphrodite.

Aphrodite looked from him to the Twins. 'We're with you, too.' Erin spoke for both of them.

Finally she turned to Stevie Rae, who wiped her eyes, sent me a big, confident smile, and then she said to Aphrodite, 'You've saved my life twice. I'm trusting that you can do the same for Zoey.'

I saw Aphrodite's face flush, her chin lift, and her shoulders straighten and knew that for the first time in a very long time she felt like an accepted part of a group.

'Okay, let's do this,' Aphrodite said. 'It's the first element, the one we all embrace from our first breaths to our last. I call wind to the circle!' Sure enough, I saw a sudden breeze begin to lift Aphrodite's and Damien's hair, and with a look of obvious relief, she moved clockwise around the circle to Shaunee.

And then I stopped paying attention – or rather my attention started to narrow, getting all gray and tunnel-vision-like around the edges.

'Zoey, are you still with us?' Darius asked as he pressed more gauze against my chest.

I couldn't answer him. My head felt really light, but the rest of my body was unbelievably heavy, like some moron had parked a Mack truck on top of me.

'Z?' Erik was saying. 'Z, look at me!'

'Zoey? Babe?' Heath looked like he was going to cry again.

Okay, I really wanted to say something to make them feel better, but it just wasn't possible. I couldn't make my body work anymore. It was like I'd become a distant spectator in the game that was going on around me. I could watch, but I couldn't play.

'All the elements but spirit have been evoked,' Aphrodite said. She was standing beside Darius. 'That's the element Zoey always personifies, and I feel weird calling it in her place.'

'Call it,' Darius said. He glanced up from me and looked around the circle at my friends. 'Concentrate the power of your element on Zoey. Think about filling her with strength and warmth and life.'

Vaguely I heard Aphrodite evoking spirit, although I didn't feel the quickening its presence usually gave me. I briefly felt a distant warmth and thought for a second that I also smelled rain and cut grass, but that was gone quickly while the gray framing my vision became thicker and thicker.

'Are you the human Zoey was Imprinted with?' I heard Darius talking to Heath. I listened, but couldn't manage to care too much about what they were saying.

'Yes,' Heath said.

'Good. Your blood would be even better than Aphrodite's for her.'

'That's the first good news I've heard in ages,' Aphrodite mumbled, wiping her eyes with the back of her hand.

'Are you willing to allow Zoey to drink from you?'

'Of course!' Heath said. 'Just tell me what I need to do.'

'Sit up here. Hold her head in your lap. Then give me your arm,' Darius told Heath.

Heath got up on the end of the table, and with Erik and Darius's help my head was soon resting against his warm thigh, like he was a living pillow. Heath held his arm out and Darius grasped it firmly. My mind was too fuzzy to make sense of what they were doing until Darius reached behind him and took the all-purpose knife/scissors/bottle opener from the first aid kit, flipped the knife partway open, and pressed the blade against the soft skin on the inside of Heath's muscular forearm.

The scent of his blood settled over me like a delicious fog.

'Press her mouth against it,' Darius said. 'Make her drink.'

'Come on, babe. Take some of this. It'll help you get better.'

Okay, my rational mind knew that Erik was standing right there beside me watching along with all of my best friends. Under normal circumstances I would never have done what I did next, no matter how delicious and amazing and enticing Heath's blood smelled.

But I wasn't currently experiencing anything that even mildly resembled normal circumstances. So when Heath pressed his bleeding arm against my lips, I opened my mouth, sank my teeth deep into him, and started sucking.

Heath moaned and wrapped his other arm around me, pressing his face into my hair as I drank from him. The world immediately narrowed so that there was only Heath and me as his blood exploded into my body. With that first drink, awareness slammed back into my chest, and with it pain so intense that I would have wrenched my mouth from his skin had he not tightened his grip on me and whispered into my ear, 'No! You can't stop. If I can stand it, so can you, Zo.'

See, I knew I wasn't just causing him to feel the exquisite pleasure feeding from a human usually caused both vamp and victim. We'd instantly Imprinted again. Even in the bad shape I was in I could tell that. Heath's whole awareness filled me along with his blood, and we were bound together through the magical fabric that was the need and attraction between human and vampyre, stitched together in a single garment of the ancient bond that was an Imprint. But I wasn't just drinking from him. I was feeding in a frenzy that was a natural instinct for survival, and through our connection Heath was feeling my pain and fear and need, everything that I'd been numb to when my body was in near-fatal shock. His blood had changed that, though. It had revitalized me, and in doing so it had wrenched me out of the deadly shock state and thrown me directly into searing pain and the realization that I was perilously close to dying.

I whimpered, still feeding from him, but was miserable because I knew what I was making him feel.

Of course, he knew what I was feeling, too, and how sorry I was that I was hurting him.

'It's okay, babe. It's okay. It's not that bad, really,' he whispered in my ear through teeth gritted against the intense mixture of pain and desire.

I don't know how much time had passed when I realized

173

that, even though the cut across my chest hurt like hell, my body was warm, and I could feel caressing me a soft breeze that carried the scent of spring rain and a hay-filled meadow. My spirit, too, felt invigorated, and I knew that Heath's blood had energized me enough that now I was able to accept the healing aid of the elements that comforted my soul as they soothed my body.

At about the same time I realized Heath had stopped talking to me. I opened my eyes and glanced up. He was kinda slumped over me but was being held upright by Darius's firm grip on his shoulders. His eyes were closed and his face was pale.

Instantly I pulled my mouth from his arm. 'Heath!' Had I killed him? Panicked, I tried to sit up, but the pain shooting through my body stopped me.

'The human is fine, Priestess,' Darius soothed. 'Stanch the wound on his arm so that he will not lose any more blood.'

Automatically I ran my tongue over the narrow slice on Heath's arm and the bigger gash I'd made when I bit him while I thought, *Heal . . . don't bleed anymore*, and when I pulled away this time I saw that the knife wound, as well as the marks my teeth had left, had completely stopped bleeding.

'You can close the circle,' Darius told Aphrodite, who was watching me with undisguised curiosity.

See, I wanted to tell her, *there are a lot of different kinds of Imprints. What I have with Heath is definitely not what you have with Stevie Rae*. But I couldn't summon the energy to say the words. Actually, I wasn't looking forward to the gazillion questions I was sure she was going to have for me. And then before she turned to Stevie Rae to begin thanking and then sending away the elements, I saw Aphrodite send Darius a sexy smile filled with promise, and I remembered that the first Imprint I'd shared with Heath had been broken when I'd had sex with Loren, and I realized that it was Darius who was going to have to field her questions. By the intimate smile he gave her in return, I was guessing he was going to like that kind of questioning wayyyy more than I ever would.

Okay, gross.

As a grinning Aphrodite closed the circle, Darius turned back to Heath and me.

'Erik, help me get him over to the bed,' Darius said.

A stone-faced Erik lifted my head out of Heath's lap. He and Darius carried him the short distance to the bed and laid his still body on the spot so recently vacated by Jack (who was watching, wide-eyed, from the side of the room while he manically petted Duchess over and over).

'Go get something to eat and drink fast. Oh, and find some more of Venus's wine,' Darius told Jack. 'But tell the red fledglings to stay away,' he added before Jack nodded and scampered off with Duchess at his heels.

'They're not gonna attack Heath,' Stevie Rae said. She came to me and held my hand. 'Especially now that he's Imprinted with Zoey again. His blood smells wrong.'

'I don't have time to test whether they will or will not right now,' Darius said. He came back over to the bed and started inspecting my wound again. 'Good. It has completely stopped bleeding.'

'I think I'll take your word for that. I don't really want to look again.' I was pleased as hell that I had my voice back, even if I did sound weak and more than a little shaky. 'Thanks, guys, for the circle,' I told my friends, who grinned at me and started to rush the table.

'No!' Darius put up a hand, halting their jubilation. 'I need room to work. Aphrodite, find some of those butterfly bandages in that kit and bring them over to me.'

'Hey, am I done almost dying?' I asked the warrior.

Darius looked up from my wound to meet my eyes, and I saw there a relief that told me exactly how close I must have been to not making it.

'You are done dying.' He paused, clearly at the brink of saying more.

'But?' I prompted.

'There's no but about it,' Stevie Rae said quickly. 'You're done dyin'. Period.'

I didn't look away from Darius, and he finally answered me. 'But you need more help then I can give you if you're going to recover fully.'

'What do you mean, more help?' Aphrodite asked as she moved to Darius's side, a handful of weird Band-Aids clenched in her fist.

Darius sighed. 'Zoey's wound is severe. The human's blood has saved her life by replacing the blood she lost and strengthening her enough that she was able to accept the energy of the elements, but not even Zoey can recover from so great a wound by herself. She is still just a fledgling, though even were she a fully Changed vampyre, an injury like this would be difficult for her to recover from.'

'But she looks better now, and she's talking to us,' Damien said.

'Yeah, I don't feel like I'm not really here anymore,' I said.

Darius nodded. 'That is all good, but the truth is you need many stitches so that the wound can close and heal.'

'What about these?' Aphrodite held up the butterfly Band-Aid packages. 'I thought that's why you needed them.'

'Those bandages are only temporary. She needs real stitches.'

'So stitch me up.' I tried to sound as brave as I could, even though the thought of Darius sewing up my flesh made me want to puke or cry, or both.

'There are no sutures in the kit,' Darius said.

'Can't we get some?' Erik asked. I noticed as he spoke, he was looking everywhere but at me. 'I could drive Heath's truck to the St John's pharmacy and Stevie Rae could do her mind control thing on a doc there. We'd bring back whatever you need, and then you could stitch her up.'

'Yeah, we can do that. I can even grab a doctor if you want and bring him down here, then wipe his memory clean when we return him,' Stevie Rae said.

'Okay, Stevie Rae, that's a nice offer,' I said, more than a little disturbed that she was talking about what amounted to kidnapping and brainwashing. 'But I really don't think that's a good idea.'

'It's not that simple to solve the problem anyway,' Darius said.

'So explain it so it is that simple,' Heath said, propping himself up on his elbows and looking totally like crap even though he smiled sweetly at me.

'Zoey needs more than a doctor's care. Zoey needs to be around adult vampyres so that the damage to her body doesn't become fatal.'

'Hang on. I thought you said I was done almost dying,' I said.

'You are done almost dying from this particular wound, but if you don't get within a coven of vampyres, and I mean more than one or two or three of us, the damage caused to your body will use up your reserves of strength and you will begin rejecting the Change.' Darius paused, letting what he was saying sink in with all of us. 'You'll die from that. You may come back to us, like Stevie Rae and the rest of the red fledglings did, but you may not.'

'Or you may come back like that stupid Stark kid and be a crazed asshole who starts attacking us,' Aphrodite said.

'So you really don't have any choice,' Darius said. 'We have to get you back to the House of Night.'

'Well, hell,' I said.

CHAPTER FOURTEEN

'BUT SHE CAN'T GO BACK! KALONA'S THERE,' ERIN SAID.

'Not to mention the Raven Mockers,' Shaunee said.

'One of them did this to her,' Erik said. 'Right, Heath?'

'Yeah, the thing was disgusting,' Heath said. He was chugging brown pop from a can Jack had handed him while he stuffed nacho cheese Doritos in his face. I was glad to see he looked lots better, almost completely like himself, which proves Doritos and brown pop really are health foods.

'Then they'll just attack her again, so taking her there won't really save Zoey. It'll just enable them to finish killing her,' Erik said.

'Well, maybe not,' I admitted reluctantly. 'The Raven Mocker didn't attack me, or at least, not on purpose. It was going to attack Heath and I kinda got in the way.' I gave Heath an apologetic smile. 'Actually, it freaked when it hurt me.'

'Because it said its dad had been looking for you,' Heath added. 'I remember. He did freak right after he cut you. Zoey, babe, I'm sorry I almost got you killed.'

'Didn't I fucking tell you!' Aphrodite practically snarled at Heath. 'What happened was your fault! You shouldn't have been here!'

'Whoa, Aphrodite, hang on,' I said. I started to put my hands up to make simmer-down motions to her, but Darius shot me a 'hold still' look. Plus, it really did hurt whenever I moved too much. So I settled for words with no hand motions, which felt kinda weird. 'You kept blaming Heath before. What gives?'

She looked at me and I swear she fidgeted. Aphrodite actually fidgeted.

I frowned at her. 'What's the deal, Aphrodite?'

When she didn't say anything, Stevie Rae sighed and said, ''Cause she's know-it-all Vision Girl, and this time she was in the dark.'

'Do not tap into my mind like that!' Aphrodite shouted at Stevie Rae.

'Then answer Z's question. She feels too crappy to pull it out of you,' Stevie Rae said.

Aphrodite turned her back to Stevie Rae. 'It's just that I expected to get a heads-up if you were going to die, that's all.'

'Huh?' I said, speaking for all of us who were staring at her with question-mark faces.

She rolled her eyes. 'Hello! I've had two death visions of you, so it's only logical to assume if you were going to be all grotesquely close to death, I'd know a little something about it, that's all. But Nyx didn't clue me in with any kind of a vision, so I figured Football Joe over there messed things up 'cause the goddess didn't expect him to be poking around where he's not supposed to be.' She frowned at Heath and shook her head in disgust. 'I mean, come on! Are you special needs, special services or what? Weren't you almost killed here once before?'

'Yeah, but Zo saved me, so I figured she'd make like a superhero again if things got bad, and we'd be okay,' Heath said. Then his cute, goofy expression changed and he looked like someone had just taken away his birthday. 'But I didn't think I'd be the cause of getting Zoey almost killed.'

'And they say football players aren't brilliant. Wherever did they come up with that?' Aphrodite said sarcastically.

'All right, that's enough,' I said. 'Heath, you didn't almost get me killed. The stupid Raven Mocker almost got me killed. Do you think I would have gone willingly with it? Hell no!'

'But I—' he began.

I cut him off. 'Heath, if you hadn't been there I would have eventually stuck my head aboveground. The gross birdman said they were looking for me, which means sooner or later they would have found me and I would have had to fight them. Period, the end. And, Aphrodite, just because you get visions doesn't mean you know everything. Sometimes stuff happens even you can't foresee. Get used to it and stop being so darn mean. Plus, this isn't just about Raven Mockers. Before it attacked, it looked like Neferet,' I finished in a rush.

'What?' Damien said. 'How could it have looked like Neferet?'

'I don't have a clue, but I promise when I looked up she was there. She smiled a terrible, creepy smile at me. I blinked, and then she was gone and there was a Raven Mocker in her place. That's all I know.' I knew there was something else I needed to remember about what had happened, but my mind was feeling fuzzy with pain and I slumped down, totally exhausted.

'We have to get her back to the House of Night,' Darius said.

'And take her right to Neferet? That doesn't sound smart,' Heath said.

'Nevertheless, she has to go there.'

I looked up at Darius. 'Isn't there some other way?'

'Not if you want to live,' he said.

'Then Zoey has to go back to school,' Damien said.

'Oh, great! So the Raven Mockers and Neferet have her exactly where they want her!' Aphrodite yelled.

I looked at Aphrodite and saw beyond the hateful demeanor she wore like armor to the sincere worry she had for me. Basically, she was scared. I couldn't really blame her. I was scared, too – for myself, for my friends. Hell, I was scared for the whole darn world.

'They want me there, but they want me alive,' I said solemnly. 'That means before they do anything else, they'll make sure I'm healed.'

'Are you remembering that the House of Night's healer is Neferet?' Damien said.

'Of course I remember,' I said irritably. 'I'm just hoping Kalona wants me alive worse than she wants me dead.'

'But what if she does something terrible to you after you're healed?' Aphrodite said.

'Then you guys will have to come get me out of there,' I said.

'Uh, Zoey,' Damien said. 'You sound like you think you're going back there alone. You're not.'

'Yeah, no way,' Erin said.

'We're not letting you out of our sight,' Shaunee said.

'Where you go, we go,' Jack said.

'That's right. We're in this together,' Stevie Rae said. 'Remember the only thing that was the same about both of the death visions Aphrodite had of you was the fact that you were alone. So we're not lettin' you be alone.'

Erik's voice sliced between us. 'We can't all go back with her.'

'Look, Erik,' Aphrodite sneered. 'We get that you're Mr Jealous and that seeing your girlfriend sucking on another guy is probably not cool with you, but you're going to just have to learn to deal.'

Erik completely ignored her. Instead, he met my eyes and I saw that he had, once again, reached into his acting bag of tricks and pulled out the character of a stranger. As I studied him, I saw absolutely no trace of the guy who wanted me so bad that his passion had gotten kinda scary. I couldn't even find any trace of the possessive Neanderthal who had wanted to kick Heath's butt and boss me around. He was able to cover all of those versions of himself and his emotions so effectively that I was beginning to wonder who the hell the real Erik was.

'Stevie Rae can't go back with you. If she goes, who will be here to control the red fledglings? Aphrodite can't go back with you. She's just a human, and as much as I'd like something to eat her, I imagine you and Nyx probably want to keep her around.'

'Before he says shit else, you need to know that I'm going back with you, no matter what,' Heath said.

Erik didn't so much as blink. 'Yeah, and you'll get your stupid human ass kicked, probably killed, even faster than Aphrodite would. And along with yourself, you'll probably get Zoey killed for real this time. Zoey has to go back, because she'll die if she doesn't. Darius is the only one who should go back with her. Anyone else is taking a big risk. For sure they'll be trapped at the House of Night. Maybe they'll even be killed.'

As usual, the room exploded as my friends yelled their own not-so-positive opinions of Erik's emotionless proclamation.

'Guys . . . guys . . .' I tried to speak over them but didn't have the energy.

'Silence!' Darius commanded, and everyone finally shut up.

'Thanks,' I said to him, then I looked at my friends. 'I

think Erik's right. Anyone who goes back with me is at risk, and I don't want to lose you guys.'

'But aren't the five of you stronger when you're together?' Heath asked.

'Yes, we are,' Damien answered.

Heath nodded. 'That's what I thought. So shouldn't those of you who have a special thing with an element go back with Zoey?'

'An affinity for an element,' Damien explained. 'That's what it's called. And I agree with Heath. The circle should stay complete.'

'It can't,' Darius said. 'Stevie Rae has to stay here with the red fledglings. If she's trapped on campus or, worst case scenario, killed, we have no way of knowing if Erik's presence, as a Changed vampyre, will be enough to keep them healthy and under control. In case Zoey and I were the only ones who noticed, let me tell all of you that Kramisha looked as if she was having trouble controlling herself around Heath. The ripple effect that might be caused by Stevie Rae's absence could be disastrous. So the circle cannot stay complete.'

'Wait, maybe it can,' Aphrodite said.

'What do you mean?' I asked her.

'Well, I can't represent earth anymore. That affinity was given back to Stevie Rae when she Changed, and the one time I tried to evoke it, the element was pissed and zapped me.'

I nodded, remembering how upsetting it had been for Aphrodite to believe that Nyx had abandoned her, which she really hadn't. But still, the girl was definitely unable to evoke earth anymore.

'But,' Aphrodite continued, 'Zoey can evoke earth, just like she can any of the five elements. Right?'

I nodded again. 'Right.'

'And I just evoked spirit without any problem. So what if we just change positions? Zoey personifies earth and I call spirit. It worked just a little while ago. I think as long as Zoey's around to help nudge spirit toward me, there's no reason it won't work again.'

'She has a point, which makes the circle complete without me,' Stevie Rae said. 'As much as I want to stay with you, Darius is right. I can't take the chance that I can't get back here to my fledglings.'

'You are all forgetting another reason the rest of you can't return with Zoey,' Darius said. 'Neferet, and perhaps even Kalona, can read your minds. Which means everything you know about the red fledglings and this safe haven, they will know, too.'

'Uh, guys, I have an idea,' Heath spoke up. 'Okay, I don't really know much about this stuff, so I might be totally wrong, but can't each of you get help from an element to, I dunno, set up some kind of road-block around your minds?'

I blinked in surprise at Heath and then grinned. 'You might be on to something. What do you think, Damien?'

Damien looked excited. 'I think we were idiots not to have thought of it ourselves.' He smiled at Heath. 'Well done, you!'

Heath shrugged and looked adorable. 'No problem.

Sometimes it takes someone from the outside to figure stuff out.'

'You really believe that could work?' Darius asked.

'It should,' Damien said. 'Or at least it should for those of us who have an actual affinity for an element. The Twins and I have called our elements to protect and shield before. It shouldn't be hard to ask them to put up barriers around our minds.' He hesitated and glanced at Aphrodite. 'But can you do it? You don't really have an affinity for spirit, do you? I'm not trying to be mean, but just because you can stand in Zoey's place and evoke the element within a circle, it doesn't mean you are actually able to conjure spirit on your own.'

'I don't have to conjure spirit to protect my mind,' Aphrodite said. 'Neferet hasn't been able to read my mind from the day I was Marked, just like she hasn't been able to read Zoey. And I have to tell you I'm getting damn tired of you guys giving me shit because I'm a human again!'

'Okay, you're right about the mind-reading part. Sorry about that,' Damien said. 'But I think we should know for sure if spirit will really work for Aphrodite, *before* we blunder back into the House of Night.'

'Yeah, Aphrodite,' Jack said. 'We're not being judgmental about you being a human and all. We just need to know if your spirit mojo works.'

I had a sudden thought. 'It doesn't really matter whether Aphrodite can conjure the element outside a circle casting, because I can. Spirit,' I said softly, 'come to me.' As easily as drawing a breath, I evoked the element and felt its wonderful presence.

'Now go to Aphrodite. Protect and serve her.' I flicked my fingers wearily in her direction, and felt spirit rush away from me. An instant later Aphrodite's big blue eyes widened and she smiled.

'Hey! It works,' she said.

'How long can you keep that up?' Erik asked me.

Annoyed at the total lack of emotion in his voice, I snapped, 'As long as I have to.'

'So the circle stays intact,' Damien said.

'Yeah, we all go with Z back to school,' Erin said.

'Together. The five of us,' Shaunee said.

'I feel like one of the dorky Mouseketeers,' Aphrodite said, but she was smiling.

'We're agreed, then,' Darius said. 'The five of you and I will return. Stevie Rae, Erik, Jack, and Heath stay here.'

'Hell no, he doesn't stay here,' Erik said, finally showing some emotion.

'Dude, you don't have shit to say about it. Anyway, I'm not staying. I'm going with Zoey.'

'You can't, Heath. It's way too dangerous,' I said.

'Aphrodite's human and she can go. So can I,' he said stubbornly.

'Moron football boy, first, I might be human, but I'm also special, so I go. Second, you can't go because they can use you to get to Zoey. You're Imprinted with her again. They hurt you; they hurt Zoey. So show some sense and take your butt back to suburbia.'

'Oh. I hadn't thought about it like that,' Heath said.

'You have to go home, Heath. We'll talk later after things have settled down.'

'Shouldn't I stay here, where I'm close to you? So if you need me you can get to me fast.'

I wanted to say yes, even with Erik watching me all dead-faced and even knowing that the best thing for Heath was if I never saw him again. Our Imprint was incredibly strong, even more so than it had been the first time. I could feel him, so close and sweet and familiar, and even though I knew it was wrong and knew I shouldn't, I wanted to keep him beside me. But then I remembered how Kramisha had looked at him, like she wanted to take a chomp outta him. I knew that his blood would taste funny to any other fledgling or vampyre because we'd Imprinted, but I couldn't be sure that would stop them from wanting to sample it. Just thinking about someone else drinking from Heath made me feel seriously pissed.

'No, Heath,' I insisted. 'You have to go home. It's not safe for you here.'

'I don't care if I'm safe or not. I care about being with you,' Heath said.

'I know, but I care if you're safe or not. So, go home. I'll call you as soon as I can.'

'Okay, but I'll be back here the second you call,' he said.

'Want me to walk him outside?' Stevie Rae asked. 'The tunnels can be kinda confusing if you're not familiar with them.'

Plus, I can stop any red fledgling who has a mind to take a bite out of him. The thought was there, but unsaid in the air between us.

'Okay, thanks, Stevie Rae,' I said.

'Erik, hold Zoey up. Aphrodite, finish wrapping this Ace bandage around her. I better go out there with Heath, too,' Darius said.

'The Raven Mocker was in the tree above his truck, kinda perched on the roof of the depot,' I told Darius.

'I'll be vigilant, Priestess,' Darius said. 'Come on, boy. You need to go home.'

'We'll be back in a sec, Z,' Stevie Rae said.

Instead of following Darius and Stevie Rae from the room, Heath came to me. He cupped my cheek with his hand and smiled. 'Stay safe, okay, Zo?'

'I'll try. You, too,' I said. 'And, Heath, thanks for saving my life.'

'Anytime, Zoey. And I mean that. Anytime.' Then, like we were alone and not in the middle of a room with my friends (and boyfriend) gawking at us, Heath bent and kissed me. He tasted like Doritos and brown pop and Heath. Through it all I could smell him, the distinct scent of his blood that was Imprinted uniquely to me and, because of that, literally the most fascinating, delicious smell on this earth.

'I love you, babe,' he whispered. He kissed me one more time. As he was leaving he waved at my friends. 'See you guys around,' he said. I was only half surprised when Jack and Damien called bye and the Twins made kissing noises at him. I mean, Heath is cute. Totally cute. Right before he ducked out the blanket door he glanced back at Erik, who was standing beside me. 'Hey, dude, I'm holding you personally responsible if anything hurts her.' Then Heath gave Erik his charming, lopsided grin. 'Oh, and how about you make my job totally easy and try to boss her around a bunch while I'm gone?' Chuckling to himself, Heath finally left the room.

Aphrodite laughed, which she tried to cover with a cough.

'Ex-boyfriend does have a way about him,' Shaunee said.

'Yes, he does, Twin,' Erin said. 'Not to mention a cute butt.'

'Uh, awkward, anyone?' Jack said.

CHAPTER FIFTEEN

THE TWINS MUTTERED HASTY APOLOGIES, SHOOTING ERIK guilty looks. Erik, looking like he was carved out of stone, told Aphrodite, 'Here, I'll lift her up a little and you can wrap the bandage around her.'

'Fine by me,' Aphrodite said.

So, without meeting my eyes, Erik slid his hands under my shoulders and gently lifted my torso off the table. While I gritted my teeth against the pain and Aphrodite wrapped the Ace bandage around me, I wondered what the hell I was going to do about Erik and Heath. Erik and I were supposedly back together, but after the scene in the basement I wasn't one hundred percent sure we should be together. I mean, he said he loved me, which was all well and good, but did loving me mean he'd turned all possessive and jerkish? And besides that, was what we had together strong enough to tolerate another Imprint with Heath, especially now that it wasn't just an abstract idea? Now that he'd seen Heath and me together, was there any way Erik and I could be together?

I looked up at him as he held me so carefully. Feeling my gaze on him, his blue eyes shifted to me. He didn't look like a stone man anymore. He just looked sad. Really, really sad. Did I still want to be Erik's girlfriend? The longer I looked into his eyes, the more I thought that maybe I did. Then where did that leave me with Heath? Back to where I was with both of these guys before I'd cheated on them and let Loren trick me into giving him my virginity.

It had been an uncomfortable boyfriend triangle then, and it was even worse now. But what the hell was I going to do? The truth was I cared about both of them.

God, it's exhausting being me.

When Aphrodite was done bandaging me, Erik asked Jack to bring him a pillow from the bed, and then he put me carefully back down with my head and shoulders resting on its softness.

'You guys had better get ready to leave,' Erik said to the Twins, Damien, and Aphrodite. 'I'll bet Darius will want to get Zoey back to the House of Night right away.'

'That means we have to get our purses from Kramisha's room,' Shaunee said.

'Like I would forget my new winter season Ed Hardy purse, Twin?' Erin said.

'Of course not, Twin. I'm just sayin' . . .' Their voices faded as they hurried from the room.

'I want to go with you,' Jack said, looking close to tears.

'I want you to come, too,' Darius said. 'But it's too dangerous. You have to stay here with Erik and Stevie Rae until we know exactly what we're up against.'

'My mind understands that, but my heart says something else,' Jack said, leaning his head against Damien's shoulder. 'It's just . . . just . . .' Jack took a deep breath and finished on a sob, 'It's just poop that I can't go!'

'We're going to step down the tunnel a ways,' Damien said, putting his arm around Jack. 'Just have Darius yell when he's ready.' Then Damien led a stricken Jack out of the room, with Duchess trailing sadly along behind.

'I'm going to go find my cat,' Aphrodite said. 'I'll see if I can find your little orange creature, too.'

'Don't you think we should leave the cats here?' I asked.

Aphrodite raised a blonde brow at me. 'Since when could cats be told what to do?'

I sighed. 'You're right. They'd just follow us back and then complain at us for years about leaving them behind.'

'Tell Darius I'll be right back.' Aphrodite ducked out through the blanket.

That left Erik and me alone.

Without looking at me he started to move toward the doorway saying, 'I'm going to—'

'Erik, don't go. Can't we talk for just a second?'

He stopped, his back still to me. His head was bowed and his shoulders were slumped. He looked utterly defeated.

'Erik, please . . .'

He spun around and I saw there were tears pooling in his eyes. 'I'm so damn pissed I don't know what the hell to do! And what's worse is that this,' he paused, gesturing to the huge Ace bandage hiding the wound that sliced across my chest, 'is really my fault.'

'Your fault?'

'If I hadn't been such a possessive asshole in the basement, you wouldn't have gone outside with Heath. You were sending him away, but I had to push things and piss you off, so you went out there with him.' He ran his hand through his thick dark hair. 'It's just that Heath makes me so damn jealous! He's known you since you two were kids. I just—' He hesitated and his jaw clenched and unclenched. 'I just didn't want to lose you again, so I acted like a jerk, and not only did you almost die, but I lost you again!'

I blinked at him. So he hadn't been acting like stone man because he didn't care or because he was mad at me. He'd been hiding his emotions because he thought all of this was his fault. Jeesh – I hadn't had a clue.

I held out my hand to him. 'Erik, come here.' Slowly he came over to me and took my hand.

'I acted like a jerk,' he said.

'Yeah, you did. But I should have shown some sense and not gone outside with Heath.'

Erik looked at me for a long time before he spoke. 'It was hard to see you with him. To see you drink from him.'

'I wish there could have been some other way,' I said. I did wish it, and not just because it had been uncomfortable for Erik to watch. I loved Heath, but I'd made the decision not to be with him again, not to ever Imprint with him again. I knew the best thing for both of us, especially for Heath, was to be out of each other's lives, and that's what I'd planned. Sadly, my life rarely goes according to my plans. I sighed and tried to put some of what I was feeling into words. 'I can't help loving Heath. He's been part of my life for a long time, and now that we're Imprinted again, he literally carries part of me with him, even though I didn't mean for it to happen.'

'I don't know how much of your human boyfriend I can stand,' Erik said.

I kept meeting Erik's steady gaze and almost blurted, *I'm not sure how much of your possessiveness I can stand*, but I was too tired. I'd save that till later, after I had more time and energy to think things through. Instead I just said, 'He's not my boyfriend. He's the human I've Imprinted with. There's a big difference.'

'Consort,' Erik said bitterly. 'It's called being the High Priestess's human consort. Many of them have one. Often they have more than one.'

I blinked in surprise. I sure hadn't gotten to that part in my Vamp Sociology class. I mean, was this consort stuff even covered in *The Fledgling Handbook?* Guess I'd have to read the darn thing more carefully. I did remember Darius mentioning something about it being difficult for a human to be involved with a High Priestess the day Heath and I had had our official breakup scene, and Darius had definitely used the word 'consort' for the human. 'Huh. Um. Does that mean the High Priestess doesn't have a vampyre, uh, consort?'

'Mate,' he said quietly. 'If he's a human who has Imprinted with a High Priestess, he's called her consort. If he's a vampyre, he's given the title of the High Priestess's mate. And no. It doesn't mean she can't have both.'

That seemed like good news to me. Clearly it wasn't such good news to Erik, but at least I was beginning to believe other priestesses had gone through this kind of boyfriend stress before. Maybe I could read up on it or tactfully question Darius when the end-of-the-world stuff was resolved. For the time being I decided to put a Band-Aid on the issue and clean up the consequences later. If there was a later. 'Okay, Erik. I don't know what I'm going to do about Heath. It's all a little too much for me to deal with right now on top of everything else. Hell, I don't know what I'm going to do about you, either.'

'We're together,' Erik said softly. 'And I want us to stay together.'

I opened my mouth to tell him I really wasn't totally sure that was the best idea, but Erik bent and kissed me gently on the lips, silencing my comment. Then someone cleared his throat and we looked at the entryway to see Heath standing there, looking pale and pissed.

'Heath! What are you doing here?' I hated how shrill and

guilty I sounded as I frantically wondered how much he'd overheard.

'Darius sent me to tell you the roads are too bad. There's no way I can get back to B.A. tonight. He and Stevie Rae went to find a four-wheel drive so that he can get you and the rest of the fledglings back to the House of Night.' He paused. I recognized a tone I'd only heard in his voice a very few times. He was seriously pissed, but he was also hurt. The last time he'd sounded like this had been when he'd told me I'd killed part of his soul when I'd had sex with Loren and broken our Imprint. 'Hey, carry on. Pretend I'm not here, just like you were doing before. Didn't mean to interrupt you two.'

'Heath,' I began, but just then Aphrodite, followed by a bunch of cats, including my Nala and her hateful white Persian, appropriately named Maleficent, came into the room.

'Awkward. Again,' Aphrodite added, looking knowingly from Heath to Erik and me.

I sighed and realized my head was starting to hurt almost as much as the cut across my chest. Then the Twins and Kramisha piled into the room, too.

'Ah, oh,' Shaunee said.

'What's ex-boyfriend doing here?' Erin said.

'The roads are too bad. Heath can't get home,' I said.

'So that means he be staying here?' Kramisha asked, giving Heath a long look.

'He'll have to. He's safer here than at the House of Night,' I said, keeping an eye on Kramisha and adding silently to myself that I wasn't convinced he'd be safe here either. 'He and I have Imprinted again,' I added for good measure.

Kramisha curled her lip. 'I know that. I can smell you in his blood. He ain't good for nothin' now 'cept for being your boy toy.'

'He's not—' I started, but Heath's sharp voice cut me off.

'No, the girl's right. That's all I am to you,' Heath said bluntly.

'Heath. That's not how I think of you,' I said.

'Yeah, well, I don't want to say shit more about it. I'm your blood donor, and that's it.' He turned away from me and I saw him grab a bottle of wine someone had left by the bed and take a big swig of it.

Damien, a puffy-eyed Jack, and Duchess (causing all of the cats except Nala to hiss like insane creatures) crowded back into the room then.

'Hey, Heath,' Jack said. 'I thought you were on your way home.'

'I can't get home. Looks like I'm stuck here with you in the left-behind pile.'

Jack frowned, close to bursting into tears again. 'Damien's not leaving me behind. Not really. I just— I just can't go with him right now this second.'

'That's right. We'll be back together as soon as we can,' Damien said, putting his arm around Jack.

'Okay, I hate to interrupt all this gay-boy romance stuff, but I wrote me some more poems when I woke up and thought you better see them,' Kramisha said.

That broke though my confusion about what to do about Heath and Erik. 'You're right. I do need to see them,' I said. 'Damien, did Jack get a chance to explain to you about Kramisha's poetry?'

'Yes. I even got a copy of the poems before Kramisha went to sleep and read them while Jack and I were on watch,' Damien said.

'What the hell are you guys talking about?' Aphrodite said.

'When you were all drunk and disorderly, Z discovered poetry written on the walls of Kramisha's room,' Erin said.

'Written by Kramisha, but all of it seemed to be about Kalona, which is totally creepy,' Shaunee said.

'It's like she's channeling abstract images about him,' Damien said. 'I think the poems in her room were meant to catch our attention, which means we need to check out everything Kramisha writes.'

'Oh, great. That's all we need. More gloom and doom poetry,' Aphrodite said.

'Well speaking of, here's two new ones.' Kramisha tried to hand me the couple of sheets of paper the poems were written on, but moving my arms up so I could hold them made me suck air with pain.

'Here.' Erik smoothly took the papers from her. Then he brought them to me and held them up so that Damien, the Twins, Aphrodite, Jack, and I could read them at the same time. The first one was baffling.

What once bound him
Will make him flee
Place of power – joining of five

Night
Spirit
Blood
Humanity
Earth

Joined not to conquer,
Instead to overcome
Night leads to Spirit
Blood binds Humanity
And Earth completes.

'That makes my head hurt. I mean, more than it already does. I cannot tell you how much I hate poetry,' Aphrodite said.

'Do you have a clue about this?' I asked Damien.

'I think it's giving us directions on how we can make Kalona flee, or run away,' he said.

'We know what 'flee' means, Mr Vocab,' Erin said.

'It's kinda depressing that it says flee instead of kill,' Jack said.

'Kalona can't be killed,' I said, speaking the words automatically. 'He's immortal. He can be trapped. He can be chased away, although it boggles my mind to think about what might make him run. But he can't be killed.'

'Those five thingies together, in a place of power, make him run,' Jack said.

'Wherever that is, and whatever they are,' I said.

'They're people who represent each of those things. Or at least that would be my first guess. See how they're capitalized? That usually means they are proper nouns, or names,' Damien said.

'They're names,' Kramisha said.

'Do you know anything else about it? Can you tell who they are?' Damien asked.

Kramisha shook her head, looking frustrated. 'No. It's just when you said that they be people, I knew you was right.'

'How about the next one?' Damien said. 'Maybe it'll help us make sense of this one.'

I turned my attention to the other sheet of paper. The new poem wasn't long, but it made my skin crawl.

She comes back
Through blood by blood
She returns
Cut deep now
Like me
Humanity saves her
Will she save me?

'What were you thinking when you wrote this?' I asked Kramisha.

'Nothin'. I was barely awake. I just wrote the words that come to me with both of 'em.'

'I don't like it,' Erik said.

'Well, it doesn't help us with the other poem, that's for sure. Actually, I think it's talking about you, Zoey,' Damien said. 'I think it's foretelling your wound and your return to the House of Night.'

'But who's speaking? Who is this "me" that's asking if I'll save him or her?' I was feeling weaker and weaker by the moment, and the long strip of my wound was throbbing in time with the beat of my heart.

'It could be Kalona,' Aphrodite said. 'That's who the first poem's about.'

'Yes, but we're not so sure Kalona ever had any humanity in him to lose,' Damien said.

I carefully kept my mouth shut, even though my first impulse was to say that I did think Kalona had not always been like he was now.

'On the other hand,' Damien continued, 'we know that Neferet has turned from Nyx, which could also mean that she's lost herself, or her humanity. It could be referring to Neferet.'

'Ugh,' Erin said.

'She has definitely lost her damn mind,' Shaunee said.

'Actually, doesn't it make the most sense that it's that new undead kid talking?' Erik said slowly.

'You may be on to something,' Damien said. I could practically see the wheels in his mind turning. 'The "Cut deep now / Like me" part could be metaphorical for his death.

Zoey's wound is definitely life threatening, and they've certainly both been drawn to the House of Night because of blood.'

'And his humanity is missing. Like the rest of the red fledglings,' Aphrodite said.

'Hey, I don't know what you talkin' 'bout. I got me plenty of humanity,' Kramisha said, clearly offended.

'But you didn't have your humanity when you first rose, did you?' Damien said.

His voice was so clinical that Kramisha's feathers instantly unruffled. 'No. You right about that. I had no damn sense about me at first. None of us did.'

'Sounds like a good guess about the meaning of the second one,' Damien said. 'And because we have Kramisha on our side, her gift with words gives us a glimpse into the possible future. The first poem . . . I don't know. I'll think about it. What we need is to spend some time brainstorming possible meanings – time we don't have right now. But that's really inconsequential. We should still appreciate Kramisha.'

'Hey, not a problem,' Kramisha said. 'It's all part a bein' the Poet Laureate.'

'The who?' Aphrodite said.

Kramisha fixed a sharp look on Aphrodite. 'Zoey made me the new Vamp Poet Laureate.'

Aphrodite opened her mouth, but I beat her to speaking. 'Actually, let's have a quick vote of my Prefect Council on whether Kramisha should be our new Poet Laureate.' I looked at Damien. 'What's your vote?'

'Yes, definitely,' Damien said.

'I say yes, too,' Shaunee said,

'Ditto. We're due for a female Poet Laureate,' Erin said.

'I already gave my yes vote,' Erik said.

We all looked at Aphrodite.

'Yeah, yeah, whatever,' she said.

'And I can promise Stevie Rae will vote yes, too,' I said. 'So it's official.'

Everyone smiled at Kramisha who looked totally pleased with herself.

'Okay, so, to summarize,' Damien said, 'we've pretty much decided that Kramisha's first poem is outlining a way Kalona can be forced to run away, even though we don't really have a good understanding of the details provided in the poem. The second is saying that Zoey's return to the House of Night might somehow save Stark.' Erik said.

'Yeah, that's what it sounds like.' I handed the pieces of paper on which the poems were written to Aphrodite. 'Would you put those in my purse, please?' She nodded and folded them neatly, tucking them into my cute little bag. 'I wish both poems had come with more instructions,' I said.

'I think you should start by paying special attention to Stark,' Damien said.

'Or at least she should be on her guard around him,' Erik said. 'The poem does mention being cut, and right now that's way more than a poetic metaphor.'

I listened while Damien semi-agreed with him and I looked away from Erik's penetrating gaze and right into Heath's sad brown eyes.

'Let me guess. Stark's *another* guy, isn't he?' Heath said.

When I didn't answer, he took a long drink from the bottle of wine.

'Well, uh, yeah, Heath,' Jack said, sitting next to Heath on the bed and looking concerned. 'Stark is a fledgling who, I guess, was kinda a friend of Zoey's before he died and then un-died. He was a new kid, so none of us had gotten to know him very well.'

'But you knew things about him no one else did. Like that his gift from Nyx was that he never missed any mark he aimed at, right?' Damien said.

'Yeah. I knew stuff about him no one else knew, except Neferet and the professors,' I said, trying not to watch Heath guzzle down the bottle of wine and avoiding Erik's sharp gaze.

'I didn't know that about his gift, and I'm a professor,' Erik said.

I closed my eyes and leaned heavily back on the pillow. 'Then maybe that was more info Neferet kept to herself,' I said wearily.

'So why would he tell you about something that was top secret?' Erik said.

Annoyed that he sounded like he was interrogating me, I didn't say anything, and against my closed eyes I easily recalled the image of Stark's cute, cocky half smile and how I'd felt a sudden connection with him and even kissed him as he died in my arms.

'Well, let's see – a not-so-wild guess says that Stark told Z about his gift because she's top-shit fledgling and he wanted her to know the real deal with him,' Aphrodite broke in. 'Can't you see you're wearing the hell out of her with all of these questions!'

As my friends – well, all of them except for my 'consort' and my possible 'mate' – mumbled apologies, I kept my eyes closed and wondered just how badly I wanted to get all healed up, because it seemed that, once again, I found myself in a 'situation' that involved three guys. And that wasn't even counting Kalona.

Well, hell . . .

CHAPTER SIXTEEN

THANKFULLY, STEVIE RAE'S RETURN STOPPED ALL OF THE
Stark speculation.

''Kay. I'm supposed to tell Erik to carry Zoey. The rest of
you stay close. Darius is right outside in the parking lot,' Stevie
Rae said.

'But we can't all fit in Heath's truck,' I said, forcing my
heavy eyelids to open.

'You won't have to. We found something that'll work
better,' Stevie Rae said. Before I could ask any questions she
hurried on. 'And Darius also said Z should bite Heath again

for one fast suck before you head out. He said she ought to be gettin' real weak about now.'

'That's okay. I'm fine. Let's just go,' I said quickly. Yes, I felt like utter poop. No, I didn't want to bite Heath again. Well, I didn't mean I really didn't *want* to. I meant I really didn't think I *should*, especially with him being pissed at me just then.

'Just do it,' Heath said. Suddenly he was there beside me, still holding the bottle of wine in one hand. He didn't even look at me. Instead he focused his attention on Erik. 'So cut me.' He held out his arm to Erik.

'My pleasure,' Erik said.

'No. I'm not okay with this,' I continued to protest.

In one blindingly quick movement Erik slashed Heath's forearm, and the scent of his blood hit me. I closed my eyes against the spike of desire and need that was driving into me with every breath I inhaled. I was gently jostled and then Heath's strong, warm thigh was again my pillow. He wrapped his arm around me so that his cut arm was just under my nose. I opened my eyes then and, ignoring the need that was screaming through my body, I looked up at Heath. He was staring across the room at nothing.

'Heath,' I said. 'I can't take anything from you you're not willing to give me.'

He looked down at me and I saw several emotions cross his expressive face, the foremost of which was a terrible sadness. In a voice that sounded almost as weary as I felt, he said, 'There's nothing I'm not willing to give you, Zo. When are you going to understand that? I'm just wishing you would leave me with a little pride.'

His words broke my heart. 'I love you, Heath. You know that.'

His expression softened into a slight smile. 'It's good to hear you say it.' Then he looked from me to Erik. 'Did you hear that, vamp? *She loves me*. And remember that no matter how big and bad you think you are, you'll never be able to do this for her.' Heath lifted his arm so that the bloody slash Erik had made in it was pressed against my lips.

'Yeah, I see what you can do for her. I might have to put up with it, but I don't have to have it shoved in my face.' Angrily knocking the blanket aside, Erik left the room.

'Don't think about him,' Heath told me softly, stroking my hair. 'Just drink from me and think about getting well.'

I looked from the doorway to Heath's sweet gaze, and with a small moan I gave in to the need that raged within me. I drank from him, sucking in energy and life, passion and desire, along with his blood. I closed my eyes again, this time because of the intensity of the pleasure drinking from Heath gave me. I heard Heath's moan echo mine and felt him curl around me, pressing his arm more firmly against my lips and whispering sweet things to me that weren't entirely understandable.

My head was spinning by the time someone pulled Heath's arm from my grip. I felt stronger, even though my wound was burning like there was a fire camped out on my chest. But I was also feeling dizzy and weirdly giggly.

'Hey, she don't look right,' Kramisha said.

'But I feel more right. Or is that righter? Which is it, Damien-Shamien?' I paused and giggled, which hurt my chest so I clamped my lips tight together to make myself stop.

'What's wrong with her?' Jack asked.

'There's definitely something abnormal going on,' Damien said.

'I know what's wrong with her,' Stevie Rae said. 'She's drunk.'

'Nuh-uh! I don't even like to drink,' I said, and then burped softly. 'Oh, oopsie.'

'Boyfriend is drunk. She just drank from boyfriend,' Shaunee said.

'So that means Z's trashed, too,' Erin said. She and Shaunee had a wobbly Heath between them and they were guiding him back to the bed.

'Hey, I'm not drunk. Yet,' Heath said. Then he collapsed onto the bed.

'I didn't know vamps could get drunk off a human's blood,' Aphrodite said. 'That's really interesting.' She handed me my purse while she studied me like I was a specimen under a microscope.

'You'd think it was less interesting if you'd eaten a wino and had a hangover headache and then burped cheap wine for days,' Stevie Rae said. 'All I can say about that is *nas-ty*.'

Aphrodite, the Twins, Damien, Jack, and I all stared at her. Finally I was able to say, 'Stevie Rae. Please don't eat any more people. It's really *dis-dis-disturbing*,' I slurred.

'She sure won't eat another wino. That last one tasted bad for real,' Kramisha said.

'Kramisha! Don't freak Zoey out. No one is eating anyone anymore. I was just usin' that one time *a long time ago* as an example of why I know Heath's being trashed made her trashed.' Stevie Rae patted my arm. 'So don't worry, 'kay? We'll be fine here, and so will the street people. Don't stress about us. You just get well.'

'Oh, yeah.' I rolled my eyes at Stevie Rae. 'I'm not going to worry 'bout a thing.'

'Hey, you have my promise. No eating people while you're gone.' Stevie Rae looked solemn and pretended to draw an *X* over her heart. 'Cross my heart and hope to die.'

Hope to die! Jeesh, I really hoped that none of us would have to die. Again. And just like that I was able to think through the wine fog that had woozied my brain, and I knew what I had to do. On purpose I gave Aphrodite a tipsy smile. 'Hey there, Afro! Why don't you guys go on out to Darius? I gotta give Stevie Rae a phone number, then I'll be right there.'

'Fine. We'll meet you out there. And do not ever call me Afro again.' In a huff, Aphrodite led the Twins, Damien, Jack, and a whole passel of annoyed cats out of the room.

As they left the room, Erik came back in. Crossing his arms, he leaned silently against the wall and watched me. I used my drunkenness as an excuse to ignore him.

'Hey, could you manage to focus? Do you want me to add a number to my phone?' Stevie Rae said.

'No,' I said stubbornly. 'I gotta write it down.'

'Okay, okay,' she said quickly, obviously humoring the drunk.

She was looking around for something to write on when Kramisha marched over to her and handed her a piece of paper and a pen. 'Here's something to write on.'

Looking utterly confused, Stevie Rae shook her head at me. 'Z, are you sure you can't just tell me the—'

'No!' I snapped.

'Okay, here, don't have a big ol' cow.' Stevie Rae slipped the paper and pen into my hands. I could feel Erik, who had come over to stand closer to my table, watching me. I gave him a boozy frown. 'Don't peek at what I write!'

'All right, all right!' He held his hands up in surrender and walked over to Kramisha. I could hear both of them talking about how goofy I acted when I was trashed.

It was hard as hell to concentrate through the ridiculous buzz Heath had passed on to me, but the pain the movement of my hands caused helped to sober me up. I scrawled down Sister Mary Angela's cell-phone number and then quickly wrote, *Plan B: be ready to move everyone to the abbey but don't tell. No one knowing = Neferet not knowing where you are.*

'Okay, here.' Stevie Rae tried to take the paper from my hand, but I held it tight, which made her look up at me in exasperation. I met her eyes, trying to look and sound as sober as possible as I whispered, 'If I tell you to move, you move!'

Her gaze went down to the note I'd just written, and I saw her eyes widen. She looked quickly up at me and then nodded almost imperceptibly. Awash in relief, I closed my eyes and gave in to the dizziness.

'All done with her secret phone number note?' Erik said.

'Yep,' Stevie Rae teased back. 'As soon as I put this in my phone, I'm gonna destroy the evidence.'

'Or it might self-destruct,' Heath slurred from over on the bed.

I opened my eyes and looked at him. 'Hey!'

'What?' he said.

'Thanks again,' I said.

Heath shrugged. 'No big deal.'

'Yeah, it is,' I said. 'Stay safe, okay?'

'Does it matter?' he asked.

'Yeah, it does. But next time I really wish you wouldn't drink.' I burped again and then grimaced when the movement hurt my chest.

'I'll try to remember that,' he said, tipping the wine bottle back to his lips.

I sighed, told Stevie Rae, 'Get me out of here,' and closed my eyes, clutching my purse and the two indecipherable poems to me.

'That's your cue, Erik,' Stevie Rae said.

Erik was suddenly at my side. 'This is going to hurt, and I'm sorry, but you really need to get back to the House of Night.'

'I know. I'm just gonna close my eyes and try to pretend I'm someplace else, okay?'

'Sounds like a good idea,' Erik said.

'I'll be right here with you, too, Z,' Stevie Rae said.

'No. Stay with Heath,' I said quickly. 'If you let anyone eat him, I'm gonna be majorly pissed. And I mean it.'

'I'm right here,' Kramisha said, 'and I heard that. I ain't eatin' your boyfriend. He don't taste good no more.'

'That's not what Zo says!' Heath slurred and lifted his almost empty bottle like he was going to toast to us.

I ignored both of them and kept my eyes on Stevie Rae.

'Don't worry. Heath'll be fine. I'll take care of him.' Stevie Rae hugged me and kissed my cheek. 'Stay safe,' she said.

'Remember what I wrote,' I whispered. She nodded.

'Okay, let's go,' I told Erik, and squidged my eyes shut tight.

Erik lifted me as gently as he could, but the pain that sheared through my body was so awful that I couldn't even scream. I kept my eyes closed and tried to breathe in shallow little pants while Erik hurried down the tunnel with me in his arms, murmuring that everything would be fine . . . we'd be there soon . . .

When we got to the iron ladder that led up to the basement, Erik said, 'I'm sorry, but this is going to hurt like hell. Just hang on, though, Z. It's almost over.' Then he shifted his grip on me and lifted me to Darius, who was reaching down for me.

That was when I fainted.

Sadly, I came to when the freezing rain and an icy wind slapped against my face.

'Ssh, don't struggle. You'll only make it worse,' Darius said.

He was holding me in his arms. Erik was walking at his side, watching me with worried eyes as we made our way toward a huge black Hummer that was idling in the parking lot. Jack was standing beside the open door to the wide backseat. I could see Aphrodite in the passenger's seat and the Twins together with a whole buttload of cats in the far-back area. Damien was sitting by the open door.

'Slide over and help me lay her down here,' Darius said.

They somehow transferred me to the backseat of the Hummer, pillowing my head on Damien's lap. Unfortunately, I didn't pass out again. Before Darius closed the door, Erik squeezed my ankle.

'You have to get well, okay?' Erik said.

I barely managed a weak, 'Okay.'

When Darius closed the door and jumped into the driver's seat and we took off, I made a conscious decision to avoid the whole Erik-Heath issue until my life was calmer and I could deal with the two of them. I admit that at that moment I left the two of them behind with a guilty sense of relief.

Most of the ride back was as dark and silent as ice-swept Tulsa had become. Darius had to battle the Hummer to keep it on the sheets of ice that masqueraded as streets, and Aphrodite only commented once in a while on a fallen limb in their way or a turn they should take. Damien, tense and speechless, held me securely on his lap, and the Twins were, for a change, not chattering with each other. I closed my eyes, trying to control the dizziness and the pain. A disturbingly familiar sense of numbness had started to creep slowly over my body again. This time I recognized it, though, and knew how dangerous it would be to give in to the numbness, no matter how restful and compelling it seemed. This time I knew the numbness was a disguise for death. I forced myself to take deeper breaths, even though each one made pain radiate throughout my body.

Pain was good. If I hurt, it meant I wasn't dead.

I opened my eyes and cleared my throat, making myself speak. My blood-wine buzz was gone and all I felt was exhausted and consumed by pain. 'We have to remember what we're walking into. It's not the old House of Night. It's not our home,' I said. My voice carried, but I sounded like a hoarse stranger. 'Besides keeping our elements close to us, I think the smartest thing we can do is to try to stick as close to the truth as possible whenever we're questioned about anything.'

'That's logical,' Damien said. 'If they sense we're telling the truth, they'll be less likely to feel the need to probe farther into our minds.'

'Especially if those minds are protected by the elements,' Erin said.

'We might very well baffle them with our supposed ignorance, and Neferet will underestimate us again,' Shaunee said.

'So we're coming back because of that text message sent from the school calling all of us back,' Damien said. 'And because Zoey's been hurt.'

Aphrodite nodded. 'Yeah, and the only reason we left was because we were scared.'

'And that's the damn truth,' Erin said.

'Totally,' Shaunee added.

'Just remember: Tell the truth when possible and keep your guard up,' I said.

'Our High Priestess is correct. We are entering the enemy's camp, and we can't afford to be lulled into forgetting that by the familiarity of our surroundings,' Darius said.

'I have a feeling we won't be tempted to forget it,' Aphrodite said slowly.

'What kind of *feeling* do you mean?' I asked.

'I think our entire world has changed,' Aphrodite said. 'No, I know it has. The closer we get to the school, the more wrong it feels.' She swiveled and looked over the seat at me. 'Can you feel it?'

I shook my head slightly. 'I can't feel anything except the cut in my chest.'

'I can feel it,' Damien said. 'It's like all the hair on the back of my neck is standing up.'

'Ditto,' Shaunee said.

'My stomach feels awful,' Erin said.

I took another deep breath and blinked hard, concentrating on staying conscious. 'It's Nyx. She's warning you with those feelings. Remember the effect Kalona's appearance had on the other fledglings?'

Aphrodite nodded. 'Zoey's right. Nyx is making us feel like crap so we don't give in to this guy. We have to fight against whatever it is about him that sucks the rest of the fledglings in.'

'We can't go over to the Dark Side,' Damien said grimly.

Darius crossed the intersection of Utica and Twenty-first Street.

'It looks really creepy that Utica Square is totally dark,' Erin said.

'Creepy and horrible and wrong,' Shaunee said.

'There's no power anywhere,' Darius said. 'Even St John's Hospital has hardly any lights, like it's barely running on generators.'

Darius continued down Utica and I heard Damien gasp. 'It's eerie, the way it's the only thing in Tulsa still lit up.'

I knew the House of Night had finally come into view. 'Lift me up. I need to see it,' I told Damien.

He hoisted me up as gently as he could, but still I had to grit my teeth so I wouldn't scream. And then the bizarre sight of the House of Night made me temporarily forget my pain. It was ablaze with flickering oil lights, illuminating the huge castle-like structure. Ice covered everything, and the captured flames glistened against the slickened stone, making it appear faceted as if it were one humongous jewel. Darius reached into his pocket and pulled out a little remote. He aimed it at the school's wrought-iron gate and clicked, and with a creaking sound it swung open, the movement sending shards of ice raining down on the driveway.

'It looks like a castle out of one of those old, gruesome fairy tales where everything has been put under a spell and frozen in ice,' Aphrodite said. 'Inside, a princess has been poisoned by an evil witch and she's waiting to be rescued by her handsome prince.'

I stared at my home that was now a familiar stranger and said, 'Let's just remember that there's always a terrible dragon guarding the princess.'

'Yes, something horrible, like a Balrog,' Damien said. 'Like in *The Lord of the Rings*.'

'I'm afraid your demon reference is more accurate than we might wish it to be,' Darius said.

'What's that?' I asked. Unable to point, I jerked my chin in the direction ahead and to the left of us.

But I hadn't needed to say anything. In seconds what had made the movement was obvious to all of us as the Hummer was surrounded. In the blink of an eye the night above us shifted and Raven Mockers dropped out of it to crouch all around us. Then from behind them one huge, scarred warrior I didn't recognize stepped into the middle of the group, looking grim and dangerous.

'*That* would be one of my brothers, a Son of Erebus, standing side by side with our enemies,' Darius said softly.

'Which makes the Sons of Erebus our enemies, too,' I said.

'Priestess, at least when you're referring to that warrior, I'm sorry to have to agree with you,' Darius said.

CHAPTER SEVENTEEN

DARIUS WAS THE FIRST OF US OUT OF THE VEHICLE. HIS FACE was set in expressionless lines so that he looked strong and confident, but entirely unreadable. He ignored the Raven Mockers, who were staring at him with their terrible eyes, and addressed the warrior in the center of the group.

'Greetings, Aristos,' Darius said. Though he clenched his fist over his heart in a quick salute, I noticed Darius did not bow. 'I have several fledglings, including a young priestess, with me. The priestess has been severely wounded and is in need of immediate medical attention.'

Before Aristos could respond, the largest of the Raven

Mockers cocked its head to the side and said, 'Which priestess returns to the House of Night?'

Even inside the Hummer I shivered hearing the creature's voice. This one sounded more human than the one that had attacked me, but that made it even more frightening.

Slowly and deliberately Darius shifted his attention from Aristos to the horrible creature who was neither bird nor man, but a mutated mixture of both. 'Creature, I do not know you.'

The Raven Mocker narrowed its red eyes at Darius. 'Son of man, you may call me Rephaim.'

Darius didn't blink. 'I still do not know you.'

'You will know me,' Rephaim hissed, opening his beak so that I could see into his maw.

Darius ignored the creature and addressed Aristos again. 'I have a priestess who has been badly wounded and several fledglings who are in need of rest. Will you allow us to pass?'

'Is it Zoey Redbird? Do you have her with you?' Aristos asked.

Every one of the Raven Mockers reacted to my name. Each of them turned their attention from Darius to our Hummer. Wings ruffling and abnormal limbs twitching with subdued energy, the things stared. I'd never been so glad for tinted windows in my life.

'It is.' Darius's response was clipped. 'Will you let us pass?' he repeated.

'Of course,' Aristos said. 'All fledglings have been ordered to return to campus.' He gestured toward the school buildings. The movement briefly allowed the side of his neck to be illuminated by the nearest gaslight, and I saw a thin red line running across his skin, as if his neck had recently been injured.

Darius nodded tersely. 'I will carry the priestess to the infirmary. She cannot walk.'

Darius had started to return to the vehicle when Rephaim said, 'Is the Red One with you?'

Darius glanced back at him. 'I do not know what you mean by the Red One,' he said blandly.

In an instant Rephaim had spread his massive black wings and leaped on the hood of the Hummer. The crackling of the metal denting under his weight was drowned out by the collective hissing of the agitated cats. Rephaim perched there, human hands curled into claws, lurking over Darius. 'Do not lie to me, ssssson of man! You know I sssspeak of the red vampyre!' As his temper spiked, his voice became less human.

'Get ready to call your elements,' I said, trying to push down the pain and speak clearly and calmly, even though I felt so weak and lightheaded that I wasn't certain I could call spirit for Aphrodite, let alone help control and direct the rest of them. 'If that thing attacks Darius, we throw everything we have at it, pull Darius in here, and drive away like hell.'

But Darius didn't seem perturbed at all. He looked up at the creature coolly. 'You mean the red vampyre priestess Stevie Rae?'

'Yessss!' The word was one long hiss.

'She is not with me. I have only blue fledglings here.

223

And the priestess among them needs immediate aid – as I have already explained.' Darius continued to gaze calmly up at the thing that looked like it had stepped out of a nightmare. 'For the final time, do you allow us to pass or not?'

'Passss, of coursssssse,' the creature hissed. It didn't get off the Hummer, but leaned back so that Darius could barely get the driver's-side door open.

'Come this way. Now.' Darius motioned for Aphrodite to slide across the seat, and held his hand out so that she could take it. 'Stay close,' I heard him murmur to her and saw her nod her head quickly. Keeping glued to Darius's side, she moved with him to my door. He leaned in, meeting our eyes. 'Are you ready?' he asked quietly. The question was filled with so much more than those three simple words.

'Yes,' Damien and the Twins said together.

'Ready,' I said.

'Again, stay close,' he whispered.

Darius and Damien managed to move me painfully into the warrior's arms. Glaring silently at the Raven Mockers, all the cats in the vehicle slunk out and seemed to melt into the icy shadows. I breathed a sigh of relief when none of the creatures pounced on my Nala. *Please let the cats be safe*, I sent a silent plea to Nyx. I felt more than saw Aphrodite, Damien, and the Twins surround Darius and me, and then, as if we were one being, we moved away from the Hummer and on to the school grounds.

The Raven Mockers, including Rephaim, took to the sky as Aristos led us the short distance to the first building on campus, the one housing the professors' quarters as well as the infirmary.

As Darius carried me through the arched wooden doorway that always reminded me of something that should stand behind a moat and into the familiar building, I thought about how it had only been a little more than a couple of months ago that I'd first arrived here and had been taken unconscious into the infirmary to wake up, not having a clue about my new future. Weird that I was in almost that exact position again.

I glanced at my friends' faces. Everyone looked calm and confident. It was only because I knew them so well that I recognized the fear in the tight line of Aphrodite's mouth, and that Damien's hands, fisted at his sides, hid their shaking. The Twins walked on my right, so close that Shaunee's shoulder brushed Erin's, which in turn brushed against Darius – as if through touch they could gain courage.

Darius turned down a familiar hallway, and because he was carrying me, I felt the instant tension in his body and knew before she spoke that he had seen her. I lifted my heavy head wearily from his shoulder in time to see Neferet standing in front of the door to the infirmary. She was beautiful in a long, body-hugging dress made of an iridescent black material that shimmered and showed hints of deep purple whenever she moved. Her dark auburn hair fell in thick, glossy waves down to her waist, and her moss-green eyes sparkled with emotion.

'Ah, so the prodigal returns?' Her voice was melodic and slightly amused.

Instantly I pulled my eyes from her and whispered frantically under my breath, 'Your elements!' I only worried for the space of a heartbeat about them not hearing and not understanding, because almost immediately I felt the light brush of a fire-warmed wind and smelled a cool spring rain. Even though Neferet could not read Aphrodite's mind, I murmured, 'Spirit, I need you,' and felt the flutter within me as the element responded. Before I could change my mind and selfishly keep the invigorating spirit for myself I commanded, 'Go to Aphrodite,' and heard the sharp intake of her breath as the element filled her. Sure that my friends were as protected as they could be, I turned my attention to our tainted High Priestess. I opened my mouth to comment on the irony of her using a Biblical comparison, when a door a few feet down the hall from where Neferet stood opened and *he* stepped out of it.

Darius stopped so abruptly it felt as if he'd suddenly hit the end of a tether.

'Oh!' Shaunee breathed.

'*Shiiiiit!*' Erin said on a long sigh.

'Don't look at his eyes!' I heard Aphrodite whisper. 'Stare at his chest instead.'

'Not a hard thing to do,' Damien said softly.

'Stay strong,' Darius said.

Then time seemed to suspend.

Stay strong, I told myself. *Stay strong*. But I didn't feel strong. I felt exhausted and hurt and utterly defeated. Neferet intimidated me. She was just so perfect and powerful. Kalona made

226

me realize my insignificance. The two of them together dwarfed me, and my head swam dizzily with a cacophony of thoughts. I was just a kid. Hell, I wasn't even a full vampyre yet. How could I hope to stand against these two amazing beings? And did I really want to fight Kalona? Did we know for one hundred percent sure that he was evil? I blinked, clearing my blurring vision and stared at him. He absolutely did not look evil. Kalona was wearing pants that looked like they were made of the same creamy brown deerskin real moccasins were made of. His feet were bare, and so was his chest. It sounds stupid to say it – that he was standing there in the hallway half-naked – but then it didn't feel stupid at all. It felt right. It's just that he was so incredible! His skin was completely free of any blemish and was the golden tan that white girls try but always fail to get by roasting in tanning beds. His hair was thick and black. It was long but not ridiculously Fabio-long. It was just kinda shaggy and had a cute wave to it. The more I looked at it, the more I could imagine running my fingers through it. Not heeding Aphrodite's warning, I looked directly into his eyes and felt a jolt of electricity sizzle through me as his eyes widened in recognition, and that jolt seemed to zap even more of my already almost nonexistent strength. I sagged in Darius's arms, so weak I could hardly hold my head up.

'She is wounded!' Kalona's voice boomed down the hall. Even Neferet cringed. 'Why is she not being tended?'

I heard the sickening sound of huge wings fluttering, and then Rephaim stepped out of the room Kalona had just been in. I shivered as I realized the Raven Mocker must have flown up to the window and then crawled in from there. *Isn't there any place aboveground that the horrid things couldn't get to?*

'Father, I ordered the warrior to take the priestess to the infirmary so that she could be properly cared for.' Rephaim's unnatural voice sounded even more obscene after hearing the majesty of Kalona.

'Oh, bullshit!' Completely shocked, I stared open-mouthed at Aphrodite, who was giving the Raven Mocker her best bitchy sneer. She tossed back her thick blonde hair as she continued, 'Bird boy kept us out there in the freezing rain while he yammered about the Red One this and the Red One that. Darius got Zoey in here despite his *help*.' Aphrodite air-quoted over the word 'help.'

There was utter silence in the hallway, and then Kalona threw back his beautiful head and laughed. 'I had forgotten how amusing human women can be.' With a graceful movement of his hand he gestured to Darius. 'Bring the young priestess here so that she may be tended.'

I could feel Darius's reluctance in the tension of his body, but he did as Kalona ordered, with my friends at his side. We reached Neferet and the infirmary door at the same time Kalona did.

'Your duty is finished here, Warrior,' Kalona told Darius. 'Neferet and I shall attend her now.' And the fallen angel opened his arms as if he expected Darius to give me to him. With that movement the enormous raven-feathered wings that had until then been tucked neatly against his back, rustled and half opened.

I wanted to reach out and touch those wings and was glad I was too weak to do more than stare.

'My duty is not finished.' Darius's voice was as tense as his body. 'I have sworn to care for this young priestess, and I must stay by her side.'

'I'm staying, too,' Aphrodite said.

'And I stay.' Damien sounded small and shaky, but I saw that his fists were still clenched firmly by his sides.

'Us, too,' Erin said, and Shaunee nodded grimly.

It was Neferet's turn to laugh. 'Surely you don't think you can stay with Zoey through my examination?' The amusement in her voice disappeared. 'Stop being ridiculous! Darius, take her into that room and leave her on the bed. If you insist, you may wait here in the hall for her, though by the look of you, the wiser choice would be for you to eat and refresh yourself. After all, you have brought Zoey home, where she is safe, so you have completed your charge. The rest of you return to the dorms. The human part of the city might be paralyzed by a simple storm, but we are not humans. Life goes on for us, which means school goes on.' She paused and gave Aphrodite a look so filled with hatred that it twisted her face into something that was too hard and cold to keep even a tiny bit of its beauty. 'But you are now a human, are you not, Aphrodite?'

'I am,' Aphrodite said. Her face was pale, but she lifted her chin and met Neferet's frigid gaze.

'Then you belong out there.' Neferet made a vague motion away from us.

'No, she doesn't,' I said. Concentrating on Neferet had broken the spell staring at Kalona had cast over me. I barely recognized my own voice. It sounded like a whispery, weak old woman, but Neferet didn't have any problem hearing me, and she turned her attention from Aphrodite to me. 'Aphrodite still has visions from Nyx. She belongs here,' I managed to say, even though I had to blink rapidly because gray spots kept messing up my sight.

'Visions?' Kalona's deep voice cut the air between us. This time I refused to look at him, though he was standing so close that I could feel the weird chill that came from his body. 'What type of visions?'

'Warnings of future disasters,' Aphrodite spoke up.

'Interesting.' He drew the word out. 'Neferet, my Queen, you did not tell me you had a prophetess at the House of Night.' Before Neferet could speak, he continued, 'Most excellent, most excellent. A prophetess can be quite useful.'

'But she is not a fledgling, nor is she a vampyre, and thus she does not belong at the House of Night. So I say she should leave.' Neferet's voice had an odd tone to it I didn't recognize at first, and then as I blinked more and my vision cleared enough for me to get a good look at her body language – she was all but hanging on Kalona – I realized with a little shock that Neferet was actually pouting.

Then, mesmerized, I watched Kalona reach out and stroke the side of Neferet's cheek, sweeping his palm along the curve of her long, smooth neck, continuing to caress her shoulder, and finally trailing off down the length of her back. Neferet trembled under his touch and her eyes dilated, as if his caress made her high.

'My Queen, surely a prophetess will be of some use to us,' he said.

Still staring at him, Neferet nodded.

'You stay, little prophetess,' Kalona told Aphrodite.

'Yes,' she said firmly. 'I do. I stay with Zoey.'

Okay, I'll freely admit that Aphrodite was utterly surprising me. I mean, yes, I was hurt badly and probably in serious shock, so I can blame my altered mental and physical state on that and hope that some of the weirdly hypnotic effect the fallen angel was having on me was because I very well might be dying. But obviously everyone else was being affected by Kalona to some degree. Everyone except Aphrodite. She totally sounded like her normal bitchy self. I just didn't get it.

'Prophetess,' Kalona said. 'You say you are given warning of future disasters?'

'Yes,' Aphrodite said.

'Tell me, what do you see in the future if we were to turn Zoey away at this moment?'

'I haven't had a vision, but I know Zoey needs to be here. She's been hurt badly,' Aphrodite said.

'Then let me assure you that I, too, have been known to prophesy.' Kalona spoke. His voice, which had been so delicious and deep that I honestly wanted nothing more than to curl up and listen to him forever, had started to change. Subtly, at first, I felt the shift in timbre. As he continued to speak to Aphrodite, my flesh began to crawl with fear. His obvious displeasure was reflected in his voice, until even Darius took a staggering step away from him. 'And on my oath I tell you if you do not do as I command, this priestess will not live another night. Leave us now!'

Kalona's words crackled through my body, causing my already dizzied senses to reel. I clung to Darius's shoulders. 'Just do what he says,' I told Aphrodite, pausing to try to catch my breath. 'He's right. I'm not gonna last long if I don't get help.'

'Give the priestess to me. I shall not ask another time,' said Kalona, spreading his arms for me again.

Aphrodite hesitated for just a moment, then she reached over and grasped my hand. 'We'll be here when you're better.' She squeezed my hand and I suddenly felt the rush of spirit re-enter my body.

I wanted to tell her no, she needed to keep the element – she needed its protection – but Aphrodite had already turned to Damien and given him a nudge toward me, saying, 'Tell Zoey bye, and give her your strongest *get-well* wishes.'

I watched Damien glance quickly at Aphrodite, who nodded slightly. Then he grabbed my hand and squeezed, too. 'Be well, Z,' he said, and when he let loose my hand I could feel a sweet breeze wrap around me.

'You guys, too,' Aphrodite told the Twins.

Shaunee took one of my hands, and Erin the other. 'We're pulling for you, Z,' Erin said, and when they turned away, I was left with the warmth of summer and the freshness of a cleansing rain.

'Enough sentimentality. I'll take her *now*.' And before I could draw another breath Kalona had taken me from Darius. Pressed against his naked chest I closed my eyes and tried to cling to the strength of the elements as I trembled at the wonderful cold heat of his body.

'I will wait here,' I heard Darius say before the door closed with a sickening thud of finality, shutting my friends out and leaving me alone with my enemy, a fallen angel, and the monstrous bird creature his ancient lust had created.

Then I did something I'd only done twice before in my entire life. I fainted.

CHAPTER EIGHTEEN

THE FIRST THING I REALIZED AS I BEGAN TO REGAIN consciousness was that the crisp sheets of the infirmary bed were cool against my naked skin, which meant I didn't have any clothes on.

The second thing I realized was everything within me was telling me to keep my eyes closed and keep breathing deeply. In other words, I needed to pretend I was still out.

Staying as still as possible I tried to take inventory of my body. Okay, the long nasty wound on my chest was hurting considerably less than it had been when I'd passed out. I searched around with my senses (except sight, of course) and could feel and smell the lingering presence of spirit, air, water, and fire. The elements weren't fully manifested and glaringly obvious, but they were there around me, soothing and strengthening – and making me worried as hell for my friends. *Go back to the others!* I ordered the elements silently, and felt their reluctant departures. All except for spirit. I wanted to sigh and roll my eyes. Instead I concentrated harder. *Spirit, go to Aphrodite. Stay close to her.* Almost instantly I felt the absence of the powerful element. I must have made an involuntary movement at the departure of spirit because from somewhere near my feet Neferet spoke up.

'She stirred. I do not doubt she will regain consciousness soon.' There was a pause, and I could hear her moving as if she were pacing as she continued to speak. 'I still say I should not have healed her. Zoey's death could have been easily explained. She was almost dead when she arrived here.'

'If what you have told me is true and she has dominion over all five of the elements, she is too powerful to be allowed to perish,' Kalona said. He, too, sounded like he was standing near the end of my bed.

'What I've told you is the complete truth,' Neferet said. 'She controls the elements.'

'Then we can use her. Why not include her in our new vision of the future? Having her allegiance would sway any members of the Council who would not readily succumb to me.'

New vision of the future? Swaying the Council? As in the High Council of Vampyres? Holy crap!

Neferet's response was smooth and confident. 'We won't need her, my love. Our plan will succeed. You should know that Zoey will never use her power for us anyway. She is entirely too infatuated with the Goddess.'

'Ah, but that can change.' His deep voice was like melted chocolate. Even though my mind was racing with the news I'd just overheard, my body was mesmerized by the sound of him; it felt good just to listen to him. 'I seem to recall another priestess whose infatuation with the Goddess was broken.'

'She is young and not wise enough to allow her eyes to be opened to more intriguing possibilities, as mine have been.' Their voices were so close together that I knew she must be in his arms. 'All Zoey can ever be to us is another enemy. I believe the day will come when either you or I will have to kill her.'

Kalona chuckled. 'You are such a delightfully bloodthirsty creature. If the young priestess is not a benefit to us, then of course she shall eventually be disposed of. Until then I will see what I can do about breaking the shackles that bind her.'

'No. I want you to stay away from her!' Neferet snapped.

'You would do well to remember who is master here. I will not be ruled or commanded or trapped, ever again. And I am not your impotent Goddess. What I give I will take away if I am displeased!' The sexy silkiness was gone from Kalona's voice, and a terrible coldness had replaced it.

'Don't be angry.' Neferet was instantly contrite. 'It is just that I cannot bear to share you.'

'Then do not displease me!' he shouted, but already the anger was fading from his voice.

'Come with me from this room and I promise I will not displease you,' Neferet said teasingly. I could hear the disgusting moist sounds of them kissing. Neferet's breathless moans were enough to make me gag.

After way too many totally R-rated nasty sound effects, Kalona finally said, 'Go to our chamber. Ready yourself for me. I will follow you there shortly.'

I could almost hear Neferet's *No! Come with me now!* shriek through the room, but she surprised me by saying, 'Come to me soon, my dark angel,' and that in a sweet, sultry voice. Then there was the swish of her clothes and the opening and closing of a door.

She's actually manipulating him. I wondered if Kalona knew it. Surely an immortal being would be wise to a vampyre High Priestess's mind games (well, and body games, too – eesh). Then I remembered the spectral image of Neferet I'd glimpsed at the depot. How had she done that? *Maybe turning to the Dark Side has given her different powers; maybe she's not just a fallen vampyre High Priestess. Who knows what being Queen of the Tsi Sgili really means?* This new thought terrified me.

A rustling around my bed interrupted my awful inner musings. I lay very still. I wanted to hold my breath, but knew that I had to keep taking deep, even breaths. I swear I could feel Kalona's eyes on me and was unbelievably glad that the sheet had been pulled modestly up over my breasts and tucked tight around my body.

I felt the familiar chill coming from his body. Kalona must be close to me. He was probably standing right there, right beside my bed. I heard the ominous rustle of feathers and could imagine him spreading those beautiful black wings. He could be getting ready to pull me into his arms again and wrap them around me, like he had in my dream.

And that was it. No matter what my instincts were screaming at me, I couldn't keep my eyes closed any longer. Sure that I was going to be looking up at his indescribably perfect face, I opened my eyes to find myself staring up at the mutated features of Rephaim. The Raven Mocker was bent over me, his terrible bird face just inches from mine. His beak was open and his tongue was flicking in my direction.

My reaction was immediate and automatic, and several things happened all at once. Shrieking my most piercing girl scream, I clutched the sheet to my chest and scrambled back so fast I smacked myself against the headboard of the bed. As I did that, the disgusting Raven Mocker hissed and spread his wings, looking like he was going to pounce on me, and the door burst open. Darius rushed into the room, took one look at the malevolent creature hovering over me, and with a move that was as graceful as it was lethal, reached inside his leather jacket to the knife he holstered there, pulled it free, and threw. The blade struck Rephaim high in his chest. The creature shrieked and staggered back, clutching at the pearl-inlaid hilt of the knife.

'You dare attack my son!' It took Kalona only two strides to reach Darius. With the strength of a god, he grabbed the warrior by the throat and lifted him off his feet. Kalona was so tall, his arms so long and muscular, that he was able to slam Darius against the ceiling of the room. He held Darius there as the warrior's legs kicked spasmodically and his fists beat ineffectually against Kalona's massive arms.

'Stop it! Don't hurt him!' Pulling the sheet with me off the bed I staggered over to the two of them, not realizing until I'd gotten to my feet how weak I still was. Kalona's black wings were unfurled, and I had to duck under one of them to get to Darius. I didn't know what I thought I was going to do when I leaped off the bed. Even if I had been myself and not hurt and drained I would have been no match for this immortal being – and right now, though I was screaming at him and pounding on his side, I could tell I was less troubling to him than an annoying mosquito would have been. But one thing did happen. As I looked up at Kalona, I saw his blazing amber eyes and how his teeth were bared in a feral smile, and I understood that he was enjoying slowly choking the life from Darius.

At that moment Kalona's true self was revealed to me. He was not a misunderstood hero who was waiting for love to bring out his good side. Kalona didn't have a good side. Whether he had always been like this or not wasn't import-ant. What he'd become – what he was now – was evil. The spell he had worked over me shattered like a dream made of glass. I hoped desperately that it was too broken to ever be pieced back together again.

Drawing a deep breath, I raised my hands, palms out, not

caring that the sheet fell away from my body, leaving me standing there naked. Then I used the last of my strength to evoke, 'Wind and fire, come to me. I need you.' Instantly I felt the presence of the two elements, and beyond their presence I could sense Damien and Shaunee and had a brief flash of the two of them concentrating with their eyes closed as they added their combined wills to strengthen their elements. That little burst of power was all I needed. I narrowed my eyes and put everything I had into my command. 'Make the winged guy get off Darius!' I threw my hands at Kalona, focusing the elements on the movement, and at the same time thinking how fire and wind had gotten me out of some pretty tight spots with those stupid Raven Mockers, so using them against their daddy should work, too.

The effect of the blast of hot air was immediate. It caught Kalona's outstretched wings and tossed him up and back, and there was a weird sizzling sound as the heated air touched his naked skin, actually causing mist to form in the air around him.

Darius had fallen heavily to the floor, but he was gasping for air while he tried to stand, putting his body between Kalona, Rephaim, and me. I couldn't do much more than try to control my breathing and blink hard to clear the weird little bright spots from my vision. Fire and wind had gone, leaving me barely able to stay on my feet.

A movement at the edge of my vision had me glancing at the open door and I gasped in surprise as Stark ran into the room, his bowstring already notched with a deadly-looking arrow. He lifted it to take aim at Darius, and then hesitated, shook his head like he was trying to clear it, and stared at me.

At the first sight of him I felt a wonderful rush of happiness. He looked like himself again! His eyes weren't glowing red. He didn't seem crazed and wasn't hollow-cheeked and skeletal. Then I realized I was standing there completely naked as he and I stared at each other. I grabbed the sheet pooling at my feet and hurriedly wrapped it around me, bath towel-style. Even in the middle of the big mess and stress that was going on around me, I could tell that my face was blazing red with embarrassment. I should have said something, anything to him, and instead my mind was frozen by the fact that *he had just seen me completely naked*.

Recovering his composure sooner than me, Stark lifted his bow again, renotching the arrow and sighting it at Darius.

'Stark! Don't shoot him!' I cried. I didn't bother to try to block his view of Darius. If Stark shot, he wouldn't miss no matter what I did. He couldn't miss. Unlike Kalona, my Goddess didn't take back a gift once she'd given it.

'If you are meaning to kill the person who threw me across the room, then that arrow will strike the priestess and not the warrior,' Kalona said. He had gotten to his feet and he sounded perfectly normal. His expression was calm, but the skin of his naked chest looked flushed and kinda odd, like he'd suddenly gotten a sunburn. Small wisps of vapor were still lifting lazily from his exposed skin, even though both elements had left the room. 'And it is not the priestess I want killed. It is the warrior.'

241

Before Stark could fire his deadly arrow, I turned to Kalona, beseeching him, 'Darius was just protecting me. It was a Raven Mocker who did this.' I pointed to the long wound across my chest that was no longer gaping nastily open, but was instead an angry, jagged red line. 'When Darius heard me scream and he saw Rephaim bending over me, it was only logical for him to assume I was being attacked again.' Kalona had held up a hand to Stark, halting the shot. With the fallen angel's attention fully on me, I continued, 'Darius has sworn to protect me. He was just doing his job. Please don't kill him for that.'

I held my breath during a long pause. Kalona stared at me, and I stared right back at him. The weird, hypnotic allure I'd felt for him hadn't returned. Not that he wasn't totally the most gorgeous man I'd ever seen. He definitely was. Then I felt a little start of surprise as I realized exactly what I was seeing as I gawked at him.

Kalona had gotten younger.

When he'd first risen from his imprisonment in the earth, he'd been utterly and completely handsome, but he'd also been a *man*. Well, one that was abnormally big and had huge black wings, but still, a man. He'd had an ageless look about him, appearing anywhere from thirty to fifty. But that had changed. If I had to guess his age, I'd say he was about eighteen. Definitely no older than twenty-one.

He's the perfect age for me . . .

Finally Kalona stopped staring at me and slowly turned to Rephaim, who was crouched in the corner of the room, his terrible human hands pressed around the knife that still protruded from his bird chest.

'Is this true, my son? Did one of my children cause the priestess's wound?'

'I have no way of knowing, Father. Not all of the sentries have returned,' Rephaim spoke between short, panting breaths.

'It is true,' Darius said.

'Of course that is what you would say, Warrior,' Kalona said.

'I give you my word as a Son of Erebus that I tell you the truth,' Darius said. 'And you have seen Zoey's wound. Surely you recognize an injury made by the claws of one of your own children.'

I was glad to see that Darius wasn't all puffed up and ready to continue the fight, like an idiot teenage boy would have been (hello, Heath and Erik!), and then I understood. Darius was still protecting me. If Kalona knew a Raven Mocker had almost killed me, without getting the rest of the story about it having been an accident, then maybe he would at the very least not leave me alone with one of them, and at the most warn his nasty children to stay away from me. That is, if Kalona still wanted me alive.

Then I quit babbling anything in my mind because Kalona was closing the space between us. I stood very still, staring straight ahead at his bare chest as he reached out, stopping just short of touching me. Slowly, with one finger he traced the path of my wound without actually stroking my skin, but still I could feel the chill that came from his body. I had to grit my teeth hard to keep myself from either shivering and cringing back or looking up into his eyes and taking the chance that I would lean forward just enough for his cold finger to touch my heated flesh.

'It is the mark of one of my sons,' he said. 'Stark, this time do not kill the warrior.' I had just heaved a long sigh of relief when Kalona added, 'Of course, I cannot allow him to wound my beloved son without redress. But I prefer to admonish him myself.'

Kalona's voice was so calm, so matter of fact, that I didn't really get the meaning of his words until, like a cobra, he struck. The warrior only had time to begin to take a defensive stance when Kalona whirled, pulled the knife from Rephaim's chest, and in one motion raked the blade down the side of Darius's face.

Darius staggered under the blow, and then fell as blood sprayed all around me, a heavy, scarlet rain in the little room. I screamed and tried to go to him, but Kalona's frigid hand closed around my wrist, jerking me back against him. I looked up at the immortal, willing the anger and horror I felt to burn through his awful appeal.

And I wasn't drawn to him! His spell didn't work on me! Young and inhumanly beautiful as he was, I still saw him as a dangerous enemy. He must have seen the triumph in my eyes because suddenly his war-like expression changed to a slow, knowing smile. He bent and whispered for my ears alone, 'Remember, my little A-ya, the warrior can protect you from all others *except* me. Not even the power of your elements can keep me from claiming what will eventually be mine again.' Then he pressed his lips against mine and the wild taste of him was like a blizzard rushing through my body, numbing my resistance and freezing my soul with a forbidden desire that utterly overwhelmed me. His kiss made me forget everything and everyone – Stark, Darius, and even Erik and Heath were frozen from my mind.

He released me and my legs would not hold me up. I crumpled to the floor as he strode from the room, laughing, with his wounded favorite son hobbling behind him.

CHAPTER NINETEEN

I WAS SOBBING AS I CRAWLED OVER TO DARIUS. I HAD JUST reached him when I heard a terrible sound coming from the doorway. I looked up to see Stark. He still grasped his bow in one hand. The other was holding on to the doorpost so tight that his knuckles had turned white, and I swear I could see his fingers making indentations in the wood. His eyes were blazing red and he was bent slightly over, as if his stomach was causing him pain.

'Stark? What is it?' I wiped the back of my hand across my eyes, trying to clear the tears from my vision.

'The blood . . . can't bear it . . . have to . . .' He spoke in broken starts and stops and then, as if against his will, he took a staggering step into the room.

On the floor beside me Darius got to his knees. He grabbed the knife from the floor where Kalona had dropped it and faced Stark. 'You should know I only share my blood with those I have invited to taste of me,' Darius's voice was steady and strong. Had I not been looking at him I would never have known that a river of blood was gushing down his face from a terrible knife slash. 'And I have offered you no such invitation, boy. Back away before what happened here gets any worse.'

There was a dark struggle going on within Stark that was reflected in his entire body. From the glowing red of his heated eyes to the feral grimace of his lips to the tightrope tension that radiated from him, he looked like he was on the brink of an explosion.

But here's the deal: I'd had just about enough. Saying my reaction to Kalona's kiss had freaked me out was the new understatement of the year. My body still ached. My head was woozy. I was so weak I didn't think I'd win an arm-wrestling contest with, well, Jack. Now Darius was hurt, and I didn't have a clue as to how badly. Seriously, you could stick a fork in me and call me so done with all this stress.

'Stark, just get the hell out of here!' I rounded on him, glad my voice sounded lots stronger than I felt. 'I don't want to zap the crap outta you with fire, but if you take one more step into this room, I swear I'm going to burn your butt up.'

That got through to him. Stark's red eyes locked on me.

He looked pissed and dangerous. There was a darkness that surrounded him like an aura, making the red in his eyes blaze. I stood, glad that the sheet was staying tucked around my body, and lifted my arms, holding them up and ready. 'Do not push me right now. I promise you won't like it if I lose my temper.'

Stark blinked a couple of times at me, like he was trying to clear his vision. The scarlet of his eyes faded, the darkness in the air around him dissipated, and he wiped a shaky hand across his face. 'Zoey, I—' he began, sounding almost normal. Darius shifted in his defensive stance, taking a step closer to me. Stark snarled at him – actually *snarled* – like he was more animal than human, spun around, and ran out of the room.

I somehow managed to stagger to the door and slam it closed, then dragged a chair from near the bedside and propped it under the door handle, just as I'd seen people do in the movies, before I went back to Darius.

'I am glad you are on my side, Priestess,' he said.

'Yeah, that's me. I'm *fierce*.' I tried to pretend I wasn't close to passing out by sounding like Christian from *Project Runway*. I was pretty sure Darius didn't know *Project Runway* from a science project, but it did make him chuckle as we helped each other over to the end of the bed, where he sat heavily and I stood beside him, concentrating on not swaying like I was drunk. Which, sadly, I wasn't anymore.

'There should be first aid supplies in the cabinet over there.' He motioned to the long stainless-steel cabinet that stretched halfway across the far wall. There was also a sink built into it and a bunch of scary hospital-looking items (they were sharp and very stainless steel) stored neatly in trays and whatnot beside the sink.

Wearily, I ignored the sharp things and started pulling open drawers and cabinets, which was when I noticed my hands were shaking like crazy.

'Zoey,' Darius called, and I glanced over my shoulder at him. He looked terrible. The left side of his face was a bloody mess. The slash extended from his temple, all the way down his jawline, messing up the bold geometric design of his tattoo. But his eyes smiled at me and he said, 'I'm going to be just fine. This is little more than a scratch.'

'Well, it's a big scratch,' I said.

'I believe it will annoy Aphrodite,' he said.

'Huh?'

He started to smile, but ended the attempt with a grimace as the movement caused more blood to pour from the wound. He pointed at his face. 'She won't like the scar.'

When I had a bunch of bandages and alcohol wipes and gauze and stuff, I came back to him. 'If she gives you crap about it, I'll kick her butt. After I've rested up.' I stared at the awful 'scratch,' ignoring the delicious scent of his blood and swallowing hard to keep myself from puking.

Okay, yes, it does sound like a total contradiction: the fact that I love the taste and smell of blood, but that seeing it pouring out of a friend's body grosses me out. Wait, no. Maybe it's not a contradiction, because, hello! I don't eat my friends! I thought about Heath and decided to amend my thought: I don't eat my friends under normal circumstances and unless they give me their permission.

'I can clean it,' Darius said, reaching for the alcohol wipe I was balling up in my fisted hand.

'No,' I said, then repeated more firmly, shaking my head to try to clear away the wooziness in it. 'No, that's ridiculous. You're hurt; I'll do it. Just walk me through what I need to do.' I paused, before I continued, 'Darius, we have to get out of here.'

'I know,' he said solemnly.

'You don't know all of why. I overheard Kalona and Neferet talking. They said they were planning some kind of a new future, and then said it would involve "swaying the Council."'

Darius's eyes widened in shock. 'Nyx's Council? As in the High Council of Vampyres?'

'I don't know! They didn't say anything else about it. I guess they could have been talking about the Council here at the House of Night.'

He studied my face. 'But you do not believe that is what they were referring to?'

I shook my head slowly.

'Sweet Nyx! It cannot be done!'

I frowned, wishing my gut wasn't disagreeing with him. 'I'm afraid there's a chance it can be done. Kalona is powerful, and he has that magical draw-people-to-him thing going on. Look, the bottom line is we can't be trapped under Neferet's control while she and the bird guy put their disgusting plan in motion – whatever that plan might be.' Actually, I was scared that they'd already put their disgusting plan in motion, but saying it out loud felt like a spell that would make it be true. 'So can't we just get you fixed up, grab Aphrodite, the Twins, and Damien, and go back to the tunnels?' I felt precariously close to bursting into tears. 'I'm all better, and I think it's worth the chance of drowning in my own blood to get the hell out of here.'

'Agreed, and I believe Neferet has healed you enough that you will not be in danger of rejecting the Change, even if you are not among a full fold of vampyres.'

'Are you okay enough to leave?'

'I told you I am fine, and I was speaking the truth. Let us get this cleaned up and then we will leave this place.'

'I like the tunnels better.' I surprised myself by admitting out loud what I had been thinking, but Darius nodded solemnly in agreement. 'It is because it feels safe there, and it is definitely no longer safe here,' he said.

'Did you notice Neferet?' I asked him.

'If you mean did I notice the Priestess's power seems to have increased – yes, I did.'

'Great. I almost wish I was just imagining things,' I muttered.

'Your instincts are good, and they've been warning you about Neferet for quite a while.' He paused. 'Kalona's hypnotic power is unusual. I've never felt anything like it before.'

'Yeah,' I said, cleaning the blood off his face. 'But I think I've broken whatever hold he was having over me.' I refused to admit, even to myself, that though the hypnotic effect was gone, I still had had a powerful reaction to his kiss. 'Hey, did Kalona look different to you?'

'Different? How so?'

'Younger, like he's not even as old as you.' I guessed that Darius was somewhere in his early to mid-twenties – or at least that's how old he appeared to me.

Darius gave me a long, considering look. 'No, Kalona appeared the same as when first I'd seen him – ageless, but not in a way that could ever be mistaken for a teenager. Perhaps he has the ability to alter his appearance to please you.'

I wanted to deny it, and then I remembered what he'd called me just before he kissed me. It had been the same name he'd called me during my nightmare. *My response to him is almost automatic, as if my soul recognizes him*, my mind whispered traitorously. A terrible fear shivered through my body, causing the little hairs on my arms and the back of my neck to stand straight up. 'He calls me A-ya,' I said.

'The name sounds familiar. What does it mean?'

'It's the name of the maiden the Ghigua women created to trap Kalona.'

Darius sighed deeply. 'Well, at least we now know why he's so intent upon protecting you. He thinks you are the maiden he loved.'

'I think it was more obsession than love,' I said quickly, not wanting to even consider the idea that Kalona could possibly have loved A-ya. 'Plus, we have to remember that A-ya did trap him, causing him to be imprisoned in the earth for more than a thousand years.'

Darius nodded. 'So his desire for you could very easily change to violence.'

My stomach clenched. 'Actually, the reason he wants me might be just to get back at A-ya. I mean, I don't know what he's actually planning to do with me. Neferet was all for killing me, but he stopped her because he said he can use my power.'

'But you would never turn from Nyx to him,' Darius said.

'And once he realizes that, I can't see him keeping me around.'

'He'll view you as a powerful enemy, one who might find a way to entrap him again,' Darius said.

'Okay, so explain to me what to do to get you fixed up, and then let's find the others and get the hell out of here.'

Darius walked me through a very gross cleaning of the long slash wound, during which I actually had to pour alcohol into his cut flesh to, as he put it, *flush out any infection that might have been caused by the Raven Mocker's blood*. I'd totally forgotten that the same knife had been imbedded in Rephaim's chest and it definitely had nasty mutant man-bird blood all over it. So I cleaned the cut and then Darius helped me find this weird but cool stuff called Dermabond, better known as liquid stitches, which I squirted in a line down the length of his cut, mushed the sides of the wound together, and, *ta-da!* except for a big not-yet-healed cut, Darius said he was good as new. I was slightly more skeptical, but (as he reminded me) I really wasn't a credible nurse to begin with.

Then he and I searched though the cabinets because I was not going anywhere with a sheet wrapped around me. Okay, you would not believe the gross, paper-thin, backless hospital 'gowns' (oh, please, they are *so* not real gowns) we found in one drawer. Why is it hospitals make you wear ugly, too revealing stuff when you already feel awful? It just makes no sense. Anyway, we finally found a pair of green hospital scrubs that were way too big for me, but whatever. They were seriously better than being wrapped up in a sheet. I completed my look with some booties. I asked Darius if he'd seen my purse, and he said he thought it was still in the Hummer. It was probably shallow of me, but I spent quite a few minutes stressing that if my purse was lost I'd have to get a new driver's license and cell phone, and wondered briefly if I'd remember the exact right shade of the cool Ulta lip gloss I was going to have to replace.

Sometime after I put on the scrubs (while Darius's back was turned) and started worrying about my purse being missing, I realized I was sitting on the bed staring off into space and almost falling asleep.

'How are you feeling?' Darius asked. 'You look ...' His words trailed off as I'm sure he tried and vetoed words like 'crappy' and 'hideous.'

'I look tired?' I volunteered helpfully.

He nodded. 'You do.'

'Well, that's a not-so-amazing coincidence because I am tired. Really tired.'

'Perhaps we should wait and—'

'No!' I interrupted. 'I meant it when I said I wanted to go. Plus, there's no way I can get any real sleep as long as we're here. I just don't feel safe.'

'Agreed,' Darius said. 'You aren't safe. None of us are safe.'

Unspoken was the understanding that we would still not be safe even if we managed to get away from the House of Night, but it was better for morale if neither of us mentioned that.

'Alright, let's get the others,' I said.

I checked the clock on the wall before we left the room and realized that it was a little after 4:00 A.M. It was a shock to see how much time had passed, especially since I must have been out for several hours, even though I didn't feel rested at all. If things were normal at the House of Night, fledglings should be finished with classes. 'Hey,' I told Darius, 'it's about dinnertime. They might be in the cafeteria.'

He nodded, moved the propped-up chair, and opened the door slowly.

'Hallway's empty,' he murmured.

While he'd been peeking down the hall, I'd been checking him out. So, instead of following him out of the room, I grabbed his sleeve and held him back. He gave me a questioning look.

'Uh, Darius, I'm thinking that we really need to change clothes before we make a grand entrance in the middle of the cafeteria, or even my dorm. I mean, you're more than a little bloody, and I'm wearing what looks like a big green trash bag. We're not exactly inconspicuous.'

Darius glanced down at himself, taking in the dried blood that was splattered all down his shirt and jacket. The blood plus the newly closed laceration on his face plus my hospital scrubs definitely equaled conspicuous, a conclusion Darius obviously came to easily.

'Let's take the stairs up to the next floor. That's where the Sons of Erebus are housed. I'll change, then get you quickly to your dorm so you can be rid of those.' He gestured at my outfit. 'If we get lucky we'll find Aphrodite and the Twins in the dorm and will just have to scout out Damien and then slip from the school grounds.'

'Sounds good. I never thought you'd hear me say that I was looking forward to getting back to those tunnels, but right now that feels like the best place to be,' I said.

Darius grunted what I assumed was guy language for agreeing with me, and I followed him into the hall, which really was deserted. It was just a short way to the stairwell. Okay, going up a flight of steps just about did me in, and I ended up leaning heavily on Darius's arm. I could tell by the worried glint in his eyes that he was seriously considering picking me up and would have (despite my protests) if we hadn't gotten to the next floor about then.

'So,' I said between gasps, 'is it always this quiet up here?'

'No,' Darius said grimly. 'It's not.' We passed a common area that had a fridge, a big, flat-screen TV, some comfy couches, and a bunch of guy stuff like free weights, a dartboard, and a pool table. It, too, was deserted. His face set into unreadable lines, Darius led me to one of the many doors that opened off the hall.

His room was just about as I'd imagined a Son of Erebus's room would be – clean and simple, with hardly any knickknacks.

He did have some trophies that were for winning knife-throwing competitions, and a whole collection of Christopher Moore's hardback books, but no framed pictures of friends or family, and the only art on the walls was of Oklahoma landscapes, which probably came with the room. Oh, he also had a mini-fridge like Aphrodite's, which kinda annoyed me. Did everyone have a fridge except me? Jeesh. There was a big, heavily draped picture window that I wandered over to, pulling back a corner of the curtains and looking out so Darius could change his clothes without causing a jealous Aphrodite to disembowel either of us.

It should have been a busy time. Classes were out and kids should have been going from the academic part of the school to the dorms, rec room, cafeteria, and just in general hanging out and being teenagers. Instead, I only saw a couple of people doing their best slip and slide down the sidewalk as they hurried from one building to another.

Even though my intuition was telling me there was way more to it than that, I wanted to blame the dead quiet of the school on the weather. The dark sky was still spitting icy rain, and despite the isolating effects of the storm, I was enthralled with how magical the shining coating of frozen water made everything look. Trees bowed under the crystalline weight that entombed their branches. The soft yellow of the gaslights flickered over slick walls and sidewalks. The coolest thing was the ice-encapsulated grass. It stuck up in brittle spikes all over, glistening when light hit it just right, making the ground look like it had grown a field of diamonds.

'Wow,' I said, more to myself than Darius, 'I know the ice storm is a pain in the butt, but it really is pretty. It makes everything look like a whole different world.'

Darius was pulling a sweatshirt on over a clean T-shirt as he joined me at the window. His frown said that he saw the pain-in-the-butt part of the storm more than the ice magic of it.

'I don't see one sentry,' he said, and I realized that his frown hadn't been directed just at the ice but at the boundaries of the walls, which we could see from his window, too. 'We should be able to see at least two or three of my brother warriors from here, but there is no one.' Then I felt him stiffen.

'What is it?'

'I spoke too soon, and you were correct. This is a whole different world. There are sentries posted. They are just not my brothers.' He pointed at a spot on the wall to our right where it curved behind Nyx's Temple, which was situated right across from the building we were in. There, between the shadow of an ancient oak and the rear of the temple, the darkness shifted to reveal the bent shape of a Raven Mocker crouched on the wall. 'And there,' Darius motioned down the wall a little way to another spot. I'd overlooked it as nothing more than a natural fold of darkness on this stormy night, but as I stared, it, too, moved slightly, revealing another terrible man-bird creature.

'They're all over,' I said. 'How are we going to get out of here?'

'Can you disguise us with the elements, as you did before?'

'I don't know. I'm so tired, and I feel weird. My cut is better, but it's like I keep getting drained and never really refilled.' Then my stomach sank further as I realized something else. 'After I used fire and wind to knock Kalona off you, I didn't have to release the elements. They just weren't there anymore. That's never happened before. They've always hung around until I bid them depart.'

'You're exhausting yourself. The ability to conjure and control the elements is your gift, but it doesn't come without a price. You're young and healthy, so under normal circumstances you probably hardly notice the drain it causes in you.'

'I have a couple of times before, but it's never been like this.'

'You've never been close to death before. Add to that the fact that you haven't had time to rest and recuperate, and that's a dangerous combination.'

'In other words, we may not be able to count on me to sneak us out of here,' I said.

'How about we call you Plan C, and we try to come up with Plans A and B.'

'I'd rather be Plan Z,' I grumbled.

'Well, this will help, even if it's just a temporary fix.' He went to the mini-fridge and pulled out what looked like two water bottles, only the bottles were filled with a thick red liquid I recognized very well. He handed me one. 'Drink up.'

I took it and frowned at him. 'You have blood in water bottles in your fridge?'

He raised his brows at me, then cringed a little as the cut

that stretched down the entire side of his face pulled. Finally he said, 'I am a vampyre, Zoey. You will be one soon. To us having bottled human blood is the same as having bottled water. Only there is a lot more kick to blood.' He lifted his bottle to me and then drained it.

I shut off my mind and did the same. As always, the blood hit my system like an explosion, giving me a kick of energy and making me feel suddenly very much alive and invincible. My woozy head cleared, and the ache that had been radiating from my wound diminished, letting me draw a big, deep, pain-free breath.

'Better?' Darius said.

'Totally,' I said. 'Let's go get me some real clothes and find the others while this buzz lasts.'

'That reminds me.' He turned back to the fridge, grabbed another bottle of blood, and tossed it to me. 'Stick that in your pocket. Drinking blood won't replace sleep and the time your body needs to heal, but it will keep you on your feet. Or at least I hope it will.'

I shoved the bottle in one of the huge pockets of my baggy scrub pants. Darius strapped on his knife holster, grabbed a clean leather jacket, and he and I left his room, hurried down the stairs, and walked to the door of the building – all without seeing anyone else. It felt wrong, but I didn't want to pause to talk about it. I didn't want to do or say anything that might keep us there for even one more second than we had to be.

As Darius reached the front door of the building, I hesitated. 'I don't think it's smart for the Raven Mockers to see that I'm up and walking around.' I kept my voice low, even though there was no one visible around us.

'You are probably right,' he said. 'Can you manage it?'

'Well, it's really not very far to the dorm. Plus, the weather's already nasty. I'll just call in some mist and increase the rain. That should do a pretty good job of hiding us. Remember to think that you're made of nothing but spirit. Try to imagine blending in with the storm. That usually makes it easier for me.'

'Will do. I'm ready whenever you are.'

I drew a deep breath, grateful that my chest was almost completely pain-free, and centered myself. 'Water, fire, and spirit, I need you,' I said. I flung wide one of my arms, as if receiving a hug from a friend, and hooked the other through Darius's arm. Immediately I felt the three elements surge around and through me and, hopefully, Darius, too. 'Spirit, I ask you to cloak us . . . hide us . . . let us blend with the night. Water, fill the air around us, bathe us and conceal us. Fire, I need you just a little – just enough to heat the ice so that it changes to mist. But not only around us,' I added quickly. 'Go all over the school grounds. Make everything soupy and misty and magical.' I smiled as I felt the elements quivering in anticipation of the tasks I'd given them. 'Okay, let's do this.' I nodded at Darius. He opened the door and, buoyed by wind and spirit and fire, we moved out into the ice storm.

I'd been right about one thing: the weather was nasty. I'd definitely liked it more looking out from inside the warm, dry building. It had been bad before, but as the elements responded to my command the storm increased in intensity. I glanced around us, trying to discover if the Raven Mockers had noticed us, but the elements were working together well, and Darius and I walked in what felt like the middle of a blinding snow globe turned to ice. The ice and wind were so bad that I would have fallen right on my butt if Darius hadn't had the reflexes of a cat and somehow managed to keep both of us on our feet.

Which reminded me, as he and I walked quickly but carefully down the frozen sidewalk, shrouded in a sudden mist that had blown up all around us, heads bent against the icy onslaught, I did not see one single cat. Okay, yeah, the weather was awful, especially after I'd messed with it, and cats don't like anything wet, but I didn't remember once in the months I'd lived at the House of Night walking anywhere on campus and not seeing at least a couple cats chasing after each other.

'There aren't any cats around,' I said.

Darius nodded. 'I already noticed.'

'What does it mean?'

'Trouble,' he said.

But I didn't have time to think about what the absence of cats might mean (and to worry about where my Nala might be). I was already feeling the drain of energy. I had to focus all of my strength and concentration to keep a running whispered litany going to wind, fire, and water. 'We are the night, let the spirit of night cover us . . . shroud us with mist . . . blow, wind, and keep evil eyes from seeing us . . .'

We were almost to the dorm when I heard the girl's voice.

I couldn't make out what she was saying, but the high, nervous tone definitely meant that something was wrong. The tension in Darius's arm, and the way he was peering around, trying to see through the elemental soup surrounding us, told me that he'd heard it, too.

As we got closer to the dorm, the voice got clearer and louder, and the words began to make sense.

'No, really! I— I just wanta get back to my room,' the frightened girl's voice said.

'You can get back. After I'm done with you.'

I froze, pulling Darius to a stop with me as I recognized the guy's voice even before the girl answered him.

'How about later, Stark? Then maybe we can—' Her words were abruptly cut off. I heard a little scream that ended in a gasp, and then there was an awful wet sound, and the moans began.

CHAPTER TWENTY

DARIUS STARTED FORWARD, PULLING ME WITH HIM. WE GOT to the little stoop that was the entrance to the girls' dorm. There were wide stairs, framed with staggered, waist-high stone walls, excellent for sitting on and flirting with your boyfriend after he'd walked you to the door and before he kissed you good night.

What Stark was doing was a twisted mockery of the good-night kissing that usually went on there. He was holding a girl in what could have been an embrace, had it not been obvious that, just seconds before his teeth had locked on her neck, she'd been trying to get away from him. I watched, horrified, as Stark, oblivious to our presence, continued his attack on her. It didn't matter that the girl was now moaning with sexual pleasure. I mean, we all know that's what happens when a vamp bites someone: The sex receptors in both the 'victim' (and in this case she was definitely his victim!) and the vamp were stimulated. She was physically feeling pleasure, but her wide, terrified eyes, and the rigidity of her body made it obvious she would fight him if she could. Stark was drinking in huge gulps from her throat. His moans were feral and the hand that wasn't holding her tight against his body was fumbling at the girl's skirt, lifting it so that he could situate himself between her legs and—

'Free her!' Darius commanded, pulling his arm from my grasp and stepping out of the pocket of concealing mist and night that had been hiding us.

Stark dropped the girl with no more thought than he would have given an empty QT Big Gulp. She whimpered and on hands and knees scrambled away from him toward Darius. Darius tossed an old-time handkerchief he'd pulled from his pocket at me, and said, 'Help her.' Then he situated himself like a muscular mountain between the hysterical girl and me and Stark.

I crouched down, realizing with a start of surprise that the girl was Becca Adams, a pretty blonde fourth former who had had a crush on Erik. As I watched Darius confront Stark, I handed Becca the handkerchief and murmured soothing words to her.

'You seem to keep getting in my way,' Stark said. His eyes

still glowed red, and there was blood on his mouth that he wiped away absently with the back of his hand. Again, I could see a darkness that pulsed around him. It wasn't completely visible, but more of a shadow within a shadow that shifted in and out of my vision, something that was actually easier seen when I wasn't looking for it.

And then it hit me. I knew where I'd noticed such strange liquid darkness before. It had been in the shadows of the tunnels, and then again in the glimpse of the spectral form of Neferet that had turned into the Raven Mocker who had almost killed me! With more sudden insight I recognized this darkness further. I was sure it had been present, pulsing like a living shadow around Stevie Rae before she'd Changed, only then my eyes and mind had just registered my best friend's need and anguish and struggle, and I'd processed the darkness she'd been moving in only as internal. Goddess, I'd been a fool! Overwhelmed, I tried to make sense of this new knowledge as Darius confronted Stark.

'Perhaps no one has explained to you that vampyre males do not abuse females, be they human, vampyre, or fledgling.' Darius spoke calmly, as if he were having an ordinary conversation with a friend.

'I'm not a vampyre.' Stark pointed to the outline of the red crescent moon on his forehead.

'That is an inconsequential detail. We' – Darius motioned from himself to Stark – 'do not abuse females. Ever. The Goddess has taught us better.'

Stark smiled, but the gesture lacked any real humor. 'I think you're gonna find that the rules have changed around here.'

'Well, boy, I think *you'll* find that some of us have rules written here' – Darius pointed to his heart – 'and rules written there aren't subject to the changing whims of those around us.'

Stark's face hardened. He reached back and pulled free a bow that had been fitted in a strap on his back. Then he took an arrow from the quiver I'd assumed was a man purse hanging over his shoulder (I should have known it wasn't; Stark isn't exactly a man-purse kind of guy). He fitted the arrow in the bow and said, 'I think I'll make sure you're never in my way again.'

'No!' I stood up and moved to Darius's side, my heart pounding like crazy. 'What the hell's happened to you, Stark?'

'I died!' he yelled, his face twisting in anger as the ghostly darkness rolled around him. Now that it was visible to me, I wondered how I could ever have missed it. Ignoring the shadowy evil, I continued to confront him.

'I know that!' I yelled. 'I was there, remember?' That made him pause. The bow dipped down a little. I took that as a good sign, and went on. 'You said you'd come back to Duchess and to me.'

When I said his dog's name, pain flashed across his face, and all of a sudden he looked young and vulnerable. But the expression only lasted an instant. I blinked and he was back to being dangerous and sarcastic, though his eyes had stopped glowing red.

'Yeah, I'm back. But things are different now. And bigger

changes are coming.' He gave Darius a look of utter disgust. 'All that old shit you believe in doesn't mean anything anymore. It makes you weak, and when you're weak you die.'

Darius shook his head. 'Honoring the way of the Goddess is never weakness.'

'Yeah, well, I haven't seen much of any goddess hanging around here, have you?'

'Yes, actually I have,' I spoke up. 'I've seen Nyx. She appeared right in there' – I pointed at the girls' dorm – 'just a couple days ago.'

Stark looked at me silently for a long time. I searched his face, trying to find some hint of that guy I'd felt such a connection with – whom I'd kissed right before he'd died in my arms. But all I could see was an unpredictable stranger, and foremost in my mind was the knowledge that if he shot that arrow he would not miss whatever he aimed at.

And suddenly that reminded me. He hadn't killed Stevie Rae. The fact that she was alive proved that he hadn't *meant* to kill her. So maybe there was some piece of the old Stark left within him.

'Stevie Rae's fine, by the way,' I said.

'That's nothing to me,' he said.

I shrugged. 'Just thought you'd want to know, since it was your arrow that made her a shish kebab.'

'I was doing what I was told to do. The boss said make her bleed; I made her bleed.'

'Neferet? Is that who's controlling you?' I asked.

His eyes blazed. 'No one's controlling me!'

'Your bloodlust is controlling you,' Darius said. 'If you weren't under its control, you wouldn't have had to force yourself on that fledgling.'

'Yeah? Ya think so? Well, you're wrong. I happen to like my bloodlust! I liked doing whatever I want with that girl. It's time vampyres stopped slinking around. We're smarter, stronger, *better* than humans. We should be in charge, not them!'

'That fledgling isn't a human.' Darius's voice was like a naked blade, reminding me that he wasn't just a big brother-type guy; he was a Son of Erebus and one of the most powerful warriors alive.

'I was thirsty and there wasn't a human handy,' Stark said.

'Zoey, get the girl into the dorm.' Darius didn't take his eyes off Stark. 'She is done serving his convenience.'

I hurried over to Becca and helped her to her feet. She was a little wobbly but able to walk. As we reached Darius, he moved forward with us, always keeping himself between us and Stark. Just as we were passing by him, Stark spoke with an angry intensity that sent a chill down the back of my neck.

'You know, all I have to do is think about killing you and shoot this arrow. Wherever you are, you're dead.'

'If that is so, then I will be dead,' Darius said matter-of-factly. 'And you will be a monster.'

'I don't mind being a monster!'

'And I don't mind dying if it is in the service of my High Priestess and, ultimately, my Goddess,' Darius said.

'If you hurt him, I'll come against you with everything I have,' I told Stark.

Stark looked at me and his lips tilted up in a ghost of that cute, cocky smile he used to have. 'You're a little bit of a monster yourself, aren't ya, Zoey?'

I didn't think that nasty comment was worth a response, and obviously neither did Darius. He kept shepherding us by Stark, opening the front door of the dorm and helping Becca inside. But instead of me following her in, I paused. Intuition was telling me that there was something I had to do, and much as I'd like to ignore my intuition, I knew I shouldn't. 'I'll be right in,' I told Darius. I could see that he was going to argue with me, but I shook my head and said, 'Trust me. I just need a second.'

'I'll be inside the door,' Darius said, threw Stark a hard look, and then stepped into the dorm.

I faced Stark. I knew I was taking a chance with what I was going to say to him, but I kept remembering Kramisha's poem and the line that said, '*Humanity saves her / Will she save me?*' I at least had to try.

'Jack's taking care of Duchess,' I said without any preamble.

I saw that flash of pain in his eyes again, but his voice wasn't touched by it. 'So?'

'So I'm just telling you that your dog's fine. She's had a pretty hard time, but she's okay.'

'I'm not who I used to be, so she's not my dog anymore.' This time I heard a quaver in his voice, which gave me enough hope that I took a step toward him.

'Hey, the great thing about dogs is that they give unconditional love. Duch doesn't care who you are right now. She'll still love you.'

'You don't know what you're talking about,' he said.

'Yeah, I do. I've spent some time with your dog. She's got a really big heart.'

'I wasn't talking about her. I was talking about me.'

'Well, I've spent some time with red fledglings, too. Not to mention that the first ever Changed red vamp is my best friend. Stevie Rae's different than she used to be, but I still love her,' I said. 'Maybe if you spent some time with Stevie Rae and the rest of the red fledglings you could, I don't know, *find* yourself again. They have.' I said this with way more confidence than I felt. After all, I had glimpsed fragments of the darkness surrounding Stark down in those tunnels, around those red fledglings, but I couldn't help believing it would be best to get him away from here, where evil seemed to come and go so easily.

'Sure,' he said too quickly. 'Why don't you take me to this Stevie Rae vamp and I'll see what happens?'

'Sure,' I said just as quickly. 'Why don't you leave your bow and arrows here and show me how to get off campus without the bird freaks knowing and I'll do just that?'

His expression hardened and he was a mean stranger again. 'I don't go anywhere without my bow, and no one leaves campus without them knowing.'

'Then it looks like I won't be taking you to Stevie Rae,' I said.

'I don't need you to show me where Stevie Rae is. She knows all about their little hideout. When she wants your friend, she'll have her. If I were you, I'd expect to see Stevie Rae a lot sooner than you thought you would.'

Warning bells were ringing like a fire alarm in my mind, and I definitely didn't have to ask who the 'she' was Stark was talking about. But instead of showing just how upset Stark's admission made me, I smiled calmly and said, 'No one's hiding out. I'm right here, and Stevie Rae is right where she's been since she Changed. No big deal. Plus, it's always great to see her, so if she shows up here, that's cool.'

'Yeah, whatever. No big deal. And I'm cool staying right where I am.' He looked away from me, out into the icy fog that was drifting lazily around us. 'I don't get why you care anyway.'

And suddenly I knew exactly what to say. 'I'm just keeping my promises to you.'

'What do you mean?'

'You asked me to promise you two things before you died. One was not to forget you, and I haven't. The other was to look after Duchess, and I'm letting you know that I've made sure she's okay.'

'You can tell that Jack kid that Duchess is his dog now. Tell him . . .' Still not looking at me, he paused and drew a shaky breath. 'Tell him she's a good dog and to take care of her.'

Continuing to follow my intuition, I crossed the few feet between us and put my hand on his shoulder, almost exactly as I'd done the night he died. 'You know it doesn't matter what you say or who you give her to, Duchess will always belong to you. When you died, she cried. I was there. I saw it. I didn't forget. I won't ever forget.'

He didn't look at me, but slowly he dropped his bow to

the ground and put his hand over mine. We just stood there like that. Touching but not saying anything. I was watching his face carefully, so I saw the entire transformation. As he pressed his hand over mine, he let out a long, slow breath, and his face relaxed. The last hint of red left his eyes, and the strange, shadowy darkness evaporated. When he finally looked at me, he was the kid I'd been so drawn to and who had died while I held him in my arms, listening to him tell me that he'd come back.

'What if there's nothing left in me worth loving?' He asked it in a voice so low that if I hadn't been standing close I wouldn't have heard him.

'I think you can still choose what you are, or at least what you are becoming. Stevie Rae chose her humanity over the monster. I think it's up to you.'

I know what I did next was stupid. I'm not even sure why I did it. I mean, I already had unresolved issues with Erik and Heath. The last thing I needed was another boy complicating my life, but at that moment there was only Stark and me, and he was himself again – the guy who had agonized over the gift Nyx had given him because he had accidentally caused the death of his mentor; the guy who had been horrified at the thought of hurting anyone again. The guy I'd felt such an immediate and deep connection to I'd thought that just maybe there really were such thing as soul mates, and had considered, at least for a few brief moments, that he might be mine. That's all I was thinking about as I stepped into his arms. When he bent and hesitatingly pressed his lips to mine,

I closed my eyes and kissed him softly and sweetly. He kissed me back, holding me so gently it was as if he thought I might break.

Then I felt him stiffen and he pulled away, taking a staggering step backwards. I was sure I saw tears in his eyes before he yelled, 'You should have forgotten me!' Stark picked up his bow and bolted away into the roiling darkness of the stormy night.

When he was gone I stood there staring after him, wondering what the hell was wrong with me. How could I have kissed a guy who had been attacking someone just minutes before? How could I feel a connection to someone who might be more monster than man? Maybe I didn't even know myself anymore. I sure didn't know what I was becoming.

I shivered. The cold dampness of the night seemed to have settled through my clothes and skin and into my bones. And I felt tired. Really, really tired.

'Thank you, fire and air and water,' I whispered to the listening elements. 'You served me well tonight. You may go now.' Fog and ice swirled around me once, and then rushed away, leaving me alone with the night and the storm and my confusion. Wearily I trudged back to the dorm, wishing I could go inside, take a hot shower, and curl up in my bed to sleep for several days.

Naturally, my wish was no one's command . . .

CHAPTER TWENTY-ONE

I'D BARELY TOUCHED THE DOOR WHEN DARIUS OPENED IT for me. His sharp look made me wonder if he'd been watching the scene between Stark and me, and I sincerely hoped he hadn't.

'Damien and the Twins are in there,' was all he said, motioning for me to follow him into the central room of the dorm.

'First I need to borrow your cell phone,' I said.

He didn't hesitate or ask annoying questions about who I needed to call and why. He simply handed me his phone, and then he walked ahead of me into the common room. I punched in Stevie Rae's number and held my breath while it rang. When she answered it sounded like she was talking into a tin can, but at least I could hear her.

'Hey, it's me,' I said.

'Z! Dang, I'm glad to hear your voice! Are ya okay?'

'Yeah, I'm better.'

'Yea! So what's going on with—'

'I'll fill you in on all that later,' I cut her off. 'Right now you gotta listen to me.'

''Kay,' she said.

'Do what I told you to do.'

There was a pause and then she said, 'What you told me in the note?'

'Yeah. You're being watched *in the tunnels*. Something is down there with you.'

I expected her to gasp or freak, but all she said was a calm, 'Okay, I understand.'

I continued quickly. 'There's a good chance the bird things will grab you if you come out of the tunnels anywhere they're expecting you to surface, so you're going to have to be really, really careful.'

'Don't worry about it, Z. I've been doin' a little secret recon-noitering of my own since you passed me that note. I think I can get everyone there without being seen.'

'Call Sister Mary Angela first and tell her you're coming. Tell her I'm coming, too, ASAP. But don't tell the red fledg-lings where you're going for as long as you can keep it from them. Do you understand?'

'Yes.'

'Okay. Give Grandma a hug for me.'

'Will do,' she said. 'And I won't let anyone tell her about your accident. It'll just stress her.'

'Thanks,' I said. 'Is Heath okay?'

'Totally. I told ya don't worry about him. Both of your boyfriends are fine.'

I sighed, wishing I could correct her and tell her I only had one boyfriend. 'Good, I'm glad they're safe. Oh, Aphrodite's safe, too,' I added, feeling a little strange about it, but thinking that since I'd checked on my Imprinted human, maybe Stevie Rae would like to check on hers, too.

Her laugh was happy and familiar. 'Oh, Z, I know Aphrodite's okay. I'd be able to tell right away if something happened to her. It's weird, but it's true.'

'Okay, good. I guess. Hey, I gotta go. And you do, too.'

'You want me to get everyone outta here tonight?'

'Now,' I said firmly.

'Got it,' she said. 'See you soon, Z.'

'Please be very, very careful.'

'Don't worry about me. I got a few tricks up my sleeve.'

'You'll need them. See ya,' I said, and cut off the tinny connection. It was a relief to know Stevie Rae was going to move all the red fledglings to the basement beneath the Benedictine Sisters' Abbey. I had to believe that the darkness I'd begun to see hovering around the tunnels wouldn't do so well in the basement of a bunch of nuns. I also had to believe Stevie Rae could get all the kids there without being captured by the Raven Mockers. If only the rest of us were that lucky, we could meet and regroup and figure out what the hell we could do about Kalona and Neferet. And I would ask Stevie Rae about the creepy dark-shadow stuff. Sadly, I had a feeling she would know way more than me about it.

I entered the common room. Normally, after school it would have been crazy-busy with fledglings hanging out, watching one of the several flat-screen TVs. Comfortable chairs and loveseats were clustered around the room, and kids should have filled them up as they relaxed after a long school day.

Today there weren't many fledglings, and those who were sitting around were unusually subdued. Part of that might be because the cable had been knocked out by the storm, but the House of Night had some major backup generators, and kids should have been watching DVDs – I mean, hello! Almost everyone had Netflix. But the few kids who were present were crouched together, speaking barely above a whisper.

Automatically I looked over at the area where my friends and I liked to gather and was relieved to see Damien and the Twins. They had Becca in the middle of them, and I assumed they were comforting the girl and keeping her from bursting into hysterical tears. When I got closer, I understood that I was very wrong.

'Really, I'm fine. It's no big deal,' Becca was insisting in a voice that wasn't shaky and scared anymore, but had suddenly changed to sounding incredibly annoyed.

'No big deal!' Shaunee said. 'Of course it was a big deal.'

'The guy *attacked* you,' Erin said.

'It wasn't exactly like that,' Becca said, waving her hands dismissively. 'We were just messing around. Plus, Stark really is hot.'

Erin snorted. 'Yeah, I usually find rapists majorly hot.'

Becca's eyes narrowed and she looked cold and mean. 'Stark *is* hot, and you're just jealous that he didn't want you.'

'Didn't want me?' Erin said incredulously. 'Don't you mean, didn't want to molest me? Why are you making excuses for him?'

'What the hell's wrong with you, Becca?' Shaunee said. 'No guy should ever get away with—'

'Hang on,' Damien spoke up. 'You know, Becca's right. Stark is one hot guy.' The Twins stared at him in shock, and he hurried on. 'If Becca says they were just messing around, who are we to judge?'

It was then that Darius and I stepped into their agitated little circle. 'What's going on? Are you okay?' I asked Becca.

'Totally fine.' Throwing the Twins an icy look, she got to her feet. 'Actually, I'm starving, so I'm gonna go find something to eat. Sorry I caused you two a hassle out there. Later.' She hurried away.

'What the hell just happened?' I asked in a low voice.

'The same thing that's happened all over this damn—'

'Upstairs!' Darius commanded, shutting Erin up.

I was semi-amazed to see my friends meekly obey Darius. We filed out of the common room, ignoring the curious stares of the few kids who were quietly sitting around. On the way up the staircase, Darius said, 'Is Aphrodite in her room?'

'Yeah, she said she was tired,' Shaunee said.

'She's probably hanging upside down from the ceiling in her usual batperch,' Erin said. She glanced over her shoulder at Darius and added, 'Speaking of Aphrodikey, she's gonna give birth to a big ol' litter of kittens when she sees that you've messed up your pretty face.'

'Yeah, and if you need comfort from her shallow hatefulness, you can try a little café mocha over here,' Shaunee said, waggling her brows at him.

'Or a vanilla smoothie over here,' Erin flirted.

Darius smiled good-naturedly and just said, 'I will keep that in mind.'

I thought the Twins were taking their lives in their hands, and I was darn sure not going to get between them and Aphrodite if she found out they'd been flirting with her man, but I was too tired to say anything.

'You know that blue cashmere pullover you just got from Saks?' Damien asked Erin.

'Yeah, what about it?'

'I call dibs on it if Aphrodite disembowels you for hitting on her man,' Damien said.

'She's just a human now,' Erin said.

'Yeah, we figure together we can take her,' Shaunee said, then she blew kisses at Darius. 'Remember that, warrior boy.'

Darius chuckled and I rolled my eyes. We were just passing my room when my door opened and Aphrodite called, 'I'm in here.'

We all stopped and filed into my room. 'Aphrodite, what are you doing in—'

'Ohmygoddess! What the hell happened to your face?' Not paying attention to anyone else, Aphrodite ran to Darius and started to flutter her hands around the long thin wound that stretched down the side of his face. 'Are you okay? Damn, it looks awful! Does it hurt?' She pulled back the sleeves on her shirt, exposing the newly healed bite marks Stevie Rae's teeth had left. 'Do you need to bite me? Go ahead. I don't mind.'

Darius took her hands in his, stilling her anxious movements, and said calmly, 'I am well, my beauty. It is but a scratch.'

'How did it happen?' Aphrodite sounded close to tears as she pulled on Darius's hands and led him over to the spare bed that used to be Stevie Rae's.

'My beauty! All is well,' he repeated, pulling her down on his lap and holding her close to him.

He said a bunch of other stuff to her, too, but I'd stopped listening. I was too busy staring at the—

'Cameron! There you are, sweetheart! I've been so worried about you.' Damien plopped down on the floor and started petting his blond tabby.

'Beelzebub, where the hell have you been?' Shaunee chastised the hateful gray creature who had chosen both of the Twins as his own.

'We figured you were chasing around after Maleficent, and sure enough here you are and here she is,' Erin said.

'Hang on,' I said, seeing Nala curled up on my bed. I looked around my room, taking inventory of the eight – *eight!* – cats that were hanging out there. 'What's with all the cats?'

'That's why I'm over here,' Aphrodite said, sniffling softly as she snuggled back into Darius's arms. 'Maleficent was acting very odd. She kept coming in and out of her cat door and making weird yowling sounds.' Aphrodite paused and blew a kiss to the awful white puffball that masqueraded as her cat. 'So finally I followed her. She led me to your room. I came in and found all these cats. Then I heard you guys in the hall.' She turned her beautiful blue eyes on the Twins. 'I heard *everything* you guys said in the hall, and do not think for one instant just because I've turned human it doesn't mean I cannot happily kick your combined asses.'

'But what are all these cats doing in here?' I said quickly before the Twins started a mini human-fledgling war.

'Hey there, Nefertiti!' Darius called, and a sleek calico female jumped up on the bed beside him and began to wind around his body.

'They're our cats,' Damien said, still petting Cameron. 'Remember when we escaped from here yesterday? They were all outside the school wall waiting for us.' He glanced up at me. 'Are we leaving again?'

'I hope so,' I said. 'But wait.' I was still taking stock of the cats. 'All of our cats are here, but what about that great big one over there, and the little cream-colored one who's sticking close to him?'

'That big cat is Dragon Lankford's Maine Coon,' Damien

said. 'His name is Shadowfax.' Dragon Lankford, who almost everyone called Dragon, is our fencing professor and is a master with the blade. Damien was a talented fencer, so it wasn't surprising he recognized Dragon's cat.

'Hey, I think that little white one is Guinevere, Professor Anastasia's cat,' Erin said.

'You're right, Twin,' Shaunee said. 'She's always hanging out during Spells and Rituals class.'

'What about that one?' I pointed to a familiar-looking Siamese whose body was the silver-white of moonlight, tipped in delicate gray ears and face. Then I realized why she looked familiar and answered my own question. 'That's Professor Lenobia's cat. I don't know her name, but I've seen her following the professor around the stables.'

'So, let me get this straight: All of our cats, plus cats that belong to Dragon, his wife, and Professor Lenobia, are suddenly hanging out in Zoey's room,' Darius said.

'Why are they here?' Erin asked.

I answered her question with my own. 'Have you guys seen any other cats today? I mean, while you were in class and at lunch, coming and going from the dorm and class to class, did you see any cats?'

'No,' the Twins said together.

'I didn't,' Damien answered more slowly.

'Not a one,' Aphrodite said.

'And you noticed earlier that we saw not one cat between the infirmary and the dormitory,' Darius said.

'I thought it was bad then; I still think it's bad,' I said.

'Why would all the cats except these disappear?' Damien asked.

'The cats hate the birdmen,' I said. 'Whenever Nala's been with me and one's been around, she's totally freaked.'

'There's more to it than that. If it was just about hating them, then the cats would *all* be hiding, and not just special ones hanging out in here,' Aphrodite said.

'Maybe that's it,' Damien said. 'There's something special about these particular cats.'

'Okay, I hate to be a bitch – or maybe I don't – but anyway, can we forget about the damn cats for a second? I want to know who the hell did this to my man's face,' Aphrodite said.

'Kalona,' I said, when it was obvious Darius was too involved with grinning at the 'my man' title Aphrodite had awarded him to answer.

'I was afraid of that,' Damien said. 'How'd it happen?'

'Darius attacked Rephaim,' I explained, 'which pissed off Kalona. He didn't let Stark kill him, but the cut was his parting gift for Darius wounding his favorite son.'

'That fucking Stark!' Shaunee said.

'He's really bad news. He and the nasty-assed birdmen do whatever the hell they want,' Erin said.

'And no one does anything about it,' Shaunee finished.

'It's like the thing you just witnessed with Becca,' Damien said.

'Speaking of,' Shaunee said. 'What was the deal with you agreeing with that bimbo about *oh, no big deal because Stark's sooooo hot!* Talk about annoying.'

'You weren't going to get through to her. Becca's on their side. As far as I can tell, Stark and the birds and Kalona do anything to anyone, and there are no repercussions for their actions.'

'It's worse than no repercussions,' Aphrodite said. Still within Darius's arms, she'd gotten herself together. 'It's like Kalona's cast a spell over everyone, and the spell somehow extends to Stark and the birds.'

'That's why I agreed with Becca and just let her go. It's not a good idea to call attention to the fact that we're the only ones not in the Kalona Fan Club,' Damien said.

'And Neferet, don't forget about her,' Aphrodite said.

'She's with him, but I don't think she's under his spell,' I said. 'I overheard them talking when they thought I was passed out, and she disagreed with him. He got big and bad and scary with her, and she seemed to back off, but what she really did was just change her tactics. She's manipulating him, and I can't tell if he knows it or not. And she's changing, too.'

'Changing? What do you mean by that?' Damien asked.

'Her power is different than it used to be,' Darius said.

I nodded. 'It's like a switch has been thrown inside her, and it's let loose a different kind of power.'

'A dark power,' Aphrodite said. We all looked at her. 'Her power isn't based on Nyx anymore. Sure, she's still using the gifts our Goddess gave her, but she's channeling energy from somewhere else, too. Couldn't you guys feel it in the hall outside the sickroom?'

There was a long silence, and then Damien spoke up. 'I think we were too busy struggling against Kalona's attraction.'

'And scared shitless,' Erin said.

'Entirely,' Shaunee agreed.

'Well, so now we know. Neferet is even more of a threat than she's ever been. Neferet and Kalona are planning a new future, and it has something to do with taking over the Council,' I said, wishing I could crawl into bed and pull the covers over my head.

'Oh my goddess! The High Council?' Aphrodite said.

'I don't know for sure, but that's what I'm afraid of. I'm also afraid her new power has given her special abilities.' I paused. I didn't want to freak out the gang before I had my talk with Stevie Rae, but they did need to be warned, so I picked my words carefully. 'I think Neferet can project her influence by moving through, or maybe manipulating, shadows.'

'That's bad,' Damien said.

'It means we have to be on guard,' Erin said.

'Majorly on guard,' Shaunee agreed.

Darius nodded. 'Remember always: Neferet is our enemy, Kalona is our enemy, and most of the other fledglings are our enemies, too.' His sharp gaze went from kid to kid. 'What about the rest of the professors?' Darius asked them. 'All of you attended classes today, didn't you? How were they acting?'

'Yeah, we went to class, weird as that was,' Shaunee said.

'It was like attending Stepford High School,' Erin said.

'It seems the professors are all enthralled with Kalona, too,'

Damien said. 'Of course, I can't tell you that for sure. We weren't ever alone with the professors.'

'Not alone? What do you mean?' I said.

'I mean those bird things are everywhere – coming and going from class, and even *in* class.'

'Are you kidding?' A shiver of revulsion quavered though my body at the thought of those terrible mutations of nature moving freely among fledglings – like they belonged here!

'He's not kidding. They are everywhere. It's like *Invasion of the* fucking *Body Snatchers*,' Aphrodite said. 'The good guys look the same on the outside, but are screwed on the inside, and the Raven Mockers are the damn aliens.'

'And the Sons of Erebus? Are they supporting this?' Darius asked.

'I haven't seen one warrior since Aristos escorted us onto campus,' Damien said. 'How about you guys?'

The Twins and Aphrodite shook their heads no.

'This is so not good,' I said. I rubbed my forehead as a wave of exhaustion engulfed me. What were we going to do? Who were our friends? And how the hell were we going to get out of the House of Night and to what I could only hope would be safety?

CHAPTER TWENTY-TWO

'ZOEY? ARE YOU OKAY?'

I looked up to meet Damien's soft brown eyes. Before I could answer him, Darius spoke up.

'She is not. Zoey must get sleep; she must rest to restore her strength.'

'How's your nasty, ugly, gaping wound?' Erin asked.

'It doesn't look like you're bleeding through that charming hospital garb, so we assumed you were fixed right up,' Shaunee said.

'I'm better, but I'm having an issue with getting my strength back. It's like I'm a cell phone with a messed-up charger.'

'You must rest,' Darius repeated. 'Your wound was almost fatal. Recovery takes time.'

'We don't have time!' I yelled in frustration. 'We need to get the hell out of here and away from Kalona until we can figure out how we can beat him.'

'Getting out of here isn't going to be as easy as it was last time,' Damien said.

Aphrodite snorted. 'As if that was easy!'

'It will be compared to what we're up against now,' Damien continued. 'Raven Mockers are everywhere. Last night they were attacking people randomly. It was mass confusion then, and that helped us slip away. Today they're well organized and stationed all over.'

'I saw them around the perimeter. They've more than doubled the guards we had before,' Darius said.

'But there aren't any of them outside the dorm, like you used to be,' I said to him.

'It's because they don't care whether we're safe. They just care that we don't leave the school,' Damien said.

'Why?' I asked wearily, rubbing at my temple where a headache was starting to pound.

'Whatever they're planning needs isolation right now,' Darius said.

'Doesn't that point more to them just taking over this House of Night, versus trying anything with the High Council?' Aphrodite said.

She asked me, but when I couldn't make myself give her

the reassuring response she was obviously hoping for, Darius spoke up.

'Perhaps, but it is too early to really know.'

'Well, the ice storm's helping with the isolation thing. Power is down everywhere. Cell-phone service is sketchy. Except for little pockets being run by generators, Tulsa's blacked out,' Damien said.

'I wonder if Nyx's High Council even knows Shekinah is dead,' Darius said.

I looked at Damien. 'What happens when the High Priestess of all Vampyres dies?'

Damien's forehead scrunched up as he thought. 'Well, if I remember correctly from Vamp Soc class, Nyx's Council meets and elects a new High Priestess. That only happens about once every three to five hundred years. Once elected, a High Priestess reigns for her entire life. The election is a big deal, especially when it's sudden like this one will have to be.'

I perked up. 'Doesn't it make sense that Nyx's Council would be verrrry interested in how Shekinah suddenly dropped dead?'

Damien nodded. 'I'd definitely say so.'

'So that might be a major reason for Kalona wanting to keep our House of Night isolated. He doesn't want the attention of the High Council,' Aphrodite said.

'Or he does want their attention – as in presenting Neferet as the new vamp High Priestess, but they are gathering their power so they can be sure of the Council's vote.'

There was a dead silence in the room as everyone stared in horror at me.

'We cannot allow that to happen,' Darius finally spoke.

'We won't,' I said firmly, hoping we'd somehow be able to back up my statement. 'Hey, is Kalona still saying he's Erebus come to earth?' I asked.

'Yeah,' Erin said.

'And even though it sounds stupid, everyone believes him,' Shaunee said.

'Did you actually see Kalona today?' I asked Shaunee. 'I mean, except for when we first got here?'

She shook her head, 'Nope.'

I looked from her to Erin.

'Ditto. I didn't see him either,' she said.

'Didn't see him,' Damien said.

'Neither did I, and I say good riddance,' Aphrodite said.

'Yeah, but you might be the only one,' I said slowly. I looked from the Twins to Damien. 'We've already said that Kalona has some kind of mojo crap he uses on everyone. It even works on us, or at least it does unless we don't look him in the eye and fight it real hard – and we were ready for him. We knew he was evil. Hell, it took me seeing him almost choke Darius to death for me to stop panting over him.'

'That bastard choked you?' Aphrodite said. 'Damn, that pisses me off! Oh, and abbreviated herd of nerd, in case you didn't get it the first time, get this: I'm not in the least bit affected by the mojo the winged freak lays on you. I don't like him. At all.'

'That's right,' I said. 'I noticed that earlier today. You really don't feel drawn to him at all.'

'What's to be drawn to? He's a big old bully. And he's never dressed properly. *And* I really don't like birds. I mean, the bird flu is supposed to be a seriously unattractive way to die. So, no. He's got nothing for me.'

'I wonder why his stuff doesn't work on you?' I mused aloud.

''Cause she's abby-normal?' Shaunee said.

'A serious freak in a human skin suit?' Erin added.

'How about because I'm exceptionally intuitive, and I see through his bullshit? Oh, that also means I see through yours, too,' Aphrodite said.

'She might have something there,' Damien said, sounding excited. 'We've all felt his draw, but we can resist him, unlike the other fledglings, right?'

We nodded.

'Well, we're all into the elements – have been physically and intuitively touched by them, much more so than the other fledglings. Maybe our extrasensory abilities give us the power to resist Kalona's allure.'

'The red fledglings said they weren't drawn to him at all, just like Aphrodite,' I said. 'And they all have psychic abilities.'

'That sounds logical, and it works for fledglings, but what about adult vampyres?' Darius said.

'Don't your psychic abilities vary, just like ours do?' Aphrodite said. 'Sure, fledglings say all vamps can do the mind thing, but it's not really true, is it?'

'No, it isn't really true, though many of us are highly intuitive,' Darius said.

'Are you?' I asked.

Darius smiled. 'Only when it comes to protecting those I have sworn to defend.'

'But that means there *is* something especially intuitive about you,' Damien said, still sounding excited. 'Okay, so what other vamps at this House of Night are the most psychic?'

'Neferet,' we all said together.

'We already know that. She's made her decision for Kalona, so we're not going to count her right now. Who else?'

'Damien! I think you *are* on to something!' I said. Everyone stared at me, but I was staring at the extra cats in the room.

And, as per usual, Damien got it right away. 'Dragon, Professor Anastasia, and Professor Lenobia! They're who I'd consider as the most intuitive after Neferet.'

'It's no coincidence their cats are here with us,' Darius said.

'They're a sign, sent to us to let us know we're on the right track,' Damien said.

'Then that's the second reason we can't get out of here tonight,' I said.

'The second reason?' Aphrodite said.

'The first is that there's no way I can control the elements long enough to keep all those Raven Mockers from seeing us; I'm just too tired. And the second is if Dragon and Professor Anastasia and Professor Lenobia can actually see through Kalona's bullpoopie, then maybe they can help us get rid of him.'

'The world is falling apart. It's really okay to cuss a little,' Aphrodite said.

'The world falling apart isn't an excuse to take up bad habits,' I said, sounding weirdly like my grandma.

'So it is agreed: We stay here one more day. Zoey, you must sleep. Tomorrow you all attend classes as you normally would,' Darius said.

'Yeah, agreed,' I said. 'Damien, can you get Dragon alone long enough to see if he might be on our side?'

'I should be able to during my fencing class tomorrow.'

'Who has Professor Anastasia's Spells and Rituals class?'

The Twins raised their hands like good students.

'Can you guys check her out?'

'Definitely,' Erin said.

'Will do,' Shaunee said.

'I'll talk to Lenobia,' I said.

'And Darius and I will scout out where all those nasty Raven Mockers are stationed around the walls,' Aphrodite said.

'Be careful,' I told her.

'She will be,' Darius said.

'I think no matter what, we should leave tomorrow. Staying here any longer than absolutely necessary feels wrong,' I said.

'Agreed. If your strength has returned,' Darius said.

'It better,' I said.

There was a pause, and then Darius told me solemnly, 'When we escape, Kalona will come after you. He will hunt you until he finds you.'

'How do you know that for sure?' Aphrodite said.

'Tell them what he calls you,' Darius said to me.

I sighed. 'He calls me A-ya.'

'Oh!' Erin said.

'Shit!' Shaunee finished.

'Now *that's* seriously bad news,' Damien said.

'He really believes you're the maiden the Ghigua women used to trap him more than a thousand years ago?' Aphrodite said.

'Apparently.'

'Do you think it would help if you told him you're no maiden?' Aphrodite flashed me a cocky grin.

I rolled my eyes at her and then, because Aphrodite's not so subtle mention of my un-virgin state made my thoughts inadvertently start to drift to the guys in my life, I added, 'Hey, I wonder why Stark's so under Kalona's spell. He has a major gift from Nyx, and before he died he seemed really intuitive.'

'Stark is an absolute asshole,' Shaunee said.

'Yeah, between what we heard from the other kids, and what went on with Becca, we can definitely say he's seriously bad news,' Erin said.

'Dying and then un-dying might have messed him up, but my vote is that he was a jerk before he croaked and then uncroaked,' Aphrodite said. 'We all need to stay far, far away from him. I think his badness is right up there with Kalona and Neferet.'

'Yeah, he's like a Raven Mocker without the wings,' Erin said.

'Eesh,' Shaunee agreed.

I didn't say anything. I just sat there and felt really tired and really guilty. *I'd kissed him. Again.* And my friends all thought he was a monster, probably because he was a monster. And if he's such bad news, which it seriously looks like he is, *how the hell could I think there is anything good left in him?*

'Okay, Z has to sleep,' Damien said, getting up with Cameron still in his arms. 'We know what we're supposed to do, so let's do it and then get out of here.' Damien hugged me. 'Forget about Kramisha's poem,' he whispered. 'You can't save everyone, especially if he doesn't want to be saved.'

I hugged him back, but didn't say anything.

'Getting back to those tunnels sounds good to me. We all need to be away from this place.' Damien smiled sadly at me and left the room with the Twins, who called goodbyes to me, too, as their cat trotted after them.

'Come on.' Aphrodite took Darius's hand and pulled him off the bed. 'You're not going back to your room tonight.'

'I'm not?' he said, smiling warmly at her.

'No, you're not. There seems to be a scarcity of Sons of Erebus around here, so I'm going to keep my eyes, and a few other parts of my body, on you.'

'Puke,' I said, but I couldn't help grinning at them.

'You just sleep,' Aphrodite told me. 'You'll need all your strength to deal with the guy-mess waiting for you. I have a feeling Erik and Heath are going to be a bigger drain than controlling the elements.'

'Hey, thanks, Aphrodite,' I said sarcastically.

'Don't mention it. I'm all about helping you out.'

'Good night, Priestess. I wish you a restful sleep,' Darius said right before Aphrodite pulled him out of the room. The last of the cats followed him out, leaving me alone (finally) with my Nala.

I sighed and dug into my pocket for the bottle of blood stashed there. I shook it up like it was one of those yummy cold Starbucks bottled drinks and downed it. The blood felt good spreading like warm fingers through my body, but it didn't give me the electric jolt I was used to. I was just too exhausted. I dragged myself from the bed, pulled off the stupid hospital clothes, and rattled around in my drawer for my favorite guy's boxers (the ones with Batman symbols all over them) and a stretched-out old T-shirt. Just before I put on the shirt I caught a glimpse of myself in the mirror and froze.

Was that really me? I looked way older than seventeen. All of my tattoos were visible, and they were like a breath of life blown across a corpse. I was so pale! And the circles under my eyes were truly scary. Slowly I allowed my gaze to drift down to check out my wound. It was awful, and so darn big! I mean, it stretched all the way from shoulder to shoulder. No, it wasn't gaping open anymore like a hideous mouth, but it was a jagged, puckered red ridge that made Darius's knife wound look like the scratch he liked to call it.

I touched the wound gently and winced at how sore it was. Would it always stay this raised? Okay, I realize it was incredibly shallow of me, but I wanted to burst into tears.

Not because all hell was coming against us. Not because Neferet had turned überdangerous. Not because she and Kalona might very well be threatening the balance of good and evil in the known world. Not because I was a confused mess about Erik and Heath and Stark. But because I was going to have a massively ugly scar, and I'd probably never be able to wear a tank top again. And what about if I ever wanted to let anyone see me, well, naked again? I mean, I'd had one bad experience, but surely some day I was going to be in a great relationship and I'd want him to eventually see me naked. Right? I stared at the nasty-looking, unhealed scar and stifled a sob. Wrong.

Okay, I seriously needed to stop thinking about this, and I definitely was going to quit looking at myself naked. It just can't be good for me. Hell! It probably wasn't good for anyone!

I hastily pulled the T-shirt over my head and muttered, 'Aphrodite must be rubbing off on me. I swear I didn't used to be this shallow.'

Nala was waiting for me on my bed in her usual place on my pillow. I slid under the sheets and curled up with her, loving how she snuggled against me and turned on her purr engine. I guess I should have been scared to fall asleep, what with the last Kalona dream-visit I'd had, but I was too tired to think, too tired to care. I just closed my eyes and gave myself gratefully up to the darkness.

When the dream started, it wasn't a meadow, and so, foolishly, I was immediately relieved and relaxed. I was on an incredibly beautiful island, looking out across a lagoon at a skyline that seemed familiar, even though I knew I'd never been there before. The water had a fishy, salty smell. There was a depth and richness to it, a sense of vastness that I recognized as belonging to the ocean, even though I've never been to the coast. The sun was setting and the sky was lit up with a fading brilliance that reminded me of autumn leaves. I was sitting on a marble bench the color of moonbeams. It was intricately carved with vines and flowers and felt like it belonged to another time and place. I ran my hand across the smooth back of it, which was still warm from the fading day. It was like I really was there, and not dreaming at all. I glanced over my shoulder, and my eyes widened. Wow! Behind me was a palace with beautiful arched doors and windows, all in pristine white, amazing pillars and wedding cake-like chandeliers peeking out of the elegant windowpanes and twinkling in the predusk.

It was enough to take my breath away, and I was really pleased with my sleeping self for making it all up, but I was also baffled. It all seemed so real. And so familiar. Why?

I turned my face back to the lagoon view, looking across at a domed cathedral and little boats and lots of other amazing stuff that there's no way I could have imagined all on my own. The soft night breeze was coming off the water, bringing the distinctly rich scents of the dark water. I breathed deeply, enjoying the uniqueness of it. Sure, some people might say it was kinda stinky, but I didn't think so, I was just—

Holy crap! A terrible skittering of fear fingered down my spine. I knew why this seemed familiar.

Aphrodite had described this place to me just a few days ago. Not in detail. She hadn't been able to remember everything, but what she had been able to tell me had made a distinct and unsettling impression. So much so that I recognized the water and the palace and the ancient feel of it.

This was the place Aphrodite had glimpsed in the second vision she'd had of my death.

CHAPTER TWENTY-THREE

'HERE YOU ARE. THIS TIME YOU BRING ME TO A PLACE OF your choosing, rather than me calling to you.'

Kalona stepped into view beside the marble bench, as if he had materialized out of the air. I didn't say anything. I was too busy trying to control the panicked beating of my heart.

'Your Goddess is quite unusual,' he said in a friendly, conversational tone after he sat beside me on the bench. 'I can feel the danger in this place for you. It surprises me that she would allow you here, especially because she must know you would call me to you. I imagine she believes she is warning you, readying you, but she is mistaking my intentions.

I mean to resurrect the past, and to do so the present must die.' He paused, and with a contemptuous gesture waved away the riches on the shore across the water from us. 'All of that means nothing to me.'

I had no clue what he was talking about and when I finally found my voice, all I could manage was a brilliant, 'I didn't call you to me.'

'Of course you did.' He was intimate and flirty, like he was my boyfriend and I was being kinda shy about admitting how much I liked him.

'No,' I spoke without looking at him. 'I did not call you to me,' I repeated. 'And I don't have any idea what you're talking about.'

'My musings are unimportant. All will be clear with time. But, A-ya, if you did not call me, then explain how I joined you in your dream.'

Steeling myself against the allure I already felt from just the sound of his voice, I turned my head to look at him. He was young again, and appeared eighteen or nineteen. He was wearing jeans that were comfortably loose and had that sexy, these-are-my-favorite-pair-because-they-fit-perfectly look. And that was it. He didn't have shoes or a shirt on. His wings were miraculous. They were the black of a starless sky and glistened in the fading light with a silky beauty all their own. His flawless bronze skin seemed to be lit from within. His body was beyond incredible. It was like his face – so hand-some, so perfect, that it was impossible to describe.

With a deep sense of shock I realized that was just like

how Nyx's appearance had seemed to Aphrodite and me. She had been so otherworldly in her beauty that we'd been unable to describe her. And, for some reason, that similarity between Kalona and Nyx made me incredibly sad, sad for what he might once have been and for what he had become.

'What is it, A-ya? What has made you look as if you would weep?'

I started to pick and choose my words carefully and then stopped. If this was my dream – if bringing Kalona to me was somehow my doing – then I was going to be nothing but honest. So I spoke the truth.

'I'm sad because I don't think you were always what you are now.'

Kalona went utterly still. It seemed the perfection of his features solidified and turned him into the statue of a god.

In the dream I felt timeless, so it might have been a second or a century before he responded. 'And what would you do if you knew that I have not always been as I am now, my A-ya? Would you save me or would you entomb me?'

I stared at his luminous amber eyes and tried to see through them into his soul. 'I don't know,' I said honestly. 'I don't think I could do either without some help from you.'

Kalona laughed. The sound danced across my skin. It made me want to throw my head back and my arms wide and embrace the beauty of it. 'I think you are correct,' he said, smiling into my eyes.

I looked away first, staring out at the ocean and trying to forget how incredibly seductive he was.

'I like this place.' I could hear the smile in his voice. 'I feel power – an ancient power. No wonder they chose to come here. It reminds me of the place of power from which I arose inside the House of Night, though the earth element is not strong here. That is a comfort to me. It is pleasant.'

I focused on the one thing he'd said I could actually understand. 'I guess it's no surprise you'd be more comfortable on an island. Being as you don't so much like the earth.'

'There is only one thing I like about the earth, and that was resting in your arms, though your embrace lasted too long for even my great capacity for pleasure.'

I looked at him again. He was still smiling gently at me. 'You have to know that I'm not really A-ya.'

His smile didn't falter. 'No, I do not know that.' Slowly, he reached out and took a long strand of my dark hair between his fingers. Staring into my eyes, he let my hair slide into his palm.

'I couldn't be her,' I said a little shakily. 'I wasn't in the earth when you got free. I'd been living *on* the earth for the past seventeen years.'

He kept caressing my hair as he answered me, 'A-ya had been gone for centuries, dissolved once more into the earth that made her. You are simply she, reborn through a daughter of man. That is why you are different from the others.'

'That can't be true. I'm not her. I didn't know you when you rose,' I blurted.

'Are you quite sure you didn't know me?' I could feel the

cold of his skin radiating toward my body, and I wanted to lean into him. My heart was beating hard again, only this time it wasn't from fear. I wanted to be close to this fallen angel worse than I'd ever wanted anything in my life. The desire I felt for him was even more than the pull of Heath's Imprinted blood. *What would it be like to taste Kalona's blood?* The thought made me shiver with the delicious, forbidden impulse. 'You feel it, too,' he murmured. 'You were made for me; you belong to me.'

His words slashed through the haze of my desire. I stood up and stepped around the end of the bench, putting the marble arm of it between us. 'No. I do not *belong* to you. I don't *belong* to anyone except myself and Nyx.'

'You always hearken back to that wretched Goddess!' The seductive intimacy evaporated from his voice, and he was once again the cold, amoral angel whose moods shifted on a whim and who could kill with little more than a thought. 'Why do you insist on being loyal to her? She isn't here.' He spread his arms wide and his magnificent wings rustled around him like a living cape. 'When you most need her, she steps away from you and lets you make mistakes.'

'It's called free will,' I said.

'And what is so wonderful about free will? Humans eternally misuse it. Life can be so much happier without it.'

I shook my head. 'But I wouldn't be me anymore without it. I'd be your puppet.'

'Not you. I would not take your will away.' His face changed instantly, shifting back to loving angel, the being who was so beautiful it was easy to understand why someone might throw away their free will just to be close to him.

Thankfully, that someone wasn't me.

'The only way you could get me to love you would be to take away my free will and then order me to be with you, like I was your slave.' I braced myself for the explosion I thought my words would cause, but he didn't yell or jump off the bench or throw any kind of fit. Instead he simply said, 'Then we are to be enemies, you and I.'

He didn't say it like a question, so I decided my best bet was not to answer him. Instead I asked, 'Kalona, what do you want?'

'You, of course, my A-ya.'

I shook my head and impatiently brushed aside his answer. 'No, I don't mean that. I mean, why are you here to begin with? You're not mortal. You . . . Well . . .' I paused, not sure how far I could push this subject safely, then finally decided I might as well go for it; he'd already said we were going to be enemies. 'You fell, right? From, I don't know, someplace that must be what many mortals would call heaven.' I paused again, waiting for some kind of response from him.

Kalona nodded slightly. 'I did.'

'On purpose?'

He looked vaguely amused. 'Yes, it was my choice that brought me here.'

'Well, why did you do it? What do you want?'

Another change came over his features. He blazed with a

306

brilliance that could only be immortal. Kalona stood, threw his arms wide as his wings unfurled, spreading around him with a magnificence that made it hard for me to look at him and impossible for me to look away.

'Everything!' he cried in the voice of a god. 'I want everything!'

And then he was there before me, a shining angel – not fallen at all, just miraculously here, within reach. Mortal enough to touch, but too beautiful to be anything but a god.

'Are you sure you couldn't love me?' He pulled me into his arms. His wings swept down and enfolded me in their soft darkness, a blanket that was in direct contradiction to the wonderful, painful chill of his body that I was coming to know so well. He bent, and slowly, as if giving me time to pull away, brought his mouth down to mine.

When our lips met, the kiss burned with cold heat through my body. I felt myself fall. His body, his soul, was all that I knew. I wanted to press myself into him, have him lose himself in me. The question wasn't, could I love him, but how could I not love him? An eternity of embracing him – possessing him – loving him – couldn't possibly be enough.

An eternity of embracing him . . .

The thought speared through me. A-ya had been created to love him and embrace him for eternity.

Oh, Goddess! my mind cried, *am I really A-ya?*

No. I couldn't be. I wouldn't let myself be!

I shoved against him. Our embrace had been such a complete and passionate surrender that my sudden rejection caught him by surprise. He staggered back, letting me slip through the double embrace of his arms and wings.

'No!' I was shaking my head back and forth like a crazy woman. 'I am *not* her! I am Zoey Redbird, and if I love someone, it's because he's worth loving, and not because I'm a piece of dirt that's been brought to life.'

His amber eyes narrowed as anger flashed across his face. He started toward me.

'*No!*' I screamed.

I was jolted awake to the sounds of Nala hissing like crazy and someone sitting on the side of my bed, trying to defend himself against my flailing arms.

'Zoey! It's okay. Wake up! Ow! Shit!' the guy said as my fist connected with his cheek.

'Get away from me!' I cried.

He trapped both of my wrists in one of his hands. 'Get a grip!' Then he reached out and flipped on my bedside light.

I blinked up at the guy who was sitting on my bed rubbing his cheek.

'Stark, what the hell are you doing in my room?'

CHAPTER TWENTY-FOUR

'I WAS WALKING BY IN THE HALL OUT THERE AND I HEARD your cat yowling and hissing, and then you started yelling. I thought you were in trouble.' Stark glanced over at my heavily draped window. 'Thought maybe a Raven Mocker had gotten in here. Cats really hate them, you know. Anyway, that's why I came busting in.'

'You just happened to be walking by my room at—' I glanced at my clock. 'At noon?'

He shrugged, and his lips tilted up in that cocky smile of his that I liked so much. 'Well, I guess it was more planned than coincidence.'

'You can let go of me now,' I said.

Reluctantly, his hold on my wrists relaxed, but he didn't actually let go of me. I had to pull my hands from his.

'That must have been one awful nightmare,' he said.

'Yeah, it was.' I scooted back so that I leaned against the headboard of my bed. Nala had settled down and was curled against my side.

'So, what was it about?'

I ignored his question and said, 'What are you doing here?'

'I told you. I heard noise from in here and—'

'No, I mean why were you outside my door to begin with? And, it's noon. All the red fledglings I know don't do well in the sunlight and are seriously sound asleep right now.'

'Yeah, I could sleep, but whatever. And there's no sunlight out there. Everything's all gray and icy.'

'Jeesh, the ice storm's still going on?'

'Yeah, another front is moving through today. It would suck to be a human trying to deal with this mess without all the generators and stuff this school has.'

What he said made me wonder whether the nuns had a generator at their abbey. I really needed to talk to Sister Mary Angela. Talk to her? Hell, I needed to go there. I missed my grandma, and I was seriously sick of feeling like I was in danger all the time. Unbelievably tired, I sighed. How long had I slept? I counted in my head about five hours. Ugh. And a bunch of that time had been spent in a weird dream place with Kalona, which couldn't be all that restful.

'Hey, you look tired,' Stark said.

'You haven't answered my question. Why did you come here? I mean *really*.'

He stared at me and blew out a long breath. Then he said, 'I needed to see you.'

'Why?'

His brown eyes met mine. He looked so much like the pre-dead undead Stark that it was disconcerting. At that moment his eyes were normal, and there was no scary darkness pulsing from the shadows around him. Only the red outline of his tattoo reminded me that he was different from the kid who had told me secrets and asked for my help in the field house just a few nights ago.

'They'll make you hate me,' he blurted.

'Who's they? And no one is going to *make* me feel anything.' As soon as I said it, a picture of me in Kalona's arms flashed through my mind, but I purposely shoved the all-too-graphic image away.

'They – Everyone,' he said. 'They'll tell you I'm a monster, and you'll believe them.'

I kept looking at him, silently and steadily. He was the first to look away.

'I gotta think that maybe you doing stuff like biting Becca and hanging around Kalona with your I-can't-miss-anything-I-aim-at bow strapped to your back and ready to shoot might have a little something to do with making *them* think you're not such a nice guy anymore,' I said.

'Do you always say exactly what you're thinking?'

'Well, no, but I try to be honest. Look, I'm really tired, and

311

I just had an awful dream. The stuff that's happening around here is not good. I'm confused about a bunch of things. And *you* came to *me*. I didn't call you up and say, "*Hey, Stark, why don't you sneak into my room?*" So I'm really not in the mood to play games.'

'I didn't sneak,' he said.

'I don't think that part is what's really important,' I said.

'I came here because you make me feel,' he blurted all in one big breath.

'I make you feel what?'

'Just feel.' He rubbed a hand across his brow like he might have a headache. 'Since I died and then came back, it's like part of me stayed dead. I haven't been able to feel anything. Or at least not anything good.' He was talking in short, clipped sentences, as if what he was saying was hard for him to get out. 'Okay, yeah, I have urges. Especially when I haven't had any blood recently. But that's not really *feeling*. It's just a reaction. You know – eat, sleep, live, die. It's automatic.' He grimaced and looked away from me. 'It's automatic for me to take what I want. Like from that girl.'

'Becca.' My voice was cold. 'Her name is Becca.'

'Okay, so her name is Becca.'

His expression had hardened. He didn't look scary and red-eyed, but he did look like a complete jerk, and I was just tired enough for that to really piss me off.

'You attacked her. You forced yourself on her. Look, it's pretty simple. If you don't want people to say bad things about you, then you need to stop doing bad things,' I said.

His eyes flashed and I saw a red light in their depths. 'She would have liked it. If you and the warrior had come along five minutes later, you would have seen her all over me.'

'Are you kidding me? You actually think mind control is foreplay?'

'Was she upset when you saw her inside? Or was she talking about how hot I am and how much she wanted me?' Stark hurled the questions at me.

'And you think that makes what you did okay? You messed with her mind to get her to want to be with you. By any definition that's a violation, and it's wrong.'

'You kissed me right after that, and I didn't have to mess with your mind!'

'Yeah, well, I've been having some seriously questionable taste in guys lately. But I can promise you that right now I have absolutely no desire to hurl myself into your arms.'

He stood abruptly, shoving away from my bed. 'I don't know what the hell I'm doing here. I am what I am, and nothing can change that.' Totally pissed, he started striding toward the door.

'You *can* change that.'

I said the words softly, but they seemed to shimmer in the air between us and wrap around Stark, pulling him to a stop. He just stood there for a while, fists clenched at his side, head slightly bowed as if he was fighting with himself. With his back still to me he said, 'See, that's what I mean. When you say things like that to me, you make me *feel* again.'

'Maybe that's because I'm the only person who's telling you the truth right now.' As I spoke, I got one of my gut-deep feelings that let me know I was saying the words Nyx would have me speak. I drew a long breath and tried to center myself, and even though I was tired and hurt and confused about many things, I followed the thread that had been unraveled before me and tried to sew together the shredded cloth of Stark's humanity. 'I don't think you're a monster, but I also don't think you're just a nice guy. I see what you are, and I believe in what you could choose to be. Stark, don't you understand? Kalona and Neferet are keeping you like this because they're using you. If you don't want to turn into a creature of their creation, then you're going to have to choose a different way and fight against them, and against the darkness they surround themselves with.' I sighed, searching for the right words. 'Don't you see, evil will win if good people do nothing.' I must have struck a nerve with Stark, because he slowly turned around to face me.

'But I'm not good people.'

'You were a good guy before all of this. I know you were. I didn't forget, just like I promised you. And you can be a good guy again.'

'When I hear you say it, I almost believe it.'

'Believing it is the first step. Acting on it is the second.' I paused, and he didn't say anything, so I filled the dead air with some of the babble that was drifting through my mind. 'Have you stopped to think about why we keep coming together?'

314

His smile was completely Bad Boy. 'Yeah, I thought it was because you're so damn hot.'

I tried, unsuccessfully, not to grin back at him. 'Well, yeah, I mean besides that.'

He shrugged. 'You being hot is enough for me.'

'Thanks, I guess. But that's not exactly what I meant. I was thinking it has something to do with Nyx and your being important to her.'

Stark's smiled faded instantly. 'The Goddess couldn't want anything to do with me. Not anymore.'

'I think you'd be surprised. Remember Aphrodite?'

He nodded. 'Yeah, kinda. She's that really stuck-up chick who actually thinks she's a love goddess.'

'That's Aphrodite. She and Nyx are like this.' I crossed my fingers.

'Are you sure?'

'Totally,' I said, and couldn't stop the humongous yawn that overtook me. 'Sorry. I didn't get much sleep lately. Between the stress going on around here, me getting hurt, and some seriously bad dreams, sleep has not been very friendly to me.'

'Can I ask you something about your dreams?'

I shrugged and nodded sleepily.

'Has Kalona been in them?'

I blinked in surprise at him. 'Why would you ask that?'

'He does that. Gets in people's dreams.'

'He's been in your dreams?'

'Nah, not me, but I've overhead the fledglings talking, and

315

he's definitely been in their dreams, only they liked it a lot more than you do.'

I thought about how sexy Kalona could be and how easy it would be for me to give in to his hypnotic appearance. 'Yeah, I'll just bet they do.'

'I want to tell you something, but I don't want you to think I'm making it up just so I can hit on you,' he said.

'What is it?' He was looking massively uncomfortable, as if what he was about to say made him really nervous.

'It's harder for him to get into your dreams if you're not sleeping alone.'

I stared hard at him. He was right. It sounded like something a guy would make up to get into a girl's bed (and panties).

'I wasn't sleeping alone the first time it happened,' I said.

'You were with a guy?'

I felt my cheeks start to get warm. 'No. I was with my roommate.'

'It has to be a guy. It's like he doesn't want to compete or something.'

'Stark, that sounds like utter bullpoopie.'

He smiled. 'Is "bullpoopie" really a word?'

'It's *my* word,' I said. 'And how the hell would you know this little tidbit about Kalona?'

'He talks a lot around me. It's almost like he doesn't notice I'm there sometimes. I heard him and Rephaim talking about the dreams. Kalona said he was thinking about putting Raven Mocker guards up between the girls' and guys' dorms to keep them apart, but he decided he wouldn't because he really wasn't having an issue with controlling the fledglings – with or without being in their dreams.'

'Gross,' I said. 'What about the professors? Are they all under his control, too?'

'Apparently. At least none of them have stood up against him or Neferet.'

I expected Stark to start to get defensive with my questioning, but he didn't seem to mind and was talking to me like it was no big deal to let me know this stuff. So I decided to see how much I could find out. 'What about the Sons of Erebus? I saw one when we first came on campus but haven't even seen him since.'

'There aren't many of them left,' Stark said.

'What do you mean?'

'I mean a bunch of them are dead. When Shekinah fell, Ate freaked and led an attack against Kalona, even though I don't think Kalona was the one who killed her.'

'He didn't. Neferet killed Shekinah.'

'Huh. Well, that figures. Neferet is a vindictive bitch.'

'I thought you were one of her minions.'

'No.'

'Are you sure?'

'Yes.'

'Does she know that?' I asked.

'No,' he said. 'I remember something you said right before I died. You tried to warn me to be careful around Neferet.'

'Yeah, I remember that, too.'

'Well, you were right.'

'Stark, she's changing, isn't she? I mean she's not just a vamp High Priestess anymore,' I said.

'She's not normal, that's for sure. Her powers are bizarre. I swear she can spy on people better than Kalona can.' He looked away from me, and when he met my eyes again, his were shadowed by a soul-deep sadness. 'I wish you had been there instead of Neferet.'

'Been there?' I asked, even though the tightening in my gut told me I knew exactly what he meant.

'You'd been watching my body, hadn't you? With that camera thing.'

'Yeah,' I said softly. 'Jack installed it. I didn't want to leave you alone and that was the best way I could think of to keep an eye on you. Then my grandma was in an accident and things got crazy . . . I'm sorry.'

'I'm sorry, too. It would have turned out differently if it had been you instead of her I opened my eyes to see.'

I wanted to ask him questions about what exactly happened with the whole dying and un-dying thing, as well as question him further about Neferet, but his face was closed off and his eyes were filled with pain.

'Look,' he said, abruptly changing the subject, 'you want to get some sleep. I'm tired, too. What if we sleep together? *Just* sleep together. I promise I won't try anything.'

'I don't think so,' I said.

'You'd rather have Kalona show up in your dreams again?'

'No, but I, well, I, uh, don't think you sleeping with me is a good idea.'

His expression got hard and cold again, but I could see the pain that was still in his eyes. 'Because you don't think I'll keep my promise.'

'No, because I don't want anyone to know you've been here,' I said honestly.

'I'll leave before anyone knows,' he said quietly.

And suddenly I knew my response to him could be what tipped him over in the struggle for his humanity. The last two lines of Kramisha's poem echoed through my mind: *'Humanity saves her / Will she save me?'* I knew what I had to do.

'Okay, fine. But you really have to get out of here early, before anyone sees you.'

His eyes widened in surprise, and then his lips tilted up in his cocky Bad Boy smile. 'You mean it?'

'Sadly, yes. Now come over here because I'm about to fall asleep in the middle of talking to you.'

'Cool! I don't have to be told twice. I'm a monster, not a moron.' He moved quickly back to the bed.

I scooted over, dislodging Nala, which pissed her off. Grumbling, she padded to the end of the bed, made three quick circles, and I swear she was asleep again before her head was pillowed on her paws. I looked from her to Stark and hastily threw my arm across his side of the bed before he could tuck himself in.

'What?' he said.

'First you have to get rid of that bow and arrow business that's practically growing on your back.'

319

'Oh, okay.' He pulled over his head the leather contraption that held the bow and quiver of arrows to his back and dropped them on the floor beside the bed. When I still didn't move my arm, he said, 'What now?'

'You are so not getting in my bed with your shoes on.'

'Crap. Sorry,' he muttered, kicking off his shoes. Then he looked down at me. 'Want me to take anything else off?'

I frowned up at him. Like he wasn't hot enough already in his black T-shirt, his jeans, and his cocky smile? But no way was I going to tell him that. 'No. You may not take anything else off. Jeesh, just get in here. I'm seriously tired.'

As he slid into bed beside me, I realized just how small my bed was when I was sharing it with a guy. I had to remind myself that I really was tired and that the whole point of Stark sleeping with me was for me to get some rest.

'Turn off the light, would ya?' I asked him, sounding way more nonchalant than I felt.

He reached over and snapped the light off.

'So, you think you'll be going to class tomorrow?' he asked.

'Yeah, I suppose.' Then, because I really didn't want to talk about why I might be going to class so soon after I'd been hurt so badly, I added, 'And I have to remember to look through the Hummer Darius drove us in here with. I think I left my purse in it. Or at least I hope I did, 'cause having a lost purse really sucks.'

'Now that scares me,' Stark said.

'What scares you?'

'Chicks' purses. Or at least all the weird stuff you people keep inside of them.'

'Us people? Jeesh. We're girls, and purses just have girl stuff in them.' His normal-sounding guyness was making me smile.

'There's no *just* about purse stuff,' he said. And I swear I felt him shudder.

I laughed out loud this time. 'My grandma would say that you're a conundrum.'

'Is that good or bad?'

'A conundrum is something that's puzzling, even kinda paradoxical. For instance, here you are this macho, dangerous, warrior guy who can't miss anything he shoots at, but you're totally squeed out by girls' purses? It's like they're your spiders.'

He chuckled. 'My spiders? What's that supposed to mean?'

'Well, I don't like spiders. At all.' I shuddered like he'd just done.

'Oh, I get it. Yeah, purses are my spiders. Really big spiders you can open up and they're filled with a whole nest of baby spiders.'

'Okay! Okay! You're totally grossing me out. Let's change the subject.'

'Sounds good to me. So . . . I think you have to be touching whoever you're sleeping with for this to really work.' His voice sounded weirdly intimate coming from the darkness beside me.

'Yeah, sure.' My stomach felt all fluttery, and not just because we'd been talking about spiders.

His sigh was heavy and long-suffering. 'I'm telling you the truth. Why do you think it doesn't keep him away if you're just sleeping with a roommate? You have to be touching. A guy and a girl. I guess a guy and a guy would work, too, if it was like Damien and his boyfriend. Or even a girl and a girl if they were into each other.' He paused. 'I think I'm babbling.'

'I think you are, too.' Actually, babbling was usually what I did when I was nervous, and it was refreshing to meet someone else who was a nervous babbler.

'You really don't have to be scared of me. I'm not going to hurt you.'

'Because you know I can kick your butt with the elements?'

'Because I care about you,' he said. 'You were starting to care about me, weren't you? I mean before all of this happened to me.'

'Yes.' On one hand, right about then was an excellent opportunity for me to mention the little fact that Erik and I were supposed to be back together. And maybe even say something about Heath. (Or maybe not.) On the other hand, I was trying to somehow fix the kid's humanity, or lack thereof, and it probably wouldn't help for me to be all: *Hey, I'll sleep with you and act like I care about you, but I kinda have a boyfriend. Or two.* And besides all that, I needed to start being honest with myself. Erik had seemed so perfect for me; he's who everyone thought I should be with. Then why have I always liked other guys, too, and that's even before he started acting all insanely possessive? It wasn't just Heath I'd been drawn to, but Loren and then Stark. The only thing I could think of was that something must be missing with Erik, or else I was just turning into a nasty skank. I mean, really. I didn't *feel* like a nasty skank. I felt like a girl who liked more than one guy.

He shifted on the bed beside me and I tried not to jump when I felt his arm lift up. 'Come on over here. You can put your head on my chest and go to sleep. I'll keep you safe. I promise.'

I pushed the Erik problem from my mind, and figuring I might as well – I mean, I was already in bed with the kid – I slid over. He put his arm around me and I tried to relax against his side with my head kinda awkwardly resting on his chest. I kept wondering if he was comfortable. Was I too heavy? Was I too close to him? Not close enough?

Then his hand lifted and found my head. At first I thought he was going to move my head (because it was too heavy), or maybe even strangle me or whatnot. So it surprised me when he started to stroke my hair like I was a skittish horse.

'You have really pretty hair. Did I tell you that before I died, or did I just think it?'

'You must have just thought it,' I said.

'I would tell you that you looked really hot today when I saw you naked, but that probably wouldn't be appropriate, being as we're in bed together but not doing anything.'

'No,' I stiffened, getting ready to pull out of his arms. 'It wouldn't be appropriate.'

His chest rumbled under my ear as he chuckled. 'Relax, will ya?'

'Then don't talk about seeing me naked.'

'Okay.' He caressed my hair silently for a little while, then he said, 'That Raven Mocker hurt you pretty badly.'

It wasn't a question, but I still said, 'Yeah.'

'Kalona doesn't want you hurt, so he'll be in for some shit when he gets back here.'

'He won't be getting back. I killed him. Burned him up,' I said simply.

'Good,' he said. 'Zoey, would you make me one more promise?'

'I suppose, but you don't seem one hundred percent happy when I keep my promises to you.'

'I'll be happy if you keep this one.'

'What is it this time?'

'Promise me if I become a real monster like them, you'll burn me up, too.'

'That's not a promise I feel comfortable making,' I said.

'Well, think about it because it might be a promise you'll have to fulfill.'

We were silent again. The only sound in my room was Nala's soft snoring from the foot of my bed, and the steady beat of Stark's heart under my ear. He kept stroking my hair, and it wasn't long before my eyelids started to feel incredibly heavy. But before I fell asleep I had one more thing I wanted him to hear.

'Would you do something for me?' I asked sleepily.

'I think I'd do almost anything for you,' Stark said.

'Stop calling yourself a monster.'

His hand stilled for a moment. He shifted slightly and I felt his lips against my forehead. 'Go to sleep now. I'll watch over you.'

I drifted to sleep while he was still slowly stroking my hair. Kalona didn't once enter my dreams.

CHAPTER TWENTY-FIVE

STARK WAS GONE WHEN I WOKE UP. FEELING MAJORLY refreshed as well as starving, I stretched and yawned, which is when I found the arrow lying on the pillow beside me. He'd broken it in half, which immediately caught my attention. I mean, I'm from a town named Broken Arrow. I know what the symbolism of an arrow snapped in half means – peace, an end to fighting. There was a note folded underneath the arrow pieces with my name printed on it. I opened it and read: *I watched you while you were sleeping and you looked completely at peace. I wish I could feel that. I wish I could close my eyes and feel at peace. But I can't. I can't feel anything if I'm not with you, and even then all I can do is want something that I don't think I can ever have, at least not now. So I left this, and my peace, with you. Stark.*

'What the hell does that mean?' I asked Nala.

My cat sneezed, 'mee-uf-owed' grumpily at me, jumped from my bed, and padded to her food bowl. She looked back at me, purring like crazy.

'Okay, yeah, I know. I'm hungry, too.' I fed my cat and thought about Stark while I got dressed for what I was sure would be a very weird school day. 'Today we're getting out of here,' I told my reflection firmly after I'd used the flat-iron to semi-tame my hair.

I hurried downstairs and arrived in the kitchen just in time to grab my favorite cereal, Count Chocula, and join the Twins, who had their heads together and were whispering and looking annoyed.

'Hey, guys,' I said, sitting next to them and pouring myself a huge bowl of chocolatey deliciousness. 'What's up?'

Keeping her voice pitched low for my ears only, Erin said, 'You'll see what's up once you sit here for just a few minutes.'

'Yeah, observe the pod people,' Shaunee whispered.

'Okayyyyy,' I said slowly, adding milk to my cereal and watching the kids around us with what I hoped was utter nonchalance.

At first I really didn't notice much of anything. Girls were busy grabbing protein bars or cereal or some other favorite breakfast food. And then I realized that it wasn't what I was seeing that was weird – it was what I wasn't. There was none of the typical joking around going on where someone makes fun of someone else's hair, and then someone else tells her to tell her mom to be quiet. No one was talking about boys. At all. No one was complaining about not having their homework done. Actually, no one was saying much of anything. They were just chewing and breathing and smiling. A lot.

I gave the Twins a WTF look.

Pod people, Erin mouthed to me while Shaunee nodded her head.

'Almost as annoying as that asshole Stark,' Erin whispered.

I tried not to sound massively guilty when I said, 'Stark? What about him?'

'The buttball walked through here while you were still upstairs. All like he owned the place and didn't care who knew he'd been raping and pillaging some poor helpless pod girl,' Shaunee said, still keeping her voice down.

'Yeah, you should have seen Becca. She panted after him like a terrier,' Erin said.

'And what did he do?' I asked, holding my breath.

'It was pathetic. He barely looked at her,' Shaunee said.

'Talk about being used and then wadded up and thrown away like a snot rag,' Erin said.

I was trying to figure out what I could say that would give me more info about what Stark had or hadn't done without letting the Twins know I cared as much as I was caring, *and* I thought I should maybe try to say a little something that would kinda somehow stand up for Stark, when Erin's eyes got all wide and buggy as she stared behind me.

'Well, speak of the damn devil,' Shaunee said in her best meangirl voice.

'Literally,' Erin added.

'Wrong table,' Shaunee said. 'Your minions are all over there and there.' She waved her hand around the room at the other girls who had stopped eating and were staring behind me, too. 'Not over here.'

I swiveled around in my chair to look up at Stark. Our eyes met. I'm sure mine were wide and startled. His were deep and warm, and I could almost hear the question he was asking with them.

Ignoring everyone else in the room, I said, 'Hi, Stark.' I was careful not to make my voice too friendly or icy. I just said hi to him like I would any other kid.

'You look better than the last time I saw you,' he said.

I could feel my cheeks getting warm. The last time he'd seen me we'd been in bed together. While I was still staring into his eyes and trying to figure out what the hell I could say to him in front of everyone, Erin spoke up.

'Big surprise that she looks better than when you were chomping on Becca last night.'

'Yeah, watching that would be enough to make anyone look a little peaked.'

Stark broke his gaze from mine. I saw his eyes flash a dangerous scarlet as he rounded on the Twins. 'I'm talking to Zoey, not either of you. So butt the fuck out.'

There was something about his voice that was deeply frightening. He didn't yell. His expression hardly changed.

Instead, he radiated a terrible sense of coiled snake, pissed and deadly and on the brink of striking. I looked more closely at him and saw a ripple in the air around him, like heat waves lifting from a tin roof in summer. I don't know if the Twins saw it, too, but they definitely sensed something. Both of them paled, but I hardly spared a glance for them. It was Stark I was keyed on because I knew I was glimpsing the monster he'd talked about. Seeing the almost instantaneous change that came over him, I was reminded of Stevie Rae – before she'd found her humanity again.

Was that why I cared about Stark so much? Because I'd seen Stevie Rae struggle with the same dark impulses and win over them, and I wanted to believe he could win, too?

Well, dealing with Stevie Rae had taught me one thing for sure, and that was that a fledgling in this position could be a very dangerous creature.

Keeping my voice completely calm, I said, 'What was it you wanted to say to me, Stark?'

I saw the struggle on his face as the kid I knew fought with the monster who clearly wanted to leap across the table and eat the Twins. Finally he shifted his gaze back to me. His eyes still glowed slightly red when he said, 'I didn't really have anything to say. I just found this. It's yours, isn't it?' He lifted his hand and, clenched in it, was my purse.

I looked from it to him, and then back at the purse again. I remembered what he'd said about being scared of purses like I'm scared of spiders. When I looked into his eyes again, I was smiling.

'Thanks, it is mine.' I took it from him, and as our hands brushed I said, 'A guy once told me that girls' purses reminded him of spiders.'

The red left his eyes like he'd thrown a switch. The terrible aura that had surrounded him was gone. One of his fingers wrapped around mine and held for just an instant. Then he let loose the purse and my hand.

'Spiders? Are you sure you heard him right?'

'I'm sure. Thanks again for finding this.'

He shrugged, turned, and slouched out of the room.

As soon as he was gone, all the fledglings except the Twins and me started whispering excitedly about how hot Stark is. I ate my cereal in silence.

'Okay, he's beyond creepy,' Shaunee said.

'Was that what Stevie Rae was like before she Changed?' Erin asked.

I nodded. 'Yeah, basically.' I lowered my voice and added, 'Did you guys notice anything in the air around him? Like a weird rippling or an extra-dark shadow?'

'No, I was too busy thinking he was going to eat me to look around him,' Erin said.

'Ditto,' said Shaunee. 'So is that why he doesn't freak you out, because he's like Stevie Rae before she Changed?'

I lifted one of my shoulders and used the excuse of a mouth full of Count Chocula to not say much.

'Hey, seriously, I know what Kramisha's poem said and all,' Erin said. 'But you gotta watch yourself around him. He's totally bad news.'

'Plus, the poem might not have been about him,' Shaunee said.

'Guys, do we really have to talk about this right now?' I said after swallowing.

'Nope, he has zero importance to us,' Shaunee said quickly.

'Ditto,' Erin said; then she added, 'You gonna check to be sure he didn't steal your stuff?'

'Yeah, whatever.' I unsnapped my purse and looked into it, pawing around a little and taking an out-loud inventory. 'Cell phone . . . lip gloss . . . cool sunglasses . . . money holder thing with, yep, all my money and my driver's license in it . . . and—' I broke off abruptly when I found the little note that had an arrow broken in half drawn on it. Below the arrow were the words: *Thanks for last night*.

'What? Did you find something he ripped off?' Erin asked, trying to peer across the table and into my purse.

I snapped it shut. 'No, just nasty used Kleenex. I wish he *had* ripped that off.'

'Well, I still say he's an asshole,' Erin grumbled.

I nodded and made little agreeing sounds as I finished my cereal and tried not to think about Stark's warm hand stroking my hair.

My classes, as my Spanish teacher, Professor Garmy, would have said, had she not turned into a good little pod professor, were *no bueno para me*. And the worst part was, if you took away the disgusting Raven Mockers, who seemed to be everywhere, I could have almost convinced myself that everything was normal. But almost can be a really big word.

It didn't help that my schedule had been changed around at semester, so that I was in classes with all different kids, none of them being Damien and the Twins. Aphrodite was nowhere to be seen, making me worry on and off about whether she and Darius were being eaten by Raven Mockers. Of course, knowing Aphrodite, they were still in her room playing doctor.

It was with that gross mental picture that I slid into a desk for my first class, which was now Literature 205. Oh, when Shekinah had moved all my classes around so that I could be in an advanced level of Vampyre Sociology, she'd failed to mention that the rearrangement had caused me to be bumped up to the next level of my lit and Spanish classes. So my stomach churned as I waited for Professor Penthasilea, better known as Prof P, to assign a piece of literature with a correspondingly awful essay that was so far over my head that it could roost.

I shouldn't have worried. Prof P was there. She looked like her gorgeous, artsy self. But she acted like an utterly different vampyre. Prof P, by far the coolest lit teacher I'd ever hoped to encounter, began the hour by passing out grammar worksheets. Yep. I stared down at the half-dozen pages, Xeroxed front and back, she wanted us to complete. The worksheets ran the range from comma splices and run-ons to diagramming complex sentences (seriously).

Okay, some kids – well, I guess the majority of kids if they had an on-level public school education – would not have been shocked at all by the assignment. But this was Prof P at the House of Night! One thing I could say for Hell High (as human kids called it) was that the classes were *not* boring. And even among the totally not boring professors, Penthasilea stood out. She'd captivated me in the first sixty seconds of the first day I'd sat in her class by saying that we were going to read Walter Lord's *A Night to Remember*, a book about the sinking of the *Titanic*. That was cool enough, but add to that the fact that Prof P had actually been living in Chicago when the ship sank, and she remembered tons of amazing details about not just the people on the ship but what life had been like in the early 1900s, and you have an excellent class.

I looked up from my totally boring worksheets to where she was sitting at her desk, bloblike, staring stone-faced at her computer screen. Her charisma in class today would definitely fall on the South Intermediate High School crap-teacher scale at about the level of Mrs Fosster, who consistently got the prize for the Worst English Teacher Ever, and had been called Queen of Worksheets or Umpa Lumpa, depending on whether she was wearing her M&M blue muumuu or not.

Professor Penthasilea had definitely been changed into a pod person.

Spanish class was next. Not only was Spanish II insanely too hard for me (hell, Spanish I had been too hard for me!), but Prof Garmy had turned into a nonteacher. Where before the class had been immersion, which means basically all the talking was in Spanish and not English, now she flitted around the room nervously, helping kids write the description of the picture she'd put up on the Smart Board of a bunch of cats, er, *gatos* getting all tangled in string, um, *hilo* – or whatever. (I seriously don't have many Spanish skills.) Her vamp tattoos looked like feathers, and she'd reminded me of a little Spanish bird before. Now she looked and acted like a neurotic sparrow, flitting from kid to kid and getting ready to have a nervous breakdown.

Pod professor number two.

But I would have chosen to stay in Prof Garmy's confusing Spanish class all day if it could have kept me from going to my third-hour class, Advanced Vampyre Sociology, taught by – you guessed it – Neferet.

Since day one at the House of Night, I'd resisted being put in an advanced level of Vampyre Sociology. At first it was because I'd wanted to fit in. I hadn't wanted to be known as the weird third former (or freshman) kid who'd been stuck in a sixth former (or senior) class because she was so 'special.' I mean, barf.

Well, it hadn't taken me very long to figure out that there was just no way for me to stay incognito. Since then I'd been learning to deal with my specialness and the responsibilities (and embarrassments) that go with it. But it didn't matter how hard I'd talked to myself about the Vamp Soc being just another class, I was still majorly nervous going into it.

Of course, knowing Neferet would be the teacher didn't help at all.

I came in, found a desk near the back of the class, and proceeded to hunker down in my seat, trying to impersonate one of those sloth-like kids who slept their lives away, waking up only to move from class to class, leaving a slug trail of yawns and bright pink spots on their foreheads.

My sloth impersonation might have worked had Neferet turned into a pod professor. Sadly, she hadn't. Neferet was glowing with power and what would appear to those less well informed as happiness. I recognized it as gloating. Neferet was a bloated spider, radiating her victory over everyone's head she had bitten off, delighted to be contemplating more carnage.

As a side note: Damien would be really pleased at my retention of the vocab words he'd been using around me.

Besides the fact that she seemed spiderlike to me, I noticed Neferet, again, wasn't wearing the insignia of Nyx, a goddess embroidered in silver with her hands raised and cupping a crescent moon. Instead, she was wearing a gold chain from which hung wings carved from a pure black stone. I wondered, not for the first time, why no one seemed to notice she was totally twisted. I also wondered why no one noticed the way she radiated a dark energy that filled the space around her like the air right before a lightning strike.

'Today's lesson is going to focus on an aspect of abilities that only a vampyre, or sometimes an advanced fledgling, can use. So you won't need your *Fledgling Handbooks* at the moment, unless you'd like to make additional notes in the physiology section. Please open your texts to page 426, which is the chapter on concealment.' Neferet held the small class's attention easily. She strode back and forth across the front of her room, looking regal and typically gorgeous in a long black dress trimmed in golden thread that looked like liquid metal. Her auburn hair was pulled back, and lovely curling tendrils of it escaped to frame her beautiful face. Her voice was refined and easy to listen to.

She absolutely scared the bejeezus out of me.

'So, I'll want you to read this chapter on your own. Your assignment will be to document in a journal all of your dreams for the next five days. Often secret desires as well as abilities surface in our dreams. Before you go to sleep, I want you to focus on your reading and think about what concealment means to you. What dark secrets do you keep hidden from the world? Where would you go if no one could find you? What would you do if no one could see you?' She paused, looking at each student as she spoke. Some smiled at her shyly. Others looked away almost guiltily. All in all, the class showed more animation than any of the others I'd been in.

'Brittney, darling, would you read aloud the section on page 432 on cloaking?'

Brittney, a petite brunette, nodded, turned the pages, and began reading:

CLOAKING

Most fledglings are familiar with the inherent ability they have to cloak their presence to outsiders, i.e., humans. It is practiced by the fledgling tradition of sneaking off campus to perform rituals under the very eyes of the human community. But this is only a small taste of the ability a mature vampyre can command. Even those without affinities can call night to them and conceal their movements from the inadequate senses of the typical human.

Here Neferet interrupted. 'Part of what you will learn from this chapter is that any vampyre can move stealthily among humans, a skill which comes in handy because humans tend to be overly judgmental of our activities.'

I was frowning down at the text, thinking that I couldn't be the only fledgling to notice Neferet's prejudice against humans, when her voice whiplashed at me from next to my desk.

'Zoey. So nice of you to join a class that is more fitting for your abilities.'

I looked slowly up into her frigid green eyes and tried to sound like any other fledgling. 'Thank you. I've always liked Vamp Soc class.'

She smiled, and suddenly reminded me of the creature in *Alien*, that totally freaky old movie with Sigourney Weaver and the really scary alien that ate people. 'Excellent. Why don't you read aloud the last paragraph on that page?'

Glad that I had an excuse to duck my face, I looked down at my book, found the paragraph, and read:

Fledglings should note that cloaking can be very taxing to their strength. It takes great powers of concentration to call and hold night for any protracted period of time. It is also important to understand that cloaking has its limitations. Some are as follows:

338

1. It is a draining practice and can cause excessive weariness.
2. Cloaking can only work with organic things, which is why it is easier to remain cloaked if one is skyclad (or naked).
3. To attempt cloaking items like cars or motorcycles or even bicycles is an exercise in futility.
4. As with all of our abilities, cloaking exacts a price. For some that price will be mild fatigue and a headache. For others it can be much worse.

I came to the end of the page and glanced up at her.

'That will be quite enough, Zoey. So, tell me, what did you just learn?' Her eyes bored into mine.

Well, actually, I'd just learned that my friends and I wouldn't be escaping from the House of Night using the Hummer unless we somehow got permission to leave campus. I didn't say that, though. Instead, I tried to look studious and said, 'That cars and houses and such can't be cloaked from humans.'

'Or vampyres,' she added in a firm voice that the uninformed (or the body-snatched) might think was concerned and teacherly. 'Don't ever forget other vampyres will see through the cloaking of inorganic materials, too.'

'I'll remember,' I said solemnly. And I would.

CHAPTER TWENTY-SIX

I HAD FENCING CLASS BEFORE LUNCH AND COULDN'T HAVE been happier. Okay, well, that's an overstatement. I could have been happier if my friends and I were about a bazillion miles away from the House of Night, Neferet, and Kalona. Since that didn't seem very possible, especially after Vamp Soc and Neferet's freaky anti-cloaking lecture, I settled for being happy that Dragon agreed I looked too tired to do more than sit and watch class.

Actually I wasn't feeling bad at all, and when I fished my mirror out of my purse to put on the lip gloss I was relieved I hadn't lost, I didn't think I looked that bad, either.

So Dragon's allowing me to sit out of class, coupled with the fact that his cat had been one of those that had shown up in my room like a furry clue, had me keeping a close eye on our fencing professor.

At first glance Dragon appears to be another of my grandma's conundrums. First of all, he's short. Second, he's cute. Really cute. As in the guy you'd pick to be a stay-at-home dad who baked cookies and could even hem his daughter's skirt in an emergency. In a world where male vampyres were warriors and protectors, a short, cute guy wouldn't normally get much attention. But his whole persona changed when he picked up his sword, or, as he'd correct me, his foil. Then he turned lethal. His features hardened. He didn't grow taller, that would just be silly (as well as impossible), but he didn't need to be taller. He was literally so fast that his foil seemed to glide and glow with a power all its own.

I watched Dragon drill the class in fencing exercises. The fledglings didn't seem so podlike in fencing class. But that was probably because it dealt with physical activity, not mental stuff. I paid closer attention and noticed that, even though the class was completing the physical motions, there was no easy banter or harmless teasing going on. Everyone was on task, which was weird as hell. I mean, let's face it. Keeping a gym filled with teenagers who had sharp things in their hands totally on task is nearly impossible.

I was frowning at a group of guys who would normally have been getting at least a couple of reprimands from Dragon, along with reminders to pay attention and not act like idiots (at the House of Night professors can call kids idiots when they act like idiots because the idiot children can't run home to their mommies and cry about it; hence there is a lot less idiot behavior at the House of Night than at most public schools), when Dragon stepped between me and my line of vision. I blinked and refocused on him.

Slowly and distinctly he winked at me before turning back to the class.

About then his huge Maine Coon padded up to sit beside me and lick one of his monstrous paws.

'Hey there, Shadowfax.' I scratched his head and felt more hopeful than I had since the Raven Mocker had almost killed me.

Even though school had turned into a nightmare and danger was all around us, lunch felt like an oasis of familiarity. I loaded up on my personal favorite, spaghetti and brown pop, and joined Damien and the Twins at our booth.

'Well, what did you guys find out?' I whispered between big bites of pasta with marinara and cheese.

'You look way better,' Damien said, his voice definitely not a whisper.

'I feel better,' I said, giving him a WTF look.

'I'm thinking we really need to go over the new vocab for the lit test next week,' Damien said loudly, opening his ever-ready notebook and taking out a number two pencil.

The Twins groaned. I frowned at him. Had he gone pod on us?

'Yeah, just because stuff is changing around here, it doesn't mean you can let your grades slide,' he said.

'Damien, you are a pain in the ass,' Shaunee said.

'Worse. You are a *damn* pain in the ass with your stupid vocab shit, and I—'

Damien slid the notebook around so that we could read what he'd written below the list of vocab words.

R.M. @ all the windows. Their hearing is <u>excellent</u>.

The Twins and I shared a quick glance, then I sighed and said, 'Fine, Damien. Whatever. We'll study the stupid vocab with you. But I agree with the Twins that you're a pain.'

'All right. Let's start with "loquacious."' He pointed his pencil at the word.

Shaunee shrugged. 'Isn't that something out of *Star Trek*?'

'Sounds right to me,' Erin said.

Damien gave them a look of disgust I knew he didn't have to act to put on. 'No, simpletons, this is what it means.' He wrote: *Dragon is on our side.* 'So, Erin, why don't you try the next word, "voluptuous"?'

'Oooh, I know what that one means,' Shaunee said, grabbing Damien's pencil before he could pass it to Erin. Beside "voluptuous" she quickly wrote: *me!* Then, farther down on the page, she scrawled: *Anastasia is 2.*

'You know I consider using texting shorthand gauche,' Damien said.

'Don't care,' Shaunee said.

'Even if we knew what "gauche" meant,' Erin said.

'I'll take the next word,' I said. Ignoring the next vocab

word, I wrote: *We gotta get out of here tonight, but can't use the Hummer. Can't cloak it.* I paused, chewing my lip, and then added, *Got to be careful. N knows we're going to try to leave.* 'I guess I don't know what that next one means after all. Can you help me out, Damien?'

'No problem.' Damien wrote: *We need to get out of here fast. Before they can stop us.*

'Okay, hang on. I'll try the next word. Just let me think about it for a sec.' We all ate silently while I thought, but not about the vocab word 'ubiquitous' (seriously, I could have thought about that forever and not figured out what it meant).

We needed to get off campus, under my cloaking, as soon as possible. But Neferet was expecting us to try to bolt; she'd made that clear. This meant she'd be listening in to our lunchroom conversations, not just via the Raven Mockers but inside Damien's and the Twins' minds the second she was physically close enough to them to make her psychic eavesdropping work. Again, I thought how relieved I was that no one but Stevie Rae and I knew I'd really be running to the Benedictine Abbey instead of the depot tunnels. Thanks to my note-passing skills and—

'That's it!'

The Twins and Damien stared at me. I grinned at them. 'I remembered what "ubiquitous" means!' I lied. 'And I have an idea about studying. I'm going to write definitions for some of the words on pieces of paper. I'll give one to each of you, which you're going to be expected to study and learn. When you learn the word, pass it back to me, and I'll give you another one. It'll be kinda like flashcards.'

'Have you lost your damn mind?' Shaunee said.

'No,' Damien said perkily. 'It's a good idea. It'll be fun.'

I was ripping strips of notebook paper and writing furiously on them: *Get to the stables*. After folding each one carefully, I said, 'Just think about the definitions we've gone over. Don't read the word I gave you until the bell rings for the end of sixth hour. I mean it.' I handed each of them their 'word.'

'Okay, okay, we get it,' Erin said, stuffing her note into the pocket of her designer jeans.

'Yeah, whatever. You two are turning into teachers. And that's not a compliment,' Shaunee said, taking her piece of paper.

'Just remember, don't peek until the bell,' I said.

'We won't,' Damien said. 'And when we do, maybe we should call our individual elements to us, just to help us focus?'

'Yes!' I said, smiling gratefully at Damien.

'Speaking of.' Shaunee grabbed the sheet of paper we'd been writing on. 'I'm going to take this to the ladies' room and do my own *studying* with my element.' She looked long and hard at me, and I nodded, understanding that she was going to call fire to her and destroy the evidence of our 'subterfuge,' which was a big word I actually knew the definition of.

'I'll go with you, Twin. You might need my, er, help.' Erin hurried after her.

'At least we don't have to worry about Shaunee lighting the school on fire from the bathroom,' Damien whispered.

'Holy shit, I'm starved!' Aphrodite breezed in and plopped down next to me. Her plate was loaded with spaghetti. She looked gorgeous, as usual, but a little frazzled. Her hair, which she normally wore long and flowing all around her shoulders, was pulled back in what might have once been a chic, puffed-top ponytail, but now looked actually messy.

'Are you okay?' I whispered, throwing a look at the window and giving Aphrodite what I hoped was a be-quiet-they-can-hear-us look.

Aphrodite followed my line of vision, nodded slightly, and then whispered back, 'I'm fine. Darius is *fast*!'

From that I understood that the warrior had probably been taking her on one of his superfast runs. I briefly regretted that he couldn't carry us all out of here, one at a time, but filed an amended version of the thought; maybe he could carry one or even two fledglings in an emergency.

'They're all over out there,' Aphrodite said so softly I almost didn't hear her.

'Around the perimeter?' Damien whispered.

Aphrodite nodded, shoveling spaghetti into her face. 'They lurk around campus, too,' she said between bites, careful to keep her voice low, 'but their focus is obviously on keeping anyone from coming or going without their permission.'

'Well, we're definitely going without their permission,' I said. I looked at Damien. 'You have to go so I can talk to Aphrodite. Do you understand?'

He started to look hurt for a second, and then I saw under-standing in his eyes as he remembered I could talk freely to Aphrodite without worrying that Neferet could break into her mind and dig out what I'd said.

'I understand,' he said. 'So I guess I'll see you . . .' His voice trailed off into a question.

'Just go over the vocab note I gave you, okay?'

He smiled. 'Okay.'

'Vocab note?' Aphrodite said after he was gone.

'It's just a way I'm getting them to meet me in the stables right after school without them knowing beforehand. Maybe if it's a surprise to them, it'll take a while for Neferet to know what we're up to.'

'And by that time we'll be out of here?'

'I hope so,' I whispered. I leaned closer to Aphrodite, not caring if the Raven Mockers were suspicious about the two of us putting our heads together. At least they couldn't get into our heads. 'Get to the stables with Darius as soon as school's out. Dragon and Anastasia are with us. So I'm hoping that means the cat clues were right, and Lenobia is on our side, too.'

'Which means she may help us get out of here from the weak part in the wall by the stables?'

'Yeah. Okay, do *not* tell anyone else this next part, not even Darius. Do you swear?'

'Yeah, yeah, whatever. Cross my heart and hope to—'

'Just saying you won't tell is good enough for me,' I said, not wanting to hear anything about hoping to die come out of her mouth.

'I won't tell. So, what is it?'

'We're not going back to the depot tunnels when we leave here. We're going to the Benedictine Abbey.'

Her gaze on me was sharp and way more intelligent than most people gave her credit for being. 'Do you really think that's a good idea?'

'I trust Sister Mary Angela, and I have a bad feeling about the tunnels.'

'Ah, shit. I hate it when you say that.'

'Hell, I don't like it either! But I sensed a darkness down there that I've been seeing too much of.'

'Neferet,' Aphrodite whispered.

'I'm afraid so.' I spoke slowly, thinking aloud. 'And I'm thinking that the influence of the nuns might repel her. Plus, Sister Mary Angela told me that there was a place of power there at the abbey, something that made my control over the elements not so surprising to her. I think she called it Mary's Grotto.' As I spoke I felt that sureness within that told me Nyx was pleased with the choices I was making. 'Maybe we can somehow use the power there, like we've used the power over by the east wall before. At the very least it might help me keep us cloaked.'

'Mary's Grotto? Sounds like something that should be in the ocean and not in Tulsa. Look, just keep in mind that the place of power by the east wall has been misused about as much as it's been tapped into for good,' she said. 'And what about Stevie Rae and her freaks? Not to mention your boyfriends?'

'They'll be there. Or at least I hope they will. The Raven Mockers have been watching the depot. Unless Stevie Rae figures out how to slip around them, I'm scared that they'll grab her.'

'Well, I can tell you from being around her for those two days that she is majorly resourceful, and some of those resources are not so nice.' She paused and kinda squirmed uncomfortably.

'What is it?' I prompted.

'Look, if I tell you, I want you to promise to believe me.'

'Fine. I promise. Now what is it?'

'Well, talking about your bumpkin BFF and her bag of tricks kinda reminded me of something. Something I found out after she and I, well, you know.'

'Imprinted?' I said, trying (unsuccessfully) not to smile.

'It's not funny, smart-ass,' she snapped. 'It's annoying. Anyway, remember when you were talking to Stevie Rae about the extent of the tunnels and whatnot?'

I thought back. 'Yeah, I remember.' Then my stomach clenched as I replayed the scene in my mind and I really did remember how Stevie Rae had looked all uncomfortable when I asked her about other red fledglings, and I braced myself to hear what Aphrodite had to say.

'She lied to you.'

I had a feeling Aphrodite had been going to say that, but knowing didn't make hearing it any easier. 'Exactly what did she lie about?'

'So you believe me?'

I sighed. 'Sadly, yes. You're Imprinted with her. That means you're close to her in a way no one else is. My Imprint with Heath has taught me that.'

'Okay, look. I do not want to do the nasty with Stevie Rae.'

I rolled my eyes. 'I didn't mean that, you dork. There are different kinds of Imprints. My bond with Heath is very physical, but I've been attracted to him for years. Uh, can I assume I'm right when I say you've never been attracted to Stevie Rae?'

'Hell yes, you can assume that,' Aphrodite said dryly.

'Both of you have psychic abilities. It's only logical that your bond would be mental, not physical,' I said.

'Yeah, good. I'm glad you get that. And that's how I know she was lying to you when she said the red fledglings she introduced us to are the only ones there are. There are more. She knows it, and she's in touch with them.'

'And you're absolutely sure of this?'

'Totally and absolutely,' she said.

'Well, I can't worry about that right now, but that could definitely explain some of the darkness I sensed down there. It's the same aura that used to surround Stevie Rae, but it's going to have to wait until we get out of here,' I said, feeling miserable and upset that my BFF felt like she had to lie to me.

'I hate to be the one to clue you in, but Stevie Rae has more secrets than Paris Hilton has purses. On the bright side, I'm betting your lying bumpkin friend, the freaks, and your boyfriends make it past the bird boys.'

'I hope so.' I sighed and messed with my napkin.

'Hey,' she said softly. 'Try not to let this thing with Stevie Rae freak you out. She's keeping secrets, but I can also tell you that she cares about you – a lot. I also know she's choosing good, no matter how hard it is for her sometimes.'

'I know that. I believe Stevie Rae must have a reason for not telling me things. I mean, it's not like I've never kept secrets from my friends before.' *Yeah*, I added silently to myself. *And you messed up big-time because of that, too.*

'Okay, so it's not just Stevie Rae that's making you look like you need some pharmaceutical help to cheer up.' Then her brows raised as she continued to study me. 'Oh, I get it. You're having boyfriend issues. Or should I say boyfriends issues?'

'Sadly, the plural seems to be the correct form of the word,' I muttered.

'Erik and I used to have a thing, but you know that's way over. You can talk to me if you need to.'

I looked at her and again thought how ironic it was that she was right. I really could talk to her.

'I'm not sure I want to be with Erik,' I blurted.

Her eyes got just a little wider, but her voice stayed nonchalant. 'He's pressuring you about sex?'

I shrugged. 'Yes, no. Kinda. But it's not just that.' I leaned forward and lowered my voice. 'Aphrodite, did he ever get possessive and überjealous with you?'

She curled her lip in a sarcastic sneer. 'He tried. I don't so much tolerate the jealous bullshit.' Then she paused and in a more serious tone added, 'Neither should you, Z.'

'I know, and I'm not.' I sighed. 'I have a lot to deal with when this mess is over.'

'Seriously. You have a mess to deal with when this mess is over.' She gobbled another forkful of spaghetti.

'Well, let's try and get this particular mess over with then so I can go back to my ridiculous personal drama. Tell Darius to be ready for some bad stuff to go down tonight. Like he said, Kalona isn't going to be happy when we get out of here.'

'No, he said Kalona isn't going to be happy when *you* get out of here. He really has a thing for you.'

'I know, and I wish he'd just get over it,' I said.

'Hey, have you thought any more about that first poem Kramisha gave you before we left the tunnels? It sounded like it was a formula for getting rid of Kalona.'

'Well, if it's a formula, I haven't figured it out.' I didn't want to admit to Aphrodite that I hadn't thought at all about Kramisha's poem – or at least not the one about Kalona. I'd been completely distracted by the second poem, and by the possibility of Stark's humanity being returned to him. And that realization made my stomach clench. What if Stark was diverting me on purpose? What if he was putting on an act when the two of us were alone so that I would be too involved with him to figure out the other poem or anything else – like a way to get out of the House of Night?

'Okay, clearly, your issues are weighing on you. And I think we can sum up your problems in one word,' Aphrodite said.

I met her eyes and we said the one word together. 'Boys.'

She snorted, and I gave a kinda hysterical little giggle. 'Let's just hope someday all of this goes away and your biggest problem is boy drama.' She hesitated and then added, 'I hope you're not still thinking about Stark.'

I shrugged and took a massive bite of spaghetti.

'Look, I did some asking around, and the boy is wrong. Period, the end. Just forget about him.'

I swallowed, chewed some more, and swallowed again. Aphrodite was still studying me.

'The poem might not have even been about him,' she said.

'I know,' I said.

'Do you? And, look, you need to focus on getting us the hell out of here, and getting rid of Kalona – or at least chasing him away from here. Figure that out now. Worry about Stark and Erik and Heath and even Stevie Rae later.'

'Yes, *I know*,' I said. 'I'll think about them all later.'

'Yeah, right. I still remember how you were the night Stark died. He got to you. But you have to remember the Stark that's strutting around here, acting like he's all that, and basic- ally using girls and throwing them aside *after* he fucks with their minds even more than their bodies, is *not* the guy who died in your arms.'

'What if he is that guy, but he just needs to Change like Stevie Rae did?'

'Well, I can promise you I'm not giving up another piece of my humanity to save his ass. Shit, Zoey, Erik's a better bet than Stark! Are you hearing me?'

'I'm hearing you.' I drew a deep breath. 'Okay, I'm going

to forget all guys right now and focus on getting us gone, and then getting Kalona gone, too.'

'Good. You can deal with boy issues later.'

'Okay,' I said.

'And you can deal with BFF issues later.'

'Okay,' I said.

'Okay,' she said.

We went back to eating. I'd meant what I'd said. I was going to deal with all my personal issues. Later. Really. Or at least that's what I told myself . . .

CHAPTER TWENTY-SEVEN

I WAS THINKING THAT DRAMA CLASS WOULDN'T BE A BIG deal. One of the pod professors would probably substitute for Erik, who had taken over temporarily for Professor Nolan after she'd been killed. I sat at the desk behind Becca, feeling weirdly déjà vu-ish, and half expecting to see Erik's pissed-off face calling me up in front of the class to try to seduce or humiliate me.

'Oh! My! God! He was not with *me!* Even though I sooooo wish he had been!'

Becca's annoying exclamation marks snagged my attention from being disgruntled at Erik. She was talking in little gaspy starts and stops to the girl across the row from her who I recognized as a fifth-former named Cassie. I kinda knew her because she'd placed twenty-fifth in the National Shakespeare Monologue Contest Erik had won, and all the drama kids tended to hang out with each other. Today, though, she wasn't acting like a Shakespearean heroine. She was acting like a pain-in-the-butt giggly girl.

'Well, he wasn't with me, either. But I can tell you, since he bit me I've been dying to do a little biting and sucking of my own on him,' Cassie said, and then dissolved into giggles. Again.

'Who are you guys talking about?' I asked, even though I was pretty sure I already knew.

'Stark, of course. He's only the hottest guy at the House of Night. Well, if you don't count Kalona,' Becca said.

'CFF – both of them,' Cassie said.

'CFF?' I asked.

'Completely freaking fine,' Becca said.

I realized afterwards that I should have kept my mouth shut. I mean, I was attempting to converse with what amounted to brain-washed pod people, but I couldn't stay out of it, and yes, I knew that some of my pissed-off-ness came from a totally inappropriate feeling of jealousy.

'Uh, excuse me, Becca,' I said, heavy on the sarcasm. 'But didn't Darius and I recently save your butt from getting raped and bit by *oooh! the hottest guy at the House of Night*? Then you were snotting and whimpering.'

Shocked at my outburst, Becca opened, shut, and opened her mouth again, reminding me of a fish.

'You're just jealous.' Cassie didn't look or sound shocked; she looked like a hateful bitch. 'Erik's gone. Loren Blake's dead. So now you don't have the two hottest guys at school on your little leash.'

I felt my face flush. Had Neferet told everyone about Loren and me? I didn't know what to say, but Becca didn't give me a chance to speak anyway.

'Yeah, just because you're all high and mighty with the elements doesn't mean you can have any guy you want.' Becca was giving me the same hateful glare she'd given Damien and the Twins when they'd tried to talk sense into her last night. 'The rest of us can actually have a chance once in a while, too.'

I clamped down on my urge to shriek at her and tried reason instead. 'Becca, you're not thinking clearly. Last night, when Darius and I broke it up between you and Stark, he was forcing you to let him suck your blood, and he was also on the verge of raping you.' I hated saying it. I especially hated knowing it was true.

'I don't remember it that way,' Becca said. 'I remember liking the sucking, and I would have liked the rest of what goes along with Stark sucking a girl's blood. You busted up something good that was none of your business.'

'You remember it like that because Stark messed with your mind.'

Becca and Cassie laughed, causing lots of heads to turn in our direction.

'The next thing you're going to say is that Kalona is messing

357

with our minds, too, and that's why we think he's so damn hot,' Cassie said.

'Are you actually saying you two can't tell that things have been different around here since Kalona broke out of the ground?'

'Yeah. So? He's consort to Nyx incarnate. His presence is bound to make things different,' Cassie said.

'And of course he came out of the ground. Earth is one of Nyx's elements. Like you don't know that?' Becca said, rolling her eyes at Cassie.

I'd just opened my mouth to try to explain to them that he'd *escaped* the earth, not been born through it, when the door to the classroom opened and Kalona strode in.

There was a cumulative sigh from every female except me. And, to be completely honest, I'd wanted to sigh and had to clamp my jaws together to stop myself. He was just so utterly gorgeous. Today he was wearing black slacks and a short-sleeved, button-up shirt that was untucked, unbuttoned, and hanging open enough that whenever he moved I could see the flawless bronze of his chest and his yummy six-pack. Someone had slit the back of the shirt, because his magnificent black wings protruded through and then tucked neatly against his broad back. His long dark hair was loose on his shoulders, making him look, despite his modern clothes, like an ancient god.

I wanted to ask Becca or Cassie how old he looked to them, because to me he again seemed only eighteen or nineteen, in the prime of his youth and strength, and not too ancient and mysterious to be out of my reach.

No! Listen to yourself! The next thing you know you'll be sounding as empty-headed as Becca and Cassie and the rest of them. Think! He's your enemy. Don't forget that. Forcing myself to look beyond his physical beauty and the hypnotic allure he radiated, I realized he'd been talking while I'd been yelling at myself.

'That said, I thought I would help direct this class, since it seems you are so very hard on your instructors.'

The class's appreciative laughter was warm and welcoming.

I raised my hand. His amber eyes widened in surprise, and then he smiled and said, 'How delightful that my first question comes from the most special of all the fledglings. Yes, Zoey, what answer may I give you?'

'With you taking over Drama I was just wondering if that meant you expect Erik Night to be gone for quite some time?' Okay, I hadn't wanted to ask him a question, but my instincts had made me raise my hand, just as my instincts were telling me what to say. I knew taunting him with the fact that Erik had escaped was dangerous, but I was doing so in a way that I hoped wouldn't give him a reason for outright anger. I just wasn't sure why I was being prompted to bait an already volatile immortal.

Kalona didn't look fazed at all by my question. 'I believe Erik Night may return to the House of Night sooner than some may think. But, sadly, I've heard he might not be in any shape to resume his duties as a professor, or as anything else for quite some time.' His smile got warmer and more intimate, and I could feel Becca and Cassie and the rest of the girls in the room shooting daggered looks of envy at me. I realized with a terrible sense of fear and disbelief that the girls hadn't really heard anything Kalona had said. They couldn't grasp that he had just threatened Erik and said that he was coming back, probably just short of being hauled here in a body bag. All they'd heard was the sound of his beautiful voice. All they knew was that he'd singled me out for his attention.

'Now, sweet Zoey, or as I like to think of you, A-ya, I give you the honor of choosing what piece of work we shall study first. Be wary! The entire class must abide by your choice. And know that I shall play the lead in whatever you choose.' He strode over to my side of the room. I was at the desk that sat second to the front, directly behind Becca, and I swear I could see her tremble at his nearness. 'Perhaps I will give you a part to play in our little drama.'

I stared at him, my heart hammering so violently in my chest that I was sure he must hear it. His being so close was hard on me. It reminded me of my dreams, where he'd come to me and held me in his arms. I could feel the tendrils of cold that snaked from his body ... wrapping around me ... making me yearn for the blanket of those ebony wings ...

He's going to hurt Erik! I clung to that thought and felt the delicious chill slither from me. No matter what was going on between Erik and me, I wasn't about to be cool with anything happening to him.

'I know the perfect play for us to do.' I was proud that my voice was calm and strong.

His smile was pure, sensual joy. 'I'm intrigued! What is your choice?'

'*Medea*,' I said without hesitation. 'Ancient Greek tragedy set in a time when gods still walked the earth. It's about what happens when a man has too much hubris.'

'Ah, yes, hubris. When a man exhibits godlike arrogance.' His voice was still deep and seductive, but I could see the anger that had begun to burn in his eyes. 'I think you will find that hubris only applies when you're dealing with mortals, and not the gods themselves.'

'So you don't want to do the play?' I said with exaggerated innocence.

'On the contrary! I believe the play will be amusing. Perhaps I shall let you dramatize Medea herself.' He broke eye contact with me and refocused his charisma on the class. 'Study this play tonight. We will begin acting it tomorrow. Rest well, my children. I look forward to seeing each of you again.' He turned and, as abruptly as he'd entered the room, he left.

There was complete silence for what seemed like a long time. Finally, to no one and everyone I said, 'Well, I guess I'll try to find some copies of *Medea*.' I got up and went to the back of the room. But not even the sound of opening and closing cabinets and pawing through files of old plays and mounds of scripts could cover the whispers that rained around me.

'Why should she get noticed by him?'

'It's not fair!'

'If this is Nyx being mysterious, then I'm damn sick of it.'

'Yeah, it's crap. If you're not Zoey Redbird, then you're not shit to Nyx.'

'Nyx gives her anyone she wants. The Goddess doesn't leave anything for the rest of us.'

On and on they muttered, sounding more and more pissed off. The guys were even chiming in. Apparently I made a handy scapegoat for what had to be a massive amount of anger and jealousy they must already have had for Kalona, but weren't allowed to take out on him because he was messing with their minds.

What was more than obvious was that Kalona was methodically tearing down the fledglings' love for Nyx, and he was using me to help him. They couldn't see the love and honor and strength of their Goddess anymore because Kalona's physical presence was blocking their view, like the sun shadows the brilliance of the moon during a lunar eclipse.

I found the box of *Medea* scripts and carried it over to Becca's desk and plopped it down. As she glared up at me, I said, 'Here. Hand these out.' Then, without another word, I left the room.

When I got outside I stepped off the sidewalk into the shadow of the school and leaned against the ice-slick side of the stone-and-brick mixture that made up the House of Night buildings and the wall that surrounded campus. I was shaking. With one appearance Kalona had turned an entire class against me. It hadn't mattered that I had obviously not been drooling over him like everyone else. It hadn't even mattered that I'd pissed him off. All that those kids had processed was his hypnotic beauty and that he'd singled me out for special attention, above and beyond any of them.

And they hated me for it.

But it was so much more than them hating me. The most frightening, most unbelievable part of it was that they had begun to hate Nyx.

'I have to get him out of here.' I spoke the words out loud, making them an oath. 'No matter what, Kalona will leave this House of Night.'

I walked slowly toward the stables, and not just because I'd left my last class early so I had time to kill before sixth hour and Equestrian Studies began. I walked slowly because I was going to slip and fall on my butt if I wasn't extremely careful. My luck I'd break something and have to deal with a cast or two along with everything else.

Someone had put a sand and salt mixture on the sidewalk, but it had little effect on a storm that just kept coming. Wave after wave of freezing rain fell, making the world look like a giant cake with crystal icing. It was still beautiful, but in an eerie, dreamlike way. As I slipped and slid and struggled the few yards I had to cross from the drama classroom to the stables, I realized there was no way the six of us were going to be able to walk out of here, not to mention the mile or so we'd have to go to get to the Benedictine Abbey on the corner of Lewis and Twenty-first.

I wanted to sit down in the middle of the cold, wet, slippery mess and burst into tears. How was I going to get us out of here? I needed the Hummer, but I couldn't cloak it.

That left only escape on foot, which wasn't fast enough under normal circumstances. During an ice storm that coated the streets and sidewalks of midtown Tulsa with ice and darkness, it was not just slow but impossible.

I was almost at the entrance to the stables when I heard the mocking *cro-oak* from the branches of the huge old oak that stood sentry outside the building. My first reaction was to slip and slide quickly to the door and get inside. I actually started to hurry, and then my anger caught up with me. I stopped, drew a deep breath to center myself, and ignored the bird-thing's terrible human eyes staring at me and causing the little hairs on the back of my neck to lift.

'Fire, I need you,' I whispered, sending my thoughts south, to the direction ruled by that element's flames. Almost instantly I felt heat brush against my skin and there was a waiting, listening quality to the air around me. I turned and looked up into the ice-crusted branches of the proud old oak.

Instead of a Raven Mocker, a terrible, spectral image of Neferet clung to the center of the tree where the massive first branches began to spread. She radiated darkness and evil. There was no breeze, but her long hair was lifting around her, as if the strands had a life of their own. Her eyes glowed a nasty scarlet, more rust than red. Her body was semi-transparent; her skin shimmered with an unearthly light.

I focused on the one thing that allowed my terror to thaw enough for me to speak – if her body looked transparent, then she really wasn't there.

'Don't you have more important things to do than spy

on me?' I was glad my voice didn't shake. I even raised my chin and glared at her.

'*You and I have unfinished business.*' Her mouth didn't move, but I heard her voice echo eerily around us.

I mimicked one of Aphrodite's haughty sneers. 'Okay, so maybe *you* don't have anything better to do than spy on me. *I*, on the other hand, am way too busy to be bothered by *you*.'

'*Once again you need a lesson in respecting your elders.*' As I watched, she began to smile, and her wide, beautiful mouth stretched and stretched and stretched until, with a horrible gagging sound, spiders exploded from that gaping maw and her image broke apart into hundreds and hundreds of seething, multi-legged creatures.

I sucked air for a huge scream, and had already started scurrying backwards, when I heard a rustling of wings and a Raven Mocker landed in the crotch of the tree. I blinked, expecting him to be overrun with spiders, but they shimmered and then seemed to soak into the night and disappear. There was only the tree, the Raven Mocker, and my lingering fear.

'Zzzzzoey,' the creature hissed my name. Obviously this was one of the bottom-feeding Mockers whose ability to speak wasn't nearly as refined as Rephaim's. 'You ssssmell like ssssummer.' It opened its dark beak and I saw the forked tongue that flicked out hungrily, like it was tasting my scent.

Okay. Enough was enough. Neferet had scared the bejeezus out of me. And now this . . . this . . . *bird boy* was going to try to bully me, too? Oh. Hell. No.

'Alright, I am sick and tired of you freaks and the way you

and your daddy and nasty Neferet think you can take over everything.'

'Father ssssays, find Zzzzzoey, and I find Zzzzzoey. Father ssssays, watch Zzzzzoey. I watch Zzzzzoey.'

'No. No. No! If I wanted a pain-in-the-butt dad to follow me around and check up on me, I'd call the Step-loser. So to you, your daddy, the rest of your bird-boy brothers, and even to Neferet, I say: Get. Off. My. Back!' I lifted my hands and flung fire at him. He screeched and took off, flapping wildly and flying erratically out of the tree and away from me as fast as he could go, leaving behind the scent of singed feathers and silence.

'You know, it's not smart to antagonize them,' a voice said. 'They're normally annoying. Once you ruffle their feathers they're really hard to get along with.'

I turned back to the stable building to see Stark standing in the open door.

CHAPTER TWENTY-EIGHT

'SEE, THAT'S ONE OF THE DIFFERENCES BETWEEN YOU AND me. You want to get along with them. I don't. So I don't care if I piss them off,' I told Stark. I channeled what was left of my fear and turned it into anger. 'And you know what? Right now I really don't want to hear anything more about it.' Still sounding pissed, I added, 'Did you see that?'

'That? You mean the Raven Mocker?'

'I mean the disgusting spiders.'

He looked surprised. 'There were spiders in the tree? For real?'

I blew out a long, frustrated breath. 'Lately I'm not sure

I can tell you what's for real and what's made up around here.'

'I did see you being pretty pissed off and tossing fire around like a beach ball.'

I saw his eyes travel down to my hands and realized that not only were they shaking, but they were still glowing with the aura of flame. I drew a deep, calming breath and willed the shaking to stop. Then, in a much calmer voice, I said, 'Thank you, fire. You may depart now. Oh, wait. First, could you get rid of some of that ice for me?' I pointed my flame-shining hands at the section of sidewalk between where I stood and the stable, and like a lovely miniature flamethrower, fire jubilantly spouted from my fingertips, and gaily licked against the thick coating of ice, causing it to turn to cold, wet mush. But at least the mush wasn't slippery. 'Thank you, fire!' I called as the flames died from my fingers and sped away to the south.

I trudged through the water and ice muck and tromped past Stark, who was staring at me. 'What?' I said. 'I was tired of almost falling and breaking my butt.'

'You're really something, you know.' He grinned his cocky, cute Bad Boy smile, and before I could blink, he pulled me into his arms and kissed me. It wasn't a groping, intrusive kiss filled with possessiveness like I'd been experiencing with Erik. Stark's kiss was more of a sweet question mark, which I answered with a definite exclamation point.

Sure, I should have been pissed. I should have pushed him away and told him off instead of kissing him back (enthusi-astically). I'd like to be able to say that my semi-ho-ish reaction to him was because I'd had so much stress and fear in my life lately that I needed to escape, and his arms were the easiest escape available, which would imply I wasn't actually totally responsible for the fact that I was sucking face with Stark right there in the doorway to the stables.

The truth is less flattering, and yet is still the truth. I didn't kiss him because of stress, or fear, or escape, or because of anything except the fact that I wanted to kiss him. I like him. Really, really like him. I didn't know what I was going to do about him. I didn't know where he would fit in my life – or even how he would fit in my life, especially if I was ashamed to admit my feelings for him in public. I could only imagine the freak-out it would cause among my friends. Not to mention the zillion pissed-off pod girls who would . . .

And thinking about the zillion pod girls Stark had been biting and whatnot finally splashed cold water on me and I managed to stop kissing him. I gave him a shove so that he stepped out of the doorway. I hurried into the field house, looking around guiltily and then breathing a sigh of relief that we were the only ones loitering and cutting class.

There was a little side room off of the main field house complex, much like the tack room in the stables. It was where the bows and arrows and targets and other field house-ish and sporting equipment and such was housed. I ducked into it with Stark close on my heels, closed the door, and took a few steps away from him. When he gave me *that look*, that sexy smile of his, and started toward me, I held up my hand like a crossing guard.

'No. You stay over there and I'll stay over here. We need to talk and that's not going to happen if you're close to me,' I said.

'Because you can't keep your hands off me?'

'Oh, please. I'm managing to keep my hands off you just fine. I'm not one of your pod girls.'

'Pod girls?'

'You know, from *Invasion of the Body Snatchers*. That's how I think of the girls you bite and mess with their minds so that they're all, "*Oooh, that Stark, he's just so hot! Ohmygod, ohmygod, ohmygod!*" It's seriously annoying. And, by the way, if you ever try any of that crap with me, I promise you I will call all of the five elements and we will kick your butt. Count on it.'

'I wouldn't try to do that to you, but that's not saying I wouldn't like to taste you. I totally would.' His voice had gone all sexy again, and he started to step closer to me.

'No! I'm serious about you staying over there.'

'Okay! Okay! What's got your panties in such a bunch?'

I narrowed my eyes at him. 'My panties are not in a bunch. All hell happens to be breaking loose around us, in case you hadn't noticed. The House of Night is under the control of something that's probably a demon. Neferet has turned into something that's probably a lot worse than a demon. My friends and I are not safe. I have no idea how to do what I need to do to begin to make this mess right, and to top it all off I'm falling for a guy who's been with a crapload of the girls on campus and used mind control on them.'

'You're falling for me?'

'Yeah, great, isn't it? I already have a vampyre boyfriend *and* a human guy I've Imprinted. As my grandma would say, my dance card is more than full.'

'I can take care of the vamp boyfriend.' Automatically Stark's hand came up to stroke the bow that was strapped to his back.

'Hell no, you won't *take care of him!*' I yelled. 'Get this through your head: That bow is not the fix-it answer to your problems. It should be your very last resort and should never, ever be used against another person, human or vampyre. You used to know that.'

His face hardened. 'You know what happened to me. I'm not going to apologize for what's become my nature.'

'Your nature? Do you mean your spoiled-brat nature, or your slut nature?'

'I mean me!' He pounded his fist against his chest. 'It's what I am now.'

'Okay, you need to hear me once and for all, because I'm not going to keep repeating this. Get a damn clue! We *all* have bad things inside us, and we *all* choose either to give in to those bad things or to fight them.'

'That's not the same thing as—'

'Shut up and listen to me!' My anger exploded around us. 'It's not the same thing for *any* of us. For some people the only thing they have to struggle with is whether they sleep in and miss first hour or get their butts up and go to school. For other people it's harder stuff – like whether or not to go

371

into rehab and stay clean or to just give up and keep using. For you maybe it's even harder – like whether to fight for your humanity or to give in to the darkness and be a monster. But it's still a *choice*. Your choice.'

We stood there staring at each other. I didn't know what else to say. I couldn't make the choice to do the right thing for him, and I suddenly understood that I wouldn't keep sneaking around and seeing him. If he couldn't be the kind of guy I was proud to be with in public, the act he put on for me in private didn't mean anything. And that was something he needed to know.

'What happened last night won't happen again. Not like that.' The anger drained out of me and my voice calmed down. I sounded quiet and sad in the stillness of the little room.

'How can you say that when you just told me you were falling for me?'

'Stark, what I'm telling you is that I'm not going to be with you if I have to hide the fact that we're together.'

'Because of that vamp boyfriend?'

'Because of you. Erik does affect us. I care about him. The last thing I want to do is hurt him, but it would be stupid of me to stay with him and wish I was with you, or anybody else, including the human guy I've Imprinted. So you need to understand Erik couldn't stop me from being with you.'

'You really do have feelings for me, don't you?'

'I do, but I can promise you I won't be your girlfriend if

I'm ashamed to be with you in front of my friends. You can't be wrong around everyone else and right around me. What you really are is how you act most of the time. I see that there's still good in you, but that good will eventually be blotted out by the darkness that's there, too, and I'm not going to hang around to see that happen.'

He looked away from me. 'I knew that was how you felt before, but I didn't think it would bother me so much to hear you say it. I don't know if I can make the right choice. When I'm with you, I feel like I can. You're so strong, and you're good.'

I blew out a big sigh. 'I'm not that darn good. I've messed up a lot. Sadly, I'll probably keep messing up. A lot. And you were the strong one last night, not me.'

He met my eyes again. 'You are good. I can feel it. You're good down deep in your heart, where it counts.'

'I hope I am. I try to be.'

'Then do this for me, please.' He closed the few feet between us before I could stop him again. At first he didn't touch me. He just kept staring into my eyes. 'You haven't completed the Change yet, but even the Sons of Erebus call you Priestess.' Then he dropped to one knee, and looking up at me, he fisted his right hand over his heart.

'What are you doing?'

'I'm pledging myself to you. Warriors have done it for ages – pledged themselves, body, heart, and soul, to protect their High Priestesses. I know I'm just a fledgling still, but I believe I qualify as Warrior already.'

'Well, I'm just a fledgling still, too, so we match.' My voice shook, and I had to blink fast to clear the tears that were pooling in my eyes.

'Do you accept my pledge, my lady?'

'Stark, do you understand what you're doing?' I knew about a warrior's pledge to a High Priestess, and it was an oath that often bound him to her service for his entire life, and was often harder to break than an Imprint.

'I do. I'm making a choice. The right choice. I'm choosing good over evil, light over darkness. I choose my humanity. Do you accept my pledge, my lady?' he repeated.

'Yes, Stark, I do. And in Nyx's name I bind you to the Goddess's service, as well as to mine, because to serve me is to serve her.'

The air around us shimmered and there was a brilliant flash of light. Stark cried out and seemed to crumple in on himself, falling at my feet with a moan.

I dropped to my knees beside him, pulling at his shoulders, trying to see what was wrong. 'Stark! What happened? Are you—'

With a wonderfully joyous cry he looked up at me. Tears were running freely down his face, but his smile was radiant. Then I blinked and realized what I was seeing. His crescent had been filled in and expanded. Two arrows faced the crescent. They were decorated with intricate symbols that seemed to glow with their new scarlet color against the white of his skin.

'Oh, Stark!' I reached out and gently traced the tattoo that forever Marked him as an adult vampyre – the second adult red vampyre there had ever been. 'It's beautiful!'

'I've Changed, haven't I?'

I nodded, and the tears overflowed my eyes and fell down my cheeks. And then I was in his arms, kissing him, and our tears mingled together as we laughed and cried and held each other.

The bell that signaled the end of fifth hour made us jump. He helped me to my feet and, smiling, wiped the tears from my cheeks and his own. Then reality broke through my happiness, and I realized everything that had to go along with this new and amazing Change.

'Stark, when a fledgling Changes, there is some kind of ritual he has to go through.'

'Do you know the ritual?'

'No, only vamps do.' Then I had a thought. 'You have to go to Dragon Lankford.'

'The fencing instructor?'

'Yeah. He's on our side. Tell him I sent you to him. Tell him you've pledged yourself as Warrior in my service. He'll know what to do for you.'

'Okay, will do.'

'But don't let anyone see that you've Changed.' I didn't know why it was important to me, but I knew he needed to keep hidden until after he reached Dragon. I looked around the storage room until I found a TU trucker's cap, which I stuck on Stark's head. With a little more searching I found a towel, which I rolled up and tucked around his neck.

'Pull this up' – I tugged the towel into place – 'and keep this brim down. You won't look too weird. I mean, there's an ice storm out there. Just get to Dragon without being seen.'

He nodded. 'What'll you be doing?'

'I'll be planning our escape from here. Dragon and his wife are in on it, and I think the Horse Master, Lenobia, is, too. So get back here as soon as you can.'

'Zoey, don't wait for me. Get away from here. Get far, far away.'

'What about you?'

'I can come and go whenever I want. I'll find you, don't worry. My body won't be with you all the time, but you'll always have my heart. I'm your warrior, remember?'

I smiled and touched his cheek. 'I'll never forget. I promise. I'm your High Priestess and you've pledged yourself to me. That means you have my heart, too.'

'Then both of us better stay safe. A heart's a hard thing to live without. I should know. I've tried it,' he said.

'But no more,' I said.

'No more,' he agreed.

Stark kissed me with such gentleness that he took my breath away. Then he took a step back, fisted his hand over his heart, and bowed formally to me. 'I'll see you soon, my lady.'

'Be careful,' I said.

'And if I can't be careful, I'll be quick.' He threw me his cocky grin and ducked out of the door.

When he was gone I closed my eyes, fisted my hand over my heart, and bowed my head. 'Nyx,' I whispered, 'I was telling him the truth. He has my heart. I don't know how that's going to turn out, but I ask that you keep my warrior safe and thank you for giving him the courage to make the choice for good.'

Nyx didn't suddenly appear before me, and I hadn't expected her to. But I did feel a brief, listening silence in the air around me, and that was enough. I knew the Goddess's hand was on Stark. *Protect him . . . strengthen him . . . oh, and could you please help me figure out what I'm going to do about him . . .* I prayed silently until the sixth-hour bell rang.

'Okay, Zoey,' I told myself. 'Let's break out of this place.'

CHAPTER TWENTY-NINE

WHEN I RUSHED INTO THE STABLES LATE, LENOBIA GAVE ME a chilly look and said, 'Zoey, you have a stall to muck.' She tossed me a pitchfork and pointed me towards Persephone's stall.

I muttered my apologies and my 'yes, ma'am – right away, ma'am' and hurried into the stall of the mare I considered my own for as long as I was in school at the House of Night. Persephone whickered a soft greeting to me and I went straight to her head, stroking her face and kissing her velvet muzzle, and basically telling her that she was the prettiest, smartest, best horse in the known universe. She lipped my cheek, blew in my face, and seemed to agree with my opinion.

'She loves you, you know. The mare has told me so.'

I turned to see Lenobia standing just inside the door of the stall, leaning against the wall. I sometimes forget how exceptionally beautiful she is, so at times like this, when I really look at her, I'm surprised again at her uniqueness. She is strength packaged delicately. Her silver-white hair and slate-gray eyes are the most striking things about her, well, except for the incredible tattoos of rearing horses that Marked her as a vampyre. She was wearing her usual outfit of a crisp white shirt and tan riding slacks tucked into English riding boots. Except for the tattoos and the silver goddess embroidered over her heart, she looked like something that should be in a chic Calvin Klein ad.

'You can really talk to them?' I'd suspected as much, but Lenobia had never been so blunt about her abilities before now.

'Not in words. Horses communicate in feelings. They are passionate, loyal beings with hearts big enough to hold the world.'

'I've always thought so, too,' I said softly, kissing Persephone's forehead.

'Zoey, Kalona must be killed.'

The abruptness of her statement shocked me to my core, and I quickly looked around, worried that Raven Mockers were lurking close by, as they had been in all of my other classes.

Lenobia shook her head and waved away my fears. 'Horses despise Raven Mockers as much as cats do, only earning a horse's hatred is more dangerous than a cat's. None of the abominable bird creatures will dare to enter my stables.'

'What about the other fledglings?' I asked softly.

'They are entirely too busy exercising horses who have been cooped up for days because of this storm to eavesdrop on us. So I repeat, Kalona must be killed.'

'He can't be killed. He's immortal.' My frustration at this unfortunate fact showed clearly in my voice.

Lenobia shook back her long, thick hair and began to pace from one side of the stall to another. 'But we must defeat him. He lures our people away from Nyx.'

'I know. I haven't even been back one whole day and already I can see how bad things are. Neferet is in on all of this, too.' I held my breath, waiting to see if Lenobia would remain blindly loyal to her High Priestess or if she would see the truth.

'Neferet is worse than any of them,' she said bitterly. 'She who should be most faithful to Nyx has betrayed her utterly.'

'She's not what she used to be,' I said. 'She's become something that's focused on evil.'

Lenobia nodded her head. 'Yes, a few of us have been afraid of that. I'm ashamed to say we looked the other way instead of confronting Neferet when she first began to behave strangely. I no longer consider her in Nyx's service. I plan on pledging my allegiance to a new High Priestess,' she finished, giving me a knowing look.

'Not me!' I practically squeaked. 'I haven't even Changed yet.'

'You've been Marked and Chosen by our Goddess. That is enough for me. It is also enough for Dragon and Anastasia.'

'How about the other professors? Are any of them with us, too?'

A terrible sadness crossed her face. 'No. All of the others are blinded by Kalona.'

'Why aren't you?'

She took her time answering me. 'I am not sure why he didn't blind me, as he has most of the others. Dragon and Anastasia and I have spoken of it, if only briefly. We do feel his allure, but a part of us was able to stay untouched by him enough that we were able to see him – really *see* him – and recognize him as the destructive creature he is. There is no doubt in our minds that you must find a way to defeat him, Zoey.'

I felt terrible and helpless and breathless and too darn young. I wanted to flail my arms around and scream, *I'm seventeen! I can't save the world – I can't even parallel park!*

And then a sweet, meadow-filled breeze caressed my face. It was warmed by the summer sun and moist as dew at dawn, and my spirit lifted in response.

'You aren't simply a fledgling. Listen within, child, and know that where that still, small voice leads you, we will follow,' Lenobia said in a voice that reminded me of my Goddess.

Her words mixed with the elements soothed me, and suddenly my eyes widened. How could I have forgotten?

'The poem!' I blurted, hurrying over to where I'd hung my purse by the door of Persephone's stall. 'One of the red fledglings has been writing prophetic poetry. She gave me one that had to do with Kalona right before I came here.'

Lenobia watched me curiously as I searched through my purse.

'Here it is!' It was wadded up with the poem that must have been about Stark. I grabbed the other poem and focused on it.

'Okay . . . okay . . . This is it. This tells me how to make Kalona flee. It's just . . . just written in poetic code or something.'

'Let me read it, too. Perhaps I can help shed light on it.'

I held the poem out so she could see it, and she read it aloud as I followed the words.

What once bound him
Will make him flee

Place of power – joining of five
Night
Spirit
Blood
Humanity
Earth

Joined not to conquer
Instead to overcome
Night leads to Spirit
Blood binds Humanity
And Earth completes.

'When Kalona rose from the earth, he wasn't being reborn, as Neferet tried to get us to believe, was he?' Lenobia said, still studying the poem.

'No. He'd been trapped there for more than a thousand years,' I said.

'By whom?'

'My grandmother's Cherokee ancestors.'

'This seems to imply that whatever it was that your grandmother's people did to bind him won't work the same way again. This time it'll make him run away. And that's good enough for me. We must rid ourselves of him before he completely erodes the ties that bind us to Nyx.' She looked from the poem to me. 'How did the Cherokee people bind him in the earth?'

I blew out a long gust of air, wishing with all my heart that Grandma was here and could lead me through this. 'I just— I don't know as much as I should about it!' I cried.

'Ssh,' Lenobia soothed, touching my arm as she would a nervous filly. 'Wait, I have an idea.'

She hurried from the stall and returned shortly with a thick, soft, curry brush, which she handed to me. Then she left the stall again and came back carrying a bale of straw.

Putting it in against the inside wall, she sat on it. Leaning comfortably back, she pulled out a long piece of golden straw and stuck it in her mouth.

'Now, brush your mare and think aloud. We will find the answer between the three of us.'

'Well,' I began as I stroked the brush down Persephone's sorrel neck. 'Grandma told me that Ghigua women, uh, those are Wise Women, from several tribes got together and created a maiden out of the earth, made especially to lure Kalona into a cave where they trapped him.'

'Wait, you said women came together to create a maiden?'

'Yeah, I know it sounds kinda crazy, but I promise that's what happened.'

'No, I do not doubt the truth of what your grandmother reported. I'm only wondering how many women came together.'

'I don't know. All Grandma told me was that A-ya was basically their tool, and each of them gave her a special gift.'

'A-ya? That was the maiden's name?'

I nodded and then looked over the mare's shoulder at her. 'Kalona calls me A-ya.'

Lenobia sucked in a shocked breath. 'Then you are the instrument through which he will be defeated again.'

'Yes, but not defeated, just chased away,' I said automatically, and then my instinct caught up with my mouth and I knew what I'd said was true. 'It is me. This time he can't be trapped because he's expecting that. But I can make him run away.' I spoke more to Persephone than to Lenobia or even to myself.

'But you're not just a tool this time. You've been given free will by our Goddess. You choose good, and good is what will make Kalona flee.' Lenobia spoke with a confidence that was infectious.

'Wait, what was that part about "five"?'

Lenobia retrieved the poem from where I'd laid it on the floor of the stall. 'It says "place of power – joining of five." And then it lists the five: Night, Spirit, Blood, Humanity, Earth.'

'They *are* people,' I said, feeling a rush of excitement. 'Like Damien said, that's why they're capitalized, because the poem is talking about people who symbolize those five things. And . . . and I'll bet if Grandma was here, she'd tell me that there were five Ghigua women who got together and created A-ya.'

'Does it feel right to you, deep in your soul? Is the Goddess speaking to you?'

I smiled and my heart soared. 'It does! It feels right.'

'The most obvious place of power is here at the House of Night,' she said.

'No!' I spoke with more emphasis than I'd intended, causing Persephone to snort nervously. I petted and soothed her and in a more reasonable voice said, 'No, inside the school the place of power has been tainted by him. It was his power joined with Neferet's and mixed with Stevie Rae's blood that released him and—' I gasped, realizing the implications of what I'd just said. 'Stevie Rae! I would have thought she'd represent earth. I mean, that's her affinity and all, but she's not earth: she's blood!'

385

Lenobia smiled and nodded. 'Very good. One down. Now all you must name is the other four.'

'And the place,' I muttered.

'Yes, the place,' she agreed. 'Well, places of power are also tied to spirit. Like Avalon, the ancient isle of the Goddess, is tied in spirit to Glastonbury. Even Christians felt the pull of the power of the place and at one time built an abbey there.'

'What?' I came around Persephone to stand excitedly in front of Lenobia. 'What did you say about an abbey and the Goddess?'

'Well, Avalon isn't literally of this world, though it is a great place of power. Christians felt it and built an abbey dedicated to Mary there.'

'Oh, Lenobia, that's it!' I had to blink hard to clear the tears of relief from my eyes. Then I laughed. 'And it's perfect! The place of power is at Twenty-first and Lewis, the abbey of the Benedictine nuns.'

Lenobia's eyes widened, and then she smiled. 'Our Goddess is wise. Now, all you need do is to figure out who the other four are, and get everyone there. The rest of the poem tells how they join together . . .' She paused. Glancing down she read:

Night leads to Spirit
Blood binds Humanity
And Earth completes.

'Blood is there already, or at least I hope she is,' I said. 'I told Stevie Rae to get herself and the red fledglings to the abbey when I found out Kalona was going to grab her.'

'Why would you think of sending her there?'

My grin was so wide I swear I almost split a lip. 'Because that's where Spirit is! Spirit is the head nun, Sister Mary Angela. She saved my grandma from the Raven Mockers, and she's been taking care of her there.'

'A nun? To represent Spirit and conquer an ancient fallen angel? Are you quite sure, Zoey?'

'Not conquer – just banish and give us enough time to regroup and figure out how to get rid of him permanently. And, yes, I'm sure.'

Lenobia hesitated only an instant, then she nodded. 'So you have identified Blood and Spirit. Think. Who have Earth, Night, and Humanity hidden within them?'

I went back to currying Persephone, and then I laughed and had an urge to hit myself in the head. 'Aphrodite. She has to be Humanity, even though most of the time she wants nothing to do with it.'

'I will take your word for it,' Lenobia said caustically.

'Okay, so, only Night and Earth are left,' I hurried on. 'As I said before, my first guess for Earth would have been Stevie Rae, because of her affinity. But I know in my heart she's Blood. Earth . . . Earth . . .' I sighed again.

'Could it be Anastasia? Her gift for spells and rituals is often grounded in the earth.'

I thought about it, and sadly didn't feel the twinge that told me I had the right answer. 'Nope, it's not her.'

'Perhaps we're focusing on the wrong people. Spirit came from outside the House of Night, which is something I would not have anticipated. Maybe Earth does, too.'

'Well, it's worth considering when you look at it like that.'

'What person – not a fledgling or a vampyre – could symbolize Earth?'

'I guess the people I've known who are closest to the earth are my grandma's people. The Cherokee have always respected the earth, versus using and owning and abusing it. The worldview of traditional Cherokee people is much different than today's worldview.' And then I suddenly closed my mouth and rested my forehead against Persephone's soft shoulder, whispering a small thank-you to Nyx.

'You know who it is, don't you?'

I looked up, smiling. 'It's my grandma. She's Earth.'

'Perfect!' Lenobia agreed. 'Then you have them all!'

'Not Night. I still haven't figured out who—' I broke off as I registered Lenobia's knowing look.

'Look deeper, Zoey Redbird, and I do believe you will discover who Nyx has Chosen to personify Night.'

'Not me,' I whispered.

'Of course it is you,' Lenobia said. 'The poem states it perfectly, "Night leads to Spirit." None of us would have ever looked to the Benedictine Abbey or its prioress to fill in the pieces of the poetic puzzle, but you led us straight to it.'

'If I'm right,' I said a little shakily.

'Listen to your heart. Are you right?'

I drew a deep breath and searched inside me. Yes, *it* was there, the feeling I knew came from my Goddess, the feeling that told me I'd gotten it right. I met Lenobia's wise gray eyes. 'I'm right,' I said firmly.

'Then we need to get you and Aphrodite to the Benedictine Abbey.'

'All of us,' I said automatically. 'It has to be Darius, the Twins, Damien *and* Aphrodite. If something goes wrong, I have to have my circle together. Plus, my reception here hasn't been great, and if getting rid of Kalona doesn't snap the fledglings and faculty out of their weird obsession, I don't think I'll be coming back to school any time soon. And, of course, we still have to deal with Neferet; I'm going to need a lot of help for all of that.'

Lenobia frowned slightly, but nodded. 'I understand, and though it pains me, I am in agreement with you.'

'You should come with us – you and Dragon and Anastasia. The House of Night is no place for you right now.'

'The House of Night is our home,' she said.

I met her eyes. 'Sometimes the people closest to you betray you, and your home isn't a place you can be happy anymore. It's hard, but it's true.'

'You sound very wise for your years, Priestess.'

'Yeah, well, I'm a product of divorce and crappy stepparenting. Who knew it would come in handy?'

We were laughing together when the bell rang, signaling the end of the school day. Lenobia was on her feet in an instant. 'We should get messages to your friends. They can meet here. It, at least, is safe from the ears and eyes of the Raven Mockers.'

'Already done,' I said. 'They'll all be here in a little while.'

'If Neferet realizes you're meeting here, it will go badly for us.'

'I know,' was what I said; *Ah, hell*, was what I thought.

CHAPTER THIRTY

DESPITE THE FACT THAT IT HAD STARTED TO SLEET AGAIN, Damien, the Twins, Aphrodite, and Darius arrived just minutes after the bell rang.

'Nice note,' Erin said.

'Very wily of you to get us here without having us think about it beforehand,' Shaunee said.

'Well done, you!' Damien said.

'But you are thinking of it now, so we need to be sure those thoughts are protected, and move fast with whatever it is we're going to do,' Darius said.

'Agreed,' I said. 'Guys, summon your elements and get them to form a protective wall around your thoughts.'

'No problem,' Erin said.

'Yeah, we've been practicing,' Shaunee said.

'Do you need me to cast a quick circle?' I asked.

'No, Z, we just need you to hush for a second,' Damien said. 'We've already had our elements primed and waiting.'

'Partial herd of nerd, get to it!' Aphrodite said.

'Shut up!' the Twins yelled at her.

Aphrodite snorted at them and went to stand beside Darius, who automatically put his arm around her. I noticed the cut on his face was almost completely healed, and there was only a thin pink line where before there had been a nasty laceration. It made me think of my own scar, and while the Twins and Damien were busy summoning their elements, and Aphrodite was nuzzling Darius, I turned my back to them and unobtrusively peeked down the front of my shirt. And grimaced at what I saw. Okay, my scar wasn't a long, thin pink line. It was puckered and jagged, and was still red and angry-looking. I shifted my shoulders. No, it didn't really hurt. It was just sore and tender to the touch. And ugly. Really, really ugly.

Whenever I thought about anyone seeing my nasty scar ('anyone' being Stark, or Erik, or even Heath, for that matter) I wanted to burst into tears. Maybe I'd just never be with another guy. It would certainly make my life less complicated . . .

'Battle scars from the war of good versus evil have a unique beauty all their own,' Lenobia said.

I jumped. She was standing close to me, and I hadn't heard her approach. I looked at her steadily. She was utterly perfect and completely *un*scarred and beautiful. 'That sounds nice in theory, but when the scar belongs to you, reality is kinda different than the theory.'

'I know of what I speak, Priestess.' She swept the curtain of her silver hair over one shoulder, turned so that I could see the back of her neck, and with her other hand, pulled aside the yoke of her white blouse to expose a terrible scar that ran from up into her hairline, down the back of her neck, and disappeared, thick and puckered, into her back.

'Okay! We're all elemented up over here,' Erin called.

'Yeah, we're ready to get down and dirty,' Shaunee said.

'So, what's the latest?' Damien said.

Lenobia and I exchanged a quick glance. 'That story will wait for another time,' she said softly. I followed her back to my friends, wondering what kind of evil she could have been fighting that could have made those awful scars.

'Zoey has named the people mentioned in the poem,' Lenobia said without any preamble. 'And the place of power at which they need to join.'

Everyone looked at me. 'It's the Benedictine Abbey. I remembered that one of the reasons Sister Mary Angela wasn't totally shocked when I showed her I could invoke the elements was that she'd felt elemental power herself. She said her abbey had been built on a place of spiritual power. I didn't think much of it then.' I paused and gave a little laugh. 'Actually, I didn't take her seriously, and thought she was just being crazy-eccentric-nun-lady.'

'Well, in your defense, the nun is kinda different,' Aphrodite said.

Darius nodded, 'At least she is for a nun.'

'She's also the Spirit the poem talks about,' I said.

'Wow, you did figure it out!' Damien grinned at me. 'Who are the rest of the personifications?'

'Blood is Stevie Rae.'

'She definitely likes it enough,' Aphrodite said under her breath.

'You're Humanity,' I told her firmly, punctuating my announcement with a big grin.

'Great. Just great. Let me state right now for the record: I. Do. Not. Want. To. Get. Bit. Again. Ever.' Then she glanced up at Darius and her expression changed, and she added, 'Except by you, handsome.'

The Twins made retching noises.

'Earth is my grandma,' I continued, ignoring all of them.

'Good thing your grandma's already at the abbey,' Damien said.

'How about Night?' Shaunee asked.

'It's Zoey,' Aphrodite said.

I raised my brows at her.

She rolled her eyes. 'Who the hell else could it be? Anyone who's not mentally impaired or sharing a brain' – she gave the Twins and Damien pointed looks – 'could figure that one out.'

'Okay, yeah, I'm Night,' I said.

'So we need to get to the Benedictine Abbey,' Darius said, going, as usual, straight to the heart of the logistics of our 'operation.' I say 'operation' because it usually feels to me like I'm flailing about hoping that somehow I'm getting enough things right that I don't totally make a mess of stuff, which isn't exactly an Operation.

'Yes, and you need to get there quickly, before Kalona and Neferet cause any more damage to our people,' Lenobia said.

'Or begin a war with the humans,' Aphrodite said.

Everyone but Darius gawked at her. And in my gawking I saw through the façade of her beauty, and how she always looked totally together, to the bruised darkness under her eyes and the vaguely reddish tint that hadn't yet faded from their whites.

'You had another vision,' I said.

She nodded.

'Ah, crap. Did I get killed again?'

I heard Lenobia's shocked intake of breath. 'Uh, long story,' I said.

'No, dork. You did not get killed. Again,' Aphrodite said. 'But I got a flash of the war – the same one I saw before – only this time I recognized the Raven Mockers.' She paused, shuddering. 'Did you know they can rape women? Not a comfortable vision to have. Anyway, Neferet hooked up with Kalona to fulfill her crazy war-with-the-humans scheme.'

'But last time you had the war vision, saving Zoey kept it from happening,' Damien said.

'I know that. I'm Vision Girl, remember? What I don't know is why this one was different, except that now Kalona has been added into the mix. And, well, I hate to clue you in about this, 'cause it's more than a little frightening, but Neferet has totally gone over to the Dark Side. She's turning into something, and it's like no vampyre we've ever known before.'

Something clicked inside me, and as the pieces of the puzzle were fitting together, I knew what was happening. 'She's becoming Queen Tsi Sgili, the first vampyre Tsi Sgili, and that's something we've never known before.' I said it in a voice that sounded as cold as I felt.

'Yeah. That's what I saw,' Aphrodite said, looking pale. 'I also know that the war starts right here in Tulsa.'

'So the Council they want to take over must be the Council at this House of Night,' I said.

'Council?' Lenobia said.

'It's too much to explain right now. Let's just say it's a good thing that they're only thinking regionally and not globally,' I said.

'It stands to reason if we make Kalona and, hopefully, Neferet with him, flee Tulsa, then perhaps the war won't start,' Darius said.

'Or at least it won't start here,' I said. 'And that might give us time to figure out how to get rid of him permanently, since he seems to be a main player in the war.'

'It is Neferet,' Lenobia said in a voice so calm it almost sounded dead. 'She is *the* impetus behind Kalona. She has desired a war against the humans for many years.' She met my eyes. 'You may have to kill her.'

I blanched. 'Kill Neferet! No way. I'm not doing that!'

'You might have to,' Darius said.

'No!' I cried again. 'If I was supposed to kill Neferet, I wouldn't have this horrible sickness in my gut just thinking about it. Nyx would let me know that it was her will, but I can't believe killing a High Priestess of hers would ever be the Goddess's will.'

'Ex-High Priestess,' Damien said.

'Is High Priestess a job you can really lose?' Shaunee asked.

'Yeah, isn't it one of those "for life" things?' Erin said.

'Plus, is she really a High Priestess if she's turning into something else, like Queen Tsi Sgili?' Aphrodite added.

'Yes! No!' I babbled. 'I don't know. Let's just get off the subject of killing Neferet. I so cannot go there.'

I saw Darius, Lenobia, and Aphrodite exchange a long look, which I definitely chose to ignore. Then Lenobia said, 'Back to getting all of you out of here. I think that is something we need to do now.'

'Right now?' Shaunee said.

'Like this second?' Erin chimed in.

'The sooner the better,' I said. 'I mean, I can feel your elements, and I know they're protecting your thoughts, but the truth is, if Neferet is trying to break into your minds, she'll know something is going on when she comes up against an elemental wall. She just won't know exactly what.' I glanced around, half expecting her to be floating like a bloated, spectral spider in the shadows. 'She's also appeared twice to me like a disgusting ghost, so I say we need to get the hell out of here. Now.'

'I don't like the sound of that,' Erin said.

'Tell me about it,' I said. 'But getting out of here is going to be a problem. The weather is definitely not helping us. I couldn't even walk from the main building to the stables without almost breaking my butt. I had to use fire to melt some of the stupid ice.' I glanced at Shaunee and smiled a little sheepishly.

'Wait, what did you say about using the element fire to melt the ice?' Lenobia broke in.

I shrugged. 'I was just sick of almost falling. So I focused some flame on the sidewalk. It melted the ice with no problem.'

'Actually, easy-peasy,' Shaunee said. 'I've done it myself.'

Lenobia looked increasingly excited. 'Do you think you could project flame specifically enough that it could melt the ice beneath your feet as a group if you moved?'

'Yeah, I think so. If we could figure out some way that it wouldn't burn our feet, too. I don't know how long I could do it, though.' I glanced questioningly at Shaunee.

She nodded. 'Sure, I could help, and it wouldn't even burn my feet. With the two of us joined together we could make it last longer than either of us trying to do it by ourselves.'

'Plus, Twin,' Erin said, 'Twenty-first and Lewis is only like half a mile down the street. Zoey's looking way better today, so you guys should be able to keep the heat going that long.'

'Even with the ice problem solved, we can't possibly move

fast enough on foot, and I can't cloak the Hummer because it's not organic,' I said.

'I think I have a solution for you,' Lenobia said. 'Come with me.' We followed as she led us to Persephone's stall. The mare was eating contentedly, and she simply flicked her ears back at us when Lenobia greeted her, went to her back leg, reached down, and said, 'Give, sweet girl.'

Persephone obediently lifted her leg. Lenobia brushed off the straw that clung to her hoof, and then, still holding the mare's leg up, she looked at Shaunee. 'Can you send flame to heat her shoe?'

Shaunee looked surprised at the unusual request, but said, 'Easy-peasy.' Then she drew a deep breath, and I heard her whisper something that I couldn't quite make out, and she pointed one glowing finger at Persephone's hoof. 'Burn, baby, burn!' she said. The glow rushed from her finger to the silver horseshoe snug against Persephone's hoof. In no time it started to glow, too. Persephone stopped eating, craned her head around and gave her hoof a curious look, snorted, and then went back to eating.

Lenobia tapped the hoof, kinda like she was checking to see if an iron was hot, quickly pulling her finger away from the glowing surface. 'It definitely worked. You can make it go away now, Shaunee.'

'Thanks, fire! Come on back to me now!' The glow swirled around the horse, making her snort again, and then came back to Shaunee whose body began to glow until she frowned and said, 'Just settle down.'

Lenobia put the horse's hoof down, patted her rump affectionately, and said, 'That is how you leave here and get to the abbey quickly. On horseback, which, in my opinion, is the best way to travel anyway.'

'The idea has merit,' Darius said. 'But how do we escape? Surely the Raven Mockers won't let us ride out the front gates.'

Lenobia smiled. 'Perhaps they will.'

CHAPTER THIRTY-ONE

'THAT IS AN INSANE PLAN,' APHRODITE SAID.

'Yet it just might work,' Darius said.

'I like it. It's kinda romantic, with the horses and all. Plus, it's the best plan we have,' Damien said.

'It's the only plan we have,' I said. At Lenobia's raised brows I hastily added, 'But I like it, too.'

'The fewer horses you take, the easier it will be for you to get away unnoticed. I suggest you ride double,' Lenobia said.

'Three is definitely sneakier than six,' Erin said.

'But how are we going to get Dragon and Anastasia in on it?' I said. 'We definitely can't all go walking over to the fencing room or Anastasia's class. And I don't want us to split up.'

Lenobia's brows went up again. 'I don't know if you've heard of this, but there is something many of us use, called a cellular telephone. Believe it or not, Dragon and Anastasia each have one.'

'Oh,' I said, feeling like a moron.

Aphrodite rolled her eyes at me.

'I'll call them and fill them in on their part of the plan. Those of you wearing skirts – you need to change. Zoey can show you where the extra riding habits are kept in the tack room. Take anything in there you might need,' Lenobia said as she hurried toward her office.

'I'll tell Dragon the diversion will start in thirty minutes.'

'Thirty minutes!' My stomach clenched.

'That should give you plenty of time to change and put bridles on three horses. You won't be able to use saddles. That would be too obvious.' Lenobia disappeared into her office just as Damien said, 'No saddles? I think I'm going to be sick.'

'Join the crowd,' I said. 'Come on,' I told Aphrodite and the Twins, 'You need to change out of those short skirts. And who the hell wears stilettos in an ice storm?'

'They're *boots*,' Aphrodite said. 'And boots are proper winter attire.'

'Three and a half inch stiletto *boots* are not sensible footwear for winter,' I said, leading them to the tack room and the riding clothes hanging neatly there among the other tack.

'Fashion-impaired geek,' Aphrodite muttered.

'Agreeing,' Shaunee said.

'For once,' Erin added.

I grabbed three bridles and shook my head at my friends. 'Just change your clothes. There are *riding boots* in that closet. Avail yourselves of their use.'

'Avail?' I heard Shaunee say as I marched out of the tack room.

'Girlfriend has been hanging around Queen Damien too much,' Erin said.

I slammed the door.

I wasn't sure what other two horses Lenobia would choose to go with us, but I knew Persephone would be carrying me, so I hurried toward her stall. Darius had moved over to one of the high stable windows and was busy stacking hay bales on top of each other. Obviously he was going to give us a weather and Raven Mocker check.

'Uh, Z, may I have one little word with you?' Damien said.

'Sure, come on in.' I went back to Persephone's stall, grabbed the currycomb, and started giving the mare a quick wipedown.

Damien stayed in the doorway. 'Here's the thing – I don't really ride.'

'Well, that's not a problem. I'll do the hard part. You just sit behind me and hold on.'

'What if I fall off? I'm sure she's a perfectly nice animal.' He sent a little hello wave to Persephone, who was still happily chewing her hay and not paying any attention to Damien. 'But she's also big. Really very big. Humongous, actually.'

403

'Damien, we are about to break out of school, run for our lives, and then try to banish an ancient immortal and a vamp High Priestess gone bad, and you're stressing about riding behind me on a horse?'

'Bareback. Riding bareback behind you on a horse,' he said. Then nodded. 'Yes, yes, I am stressing about it.'

I started giggling and had to lean against Persephone because I was hurting myself. Okay, here's the life lesson I've *really* been learning: If you have good friends, no matter how much life is sucking, they can make you laugh.

Meanwhile, Damien was frowning at me. 'Just so you know, I'm going to tell Jack you were laughing at me, and he'll get mad at you. That means the next time I purchase a gift for you, he will go on strike and *not* supervise its tasteful wrapping.'

'Jeesh, that's kinda harsh,' I said, then burst into giggles again.

'Would you guys get serious! We have a war to win and a world to save.' Aphrodite was standing with her hands on her hips just outside Persephone's stall. She was wearing her cropped black designer tank (with the gold *JUICY* label across her boobs) and her borrowed tan riding pants tucked into flat English riding boots. With no heels. None.

I took one look at her and started to giggle again. Then I caught sight of the Twins, who were standing behind her. Both of them had on Dolce & Gabbana animal-print silk tunics (probably from Saks Fifth Avenue or Miss Jackson's, jeesh). Their butts were snugged with spandexy tan English riding leggings (hee hees), tucked into brown and tan English riding boots.

It was priceless. This time Damien joined me in my hysteria.

'I hate both of them,' Aphrodite said.

'Girlfriend, we're finding we have more and more in common with you,' Erin told Aphrodite.

'Ditto,' Shaunee said, scowling at Damien and me.

Sadly, Lenobia's words threw cold water on my giggly good time.

'I spoke with Anastasia. Everything's ready to go, even though Dragon was temporarily unavailable. He was dealing with an unusual case of vampyre Change. I was told to pass word along to Zoey that Stark arrived and has been taken care of.'

'Did she say Stark?' Damien asked.

'Huh?' the Twins said.

'Oh, shit,' Aphrodite said.

'The weather still looks bad, and I can see stirrings in the trees. I think their plan is to grab us as we leave the stables. We better get going,' Darius said as he rejoined our group. He paused as he saw everyone staring at me. 'Obviously I missed something.'

'Yes, and Zoey was just getting ready to fill us in,' Damien said.

I gnawed my lip and looked from friend to friend. *Well, hell.* 'Okay, here's the deal. Stark Changed. He's the second red vampyre there's ever been.'

'Whoop-de-fucking-do,' Erin said. 'He's still an assbucket.'

'Yeah, and why would you know shit about him Changing?' Shaunee said.

'You have to stop thinking of him like he's Stevie Rae. They're worlds apart,' Damien said, more gently than the others.

'She loves him,' Aphrodite blurted.

'Aphrodite!' I yelled.

'Well, someone had to clue the dorks in to your pathetic infatuation with him,' Aphrodite said.

'You're not helping me,' I said.

'Wait. Rewind. Zoey is in love with Stark? That is the stupidest thing I've ever heard in my entire life,' Erin said.

'Well, except for the whole graduated driver's license law thing in Oklahoma, Twin. Let's get serious. *That's* the stupidest thing we've ever heard of in our entire lives,' Shaunee said.

'True. Besides that, though. And, Aphrodite, we say: You. Have. Lost. Your. Damn. Mind,' Erin said.

'Again,' Shaunee finished.

Everyone looked at me.

'I think the graduated driver's license thing is stupid, too,' I lamely said.

'See! I told you!' Aphrodite said. 'She has a serious thing for Stark.'

'Serious shit,' Erin said.

'I would never have believed it,' Shaunee said.

'Let her explain!' Damien yelled.

Everyone got really quiet.

I cleared my throat.

'Okay. Well. Remember the poem?' All of my friends narrowed their eyes at me, which I didn't think was very fair. But I continued anyway. 'It said I was supposed to save his humanity? And I did. I think. I hope.'

'Priestess, we caught him abusing a fledgling. How can you condone that?' Darius said.

'I don't condone it. It makes me sick. But I remember when Stevie Rae was fighting to keep her humanity, and she was awful.' I looked at Aphrodite. 'You know what I'm talking about.'

'Yeah, and I'm not one hundred percent sure you can trust her today. And I say that as the human she's Imprinted.'

I expected the Twins and Damien to blow up at her, but they stayed very quiet. Finally I turned to Darius. 'Stark gave me his Warrior's Oath.'

'His Warrior's Oath! And you accepted him?' Darius said.

'I did. It was right after that he Changed.'

Darius sighed deeply. 'Then Stark is bound to you until you release him from his oath.'

'I think that caused his Change,' I said. 'I think with the red fledglings their Change has something to do with the choice between good and evil.'

'By pledging to you, Stark chose good,' Darius said.

I smiled. 'I like to think so.'

'So that means he isn't an asscake anymore?' Erin said.

'I thought you called him an assbucket,' Shaunee said.

'Twin, it's the same thing,' Erin said.

'It means I trust him,' I said. 'And I wish you guys would give him a chance.'

'Giving the wrong person a chance right now could get us killed,' Darius said.

I drew a deep breath. 'I know.'

'A newly Changed vampyre needs to be secluded in Nyx's Temple. Dragon assured me Stark is safely there.' Lenobia glanced at her watch. 'We have exactly ten minutes. Can we not get on with more important things and leave the question of Stark's trustworthiness until a better time?'

'Definitely,' I said. 'What's left to do?' All I could hope was that Dragon really had the newly Changed Stark safely locked away in Nyx's Temple, and that we would actually chase Kalona out of here, thereby getting rid of Neferet, too, so that we would have a chance to deal with his trustworthiness at a better time.

We quickly got bridles on two other horses, appropriately named Hope and Destiny. Then the hard part of our plan started.

'I still say it is not safe,' Darius said, looking like a thundercloud.

'I have to do it. Stevie Rae's not here, and I'm the closest thing we have to a pure earth affinity,' I said.

'It really doesn't sound that hard,' Aphrodite said, trying to reason with the irate warrior. 'All Zoey has to do is sneak out to the wall, tell the tree that's already smushing it to push harder, and then sneak back here.'

'I will take her there,' Darius said stubbornly.

'With your mega-quickness that'll be perfect,' I said. 'By the way, I'm ready.'

'How will I know you've succeeded and it's my time to start the next part of the plan?' Lenobia asked me.

'I'll send spirit to you. If you feel a jolt of something good, you'll know we're fine and it's time to tell Shaunee to get ready to let fire loose.'

'But she must remember that only the *shoes* of the horses should be afire,' Lenobia said, giving Shaunee a stern look.

'I know! It's not even hard. Just go on about your business. Destiny and I are making friends.' Shaunee turned back to the big bay mare who would carry her and Erin, and continued to chatter to the horse as Erin brushed her and talked about sugar cubes and something called a Jazzy Apple.

'Just keep her safe and get back here to me,' Aphrodite said. She kissed Darius on the mouth and then walked toward Hope to help Lenobia finish buckling the last of the mare's bridle straps.

'Well, Priestess, shall we?' Darius said.

I nodded and let him lift me into his arms. Darius took one step out into the frigid, stormy night, and then everything blurred around us as he moved kinda diagonally across the rear grounds to a part of the big wall surrounding the school that had an even bigger oak lying across it. Somehow in one of Tulsa's last winter disasters, the tree had succumbed and fallen down. Kinda. Word had it (from Aphrodite) that under normal circumstances it was an excellent place to sneak off campus undetected, and I knew from personal experience that she'd been right.

Today we were not dealing with normal circumstances.

Darius came to a halt way too fast beside the fallen tree, shoved me under it, and whispered, 'Stay there until I'm sure it is safe.' And off he went.

So I crouched under the tree and thought about how wet and cold it was and how annoying guys were. Then I heard the nasty wing-flapping sound, and I decided to uncrouch – quickly.

I emerged from under the side of the tree just in time to see Darius grabbing a Raven Mocker by his wing, jerking him to the ground, and then slitting his throat.

I looked away fast.

'Zoey, come on. We have no time.'

Trying to ignore the corpse of the Raven Mocker, I hurried to the half-toppled tree. I placed my hand on it and closed my eyes. Centering myself, I searched for my internal north – the site of earth – and then invoked, 'Earth, I need you. Please come to me.' In the midst of an ice storm, in the dead of winter, I was suddenly, miraculously, surrounded by the scents of a spring meadow . . . ripe wheat . . . a mimosa tree in full bloom. I bowed my head gratefully and continued. 'What I need you to do is hard, and I wouldn't ask it of you unless it was an emergency.' I drew a deep breath, and focused on the ice-slicked bark beneath my palm. 'Fall,' I commanded. 'Forgive me, but I have to ask you to fall.' The skin of the tree shuddered under my hand, so violently that I fell backward, and with a crack that I swear I could hear a dying scream within, the old oak fell, crashing against the already weakened wall, sending blocks of stone and bricks tumbling down, and creating a break in the barrier that surrounded the school, a break it would seem logical for us to try to escape through.

I was breathing heavily and feeling more than a little shaky, but I automatically sent spirit to let Lenobia know I was successful. Then I picked myself up, staggered to the fallen tree, and put both hands on its bark. 'Thank you, earth.' Then a sudden thought had me adding, 'Go to Stevie Rae. Tell her we're coming. Tell her to be ready.' I felt the usual listening sense I got when I commanded an element to do something. 'Go now, earth. Thank you again for helping me, and I'm really sorry I had to hurt the tree.'

'We must return to the stables.' Darius strode over to me and lifted me in his arms. 'You did well, Priestess,' he said.

I put my head down on his friendly shoulder, and only knew I was crying because I could see the wet streaks on his jacket. 'Let's get out of here.'

CHAPTER THIRTY-TWO

THE THREE BRIDLED HORSES WERE WAITING FOR US. ERIN and Shaunee were already mounted on Destiny. Shaunee was 'driving.' She'd taken English Hunter/Jumper classes at her private prep school before she was Marked, and so she'd proclaimed herself 'an almost mediocre rider.' Aphrodite and Damien stood near Persephone and Hope. Damien looked like he might be sick at any instant.

'I felt spirit's touch and am assuming all went well,' Lenobia said as she breezed by us and began rechecking the horses' tack.

'The wall has been broken, but I was forced to kill a

Raven Mocker. I'm quite sure he'll be discovered soon,'
Darius said.

'Actually, that's good. It will just give more credence to the
thought that the fallen wall is how you'll try to escape,' Lenobia
said. She glanced at her watch. 'Time to mount up. Shaunee,
are you ready?'

'I was born ready,' Shaunee said.

'All right, how about you, Erin?'

Erin nodded. 'Ditto. I'm ready.'

'Damien?'

He answered Lenobia, but he spoke to me, 'I'm scared.'

I hurried to his side and took his hand. 'I'm scared, too.
But it's a lot less scary if I remember we're together.'

'Even if we're together on a horse?'

I smiled. 'Even if. Plus, Persephone is a perfect lady.' I took
Damien's hand and pressed it against the graceful curve of
my mare's neck.

'Oooh, she's soft and warm,' he said.

'Here, I'll give you a knee up,' Lenobia said, bending beside
us and offering Damien the cradle her hands were making.

With a long-suffering sigh he put his knee in her hands
and tried (unsuccessfully) to stifle a very gay squeal as she
boosted him up on Persephone's broad back.

Before Lenobia helped me up she put her hands on my
shoulders and looked into my eyes. 'Follow your heart and
your instinct, and you will not go wrong. Make him flee,
Priestess.'

'I'll do my best,' I said.

'That is why I have such faith in you,' she said.

Once we were all mounted, Lenobia led us to the rollaway doors that opened into the exercise corral. Earlier Lenobia had quietly gone out and opened the outside gate to the corral. Now nothing stood between us and the world except a lot of ice, the front gates of the school, a bunch of Raven Mockers, their daddy, and a crazy-assed ex-High Priestess.

As you can well imagine, I was pretty concerned about having a raging case of nervous diarrhea. Thankfully, I didn't have enough spare time for my body to give it much thought.

Lenobia slid the doors open. She'd already extinguished the lights in this part of the stable, so that we wouldn't be silhouetted, all sitting-duck-like. We peered into the icy darkness, imagining the storm to come.

'I'll give you just a few minutes to call the elements,' Lenobia said. 'The sudden increase in intensity of the storm is Anastasia's cue to begin the confusion spell on the other side of campus, and don't forget that Dragon has stationed himself at the school gate. He will cut down the Raven Mocker who is sentry there as soon as he hears hoofs approaching. Shaunee, when you're ready, set the stall on fire. When I see the flames, I'll free the rest of the horses. They already know that they are to stampede around the school grounds and create as much havoc as possible.'

Shaunee nodded. 'I got it.'

'Then refocus flame on these horses' hoofs.' Lenobia paused and reiterated, 'I mean the horseshoes on their hoofs. I'll tell Persephone when to go. All the rest of you need do is to hold

on and follow her lead.' She patted my sorrel mare affectionately. Then she looked up at me, 'Merry meet and merry part,
and merry meet again, High Priestess,' she said. Fisting her
hand over her heart, she bowed to me.

'Brightest blessings to you, Lenobia,' I said. As she began
to walk quickly away, I called after her, 'Lenobia, please recon-
sider leaving here. If we don't get rid of Kalona, you and
Dragon and Anastasia have to get underground – the tunnels
under the depot, the abbey, or even the basement of one of
the downtown buildings. That's really the only chance you
have of being safe at all.'

Lenobia paused and looked over her shoulder at me. Her
smile was serene and wise. 'But, Priestess, you will succeed.'
And she hurried away.

'Jeesh, she's stubborn,' Shaunee said.

'Let's just be sure she's right,' I said. 'Okay, are you ready?'
My friends nodded. I drew a deep breath and centered myself.
We were pointed north, so I kneed Persephone to the right
so that we were facing east. There was no time for flowery
words or inspiring music; there was only time for action.
Quickly I invoked each of the elements, feeling my nerves
steady as they filled the air and created a glistening circle that
bound us. When spirit swelled within me, I couldn't stop
myself from laughing aloud.

Still sounding giddy, I said, 'Damien, Erin, put your
elements to work!'

I felt Damien raise his hands behind me, and watched Erin
do the same. I could hear Damien whispering words to air,

asking a freezing wind to swirl and blow, toss and tussle, everything around us. I knew Erin was asking something similar of water – commanding that it increase the sleet and drench the world around us.

I braced myself to help them channel and control their elements so that we would (in theory) be moving inside a little bubble of calm in an otherwise elemental maelstrom.

Both elements responded instantly. We looked out to see the night in front of us erupt into a storm that probably knocked Doppler 8 on its butt.

'Okay,' I yelled above the wind. 'It's flame's turn.'

Shaunee lifted her arms, tossed back her head, and like she was throwing a basketball, hurled the fire that glowed between her palms at the empty, straw-filled stall Lenobia had told her to destroy. The stall burst into angry flame.

'Now the horses' hoofs,' I cried.

She nodded. 'Help me keep it up.'

'I will, don't worry.'

Shaunee pointed down at our horse's hoofs. 'Heat up their shoes!' she yelled.

Persephone snorted. Her head bowed, and as the sawdust of the stable yard began to smoke under her feet, she pricked her ears at her hoofs.

'Oh, man . . . We need to get out of here before their feet burn everything up,' Damien said. He was clutching me so tight it was a little hard for me to breathe, but I didn't want to say anything that might cause him to topple sideways.

I was just thinking that we really might light the sawdust

on fire when I heard a huge commotion behind us that I knew must be Lenobia freeing the horses to bolt around the main grounds of the campus, as if they were utterly crazed by the stable fire. Persephone tossed her head and snorted. I felt her muscles bunch and had just enough time to squeeze hard with my thighs and yell back at Damien, 'Hold on! Here we go!' And then the mare lunged out of the stables and into the raging night.

The three horses, side by side, galloped through the corral and out the gate Lenobia had left open. They turned hard to the left, circled around behind the main school building, and sooner than I would have imagined possible, there was steam hissing and mist rising in waves around us as heated hoofs met the ice that covered the asphalt of the parking lot.

Behind us I could hear the screams of panicked horses and the terrible cries of the Raven Mockers. I gritted my teeth and hoped Lenobia's mares were taking out a bunch of the birdmen.

Persephone's hoofs hissed against the slick road that led down the drive to the school.

'Oh, Goddess! Look!' Damien cried. He pointed from over my shoulder ahead and off to the left in the line of trees that framed the lane. Dragon was there fighting three Raven Mockers. His blade was a silver blur as he lunged and parried and whirled. As we came into view, the birdmen tried to shift their attention to us, but Dragon redoubled his attack, skewering one of them instantly and causing the other two to turn, hissing, back to him.

417

'Go!' he cried as we galloped past him. 'And may Nyx bless you!'

The gate was open, Dragon's doing I was sure. We surged through, turned to the right, and galloped down deserted, icy Utica Street.

At the Twenty-first Street light, which was not working, we turned the horses to the right, positioned them in the middle of the street, and gave them their heads.

Midtown Tulsa had turned into a frozen ghost of itself. If I hadn't been focused and hadn't been absolutely sure our horses were in a flat gallop down Twenty-first Street, I would have thought we were utterly lost in a strange, post-apocalyptic ice world. There was nothing in the least bit familiar around me. No lights. No cars moving. No people. Cold and darkness and ice reigned. The beautiful old trees of midtown were shrouded in so much ice that many of them had literally splintered down the middle. Power lines were down, snaking across the street like lazy vipers. The horses paid no attention to them. They leaped over downed limbs and lines, their flame-heated hoofs slicing through the ice to strike sparks against the surprised pavement.

And then, above the din of striking hoofs and the hiss of flame on ice, I heard the terrible flapping of wings and the cry of first one and then another and another Raven Mocker.

'Darius,' I yelled. 'Raven Mockers!'

He looked behind us and up, and nodded grimly. Then he did something that completely shocked me. Out of his jacket pocket he pulled a black gun. I'd never seen any of the Sons

418

of Erebus carry modern weapons, and it looked completely out of place in his hand. He said something to Aphrodite, who was pressed against his back. She slid to the side a little, allowing him to swivel around. He lifted his arm, sighted, and squeezed off half-a-dozen shots. The sound was deafening in the frozen night, but not half as eerie as what followed it – the screams of wounded Raven Mockers and the *thud! crash!* of bodies as they fell from the sky.

'There!' Shaunee cried, pointing in front of us and to the right. 'I see flames!'

At first I didn't see anything, and then through a stand of ice-enslaved trees I caught sight of a huge display of candle-flickering welcoming light. Was that it? Was that the Benedictine Abbey? Visibility was terrible, and everything was so disorientating and dark, that I couldn't tell if it was the abbey or just one of the houses-turned-plastic surgeon offices that lined this part of the street.

Concentrate! If it's a place of power, I should be able to feel it.

I breathed deep and reached out with my instinct, and I felt it – the unmistakable draw that came from the combined power of spirit and earth.

'That's it!' I yelled. 'That's the abbey!'

We yanked our horses' heads to the right and plunged off the road, through a ditch, and then up an embankment dotted with trees. The horses had to slow to dodge around fallen limbs and dead, downed power lines, and then we popped through the trees and into a clearing. Directly in front of us was a huge old oak. Its lower branches were filled with little glass cages holding cheerily burning candles. There was a carport farther behind the tree, and beyond it I could just make out the looming hulk of the brick building that was the Benedictine Abbey, or at least I could make out its windows, because there were candles lit in each one of them.

'Okay, you guys can lay off the elements now and let things calm down.' The Twins and Damien whispered to their elements, and the madness of the storm began to quiet to a cold, cloudy night.

'Whoa!' I called, and our obedient, loyal mares skidded to a stop just before an awe-inspiring figure clothed in a dark robe and wimple.

'Hello, child. I heard you were coming,' she said, smiling up at me.

I slid from Persephone's back and threw myself into her arms. 'Sister Mary Angela! I am so glad to see you!'

'As I am glad to see you, too,' she said. 'But, child, perhaps we should put off our hellos until we've dealt with the dark creatures filling the trees behind you.'

I spun around in time to see dozens of Raven Mockers landing in the trees. Except for the sounds of their wings they were absolutely silent, and their red eyes glowed like watching demons.

'Well, hell!' I said.

CHAPTER THIRTY-THREE

'Language,' Sister Mary Angela said serenely.

Darius had already dismounted and was helping Aphrodite and the Twins down. Damien hadn't waited for help, but dismounted almost as quickly as I had, and was standing beside me.

'Priestess,' Darius addressed Sister Mary Angela, 'you don't, by any chance, keep firearms at the abbey, do you?'

Her laughter sounded completely out of place yet utterly comforting. 'Oh, Warrior, of course we do not.'

'There aren't enough of us to fight them, but we have the circle,' Darius said as he studied the bird-filled trees. 'If you stay within it, you stay safe.'

Darius was right, of course. Our circle was intact. Though weirdly off-center, the silver thread that bound us together still glowed between us.

'I will run back to the House of Night and bring help,' Darius said.

I heard the frustration in his voice. What help was he going to bring? I hadn't seen any of his brother warriors since we'd entered the school grounds. Dragon was great with a sword, but even he wouldn't be a match for all of these Raven Mockers. The trees that bordered the Twenty-first Street side of the abbey were filled with the dark shapes. Already groaning under the burden of ice, the additional weight of the Raven Mockers was more stress than many of them could bear, and the cracking and breaking of limbs was as terrible as the birds' mocking cries.

'Hey, I hear y'all need some help out here.'

In my entire life, I had never been so happy to hear any voice as I was at that moment to hear Stevie Rae's Okie twang. I hugged her hard, not caring about the secrets she was keeping from me in the joy of seeing her safe. Breathing a sigh of relief, I saw the red fledglings step out of the darkness behind her.

'They is nasty!' Kramisha said, squidging up her face at the Raven Mockers.

'Let's kick their asses,' Johnny B said, looking all testosterone-filled and muscle-y.

'They're nasty alright, but they aren't doing anything except watching us,' said another familiar voice.

422

'Erik!' I cried. Smiling, Stevie Rae let go of me, and Erik pulled me into his strong arms.

There was a blur to my right and Jack launched himself at Damien.

I looked up at Erik, and even in the middle of the mess we were in, I wished it could be simple and easy between the two of us. For that instant I did wish it could just be Erik and me, instead of Erik and Stark and Kalona and Heath . . .

'Heath?' I asked, stepping out of his embrace.

Erik sighed and jerked his chin back at the abbey building. 'He's in there. He's fine.'

I smiled a little sheepishly and didn't know what to say.

'Zoey, Kalona will be here soon. The reason the Raven Mockers aren't attacking is because we're not trying to get away anymore. They're just keeping watch on us for him. Do not forget what you have to do,' Darius's voice broke through the new awkwardness between Erik and me.

I nodded and turned to Sister Mary Angela. 'Kalona will follow us here. Remember I told you he's immortal?'

'A fallen angel,' she said, nodding.

'And remember I told you about our High Priestess? Well, she's definitely gone bad, and I'm sure she'll be with him. They're equally dangerous.'

'I understand.'

'So, he can't be killed, but I do think I know how to chase him away from here and, hopefully, Neferet will go with him. But I'll need your help.'

'Whatever I have is yours,' Sister Mary Angela said.

'Good. What I need is you,' I told her, then I turned to Stevie Rae, 'And you.'

Aphrodite stepped up beside me. 'And me,' she said.

'And I need Grandma. I know it's going to be hard for her, but I need her out here, or at least wherever it is that's the center of this power I feel around us.'

'Kramisha, child, would you get Stevie Rae's grandmother?'

'Yes, ma'am,' Kramisha said, and hurried away.

'Mary's Grotto is the seat of our power.' Sister Mary Angela pointed behind me and to the side of where we were standing – a place that was between us, the north-westernmost edge of the neatly cut lawn, and the monster-filled grove of trees.

I turned to see what she was pointing at and gasped in surprise, wondering how I hadn't noticed it before now. It was the biggest shrine I'd ever seen. It was made of large pieces of Oklahoma sandstone. Each stone had been chosen carefully to fit snugly against its neighbors. It was bowl-like in shape, reminding me of pictures I'd seen of famous outdoor theaters. There was a bench sitting protected inside it, as well as several natural rock ledges running around the curved inside at various places, and every available surface was covered with candles, so that the entire shrine was glazed in candlelight and ice. As I walked toward it, I looked at its gracefully arched top, which stretched several feet over my head, and sucked in my breath. There, nestled toward the top of the structure, was the most beautiful statue of Mary I'd ever seen. Her face was serene in prayer, almost smiling as she looked up. And at her feet a riot of gorgeous roses twined around her as if they had given birth to her. I studied Mary's face and felt my heart give a little stutter beat. I recognized this Mary. How could I not? She'd appeared to me just days before in the form of my Goddess.

'I can feel the power of this place,' Aphrodite said.

'Wow, that statue of Mary is really, really pretty,' Jack said. He and Damien were holding hands and gazing up.

'Check out the sidewalk – it's perfect,' Stevie Rae said.

I looked down. The sidewalk that led from where we'd left the horses changed when it reached the front of the shrine. Here it got lots bigger and formed a circle. I grinned at Stevie Rae. 'It's definitely perfect.'

'What is it you need us to do, Zoey?' Sister Mary Angela asked, but before I could answer, the roar of an engine pulled everyone's attention back to the bird-infested trees and the road beyond.

With growing fear, I watched the big black Hummer, the very one I'd been taken back to the school in, leave the road. Gunning its engine, the vehicle lurched down the ditch, then up the other side and made its growling way through the grove of trees, causing the Raven Mockers to beat their wings and croak in a frenzy of encouragement.

'Sister, stay close to me,' I said. 'Aphrodite, Stevie Rae, I need you beside me, too.'

'We're here,' Aphrodite said as Erik and Darius stepped out of the way and the two of them moved into position beside me.

'I need Grandma,' I said.

'She's coming. Do not fear,' Sister Mary Angela said.

Finally, the Hummer rolled to a stop, so close to the horses that they snorted at it and backed away until they were standing under the carport. The doors to the vehicle opened, and Kalona and Neferet stepped out together. She was wearing all black – a floor-sweeping silk dress with a neckline that plunged to expose the onyx winged pendant resting between her breasts. A dark aura pulsed around her, making her thick hair lift and move around her shoulders.

'Holy shit,' Aphrodite whispered.

'Yeah, I know,' I said grimly.

Kalona strode at her side. He was wearing black pants and nothing else. As he moved away from the Hummer with Neferet, his wings rustled and opened a little, showing just a hint of their magnificence.

'Oh, blessed Mary!' Beside me Sister Mary Angela gasped.

'Don't look in his eyes!' I whispered to her. 'He can have a hypnotic effect on people. Don't let him get to you.'

She hesitated, studying the winged man, and then said, 'He does not draw me, but I do pity him. He has certainly fallen.'

'How old does he look to you?' I couldn't help asking her.

'Ancient. Older than the earth.'

I didn't have time to tell her he looked about eighteen to me; it was then that the driver got out of the Hummer and joined Kalona and Neferet. The driver was Stark. His eyes found mine instantly, and ever so slightly, he bowed his head to me.

I heard Stevie Rae's quick intake breath of surprise and the movement of the red fledglings behind us.

'That's the kid that shot me, isn't it?' she said.

'Yes,' I said.

'He's Changed,' Stevie Rae said. 'He's a red vampyre.'

'He's also a fucking rat,' Aphrodite muttered, then hastily added, 'Sorry, Sister.'

'Do not trust him, Zoey.' Darius's voice came from directly behind me. 'You see where he has placed his allegiance.'

'Darius,' I said sternly, without turning to look at him. 'You need to trust *me*, and that means trust my judgment.'

'Sometimes your judgment is wacked,' Erin said.

'Not when I'm listening to Nyx,' I said.

'Are you listening now?' Shaunee said.

I stared at Stark, trying to see any hint of darkness around him. There was nothing – just Stark and the way his eyes met mine steadily. 'I am absolutely listening to Nyx. Now, form the circle up around us.' Instantly the Twins and Damien moved out of the crowd behind me. Damien walked to the eastern edge of the cement circle. I felt rather than saw Shaunee move into place behind me, and Erin situated herself on our left. For a second I was concerned that I would have to step away from Aphrodite, Stevie Rae, and Sister Mary Angela and take earth's place, but then I realized that Mary's Grotto was firmly positioned in the north, and that the beautiful silver thread that bound our circle now included her shrine.

'You cannot maintain that circle for eternity,' Kalona said as he walked slowly toward our little group. 'I, on the other hand, can maintain my pursuit of you for eternity.'

'My fledglings,' Neferet said, walking beside Kalona and, except for the darkness that throbbed around her, she looked beautiful and serene and very High Priestess-like. 'You have allowed Zoey's misguided quest for power to put you in a perilous situation, but it is not too late for you. You need simply to renounce her, close the circle, and you will be accepted back in the bosom of your High Priestess.'

'If there wasn't a nun here, I'd tell you what you could do with your nasty bosom,' Aphrodite said.

'Zoey isn't the one who's turned away from Nyx,' Erin said.

'Yeah, we all know you have. It's just that Zoey was the first to know it,' Shaunee said.

'See how her evil words have tainted your judgment?' Neferet sounded sad and very reasonable.

'And what has tainted my judgment?' Sister Mary Angela spoke up from beside me. 'I barely know this child. Her words could not taint me, could not make me imagine the darkness I sense radiating from you.'

Neferet's calm façade cracked as she scoffed at the nun. 'Human woman, you are a fool! Of course you sense darkness from me. My Goddess is Night personified!'

Sister Mary Angela's serenity wasn't a façade, so her demeanor didn't change. She simply said, 'No, I am acquainted with Nyx, and though she personifies Night, she does not traffic with darkness. Be honest, Priestess, and admit you have broken with your Goddess for that creature.' The nun's hand swept toward Kalona, causing the dark folds of her habit to billow gracefully. 'Nephilium, I recognize you. And in Our

Lady's name I speak words you already know: You should leave this place and return to the realm whence you fell. Repent, and perhaps you may still be allowed to know eternity in paradise.'

'Do not speak to him, woman!' Neferet shrieked, all pretense of serenity gone. 'He is a god come to earth. You should worship at his feet!'

Kalona's laughter was terrible, and it caused the Raven Mockers to hiss as they moved restlessly all around us. 'Ladies, do not battle over me. I am a god! There is enough of me for all of you to share.' He spoke in response to Neferet and Sister Mary Angela, but his amber eyes stared straight at me.

'I will never be with you,' I told him, ignoring everyone around us. 'My choice will always be for my Goddess, and you are the opposite of everything she stands for.'

'Do not presume—' Neferet began, but Kalona lifted one hand and cut off her words.

'A-ya, you misjudge me. Look deep within yourself to the maiden who was created to love me.'

Something behind me stirred the crowd and I felt a little blip that told me our circle had been crossed, which could only happen if the Goddess herself allowed someone through. I wanted to look back and see who had joined us, but I couldn't take my eyes from Kalona's hypnotic gaze.

Then her hand slid into mine and love broke Kalona's spell. With a glad cry I glanced down to see Grandma sitting in a wheelchair that Heath had pushed up to me. She looked like she'd been through a war. Her arm was in a cast, and her head was bandaged. Her face was still swollen and discolored with bruises, but her smile was her own, as was the sweet sound of her voice.

'Did I hear you have need of me, my *u-we-tsi-a-ge-ya*?'

I squeezed her hand. 'Grandma, I'll always need you!'

I glanced back at Heath, who smiled at me. 'Kick his butt outta here, Zo,' he said; then he moved back to join Erik and Darius.

Grandma, meanwhile, had somehow risen to her feet. She took two slow steps forward, staring out at the grove of trees and the Raven Mockers swarmed there.

'Oh, sons of my mothers' mothers!' she cried and her voice carried like the sonorous beat of a tribal drum out into the night. 'What have you allowed him to make you become? Do you not feel your mothers' blood? Can you not imagine their hearts breaking for you?'

Amazed, I watched several of the Raven Mockers turn their heads, as if they were unable to face my grandma. In others the red glow began to die in their eyes, and I recognized sorrow and confusion in their human depths.

'Be silent, *Ani Yunwiya!*' Kalona's voice boomed around us.

I knew Grandma recognized the ancient name of the Cherokee people. Slowly, she turned her attention to the winged being. 'I see you, Old One. Will you never learn? Must women, once again, come together to defeat you?'

'Not this time, Ghigua. You will not find me so easy to trap this time.'

'Perhaps this time we will simply wait for you to trap

yourself. We are a very patient people, and you did it before,' Grandma said.

'But this A-ya is different,' Kalona said. 'Her soul calls to me from her dreams. It won't be long before her waking body calls me, too, and then I shall possess her.'

'No,' I said firmly. 'Thinking you can possess me, like I'm a piece of property, is your first mistake. My soul is drawn to you,' I finally admitted aloud, and found a surprising strength in my honesty. 'But like you said, I'm a different A-ya. I have free will, and my will is *not* to give myself to the darkness. So, here's the deal: Leave now. Take Neferet and the Raven Mockers and go someplace far away where you can live in peace and not hurt anyone else.'

'Or?' he asked, looking amused.

'Or I will, as my human consort put it, kick your butt out of here,' I said firmly.

His look of amusement widened into a charming smile. 'A-ya, I do not believe I will leave this place. I find I like Tulsa very much.'

'Remember that you brought this on yourself,' I said. Then I spoke to the women surrounding me. 'The poem says: Joined not to conquer, instead to overcome. I'm Night. I've led you to Sister Mary Angela – she's Spirit.' I held out my left hand and Sister Mary Angela grasped it firmly. 'Stevie Rae, you're Blood. Aphrodite, you're Humanity.'

Stevie Rae walked over to Sister Mary Angela, and took the nun's other hand, and then she looked at Aphrodite, who nodded and grasped her offered hand.

'What are they doing?' Neferet's voice came from closer than she was before. I looked up to see that she was moving quickly toward us.

'A-ya! What foolishness is this?' Kalona didn't sound amused anymore, and he, too, was approaching our circle.

'And Earth completes.' I held my hand out to Grandma.

'Do not let the Ghigua join them!' Kalona cried.

'Stark! Kill her,' Neferet commanded.

'Not A-ya!' Kalona shouted. 'Kill the old Ghigua.'

I held my breath and met Stark's eyes as Neferet said, 'Kill Zoey. No mistakes this time. Aim for her heart!' As she spoke, darkness slithered from the shadows around her. Stretching over to Stark, I watched them wrap around his ankles and begin to move up his body. I saw clearly the struggle that was going on within Stark. Neferet's dark power could still affect him. My stomach clenched. Was his Warrior's Oath to me enough to break that hold? I wanted to trust him. I'd decided to trust him. Had that been a stupid mistake?

'No!' Kalona roared. 'Do not kill her!'

'I will not share you!' Neferet cried. Her hair was whipping around her, and she seemed to grow bigger as I watched. I had been right to believe she was no longer what she once had been, not in body and not in soul. She whirled from Kalona to Stark. 'By the power with which I awakened you, I command you hit the mark. Shoot Zoey through her heart!'

I was staring at Stark, trying to will him to choose good – to keep choosing good and to turn from Neferet's cloying darkness, so I saw the exact moment he understood his way out.

As if he and I were back in the little room off the field house again, I heard myself saying to him, *You have my heart . . .* And his response: *Then both of us better stay safe. A heart's a hard thing to live without . . .*

'That's what my aim won't miss.' Stark spoke across the icy distance to me as if he and I were alone. 'The part of my lady's heart I hold as my own.' The shadows that had gripped his body were instantly washed from him as he made his decision.

And with a rush of panic I understood what he was going to do.

Aiming straight at me, he drew the bow and shot.

As he let loose the arrow, I cried, 'Air, fire, water, earth, spirit! Hear me! Do not let that arrow touch him!' I flung my power out toward Stark, channeling all five of the elements. The arrow did a weird shimmer, and suddenly it was not heading in my direction, but speeding back toward Stark's heart. It was mere inches from his chest when the elements blasted it, disintegrating it with such force that Stark was thrown back and lay crumpled, but not skewered, on the ground.

'You bitch whelp!' Neferet shrieked. 'You're not going to win this!'

Ignoring her, I held my hand out to Grandma. 'And Earth completes,' I repeated.

She took my hand in hers and, joined together, we faced the on-rush of Kalona and Neferet.

'Do not curse them.' Sister Mary Angela's voice was so

serene it seemed otherworldly. 'He is all too familiar with darkness and anger and curses.'

'A blessing,' Stevie Rae said.

'Yeah, people who are filled with hate don't know how to handle love,' Aphrodite said, meeting my eyes briefly and smiling.

'Bless him, Grandma. We'll join you,' I said.

Then my grandma's strong voice rang out, amplified with the power of spirit and blood, night and earth, all joined through the humanity of love.

'Kalona, my *u-do*,' she used the Cherokee word for 'brother.' 'This is my blessing to you.' Grandma began to recite an ancient Cherokee blessing so familiar to me its words were like coming home. 'May the warm winds of Heaven blow softly on your home . . .'

The five of us repeated, 'May the warm winds of Heaven blow softly on your home . . .'

Grandma continued. 'And the Great Spirit bless all who enter there . . .'

This time, as we repeated the blessing, Damien and the Twins recited it with us.

Grandma's voice stayed strong and steady. 'May your moccasins make happy tracks in many snows . . .'

When our voices rose to repeat Grandma's words, everyone within the circle had joined us. The blessing even echoed from behind us, and I knew the Benedictine nuns had left their sanctuary to add their prayer to ours.

As Grandma spoke the last line of the poem, her voice was

filled with such love and warmth and complete joy, it brought tears to my eyes. 'And may the rainbow always touch your shoulder . . .'

Then over the sound of our voices joined in blessing, I heard Kalona's agonized cry. He had staggered to a halt only feet away from me. Neferet was at his side, her beautiful face twisted in hatred. He reached one hand out to me.

'Why, A-ya?' he said.

I gazed into his incredible amber eyes and banished him with the truth. 'Because I choose love.'

A blinding light, made of the glowing silver thread that bound our circle, whipped from me and wrapped around Kalona and Neferet. I watched as the noose it made began to tighten. I knew the silver thread was not just made of the elements, but was also strengthened by Night and Spirit, Blood and Humanity, and grounded in Earth.

With a terrible cry, Kalona staggered back. Neferet clung to him. The darkness that pulsed from her twitched and writhed as she shrieked in agony. Though he never took his gaze from mine, he wrapped his arms around Neferet, unfurled his mighty, night-colored wings, and leaped into the sky. He hovered there for an instant, as his wings beat against gravity, and then the silver thread reared back, gaining momentum, before it snapped, whiplike, at them, lifting the winged man and the fallen High Priestess up and up until they disappeared into the clouds with the Raven Mockers screaming and following behind.

The instant he disappeared from view, I felt a familiar

burning spread across my chest, and I knew next time I looked at myself in the mirror, I would see another Mark of my Goddess's favor, though this one would be mixed with scars and deep, heartbreaking pain.

Afterward

NONE OF US SAID ANYTHING FOR WHAT SEEMED LIKE A LONG time. Then, moving automatically, I thanked the elements, closing our circle. Numbly, I helped Grandma back to her wheelchair. Sister Mary Angela began mothering everyone, clucking about how wet and cold and tired we all must be, and herding everyone toward the abbey, where she promised hot chocolate and dry clothes awaited us.

'The horses,' I said.

'Already cared for.' Sister Mary Angela nodded toward two nuns I recognized from my volunteer work at Street Cats as Sister Bianca and Sister Fatima, who were leading the three horses to a little side building that was now a greenhouse but had a heavy stone foundation that made it look like it could once have been a stable.

I nodded, feeling utterly exhausted, and called to Darius. Then, followed closely by him, Erik, and Heath, I walked out to Stark's still body.

He had crumpled to the ground beside the Hummer and was clearly illuminated by the big vehicle's lights. The shirt had been burned away from his chest, and there was the bloody brand of a broken arrow over his heart. The wound looked terrible. Not only was it raw and bleeding, it was also bruised, like a hot iron had been punched into him. I steeled myself. I'd seen him die once, I could bear witness to his second death. Drawing a deep breath, I knelt beside him and took his hand. I'd been right. He wasn't breathing. But as soon as I touched him, he drew a deep breath, coughed, and opened his eyes as he grimaced with pain.

'Hey,' I said softly, smiling through my tears and silently thanking Nyx for this miracle. 'Are you really okay?'

He looked down at his chest. 'Weird burn, but besides feeling like I've been run over by five elements, I think I'm fine.'

'You scared me,' I said.

'I scared myself,' he said.

'Warrior, when you pledge yourself to the service of a High Priestess, the goal is not to frighten her *to* death but to protect your lady *from* death,' Darius said as he offered Stark his hand.

Stark took it, and stood, slowly and painfully. 'Well,' he said with that cocky smile I loved so much, 'serving this lady might be cause for a whole new book of rules to be written.'

'You're telling us?' Erik said.

'Yeah, not something we don't already know,' Heath said.

'Well, hell,' I said, shaking my head at all of my boys.

'Zoeybird! Look up!' my grandma called to me. I glanced up and drew a deep, wondering breath.

The clouds had completely dissipated, leaving the sky clear to expose a brilliant crescent moon that shone so bright it burned away any lingering confusion and sadness Kalona had planted in my heart.

Sister Mary Angela joined me. She, too, was gazing up, but her face was turned to the statue of Mary, on which the moon had cast a single, beautiful beam of light.

'It isn't finished with him or with her yet, you know,' she said softly, for my ears alone.

'I know,' I said. 'But whatever happens, my Goddess will be with me.'

'As will your friends, child. As will your friends.'

About the Authors

P. C. Cast is an award-winning fantasy and paranormal romance author, as well as an experienced speaker and teacher. She lives and teaches in Oklahoma.

Her daughter, **Kristin Cast,** has won awards for her poetry and journalism. She also lives in Oklahoma, where she attends the University of Tulsa as a communications major.

For more information on the series visit www.pccast.net

You can also find out more about P. C. Cast and Kristin Cast, plus other Atom authors, at www.atombooks.co.uk